To Rosie
With love

Freddie '09

Burned

How a Firefighter was Railroaded by Political Conspirators

RICH JOSU AND MATT MAHADY

authorHOUSE®

AuthorHouse™
1663 Liberty Drive, Suite 200
Bloomington, IN 47403
www.authorhouse.com
Phone: 1-800-839-8640

First published by AuthorHouse 5/7/2008

ISBN: 978-1-4343-6748-8 (sc)
ISBN: 978-1-4343-6749-5 (hc)

Library of Congress Control Number: 2008902033

Printed in the United States of America
Bloomington, Indiana

This book is printed on acid-free paper.

This novel is dedicated to Jason, Freddie and Clint .Throughout all kinds of trials and tribulations ,they have been supportive, hard working sons that had to tolerate ignorance, bad press and loss of friends while watching their parents go through a painful divorce. I can't image the venom they endured from negative comments at school and the fights they were goaded into. Through it all they were courageous and stood up to the slanders and criticism.

This book is also dedicated to Sage Mahady (1991-2005) a brilliant, sweet and amazing son whose life was cut short too soon.

This fictionalized account is based on the shocking true story of an up-and-coming firefighter, the rising star of the department. Over the course of an accolade-laden career, he shoots up the ranks toward the position of captain as he demonstrates a tremendous amount of uncommon courage and valor. On the fast track toward becoming chief, it seemed there was nothing that could stop his dizzying ascent toward success. That is, until the political winds changed in his town and corruption began to reign. *Burned* is the story of how a good man's life was first disrupted and then destroyed because he would not compromise or "play ball" with rampant organized crime and political wrongdoing. It is an important parable of good versus evil in today's society, showing that, unfortunately, the good guys don't always win. If it happened to this man, under these circumstances, it could happen to you.

Chapter 1

More asleep than awake, Eddie rolled over on his cot and reached for his gear. The metallic clang of the firehouse bell seemed to echo against his skull as he dressed. A blur of rushed stumbling, latching, fastening, lacing. Although he knew it by rote and there was an automatic, automatonic professionalism about the manner in which he went through the motions of preparation, there was freshness, exuberance, an almost childlike excitement—sharpened by a slight bite of fear— that no amount of time on the job could suppress.

Rubbing the sleep from his eyes, he navigated through slaloms of hustling figures, rode the pole down to the garage, and took his position on the truck. He was still catching his bearings as the engine fired up and lurched out into the deserted boulevard, sirens strobing and wailing through the cool New Jersey night.

Eddie felt a rush of adrenaline pulse through him as the rig gathered speed. He shuddered involuntarily at the almost electrical charge that coursed through him. The truck cornered sharply, and Eddie gripped the rail tightly. There were goose bumps rising on his arms and legs and a faintly bitter taste in his mouth. He began to retreat into his own thoughts but there was no time. The early stages of Eddie's drift into reverie were cut short by a sudden lurch and locking of brakes. The team moved into position like a well-trained cadre of bees in a hive. Most of the men were starting toward their posts before the small convoy of vehicles had even come to a complete stop.

Snapping to attention, Eddie went about unfurling hoses with a veteran's cool efficiency. Tonight he was the nozzle man. This was fine, albeit a bit frustrating. Eddie preferred more hands-on work. He thrived on the thrill of the danger associated with his job. He had dreamed of it since childhood. And unlike the other much-hyped but ultimately disappointing major firsts in life—first kiss, sex, first drink, driving, diplomas, money, marriage, children, etc.—firefighting alone had not disappointed.

His first fire took his breath away. He was still just a volunteer. And so young. (God, had he ever been that young!) They had been playing chess when the radio crackled with the assignation. Ed had been nervously waiting for it all night. At that point, he'd been wondering if he'd gotten all keyed up for nothing. There he was two-thirds of the way through the shift. There had been nothing but a treed cat and a false alarm. When this call came through, however, there was urgency in the dispatcher's voice that told him and the rest of the house it was finally "showtime."

He'd thrown up at the station. It came out of nowhere. He had to dash to the toilet. At first Eddie was red-faced, but his crewmates quickly helped him get rid of any shame or embarrassment he may have felt. As soon as he exited the head, they mobbed and surrounded him for the rest of the short time they had left, slapping his back and laughing and joking. If there was one thing they understood, it was pre-fire nerves. Their confidence in him gave him confidence in himself. *Maybe they all went through this*, he thought. *Maybe they still do.* Despite the esteem boost and the private pep talk, there were dry heaves on the truck. There was bile in his throat. There was sweat upon his brow. There were one thousand half-panicked thoughts racing erratically through the speedways of his mind.

Soon he would see his first action. Like a '44 dogface in a troop-ship launch vessel in the eye before the storm, storming the beach at Normandy, he wondered how he would hold up, if he could do it, if he would function when the crucial time came. He had his doubts. But once the blaze was before him, the training kicked in, along with something else, something that had been there all along, and he knew what to do. He felt almost supernatural, working in near-perfect tandem, supporting and being supported by his team: a small, disciplined crew of professionals. Within the hour, they had succeeded in bringing the blaze under control. About twenty-five minutes later, the last flames had been snuffed completely.

So yeah, even since the beginning, since before the beginning, Eddie was a frontlines junkie. It wasn't just for the drama (although the drama was definitely a part of it), but for something else as well. He liked the part about helping people. He felt called to serve his community in his way. Because he was good at it, because he had a God-given gift; it was his destiny to use it. That's how he felt about it anyway. Those who knew him knew that he would have been one of those guys on 9/11 that raced headlong into the swaying deathtrap of Tower 2, even though they knew what was likely to happen. (One of the problems the Dept. faced and he faced was some of the guys were more concerned with getting to their part time jobs than doing the job the tax payers hired them to do).

He thrived on the glory of actually entering the burning structures. Smoke everywhere, blinding heat, burning rafters raining from above like bubbling Old Testament brimstone, that sort of thing. The sort of thing that he wouldn't be doing while stuck outside on the nozzle. Still, it was both an important and potentially tricky operation that required good aim and not a small amount of finesse and skill. So he got down to it, shelving the rest of his secret soliloquy for later, channeling all mental energies to the task at hand.

The task at hand was to put out the fire. Eddie and his backup manned one of four hoses. While his line was being trained on the fire. It gave just enough time for some of his comrades to grab the other lines and make entry. The action takes place amid a backdrop of deep blues, pale oranges, and monochromatic slabs of gray. Thick swirling tides of aquamarine night shade a shoreline of flickering combustion. Creaking joints collapsing into blankets of billowing smoke, trapping blisters of pure heat that fester in sullen nimbus clots, then slowly disperse into the sky. Flashes of movement, frenetic but deliberate: a choreography of purposeful speed. Backlit in floodlights and florescent, almost like a film set, the men loom statue-tall, imposing and heroic in the artificial light. Features abstracted and generalized like a socialist realist painting. As if wrestling willful constrictors, the men quickly twist, coax, and yank the hoses into their precise positions.

The slightest perceptible pause ... a swift smatter of random city sounds splash their pulse-pounded eardrums. All senses heightened and sharp. The signal is given. The juice surges through the lines. The hose kicks like a gun. Everybody jolts or jukes to varying degrees. The hose, however, holds steady. The men holding the hose maintain laser-precise aim, and a slim stream of highly pressurized water shoots through a broken picture window and into the pinpointed heart of the blaze.

Eddie was all concentration and determination, moving methodically in concert with his crew. He manned the second line in, directly behind the captain, who delivered the "go" signal. The hose lineup more or less mirrored the house hierarchy. In those days—this was October '78—there was one captain to each house. The senior captain, Jeff, was the guy in front of Eddie. The lieutenant, Tom, was working a neighboring hose.

The place they'd been summoned to was an imposingly large building. Not big enough to be a factory, not small enough to be a house. In fact, it was a type of hybrid structure built as a result of a civic zoning experiment designed to widen the tax base without attracting the cavernous industrial parks that tend to accompany certain forms of business development. According to a *Newark Star-Ledger* that Eddie would read later, back at the firehouse, the structure had been divided into a residential area and a business area. Apparently some sort of manufacturing operation occupied the bottom floor. There were three stories. It was a tall, wide behemoth of a shelter, a chancre on the smooth, ivory skin of the cottage and A-frame-heavy village of the township of Corrunoside -on-the-Raritonia River—if you asked any of its rather highbrow inhabitants.

4

One of the neighbors had told a local paper it was "like the oversized lair of a monster troll squatting vulgarly and looming menacingly over our prim and proper rows of miniature doll houses." That may well have been true. Surveying the building's exterior, one tended to come away with a definite warehouse vibe. Viewed from the outside, it looked like a place where rough-muscled guys in steel-toed boots and hardhats worked on clanging assembly lines amid puffed-out clouds of stinking sulfur fog and blurred wavy geysers of liquefied heat.

Inside, however, were windows with coveted panoramic views, airy loft space, and wood, bare wood where artists were building bodies of work, studios, and lives. There was faintly stained wood of a Pine-Sol-shined floor where a young couple recently stretched out together to share a bottle of Spanish red and an old Bogart film on their first night in their first apartment. New wood in yet-to-be occupied office corridors smelling faintly of sawdust. Old wood creaking like old bones in the ground-floor studios that had been there for years. Painted wood on painted walls that served as a backdrop for multiple scenes and situations. Wood in a dizzying array of varied shapes and sizes and smells. Wood of all kinds and types and grades and grains and finishes and thicknesses. Wood in all its diverse permutations. All with little in common accept its potential for flammability. Burning wood, rendered uniform in death, each unique plank and panel converted into fuel for the almighty fire. Crackling wood, raging furious as a bonfire on a chilly homecoming eve. Burning wood, burning with a vengeance. The genie was out of the bottle. In a big way.

After all the Hollywood film that's been expended capturing the lore and legend of the urban fire, it has become a cliché to say that flame is almost a living thing. That it breathes. That it has a mind of its own. Still, some form of that metaphor crossed the mind of many of those working the fire that night. It sure looked alive to those who watched while it raged almost out of control, like some half-caged satanic beast threatening to grow and spread and escape.

Of course that was before they'd watered it into submission. It had peaked, losing the intensity and immensity that only minutes before would have inspired awestruck comparisons to mysterious creatures or wild, howling beasts. Now it had become just a fire. They were starting to wrap up. The adrenaline was withdrawing. Was looking like another routine call. Judging from the initial size and scope of the blaze, it easily could have been more, but they'd handled it quickly and competently, starving it, leaving the fire no food, no fuel, and no room to maneuver into something daunting and dangerous.

This made the sudden explosion even more of a surprise. A thunderous monster slab of severe sound crashed, releasing a splattering shatter of sharp, shrieking shockwaves that stabbed at the men's eardrums with a million tiny spearheads. The deafening blast seemed to suck the very air from the sky, aurally zinging all surroundings, turning everything into instant noise. It was like God's own car door being slammed up in heaven.

Then it was over, as abruptly as it had occurred. The men on the hose line gave a visible start, almost as if they were infantry ambushed by an utterly unexpected artillery attack. Some looked ready to drop what they were doing, hit the deck, and take cover. But not one member of the steely team succumbed to panic. All held their positions; marshaling the uncommon, unspoken courage they all shared. It was this communal courage—this brotherhood of balls—that steadied their shaking hands and held their feet firmly in place. It was this courage that drowned out the jarring reverberations still ringing in their ears and reminded them all that they had a job to do there, a job that had just gotten exponentially more urgent and treacherous.

Although distracted for an instant by the stunning sonic rupture, the men quickly retrained their attention on pressing practical matters. An army of yellow coats sprang into action like agitated ants. This was supposed to be a by-the-numbers operation; now all bets were off. Crews were being redirected on the fly, and contingency plans were executed. Once the immediate shock of the situation subsided, the first lucid thoughts of most men in the company were for their brethren inside.

Eddie overheard the two officers confer, agreeing that a search party should be assembled to enter the building to ensure that no one who had been inside at the time of the blast had been injured or trapped. Jeff had assigned leadership of the four-man expedition to Tom. The lieutenant accepted, but there was a shaky hesitancy in his voice that turned Eddie's head and grabbed his attention. He knew that fear was contagious. Eddie worried that Tom's tentativeness would spread. That didn't bode well for the success of what had the potential to be a fairly hazardous mission.

In his mind, Eddie cursed Tom's ineptness and cowardice and figured he should steer clear of the issue. After all, it is a leader's job to lead. Eddie was fairly new to the company (only a year ago he'd still been part of the volunteer squad), and logic told him it was not his place to pipe up or intervene in any way. In his heart, however, he knew he had to do what was right ... even if that meant stepping on toes. Duty was duty. Its demands were simple, clear, and unchanging. It didn't make excuses. It didn't shirk off to safety.

Eddie caught up to Tom at the back corner of the truck after he'd suited up and was checking and double-checking his gear (taking just a bit more time and care than was necessary). He grabbed Tom's shoulder and spun him around in order to get his attention amid the din of hustling men at work. He indicated that he wanted to talk and discreetly motioned Tom to step a few feet away so they were out of earshot of the rest of the men.

"You ok?"

"Yeah sure."

But his blood-drained face and sheepish tone of voice belied his gruff reassurances. There was little time for further conversation. Eddie had to make an immediate decision. As if to emphasize the ticking clock, two men from Engine Company #13 came running toward the truck, all the way from the far perimeter of the fire. They were looking for the captain, trying to contain themselves, but their expressions betrayed red-alert-level alarm; there was something wild and frantic in their eyes and general manner. After searching through the men to no avail, one soot-stained guy climbed the side steps of the truck until he was visible to the most of the group. Without waiting for anyone's attention, he blurted the message that had quickened his feet and chilled the blood in his veins:

"Listen, guys, the explosion caused some kind of cave-in, and there's four men trapped inside. Two civilians and two of yours, best I can tell. I'm not even sure of the exact situation, but here's what we know."

Without waiting for the rest of it, Eddie grabbed the ax from Tom's white-knuckled grip. The decision had been made for him. He was going in. Within a matter of seconds, he put on whatever extra flame-retardant gear was immediately handy, grabbed his oxygen tank and regulator, gathered up the search and rescue team, and began marching in earnest toward the conflagration's fiery core. Jeff looked over from the hose battery with a "what-the-hell-is-going-on" expression. Eddie shouted something succinct over his shoulder and kept moving forward. There was no time to explain. Lives were at stake.

A moment later, Eddie was rounding the corner of the building with his four guy's right behind him. While looking for the most expeditious point of entry, he stole a furtive glance at his team. Whatever natural apprehension they were all feeling had been superseded by their abiding sense of duty and commitment. In Tom's eyes, he had sensed the panic of a man looking for a way out of an obligation. On the countenances of these men, he could detect nothing but grit and grim determination. They were as solid a crew as he could ask for. He felt confident putting his life in their hands and hoped he had earned the same respect from them. If the unquestioning manner with which they had accepted his taking over the reigns of this expedition was any indication, he had.

Roughly twenty yards to the left of the front door, there was a huge double window frame that had been removed to facilitate the original breach of the bottom floor. Eddie gestured over his shoulder to indicate his intended course of action, but the men had already anticipated his next move and were right on his heels as he stepped through charred ash, broken glass, and other miscellaneous debris.

8

Inside was a world of choking haze and molten humidity. At fifteen paces, the heat was already stifling; the air a soup of soot and visibility terrible. Flashlights clicked on to cut the coal-mine darkness, but within a matter of yards the beams were swallowed by the gaping gray-black jaws of swirling smoke phantoms. Gingerly but purposefully, they continued to advance, penetrating an inferno that grew more hazardous with each successive step.

Eddie was on point; Joe, a grizzled, gray-haired veteran on the cusp of retirement, was two steps behind him. Out of nowhere, Joe lunged forward, grabbed Eddie in a bear hug, and heaved him to the ground. Eddie thought Joe had lost his mind and was just about to retaliate with a roundhouse left, when he saw the flaming plank tumble end over end to spear the exact spot where Eddie had been standing just a moment before. The plank grazed Joe's arm close enough to have singed his sleeve had he not been wearing his suit, but thanks to his lightning reflexes, the team had been otherwise unaffected.

The only thing hurting Eddie, after the initial jar of Joe's take down, was his pride. He was on point. He was the leader of this operation. He should have been the one to see the falling beam. He cursed himself but quickly shook it off. The only thing beating himself up would do was heighten the probability of another mistake. This time, they'd been lucky. Firemen couldn't afford to rely on luck. So Eddie did his best to put the lapse behind him and refocus. Plotting a careful course, the team formed a tight line behind Eddie as he led them forward in a straight, steady path. They progressed without incident, pausing at the first doorway. The door was closed and the handle was hot enough to the touch to transmit warmth through asbestos gloves.

Eddie opened the door. A blast of heat backed him up several steps. On the other side, the men were met with a small residual blaze. It was too big to put out with the small extinguisher they had carried in but too small to wait for backup, not when there were company men trapped close by. Eddie took a deep breath and lunged through the flames. The men followed without hesitation. Once they made it through and patted each other down, they found themselves in a long, dark hallway. Following it to the end, they found what looked like the source of the cave-in: a rubble-obstructed stairway leading down toward a basement.

Directly above the stairway, the ceiling had collapsed, exposing the beams in the adjoining walls. The insides of what remained of the walls were twisted and rent. Although they still couldn't determine the nature of the explosion, the men had clearly found its source.

The men turned their attention to the cave-in. The stairwell was almost completely filled with chunks of concrete and charred, broken beams. The smaller pieces of rubble were sandwiched beneath a huge unbroken piece of ceiling material and a steel girder that bridged the entire span of the stairs; only the first two steps were visible. Eddie shouted for a response. Nothing. Joe stepped up and tapped on a pipe that led to the underground floor. Their hearts lifted when his tapping was answered with an identical pattern.

Joe turned and grabbed Eddie's arms.

"We found 'em. We found 'em."

Old Joe was almost hopping up and down. His face glowed through its patina of grime, and his voice contained an almost prepubescent glee. Eddie didn't want to bring him back down to earth, but he had to. They had a hellishly hard task ahead, with no guarantee of their ultimate success.

"Joe … Joe! Settle down. Finding 'em was the easy part."

Joe nodded his head, and the team got down to the dirty and dangerous business of digging through the staircase ruins. It took every ounce of strength from all four of them to hoist the huge piece of ceiling that lidded the catastrophe. Although the slab had been left more or less intact by the fall, there were jagged areas all along its edges. As a result, the guys had a hard time maintaining their grip. Brick-sized chunks of crumbled drywall and other materials flaked off in their hands as they searched out tenable handholds.

To make matters worse, the piece was resting in a flimsy awkward position. Its middle was pressing down on the rest of the rubble, while its edges rocked back and forth, creating an unstable, potentially deadly see-saw. If they dropped the slab once they lifted it, there was a good chance its impact could cause a domino effect, causing a further cave-in below and endangering the trapped party downstairs with an instantaneous crush of concrete and wood. There was also the strong possibility that the crack running down the middle of the slab could be aggravated to the point of rupture once lifted, thereby threatening Eddie and his men with live burial, deep contusions, and/or broken bones.

Eddie and his men looked at each other. They all knew the risks. If they were going by the book, now was the time to bring in backup and heavier equipment. They were not, however, going by the book. When the book concerned the matter of brothers entombed beneath their boots, the book was discarded. Without saying a word, they all nodded agreement to the obvious question before them. Two of the men picked through the debris at the far end of the stairs, gently descending into the rubble as they cleared space. Eddie and Joe propped themselves against a twisted track of railing buried deep enough to anchor their weight. On three, they lifted, Iwo-Jima-ing the thick sheet of ceiling over their heads. While straining against the weight, they pushed with all their might until the harden muscles in their chests and upper bodies screamed with power enabling them to clear the way.

Later, over Budweiser's at the corner bar, Joe, with a reverent and faraway gaze, would call it a miracle. "There's just no way … no way should we have been able to lift something so heavy and ungainly," he'd say many times over, shaking his head in disbelief. The rest of the guys may have rolled their eyes, but no one who had been present in that hellhole had the heart to contradict him. In one fluid motion, the slab was clean jerked up and out and tilted toward an out-of-the-way corner. With a collective grunt, the men shot-put the piece forward, then ran for dear life as it cannonaded against the ground with a loud, hollow, echoing thud, sending its shrapnel through the room like a two-ton grenade. They all ducked and took cover. Amazingly, they all rose intact. A few abrasions and bruises, but that was it.

The rest of the job was a little easier. They were not yet out of the woods, however, not by a long shot. What remained to be done was a trapeze act of balance and high tension. Every extraction could have caused a devastating avalanche of building materials. It was slow and tedious work requiring acute concentration and finesse.

After about an hour of rock mining and reverse Jenga, the men heard voices on the other side and knew they were close. "Hello?" Eddie yelled, "Hello?" An uproar of jubilation erupted from the other side of the obstruction. Words of encouragement were exchanged through the slowly shrinking wall of debris. Following a brief lull, one of the trapped firemen spoke up.

"Hey Mac."

"Eddie."

"Eddie."

"Yeah. What can I do for you?"

"Listen, I know the procedure in these deals. I know you got to take your time and be extra delicate and all, but if you could just speed it up a little bit, we'd appreciate it."

"Getting claustrophobic in there are you?"

"I got a lady down here. Bad burns and heavy blood loss. My gut says she's running out of time. I don't want to give you more pressure than you already got on you but … a few minutes might make the difference. Understand?"

"Understood. We'll get a move on."

"Thanks."

"It's my job. No thanks necessary."

Eddie stared up at Joe, silently soliciting his opinion on the situation. Joe shrugged his shoulders.

"Way I see it, we got to step it up; we got no choice. We can't let her die."

"Yeah Joe, that's what I'm thinking. But if we screw this up, we jeopardize the rest of them, and they're all healthy from the sound of it."

"Well then, we can't screw up."

Eddie grinned and made way for Joe, who had pulled a mini-crowbar from a holster at his belt. They signaled for the other two men to join them and began to double-time it through the destruction, trying to increase their speed without decreasing the care they were taking. This was, of course, impossible. The men's haste caused several scary slides and other close calls. At one point, the men brought a pummeling shelf of sheetrock and brick down upon themselves. Eddie's efforts had earned him a direct hit in the head. He felt woozy and weak at the knees from the impact. But he continued without pause. A few minutes later, there was a nausea-inducing groan and crack as a cluster of materials sagged forward, snapping a piece of rebar and sending a spray of building materials into the basement air pocket. Two of the men yelled out sharply, and then a sickly silence spread across both sides of the crumbling wall.

"You guys ok?" asked Eddie.

In the gap between inquiry and response, there was a brief hesitation as the battered and slightly shell-shocked trapped men caught their breath and waited for the rush of pain they'd been splashed with to crest and crash. In that hesitation, which seemed a decade long, Eddie lived a lifetime of guilt and second-guessing. In that hesitation, he aged at least a year. Finally, their voices grunted through the barrier. Their injuries were minor. The wounded woman was unaffected by the incident.

The men made quick work of the rest of the pileup. There were no further complications. Eddie tunneled into a collapsed edge of wood frame. When he had pulled it free, he realized he had broken through to the other side. Minutes later, the hole he'd dug had grown to man-sized dimensions, and Eddie had squeezed his way through.

Inside he was met by a pair of uniformed firefighters, a man who under several layers of dirt and grime was casually dressed in street clothes, and the injured woman, who was stretched out on the floor at the far edge of the tiny pocket.

The rest of the extraction was fairly uneventful. The two firefighters had sustained only minor injuries, and the male civilian had broken his arm. Eddie and Joe stayed with the hurt woman, who was floating in and out of consciousness, doing their best to talk her through while the other team members escorted the group outside, expertly navigating the myriad pitfalls of the burned-out structure. A stretcher was fetched in a hurry and Eddie and Joe carried the woman out to a waiting EMT crew.

As they crossed the threshold to the fresh air outside, they were greeted by a gathered semicircle of comrades and neighborhood onlookers who gave them a hero's welcome, spontaneously breaking into a heartfelt round of cheers and applause. This was no show for the arriving press vans. It was personal to everyone there who was on the job. They all knew it could just as easily have been them caught in that basement collapse and were relieved to see everyone make it out alive and that almost everyone survived the ordeal relatively unscathed.

It was too soon to determine the full extent of the rescued woman's injuries. She'd been prepped and rushed to the hospital before Eddie had been able to wrangle a clear assessment out of the paramedics. Another crew of paramedics had remained at the scene, treating some of the men and victims for minor smoke inhalation and for scrapes and bruises that weren't serious enough to warrant emergency room attention.

Eddie made his way toward the second ambulance to see if they could relay some information about the woman's condition. Making slow progress through the thickening crowd of back-slapping admirers and congratulators, he felt a firm hand grip his shoulder from behind. He turned with a humble nod, trying to be as low-key as he could without seeming dismissive, expecting to bashfully but sincerely acknowledge someone's expression of praise. Instead, he found himself face to face with the chief of the entire department. Judging from the sour look on the chief's face, it didn't look like he had caught up with him in order to shower him with compliments.

"Can I have a word?"

"Sure, sir."

"In private."

"All right but …."

"But what?"

"I was wondering if I could just have a minute. It looks like the EMTs are packing up and I wanted to ask … I mean I was headed over to the … just wanted to …."

"There's no new information about her status, son. I'm in radio contact with the hospital, and I'll let you know the minute I know."

"Thanks."

"Don't mention it. But do you require any medical attention before they go? Do you want to have them look you over just to be sure?"

"No. I'm all right.

"Follow me then."

Eddie's nerves had shifted into overdrive. Through the entire saga of the fire and rescue he hadn't felt like this. There was a cold cannonball of worry bouncing up and down in his stomach. They walked over to the fire chief's squad car. At the far edge of his peripheral vision, Eddie could see Tom and Jeff waiting apprehensively in the on-deck circle of official inquisition.

Chief Rumpkey leaned against his hood and stared Eddie hard in the eyes with a penetrating gaze that made Eddie want to crawl under the chassis of the vehicle.

"Eddie, I'm going to get right down to it. What you did was a violation of policy and procedure. I had specifically ordered your station captain to lead the entry team. How did you end up running the show?"

Eddie glanced over at Tom, still exhibiting the zombie-like pallor. The stain of cowardice was splotched across his face like acne on a teenager. Assuming both their jobs were at stake, all Eddie had to do was tell the chief exactly what had happened and he'd be exonerated. There was nothing wrong with taking initiative and grabbing the reins from a commander who had obviously been too petrified to discharge his duties.

Jeff was already ringed with the aura of defeat, as if he knew what Eddie was thinking. He snuck Eddie a nod to let him know he understood and to indicate that it was ok for Eddie to do what he had to do. Apparently Chief Rumpkey caught the unspoken exchange.

"Don't look over at your captain. Look at me. I want an answer— from you. I'll hear from them in a minute. Why did you seize the helm of this operation?"

The explanation was clear, but not simple. Eddie might be a lot of things, but he wasn't a rat. No matter what his problems with and criticisms of Tom were (and there were many), there was no way he was going to air private laundry publicly and sell his station mate down the river.

"Well?"

"I don't have an answer for that."

In the chasm of silence that followed, Eddie felt the vertigo of a man falling from grace. Chief Rumpkey looked Eddie up and down thoughtfully, regarding him carefully, taking the full measure of the man. Eddie felt naked before him. He thought about what it would feel like to clear out his locker and say good-bye to the station, leaving under a cloud of insubordination and disgrace. It was so unbearable that he almost broke in that moment almost blurted out the truth. It was on the tip of his tongue. But honor and loyalty sealed his lips and shut him up.

"You don't have an answer for that?"

"I don't have an answer for that."

"Well I do."

"You do?"

"Yes. You did it for the men, and you did it because you recognized that you were the best man for the job. That's why, I assume, Tom made no move to intercept you beyond throwing out a token question after you already passed him by. You were covering for your chicken-shit lieutenant, and you decided that the lives of two firefighters, not to mention two civilians, were too precious to gamble on some inept pansy that got his position from patronage."

"That's not what."

"Zip it! Quit while you're behind, or at least quit while you still have a job."

"So I still have a job?"

"Of course you do. I didn't haul you over here to discipline you. I brought you over here to gauge your body language and reactions in order to confirm what I had already assumed. And don't worry about Tom; I can't touch the weasel motherfucker no matter how bad I want to. Let's just say he's got friends in high places."

"So that's it?"

"That's it. As you were."

Stunned and shaken, but relieved, Eddie wanted to get the hell out of there before Chief Rumpkey changed his mind. He was stopped in his tracks.

"One more thing."

"Yes sir?"

"Listen Eddie, I just want to say that men like you are rare and getting rarer. It's my job to cultivate courage, not crush it, but in the future, you can't just follow the orders that make sense to you. The unit can't function that way. Kapesh?"

"Understood."

"If you can handle that part of it, there's nothing in your way. Nothing. You've got an amazingly bright future with this company as long as I have any say over it, and that's likely to be for a long time. If you can just learn to follow orders, you'll be giving the orders before you know it. Maybe you should already be giving the orders, I don't know, but there's nothing I can do about that right this minute. You're still too green and have to get some seniority under your belt. But just between you and me—and don't take this as a green light to ever, ever do something like this again—but just between you and me, I'm impressed. I questioned you to ask why the lieutenant didn't go in on that rescue, and standing here talking to you, I'm realizing ... that a Captain did."

"Thank you sir. Thank you very much. I'm speechless. I'm honored by the confidence."

"Ok, ok, enough. What happened to speechless? Speechless means speechless. Shut up about this already. Just know you got a guardian angel high up in the squad and that he's looking out for you. Be patient; accept authority, even boneheaded authority, and I'll make sure you advance. But keep it under your hat or I'll bust your ass."

"Yes sir."

"It's Chief Rumpkey, not sir. Now tell that yellow-bellied rat bastard I want to see him next."

"Excuse me?"

"Jeff. Get Lieutenant Tommy over here. And remember, not a word of this. If the guys ask, I reamed you a new one."

"Got it."

"You better. Now get out of my sight."

Eddie was doing just that, beating a path toward Jeff when he heard the chief's radio crackle to life. A few moments later, before Eddie was out of earshot, the chief called out to him across the street. Eddie cupped his hand to his ear so he could hear him through the din of aftermath.

"What'd you say Chief Rumpkey?"

He couldn't make out everything that was said, but he made out enough to get the message Rumpkey was transmitting. It was about the girl. She was in ICU, but she was listed as stable. She was going to make it.

Chapter 2

Eddie and his wife pulled into the banquet hall parking lot and searched for a space. The place was packed. After several futile and frustrating revolutions around the blacktop, he decided to make his own spot, squeezing into the end of a row, between a concrete piling and a motorcycle. The fit was a tight one but Eddie maneuvered skillfully, navigating between the two obstacles without bumping either one.

One last glance in the rearview mirror and he was ready to go. Exiting the car, Eddie surveyed his handiwork. The passenger side was crammed snug against a Yamaha with only a fingernail of separation between the Impala's door handle and the bike's throttle. On the driver's side, there was enough room to open the car door just wide enough for Eddie and his wife to wriggle out of the vehicle. Half the car occupied the space the bike had left empty; the other half rested upon a criss-crossing maze of foreboding yellow lines, which gave Eddie second thoughts about parking there. A glance at his watch, however, vetoed the idea of moving. He couldn't be late to his own commendation ceremony. People would notice. He figured he'd pay the damn ticket if he got one.

Walking toward the hall, an ill-defined uneasiness beset him. He tried to remind himself that it wasn't, after all, exactly "his own" commendation ceremony. It had been luck to be in the right spot at the right time to have helped with the basement rescue right before the annual winter holiday banquet, which was held between Thanksgiving and Christmas... Since they had a commendation to give him and the other guys involved, the brass had decided to roll their ceremony into their annual holiday bash. So, it wasn't like "the Eddie show," with him as the only focus. He reassured himself that this crowd would be here, and that this parking lot would be full, whether he and his men had done their thing that fateful night or not. Still, it didn't help matters much. Eddie did not like to be at the center of attention for any reason; not even a little bit. It made him nervous and uncomfortable.

To make matters worse, he was being recognized for doing what he considered to be his duty. *It didn't make much sense*, thought Eddie, *to single out and spotlight a man for special acclaim just for doing his job.* The whole thing seemed somehow unseemly. In fact, it embarrassed him. From his perspective, lavishing praise on a firefighter for fighting fires and saving lives was like throwing a parade for an accountant who correctly filed a client's tax returns. It was what he did for living and that was that. Period. The end.

Eddie was also unaccustomed to the formal clothing the occasion called for. His shoes were tight and pinched his feet below the ankles. His belt was dug into his waist, and his tie tugged at his neck like a noose. All in all, he had a good mind to turn around; change into some sweats, and head for the neighborhood pub for a burger and a beer. But it was too late now. He'd been spotted. A boisterous and friendly voice shouted out his name across the lot. Turning toward the source of the greeting, Eddie and his wife saw four of his buddies from the house approaching.

The sight of Steve, Jerry, Keith, and Dennis immediately relieved much of Eddie's anxiety. Their playful jibes and backslapping camaraderie help to alleviate the fish-out-of-water feelings. These guys had been his good friends of his since his days as a probie.

Steve and Jerry were identical twins who'd grown up in Elmwood Park, New Jersey, a relatively small old-school Italian-Polish working-class factory town on the Passaic River directly east of Paterson and a stone's throw from New York City. Growing up, they had enjoyed a fair amount of local celebrity as carbon-copy all-around athletes. In high school, Steve lettered in football, baseball, and wrestling; Jerry had been a basketball phenomenon who also excelled in soccer, football, and wrestling.

Both boys had attended Penn State with visions of pro-sports level fame and fortune that never quite materialized. Jerry blew out his knee during his senior year. By the time he recovered, interest in his skills had waned. Scouts who had once courted him with promises and visions of the big time quickly moved on to younger faster prey. Because his injury had occurred during (indeed, toward the end of) his final year of athletic eligibility, he lacked a venue to prove that, post injury, he was still the same player whose that 17.6 points/12 rebounds per-game averages had led Penn State to two NIT and one NCAA tournaments. Steve played minor-league baseball for four seasons but never made it past double A before hanging up his cleats.

Despite their identical frat-boy chic style of dress, flat-top crew cuts, and apple-cheeked, strong-jawed, still-boyish faces, the two cut very different figures. Once you got to know them, it was pretty easy to tell one from the other. The twins had walked away from their athletic pursuits with very different attitudes.

Steve was embittered by his experiences. He tended to bristle at the very mention of the subject of sports. If the guys happened to be discussing the previous weekend's football or baseball game, they'd change the subject if Steve entered the room. He stomped sullenly through life like a comic-strip kid with a black cloud perpetually drawn above his head. It was rare to see him smile, even rarer to hear him laugh.

Conversely, Jerry seemed to take his experiences in stride. He seemed almost relieved that the constant intense pressure to perform that had squeezed him since early childhood as a pint-sized pee-wee league standout had been eased. Now he could just exist. He seemed quite content with his lot in life. Whereas Steve had been haunted and curdled by his near miss with the majors, Jerry was proud of the accomplishments he'd been able to paste into his scrapbook. He'd even be glad to show it to you if you asked. It was a part of his identity that he was at peace with. Although he did not live off of past glories, he enjoyed reminiscing about his jock days and often regaled the guys with insider stories of college ball: road trips, locker rooms, final seconds on the foul line, March madness at the big dance, that sort of thing.

Keith was the cut-up of the crew, an old-school character with Irish-Italian roots and a strict Catholic upbringing that he seemed to still be rebelling against. A big blustery mouth bubbled over with blarney portioned out by a razor tongue that had nearly started more than one barroom brawl. His unruly, bushy black hair always poked out from his Yankees cap. Keith had pale blue eyes with a spark in the middle and fair, freckled skin that went lobster in the sun. He was a lanky 6'4", with a Nautilus build from the gym down the street. When the other guys were pounding shots, he was pounding pavement; he ran five miles a day, just after sunrise every morning. You could set your watch by it. Outgoing and charming, he had a way with women and a way with words. He was the ladies' man of the bunch that was for sure. It was a blessing and a curse, as he would be the first to tell you.´

Dennis was the most nondescript of them all. It wasn't easy to fit him into a ready character mold. In fact, they had all once joked about it, much to his chagrin. It was about a year after they'd all met and a few months since they all started hanging out regularly. They were at Jerry's newly installed aboveground pool for a barbeque. Keith was stretched out on the lawn chair, holding court, trying in earnest to impress them and his girlfriend at the time (some tiny firecracker of a redhead bartender he'd picked up at Seaside the month before).

Keith had looked them all over, acknowledging them one by one with his chilled bottle of Bud, and had shaken his head before saying, "Well, look here. The boys all here. What a motley crew! We've got Eddie over there at the Weber, the firefighter for life, the world's last decent man if there was one. Then there are our beloved twins, both in the pool. Of course they're in the pool. You'd think they'd been born with webbed feet, the bastards. The alpha and omega of sport, they are. Me, I guess I'm the resident mess, some kind of buffoon for you all's amusement." And on it went. They all had a few so maybe it seemed funnier than it was, but Keith's little personality tirade had them in stitches.

Only thing was, when he got to Dennis, he could think of no box to put him in. Pro or con. And it wasn't because Dennis was just so diverse he defied description. He was a pleasant enough guy; he did his job and he was one of them. They could relate to him; they all more or less liked him. In fact, and maybe precisely because he wasn't "Dennis the star athlete" or "Dennis the lady killer," it was Dennis who Eddie usually confided in, private, under the carpet things that he would not have felt comfortable telling the rest of the group.

It was Dennis, after all, who had brought Eddie into the fold when he'd first joined the department and everyone else was still hazing him. Dennis was the first friend Eddie made, and if he had to choose, he'd say Dennis was his closest friend of them all. There was a trust there and an unspoken understanding. So it wasn't that there was something the matter with Dennis or he was the odd man out, on the outside looking in. There was just nothing you could put a handle on as far as discernable character description.

Keith's rant had come to an abrupt end at the nondescript, bricked-up wall that was Dennis. He had drawn a blank when it was Dennis's turn to be roasted, and for once, he'd gone speechless. Dennis didn't really show it at the time (he'd been playing fetch with Jerry's lab and pretended not to have been listening), but the minor, trivial incident had nevertheless both hurt his feelings and pissed him off. He made a secret promise that day that they'd all end up remembering him for something, no matter what.

Actually, if the guys had dug a little deeper, there was one tag you could have put around Dennis's neck that would have fit snugly. It could be accurately stated that he was a formidable schemer. In this arena, his vanilla facelessness served him well. He was sharp in business. He cleaned up well in a suit, he talked the talk, and he inspired confidence. Eddie learned everything he knew about stock tables and Wall Street from listening to Dennis over meals. The entire time Eddie had known him; Dennis had been chasing or running from one can't-lose-get-rich-quick dream to another. No matter how many of them imploded, there was never a shortage of investors clamoring for action in the next one. Many of them were solid propositions, and Dennis could have made a go of several.

The problem was (and only Eddie knew this) that there was a dark side to their friend, the uber-capitalist. Dennis had a habit of cutting corners on deals. When there was enough to go around, Dennis was everyman's cash cow. When there wasn't, sometimes people got screwed. Somehow Dennis always seemed to get his. It was never outside the law, but probably outside certain ethical realms.

And speaking of ethical realms, there was definitely some quantity of vague shadiness in Dennis's past (a substantial amount of which continued to ooze up into his present). Most of the time, Dennis was a nice enough person that you could ignore the reek of the rot without too much effort. But sometimes, he was so obvious and transparent about his avarice that one could not help but notice something foul going on. The only non-Jersey native, he had moved from Florida under a cloud of bankruptcy and a set of other circumstances that had never quite been made clear, even to Eddie, who pretty much knew it all when it came to Dennis.

It was Eddie, and only Eddie for example, who knew that Dennis had experienced I.R.S. problems in the past and that he'd come within a whisper of going to the joint. And it was Eddie who knew that Dennis had an ongoing gambling problem. That was why some of Dennis's more viable business plans had suddenly gone belly-up. It was an almost discernable pattern: there'd be some tough guys with chalky voices regularly calling or coming by the house looking for Dennis. They were heavy operators who would have Dennis sweating and double-talking for about a week or two. "Heard you had a good year," Eddie had overheard one of the goons saying to Dennis when they thought they were out of earshot. Then, all of a sudden, Dennis wouldn't be having a good year. Everything he'd worked to build would have been liquidated overnight. There would be no more thriving new start-up. But there would also be no more muscle-bound monkeys on Dennis's back.

Dennis would refuse to talk about it when Eddie tried to bring it up. They'd all shrug their shoulders, keep quiet and out of his business like they'd been told to do, and get back to what they did best, fighting fires and raising hell together. Then, in a couple months, Dennis would start talking about the next opportunity of a lifetime, and the merry-go-round of greed would crank up all over again while they all tried to stay out of his way—But not so far out of his way that they couldn't come to his aid and save his ass if he needed it. They were tight like that.

Entering the hall together, the five friends caused a minor stir. There was a smattering of restrained applause followed by a hushed crescendo of cupped mouth whispers and not-so-subtle pointing in their general direction. Guys came over from across the room, ostensibly to congratulate Eddie on his commendation, but really just to be seen mingling with what was fast becoming one of the most popular groups of guys in the community. And why not? They were handsome, they were brave, most of them were single, they had personality, and they knew how to have fun.

Eddie and his wife Renee sought out Joe, who was also being honored that night. He was at the edge of the bar, nursing a drink and staring off into the distance. When he saw Eddie, his eyes lit up. They clasps hands warmly, then Joe motioned him to follow.

"Come here. I got someone to introduce you to."

Eddie followed Joe to a corner table where he recognized one of the firefighters they'd pulled out of the cave-in that night.

"Eddie meet Stan. Stan, Eddie. Listen, guys, I'll be back in a bit. I got to run and see if my folks are here yet. If I don't catch up in time, I'll see you guys up on the stage there."

And with that, Joe had ambled off, disappearing into the crowd, leaving Eddie and Renee standing with a guy and no idea of what to say. Stan was sitting with his family, looking almost as uneasy with all the fuss as Eddie felt on the inside. After being introduced to Stan's wife and preschool-aged daughters, Eddie and Renee took a seat beside them and forced out some strained small talk. They sat around awkwardly talking about lawn care, current events, and a couple of other topics that were as arbitrary as they were mundane. After a polite interval, Eddie excused himself and they retreated to the bar. He ordered a Bud and turned to survey the crowd of attendees. While waiting for his beer, he felt a tug at his sleeve. Keith was at his elbow with a broad grin creasing his face:

"Good times, eh?"

"I guess. Really, though, I could do without all the prom night bullshit. Could think of about 1,000 better ways to spend an evening."

"Amen to that. Ain't all bad though. Quite a bit of talent afoot. Fish in a barrel. So how does it feel being the man of the hour and all?"

"Ok, listen. You can cut that shit out right now. I'm not."

"Relax, man. I'm just busting balls."

"That seems to be a particular area of expertise for you."

"It's a gift."

"It's something all right."

"No, that's something," said Keith, indicating a leggy blonde with a nudge and a nod.

"C'mon, man … behave yourself. This is a family function, no boys' night out, getting' blown after the council meeting. There's press here, community leaders. I mean, for all practical purposes, we're on the clock."

"Don't mean I can't make a little time does it?"

"Hey, don't ask me, I'm not your boss. I'm just looking out for you. Or at least trying to."

"Friendly advice?"

"Friendly advice. You can take it or leave it."

"No, I know. You know I'm just pulling' your chain. But even on a serious level, I hear you. I get what you're saying. You don't think I'm hip to this whole dog-and-pony show? They put us in these community slash social situations and then they watch us from afar … judge us on our poise and present ability. It's like scouts at a bowl game; they're looking to see who's got management potential—the right stuff. Some of us will be deemed executive material, and some of us will continue to serve as dry wood for the fire from now until the end of our careers."

"Oh, man, you're bringing me down even further than I was when I got here. I didn't think that was possible."

"Forget it man, don't worry about it. Certainly no need to dwell on it."

So, anyway, I seen you over there talking to that guy you pulled out. What's his name?"

"Stan."

"Why don't you invite Stan over to our table?"

"Aw, he's here with his wife and kids and all. I think you'd be a little too rowdy and inappropriate to qualify for family hour."

"Speak for yourself."

"I am. Before I have to go up on that Dias, I plan on tying one on."

"Well then, you better take that skirt off and get started. I do believe I've lapped you by at least two beers already."

"Yeah, yeah, all right. But for real, man, I got to say, it's a strange thing. It bothers me."

"What? Tonight? The whole thing?"

"Well, yeah, of course, but you mentioned the thing with Stan. How do you make small talk the second time you meet a guy who you faced death with the first time you met him? That was strange enough. But I mean, even with Joe, I saw him a minute ago and it's like we barely have any rapport. When we're on the job, there's this unspoken groove. I mean we are in sync to the point where we're like reading each other's minds and working in perfect coordination. Then I see him at some kind of a social function like this, or in any other out-of-work type situation, and it's like pulling teeth for us to say two words to each other. You should have seen us over there before. It was weird. I mean, I couldn't wait to find an excuse to get away from him, and he hightailed it the first chance he got."

"Hey, on the job, we're all pros. You know that. We're a well-oiled machine. Off-duty, some guys click and some guys don't. Don't sweat it. It's completely natural."

"Natural? You think it's natural to trust a guy so completely you'll put your life in his hands on Tuesday, and then on Wednesday you don't know what to say to him? You call that normal?"

"Yeah, it's just one of those things. Like I said, don't worry about it."

"I got to worry about it. I got to be up on the Dias with him in five minutes acting like we're lifelong best friends and brothers-in-arms."

"You know, if I can now give you a bit of friendly advice, I think you tend to overanalyze these things. All they want you to do is go up there, flash those wholesome pearly whites for the cameras and the crowd, cut a dashing, clean-cut figure, give a short, sweet speech, accept your little plaque, acknowledge the applause, and sit back down. It ain't the freakin' Oscars. You know—and this is not to in any way diminish what you did in that basement the other day because I got balls of steel and I honestly don't know if I could've hacked that situation—but you know, the department, they put on these type of glorified photo ops about three or four times a year, anytime one of us gives them even a remotely plausible reason to do so. It's how things are done."

"But why?"

"Why? Hello! It's about money. Cold, hard cash. Budgetary prerogatives. You think they put on these little soirees for our benefit? It's done to ensure that current levels of funding are maintained or even increased, especially during tough economic times when everyone else is being expected to tighten their belts. It's done to justify the occasional raid on taxpayer coffers for new toys and technologies that we may or may not really need. You happen to be this year's poster boy. You certainly earned it; now roll with it. You, my friend, are a rising star in this department. The only thing in your way is you … your warped old-fashioned sense of moral whatever. Just play ball. You got to learn to play the game, Eddie. You got to learn to play the game."

"What if I don't want to? What if it's not a game to me? What if this game shit makes me sick? Fire and rescue is not just a clock I punch; it's a calling. It's the best way I know to serve my community, my family, my country, my God."

"Whoa. Calm down, Eddie, calm down. We're just talking here. No need to get riled."

"I'm calm, Keith, I'm calm. It just vexes me, that's all. I realize you mean well. Hell you may even be right about the way things work and the way things are, but I swear I hate to hear it put like that. It cheapens everything that this brotherhood is about. It just boils my blood."

"Well then the unfortunate reality is that you're not going to travel very far up the departmental ladder with that attitude, which, if you ask me, is a damn shame."

"Yeah, a damn shame," Eddie replied sarcastically.

"Yes Eddie, a damn shame. Look around. You got more potential than any one of us. Out of the whole bunch of us, you and you alone got the total package. You can go all the way. Chief. The sky's the limit. You're photogenic, outgoing, you got the youth, the education, the articulation, the right connections, the skills, the courage, the competence … no blemishes, no enemies. You are in a unique position to move up the ranks. Plus you are now a bona-fide hero. No one can take that away from you. I'm just saying don't blow it all for some abstract bullshit principle, this virginal purity of soul, this snow white act."

"I don't act."

"I know, that's not my point. Point is, around here, the high road is going to get you nowhere but right back to where you started. Mark my words, you will never get anywhere in this department if you are one of those guys the other guys feel uneasy around. If the men feel they got to watch their ass or their mouth, around you, if voices lower when you walk into the room, then you are going to have a problem career-wise. You know what I'm saying?

"Yeah, I think I know exactly what you're talking about."

"Now don't get all like that and turn it around on me. You think I want to say these things to you? I'm telling you 'cause I'm your friend and I want to see you get what you deserve. I'm not saying be corrupt and crooked and evil and fucked up. I'm just saying go along to get along. I'm just saying this is the township of Corrunoside baby. Play ball."

Eddie opened his mouth to respond, but hesitated when he saw Keith give a discreet nod to his left. Turning his head in that direction, Eddie caught the approach of the rest of their clique. The discussion was abruptly tabled and conversation shifted to lighter subject matters as they made their way over to the dining area to find an open table.

When the time came for Eddie to be called up to the Dias and accept his commendation, he swallowed his misgivings like a shot of rough tequila and followed Keith's advice. As flashbulbs whirred and cameras clicked, he grasped hands and clutched shoulders with a hearty smile and enthusiastic manner, first with Joe and the rest of his colleagues who had entered the building, then with Stan and the rest of the people who'd been trapped, then with the various luminaries who'd attended the event.

The whole episode seemed a blur, like a half-forgotten childhood memory of playacting at recess. And play acting was what it was, at least to Eddie, who was afraid the frozen smile affixed to his face might harden and stay there permanently. When it came his turn to speak, however, there was nothing fake about the words he spoke. They were from the heart. They brought down the house.

He didn't brag or boast about what he'd been a part of doing. Neither had the other guys, but where they had each narrated their roles in the mini-drama of the fire, with a varying degree of storytelling skill and flair, Eddie decided he'd leave the reporting to News 12. Instead, he spoke about the job and the life he mostly loved but occasionally hated, and its attendant ups and downs, its interminable periods of waiting punctuated by life-and-death bouts against heat and smoke and chemicals and heights. He spoke about the traditions that helped to mortar the bricks of their respective firehouses and about the characters and champions who had slept under those roofs. The anecdotes he chose alternately (and sometimes simultaneously) conveyed humor and tragedy, fun and fear, excitement and mind-numbing routine. Through it all the common thread was the ball-busting labors that they continually complained about but dared not live without.

It was a funny thing, but when he had mounted the podium, he'd been so nervous his note cards were shaking in his hands. Thank God Renee was there for moral support. However, when he looked out and realized that the crowd was almost completely made up of guys who were just like him, who spoke the same language and shouldered some of the same burdens, he felt much of his anxiety disperse. These were his friends and colleagues, not some tough crowd of strangers. He decided he'd be better off getting rid of the cards and just winging it.

So that's what he did. He didn't end up giving a speech per se. Instead, he just talked to them. He pointed out the intangible bond that joined them together because they were engaged in an elite undertaking, sharing a set of experiences so unique that no amount of flowery frilly fifty-cent words could quite succeed in describing it to an outsider. They were a fraternity in the truest sense of the word. Screw the keggers and secret handshakes and Greek-letter T-shirts; **some** of these guys would die for one another.

Without overstaying his welcome, Eddie managed to cover a wide range of vividly described ground, touching on the aspects of firefighting that, for him, had transformed it from a job into a calling. Where the other guys had to strain to keep their egos in check and make an effort to keep from patting themselves on the back, Eddie transfixed the room with a soft-spoken, sincere humility. He considered himself blessed to be able to do what he did for a living, and it showed.

Soon (indeed, sooner than most), Eddie had finished speaking his piece. His concluding statement was met with thunderous applause. "Passion will make you crazy," he had paused before asking, "but is there any other way to live?"

In one ineffable moment, as Eddie stood behind the podium, his understated presence, his youth and vitality, his realness and natural charisma had merged. In the process, he had managed to eclipse every other firefighter, politician, and civilian who had stood or sat on that stage that night. This was unconsciously acknowledged in an off-the-cuff exchange between Jerry and his brother, Steve, as they waited for Eddie to return triumphantly to their table.

As they were standing and clapping out Eddie's ovation, Jerry nudged Steve in the ribs and pointed up at Eddie. "Meet your new lieutenant," Jerry commented with a wink.

"What're ya talking about?" Steve scowled.

"Maybe not today, maybe not tomorrow, but mark my words. If ever there were a promotion in waiting, he'll get it."

With the unexpected success of his speech and the ceremonial rituals out of the way, Eddie found himself having a better time. After all, there was no group he'd rather be with than these guys. And whatever the pretense, here they were. He decided to stop being such a spoilsport and make the most of it. Plus, now that the spotlight was off him a bit, he could relax. Eddie, Renee, and their group of friends held court at a corner table until the wee hours. Somewhere during one of his journeys back and forth to the bar, Eddie had been pulled aside by some very important men who made some very important promises. Even his inept deputy chief (all he did was save the rubber bands and string from the towels and made balls out of them) had stumbled over to let him know he'd done a good job. Chief Rumpkey made a special effort to seek him out in order to repeat predictions of a bright future.

Eddie was as levelheaded as they come, but that much acclaim can't help but get to a man's head, especially if it's been softened a bit by good food and strong beer. He decided it was a good time to go home and sleep off the dual buzz of alcohol and praise. Part of him wanted to let go, let loose, and push the night to its furthest possible limit, but as Keith was fond of saying, that's when someone can get hurt. He looked around for a familiar face and spotted Dennis nearby. With a jocular slur in his voice, he grabbed Dennis's elbow to get his attention amid the din of laughter, voices, and music.

"Jesus, were getting out of here. I'm almost buying into my own hype," he confessed.

Dennis regarded Eddie with a wry smile that made him feel exposed. It seemed as if he was assessing a math problem in his mind, weighing pros and cons. Then, as if someone snapped his fingers and woke him from a hypnosis session, whatever it was Dennis had been wavering about was over. He snapped to attention and spoke up:

"Yeah, let's take off."

Dennis scoured the room for Keith, who he knew would be more or less sober. Keith was nowhere in sight, probably on his way home with a local fire groupie. After a quick self-assessment, Dennis judged himself fit to drive. He could see that Eddie was borderline, so Eddie's wife drove. He didn't even want to think about repercussions of a roadside stop with someone in that condition behind the wheel. It wasn't compassion that Dennis felt. He wanted so talk to Eddie so he followed them home. Once there he asked Eddie to get into his car because he needed to talk about something. He knew if he got him alone, he'd be a captive audience.

Dennis was the kind of guy who didn't like to waste time with unnecessary banter or beating around the bush. He wanted to be delicate with Eddie in the timing of his approach. But delicate wasn't his thing; neither was timing. Once he got an idea in his head, the only way he could stop it from bouncing around in there was to let it out. That's why what he had to say didn't wait very long. Just as Eddie got into the car, Dennis turned down the radio and stared at him until he had his attention. "Let's go for a ride, ok?"

"What?"

"Listen, do me a favor."

"Anything."

"I know you must be beat. I am too, and I didn't even really drink."

"But?"

"But I want ... I need to talk to you about something."

"Is it important?"

There was brief pause as the engine revved and they were off. Dennis didn't want to spook Eddie, who was easily spooked. But time was money and there was urgency. They had to move soon, or at least he had to know soon whether or not there was a "they" in order to give his embryonic idea even a remotely viable possibility of being born.

"Yeah. Let me swing on by the Parkway Diner. We'll get a cup of coffee on the arm. Fifteen minutes of your time ... that's all I ask."

"Why? Are you in trouble?"

"No, no. Nothing like that."

"Well?"

"I got a little proposition for you is all. Business. You interested?"

"That depends. This all on the up and up?"

"I'm insulted you would even ask."

The truth was that Eddie felt out of place asking. He wondered if the fact he had to ask meant that maybe something inside him was trying to tell him something. Dennis was a little infamous for quasi-shady dealings. Nothing recent and nothing that stuck ... just rumors flying around the station. Then again, there were rumors flying around about everyone. And besides, Eddie needed to come up with some kind of moonlighting gig. He had simple desires: a house for his family and a comfortable retirement. But in late '70s Jersey, with inflation the way it was and all, coupled with probably more fire department budget cuts coming down the pike, even a simple man was mightily challenged to eke out a middle-class existence on a firefighter's salary. That was a primary reason he'd even been slightly interested in moving up the ranks. Better pay. Better benefits. If he stayed where he was ... God ... well it was just that everybody—well everybody except the guys who had money in the first place—moonlighted, did something else. Why not do something with a buddy who'd proven himself to be business savvy in the past? Maybe there could be some real upside. Maybe they'd have some fun working together and it wouldn't be such a grind. He guessed it couldn't hurt just to hear Dennis out. He could always say no.

"I ask again. This all on the up and up? I never got an answer."

34

"Of course. Just hear me out ok?"

"I don't know, man."

"It could mean a lot of money. Legit money, you have my word on that."

One thing Dennis didn't bullshit about was money.

"I have your word?"

"You have my word. I'm not going to jeopardize my career. You worry too much."

Without another word, Eddie nodded in hesitant assent. Soundlessly, Dennis looped his Cutlass into a dark swath of diner parking lot. A problem with his power steering caused him to struggle with the steering wheel as he cut a sharp angle between a Honda and the diner's dumpster. The car angled in. Dennis cut the lights and killed the ignition. Eddie had been looking out the window, drifting, high on realness and sense of purpose, and knowing his place in this world. Something in the sound of Dennis's voice as he said "c'mon" jolted him out of his cerebral clouds.

They exchanged a tentative glance as they reached for their respective door handles. The light shining on Eddie's face blinked on and off, giving him the appearance of a shooting star backlit in neon with each on-off flicker of the huge, garish, campy Parkway Diner sign. Dennis was just beyond range of the restaurant lights; his face was swaddled in constant impenetrable shadow.

Chapter 3

Eddie was out of the car while Dennis was still behind the wheel fumbling with his seat-belt latch. "Damn thing sticks sometimes," he explained in a tone that was meant to sound off-handed and casual but was not quite able to conceal the rampaging stampede of his onrushing vexation. The comment was followed by a stream of expletives and the thud of Dennis's fist against the dashboard.

When Eddie bent down to peer into the car, he noticed that Dennis's infamous "anger veins" were already beginning to protrude in a downward diagonal direction from the edge of his hairline to the upper arches of his eyebrows. Eventually they'd swell into the familiar, throbbing V that typically creased Dennis's forehead whenever he was just about to go all kinds of ballistic.

Eddie had long since gotten used to Dennis's periodic eruptions. Around the firehouse, it was more or less accepted as a fact of life that Dennis tended to lose his temper easily and often. There was no question about it; Dennis was something of a hothead. It was a character flaw that, over the years, had alienated many. It had never bothered Eddie though. Since Dennis had never directed ire of any kind in his direction, anger management–type issues had never arisen between them. When Dennis raged, some of the guys reacted by getting pissed off. Eddie would just shrug his shoulders and step out of the way. The guy had a short fuse. So what? So do lots of people.

When the other guys would start talking negatively about Dennis (or anyone else for that matter) behind his back, Eddie made a habit of leaving the room, often punctuating his exit by slamming the door behind him. He'd been raised to steer clear of gossip, but even if that hadn't been the case, it's highly doubtful that Eddie would have opted to participate in any "knitting circles" (a term he employed generically to describe any gathering that he found to be short on good-natured fellowship and long on pretension, jealous sniping, grandiose boasting, and catty commentary). He was a man who had a powerful aversion to the runaway gallop of unbridled tongues.

Actually, it was powerful aversion that probably failed to adequately capture the seething intensity of Eddie's enmity toward the giggling gaggles of shameless scandal mongers who got off on impugning and ruining the reputations of others. In his book, they were little better than vampires, the way they would gather, a thirst in their eyes, eager to feed off secondhand accounts of outrageous behavior, daring to experience thrills and adventures only by proxy through the very people they wound up passing their most severe judgments upon.

What bothered him most about these loose-lipped legions he'd seen congregating in the break rooms and around the water coolers of every job he'd ever had was the absolute lack of accountability. It was, in fact, the essential element that enabled their corrosive pastime to flourish. Any idiot with a decency deficiency and an ax to grind, a confidence to betray or a shred of salacious information to share, regardless of their motivation, regardless of their source, regardless of whether the information being purveyed was in context, exaggerated, or even, for that matter, true was permitted—no, encouraged—to launch an invasion into their neighbor's privacy, assured of protection from detection, hiding behind the coward's shield of anonymity as they broadcasted blind speculations and lurid allegations to a salivating audience eager to gobble it up, without question or challenge, as if it were gospel truth.

Maybe Renee had been right when she'd advised him to pay it no mind. Maybe his co-workers were right when they urged him to lighten up. Maybe it was no more than empty chatter that no one took seriously. Harmless banter. A way to connect. Something for people to talk about, like the weather. Except he'd seen what could happen when the seeds spread by this so-called harmless banter, pollinated by endless repetition, managed to take root like some noxious weed and strangle the good names of good people, indiscriminately destroying lifetimes of careful cultivation in the process.

So what if some poor innocent slob was unjustly subject to public humiliation? So what if a reputation got ruined? A career derailed? A marriage dissolved? A family dismantled? So what if the unsuspecting target, who, of course, was always tried and convicted in absentia, was never even given an opportunity to answer in his or her own self-defense? So what if there was no face-to-face confrontation between accuser and accused? That's how the game was played. It wasn't meant to be malicious; it was meant to pass the time. No one was supposed to get hurt. People talked. That was just human nature. Gossip was inevitable … as much a fact of life as death and taxes. Making a big deal about it was as useless as tilting at windmills. The whole thing left Eddie with a sour taste in his mouth.

That sour taste was a key reason why, even before they'd been introduced to one another, Eddie had never paid any attention to the negative scuttlebutt that often followed the mention of Dennis's name. As far as Eddie was concerned, Dennis had entered into their friendship with a clean slate. So far, he'd done nothing to besmirch it.

Early on, Eddie had pegged Dennis as a mostly harmless rowdy whose many rough edges were balanced by a big heart that usually led him to do what was right and come through when it mattered. A typical Jersey kid who'd grown up with a typical Jersey chip on his shoulder but, all things considered a brave, competent asset to the department and a loyal friend.

Nothing had shaken this initial assessment. Not the whispers about questionable ethics. Not the high-decibel locker-room stories about wild behavior. Not even the Tony Soprano stereotypes who periodically called the house to "ax" where Dennis was, using voices and vocabularies that sounded like they'd been swiped from central casting. Nothing.

Until now. At the precise moment he found himself leaning against the passenger door of Dennis's late-model American behemoth, a queasy uneasiness began to creep up from the pit of Eddie's stomach. He could hardly believe the spectacle he was witnessing: a grown man allowing himself to become half-unraveled by the temporary malfunction of a defective seat-belt component.

The entire duration of Dennis's bug-eyed, tomato-faced struggle with his gummed up seat-belt button had lasted ten seconds at the most, but it had made an impression nonetheless. In the span of that brief interval, an alarming array of unpleasant questions forced Eddie to face doubts and misgivings that had been building inside him for a while.

Watching Dennis lose his composure so quickly and easily, over something so trivial, had sharpened nebulous question marks into focus, allowing vague apprehensions to take shape and form a series of concrete queries: Did Dennis have his shit together? In a partnership situation, how much potential liability could his fiery temper and/or tendency toward lazy shortcuts expose them to? Could he be depended on when the chips were down, not just in a high drama emergency situation with sirens wailing and adrenaline flowing, but also during the type of mundane, everyday kind of crisis that would be more likely to arise in a business setting? Was there any credence at all to the endless rumors he had so scrupulously ignored? Did he really know this man? Were they close, or did they just spend a lot of time together? By deepening his involvement with this man, was he recklessly putting his life savings and his future and his family at risk? Was this really a man he wanted to go into business with?

If only he had listened, right then and there, to the voice in his gut. Had he done so, you would not be reading the words on this page. There would have been no reason to write this book. There is truth in the oft-repeated cliché that hindsight is 20/20. That's why Monday-morning quarterbacks complete all of their passes and never lose a single game. However, that night at the Parkway Diner, Eddie didn't have the benefit of a crystal ball. So he did the logical thing.

He quieted his internal warnings, wrote them off as false alarms. After all, the fundamental question he was mulling—Were they compatible business partners?—was exactly what they had come to discuss. There was no harm in hearing Dennis out. He hadn't signed anything. If he didn't like what Dennis was proposing, he could simply walk away.

At the same time, Dennis displayed almost uncanny perceptive powers, as if he'd read Eddie's mind and knew that he needed reassurance. As fast as he'd blown his cool, he rallied his reserves of calm and collected himself. Expertly twisting two of his fingers into a delicate pirouette, he danced them across the tiny stage of Detroit steel on his lap, gently coaxing the buckle button to click him loose. He then proceeded to finesse Eddie with the same ballet-like grace and dexterity he'd employed on the seat belt. With a glad-handed gesture toward the entrance of the twenty-four-hour eatery, Dennis started walking with the serenity of a retiree on a Sunday stroll.

"Sorry to overreact like that, man. I don't know what got into me. Got a lot on my mind these days."

"No problem."

"Usually when folks say 'no problem,' that means there is one."

"Well I mean what I say and I say what I mean."

"Hey man, I was just playing around. You mad at me or something?"

"Of course not."

"You're not getting cold feet now that you got a chance to put your money where your mouth is, are you?"

"Of course not. I just to know that if I decide to take that leap, I'm jumping with a level-headed partner."

"I hear you loud and clear. That's why I felt the need to apologize. For real. I mean, this is me talking, Dennis. Your bro'. You know me. And that was not me back there."

"Don't sweat it. We're cool."

And they were again. Eddie's doubts had subsided almost as quickly as they had arisen. Dennis helped speed the process along, quelling his temper tantrum just in time. Although it had barely lasted long enough to warrant comment, he'd made a point of commenting anyway, striking precisely the right tone and saying exactly what Eddie needed to hear to ease his mind. In fact, Dennis managed to hit all the right notes, turning in a near-flawless performance for the rest of the night.

Of course Eddie didn't view it as a performance, even though, looking back, that's exactly what it was. Not even coach Parcell's could have cynically identified the verisimilitude involved. Where Eddie saw nothing more than the sincere words of a sincere friend and the ambitious plans of an ambitious entrepreneur, hindsight would have exposed the multilayered facade, pulling back the curtain to reveal an Oscar-worthy actor, a commission-hungry stockbroker, and a politician pandering for votes. But Eddie was still relatively young: young enough to still be free from the ravages of bitterness; young enough to be blessed with a strong set of ideals that had yet to be stomped into sawdust-fine slivers and spread across some barroom floor. There was something refreshingly fresh and unspoiled about Eddie.

Maybe his ways lacked a certain urbane sophistication. Where others may have found nuance and shades of gray, it was true that he looked at life through black-and-white lenses. Right and wrong. Good and evil. But whatever he may have lacked in subtlety and flexibility, he more than made up for with heart and soul and authenticity.

The bottom line on Eddie was that he belonged to a rare and dying species: he was a decent, honest man. He trusted. There was innocence about him, purity. In the not-so-old-days, maybe even less than a generation ago, those were characteristics that would have been valued, held up as an example, seen as qualities to be envied and strived for. Nowadays, unfortunately, nice guys often seem to finish last. Trusting souls are no longer praised as paragons of virtue; they are derided as gullible. You can choose to see Eddie as a trustworthy guy, who, in turn, was naturally trusting of others. Or you can dismiss him as a naive anachronism. In the end, it really doesn't matter what word is used to describe Eddie's values. Nowadays, the guy with the strongest values is the same guy who usually ends up holding the bag.

Once again, however, these are words that are being written well after the fact. The full story has been told to me, and now I'm conveying it to you. The wisdom of the writer is not authentic wisdom. It's merely that I already know how this is going to end. In a nutshell: hindsight. Also, Eddie may put too much faith in his friends and grant the gift of his trust too easily. But don't get the wrong idea. This is a native New Jersey survivor we're talking about here. This ain't any hayseed. No sucker. No fool. On his first field trip to Manhattan, he was one of the few boys who did not lose his spending money playing three-card Monty against the cardboard box con men who lined the sidewalks outside the Port Authority. While many of his high school classmates were busy getting ensnared in the nets cast by the local street corner poison pushers, he was busy walking his textbooks to library.

The point is that no amount of superior street smarts, skepticism, common sense, or bullshit detection can make one immune to the deception of a close friend, especially one as clever, crafty, and convincing as Dennis. It's entirely possible, if not probable, that you or I or anyone else may have easily fallen hook, line, and sinker had we been the target audience for Dennis's act that night.

Dennis was persuasive. He had a face that made you want to believe, even when you knew he was full of shit. Dennis was a natural-born hustler blessed with a hustler's charm. He was among the best in the game. You wouldn't realize he'd gotten a leg up on you until he'd gotten all the way over. The man could sell sunshine to vampires. He was on it like that. He walked around as if privy to a secret that you should know. Even when folks had an inkling that whatever he was cooking up wasn't quite kosher, they still felt an urge to be a part of what he was putting together.

Dennis projects were always time-sensitive. This was by design, in order to create urgency. People felt a rush to get on board and grab a piece of the action before the ship sailed and it was too late. Same principle as those! You must call now! Adverts they show on cable late at night. You know the ones. The ads that are constantly belittled and mocked. The ads that serve as perpetual Letterman and Leno fodder.

Funny thing about those ads, however. By every objective measure (sales, branding, and viewer ship), they work; they are effective. As was Dennis.

So, reader, before you dare pass judgment on our protagonist, either now or at some point as this sad and sordid story continues to unfold, ask yourself if you've ever been taken, hoodwinked, fooled. Then put your stone down, get back inside your glass house, and read on.

As they approached the greasy spoon, a gust of chill wind swept the restaurant parking lot, cutting through Eddie's windbreaker, causing him to shiver and thrust his hands deep in his pockets. Although the men had walked in silence, Eddie couldn't help but notice that Dennis was chomping at the bit with anticipation as they walked up the diner's concrete entrance ramp. Like a mischievous kid who has just dreamed up the mother of all pranks, Dennis could barely contain himself. Despite the longness of the night, the lateness of the hour, effects of the alcohol and the thick weariness that spread through Eddie until it felt like he had molasses for bone marrow, Dennis acted as though he were trying to keep a lid on a pot bubbling over with pure, percolating energy. His body language was a jerky mélange of spastic exuberance as he impatiently reached forward to open the door, and invite Eddie to enter first with a broad, theatrical sweep of his arm.

Eddie ambled in ahead of Dennis, senses assailed by a rush of oil heat, blipping video games, appetizing smells, and muffled cash register bells as he worked his way forward. When they reached the "please wait to be seated" sign, the two men came to a stop, following instructions despite an abundance of empty tables. It was just something they were conditioned to do. A harried-looking middle-aged hostess rushed by, promising to be with them in a minute.

If Dennis had something to say, he'd usually hold it close to his vest until he felt secure, until he was sure that he would not be overheard. For this reason, Eddie found it a bit remarkable when Dennis began laying out his proposal right where they stood. He'd expected that Dennis would wait to start talking until they were comfortably ensconced in the brown faux leather of a secluded corner booth. Even then, one could expect to sit through a fair amount of beating around the bush before anything resembling substance would be brought up.

Tonight was different. Dennis cut directly to the chase. By the time they were shown to their seats, Eddie had gleaned the gist of Dennis's proposition. Even more remarkable, he liked what he was hearing. A lot.

Much to Eddie's astonishment, Dennis's business idea actually seemed to be solid, well thought out, and complete. Once Dennis laid out his plan, he encouraged Eddie to share his input... Eddie said that he had no clue about the business or its operation so what ever you want me to do. Dennis said you just take care of the books, writing the checks, paying the taxes and I'll do all the rest buying, selling hiring etc. Is that ok with you? Sure ok.

"So that's basically it. I mean there are still some small details to iron out but what do you think so far?"

"I'm interested."

"I know that much. Else you'd be home curled up with your wife instead of hanging out in this dive staring at my ugly mug."

I'd like to sleep on it and work the numbers through when I'm a little less bleary eyed before I make a final decision, but I'm intrigued. I think you've got something here."

"But what are your reservations? Be honest. Don't hold anything back. I kind of figured the way this would go was that I'd show you what I've been putting together and then you do your best to knock it down. Remember this was my father's business."

"I don't get it. You want me to help you make this work, or do you want me to tell you why it won't work?"

"Both. I want—I need—you to be brutal. Merciless. No holds barred. Your role at this point is to poke holes wherever they can be poked. Be like a ... whattayacallit ... a troubleshooter. Troubleshoot away. This is my baby. I'm way too close to it to see it objectively. So you've got to play the critic here. What can we improve? What have I missed? What am I forgetting? What's the worst case scenario? Where are the weak spots? I figure we throw all that into the mix, stir it together, and see what we end up with. And don't worry about hurting my feelings."

"I didn't know you had any."

"I don't. Look, all kidding aside, the bottom line is to improve this thing as much as we can before it even gets off the ground, anything you can think of that'll make us better, improve our chances. I don't know about you, but assuming we do decide to pull the trigger, I'll have a lot riding on this. A lot to lose."

"You? I could lose everything I've broken my back to work for so far. We do this, I'm all in. And I'm not just talking about my life savings. I've got a family to worry about."

"And I don't? Don't forget the shoes I'll be trying to fill. This is the closest thing to a family heirloom I'll ever inherit. We screw this up and I'll."

"I don't even want to think about it."

"That's why we've got to pull out all the stops, tear this thing apart and put it back together again; figure every conceivable angle in advance. I want to keep pushing and pulling and tinkering until it's as close to perfect as we can get it."

As the night deepened and faded into the wee hours of morning, Eddie did his best to fight off fatigue and do everything he could to contribute. He pointed out some minor flaws and helped revise a few small details, but there was nothing glaring or substantial for him to attack. The harder he looked to find vulnerabilities, the more elusive they became. No amount of scrutiny could shake the foundations of the structure Dennis had put together. It wouldn't budge. This was a strong idea and a solid plan they were talking about. Dennis didn't have to convince him; he was convincing himself. By the time the men had finished nursing their apple turnovers and coffee, Eddie was sold.

Back when they'd still been waiting to be seated, Dennis had looked at him and spoke two words: "dented cans." Eddie stared back at him in disbelief, wondering if he was with a crazy man and what he was doing wasting his time there. He remembered how his first instinct was to mumble some half-baked excuse and bolt for the door.

He decided, however, that since he was there already, he might as well hear Dennis out. (The fact that Dennis had driven them there may have also had something to do with his decision to stay put.) The more Eddie listened and the more Dennis talked, the more the whole thing seemed to make sense.

It was true that the buying and reselling of dented cans were at the core of Dennis's concept. However, the full scope of his vision was far more extensive. Yes, cans would serve as the basis of the operation, at least at first. But cans were designed only to serve as a means to an end.

The general idea was to establish a shop that sold a diverse array of secondhand, repurchased consumer goods, mostly canned foodstuffs, at discount prices.

Cans were a key component of the business plan because they had an extensive shelf life, would attract a regular, loyal customer base (such as area seniors on fixed incomes who sought out bargains and returned to the places where they found them), and could be sold for next to nothing while still yielding a worthwhile profit margin.

Eddie had already been leaning toward making a commitment to the project, when, shortly after they were seated, Dennis revealed the "ace in the hole" that more or less sealed the deal between them. Thinking back on it years later, Eddie recalled how impeccable Dennis's timing had been. How he'd set the hook at precisely the right moment. In hindsight, it was easy to see that this had not been accidental or unintentional. Dennis read people the way bookworms read books. The conversation had gone something like this:

"I got to admit, I thought you had lost your marbles there for a while, but —"

"But what, Eddie?"

"I must say that I really, really think this thing has major potential."

"Yeah?"

"Yeah, but my only concern is—"

"Wait a minute, hold on, hold that thought. I don't know how I forgot to mention. You haven't even heard the best part yet. You ready for this?"

"Shoot."

"Well, remember how when we first started talking about how smart it would be to start our own thing, I used to use my father as an example, always talking about how much money he made with his sideline business and how he was able to set it up in a way that it didn't interfere with his police work?"

"Sure. I remember."

"Did I ever tell you what that business was … is?"

Sure it was your dads.

"Right it was dented cans, Eddie. He bought and resold salvaged goods."

"Ok, so we know it can be done."

"No, well, yeah, but no. That's not my point."

"What is your point?"

"The point is that he just retired. When he retired from the force, he quit running the business as well. But the thing is—and this is a big part of why I'm coming to you now with this proposition and a big part of why we should jump on this thing right away if we're serious—that he still has a massive amount of viable inventory. We could get our hands on it for a less than a steal. So, boom, in one fell swoop, there goes a big chunk of our overhead problems. We'll be able to stock the store adequately from day one, and it won't take us forever to open either. Also, if we move fast, we'll benefit from all his connections and his already-established network of product acquisition channels. That entire infrastructure is still in place, plus we've got my father as a resource. He's willing to help us out. He knows the truckers, flea-market people, all the salvage centers, plus the insurance salvage. We'll never have to shop and search and haggle. Never have to wonder where our merchandise is coming from or worry about killer variables like price hikes or shortages or anything like that. Later we can branch out, get more diverse with the products we offer, get into selling bigger-ticket merchandise if we want. It's all up to us. Put it together and it spells out a huge competitive advantage. Don't you see what kind of an edge this gives us? How much the arrangement lowers our levels of risk? Instead of being out on a limb like most start-ups, instead of starting a business totally from scratch, it's like we're taking over the reigns of an already-established company. All we have to supply is the retail space. But it will be ours. All ours. I'm talking a total partnership here, fifty-fifty, right down the middle."

Despite their late start and despite the fact that Dennis had gotten to the meat of his proposal quickly, their meeting had been anything but short. There was much to discuss and hash out. Even though the operation under consideration was relatively straightforward, the minutia that had to be covered when planning to put together a business (details within details, logistics, what-ifs, potential locations, etc.) seemed endless.

Over and over, no matter how he sliced it, Eddie didn't see how they could lose. The plan was simple, flexible, and well thought out. Clearly Dennis had done his homework. Eddie was also pleased that, although Dennis was clearly excited to get things moving, he never once, throughout the entire conversation, pressed Eddie for a final answer on his commitment to the endeavor. At the time, Eddie thought the reason for this was consideration—to give him space and time to consult with his wife and be sure he was sure before making such a monumental move. The truth was that Dennis didn't feel the need to close the deal verbally. By the time he was pouring sugar in his coffee, he knew the collaboration with Eddie was in the bag.

When it was all said and done and they were waiting on the check, a weary lull in the conversation occurred. Even Dennis, jacked up as he was, yawned and rubbed his eyes, seeming to sink into his own thoughts. Eddie took advantage of this intermission to lean back, rest his eyes, and relish the silence. He saw no need for idle conversation or time-killing small talk now that they were done saying what they'd come there to discuss. However, before he could even drift off into the refuge of a daydream, Dennis caught a second wind from somewhere and was off and running again.

Only the subject matter that was being discussed had changed. The pace and intensity with which Dennis unleashed his words remained fixed at a level so high it seemed it would be impossible to sustain for much longer. Eddie listened passively, contributing as little as possible (with the exception of a stray "um-hmm" or "right" or "yeah" or "you can say that again" tossed in at odd intervals so as to feign interest and simulate rapt attention) while Dennis talked shop, using almost the same passionate urgency to animate the tone of his voice that he had used just five or ten minutes ago when he had been discussing a decision that was likely to have a profound impact on their lives, families, and futures.

The rap that Dennis was laying down consisted of fairly generic firefighter talk. Eddie had pretty much heard, or more accurately, did his best to avoid hearing it all before. It was the station-house gossip he so despised. Who's on the rise, who's screwing up, who's getting married, and who's getting divorced, same as any workplace anywhere. Since Eddie felt so strongly about not getting involved in talking about people who weren't present, he had little interest.

Quickly sensing this, Dennis guided the conversation toward a blow-by-blow recap of the banquet they'd attended earlier that evening. This shift offered Eddie little reprieve. His face was a mask of resigned endurance as Dennis took him from the gathering's alpha to its omega, revisiting moments that had made him squirm and sweat the first time he was obliged to endure them.

Dennis's rehash of the recent past had only served to remind Eddie of how long a night it had been, how tired he was, and how badly he yearned to get home, brush his teeth, and slip under the sheets where the warm form of his wife would be waiting for his embrace. At last, the waitress dropped the check on the table.

To Eddie's surprise, Dennis picked up the tab. When he attempted to contribute his share, Dennis waved him off decisively. He wouldn't hear of it. The calculated investment more than paid for itself. It left the intended positive impression. As the men rose to make their way home, Eddie scolded himself for questioning his confidence in his soon-to-be partner.

For him to view the tiny and inconsequential incident that had happened earlier as some sort of symbolic talisman was unfair and unjust. Dennis was a good man. It was he, Eddie, who had judged harshly and thought ugly thoughts. On the way out, both men tried to act reserved and regard the totality of the plans they'd just discussed with poker-faced countenances. In truth, both were walking on air as they exited the diner.

By the end of the following week, Eddie and Dennis had hammered out a viable and equitable agreement. They were to be partners. Profits and ownership were to be split right down the middle.

The pair jumped into the secondhand merchandise game in earnest. They formulated and agreed on a blueprint for near-term action and concentrated their early efforts on following it. The two partners made an efficient team, working well together to fulfill the objectives they'd set. One of the first major tasks before them was to evaluate the quantity and quality of what Dennis's dad had to offer. At the time, Dennis's old man had consolidated all remaining merchandise into a series of trailers. They arranged to get together and look over the swag that Mr. Thefmor had collected.

Although hopelessly disorganized, much of the stuff was useful product. A few days of hard work and elbow grease in the trailers set them up with most of the stock they'd need to open their doors. Mr. Thefmor just wanted to rid himself of what was now useless clutter to him. He let it go for a song. It appeared that he could be depended on to be a valuable resource for them, then and in the future. While the guys were working, he gave a lot of good advice, employing the benefit of his own experience in the business; sharing moves he'd made that had proven fruitful as well as ones that backfired. They were also able to reach a formal agreement with him whereby he'd get a regular and set commission for continuing to help replenish their shelves.

After a few weeks of intense moonlighting, the new partners had made much better than expected headway. They found a shop where they could show and sell their wares. Their base of operations was far from ideal; the place was small and would require more than a little fixing up. Both the surrounding neighborhood and the structure itself were run down. The rent, however, was reasonable and the location was promising.

The place boasted high visibility, ample parking, and was perched on a prominent corner that boasted a high degree of both foot and vehicle traffic. Poor folks and youths from around the way would often congregate on the steps of a brownstone apartment building halfway down the block. The adjoining boulevard that pushed up close against the East side of the building was a bustling, popular thoroughfare accessed by professionals in nice cars from the correct side of the tracks. The area was centrally located and therefore a popular shortcut for people cutting across town. Savings offered by the store would appeal to both those who were forced to adhere to a budget and more affluent customers who were still interested in obtaining a quality bargain.

Eddie and Dennis spent roughly two months of off-days in the shop cleaning out yesterday's forgotten junk, wiping away layers of dust and tapestries of grime, scrubbing floors, mopping floors, painting walls, Lysoling long-padlocked storage rooms, and performing quasi-miraculous feats of light carpentry on several wood rot–afflicted ceiling beams that were sagging sadly earthward.

One Sunday morning, Eddie and Dennis had just finished hanging shelving and were admiring their handiwork. Dennis was preparing to leave; he had a shift in a few hours and was hoping to steal a nap. "Before I go," he suggested, "let's look this place up and down and see where we're at. I don't think there's that much left to do." Combining the prying eyes of the inspectors they'd soon face and the protective gazes of the parents they felt like after creating the space they were standing in, they walked every square inch methodically assessing the condition of the place and checking to see if there was anything they'd overlooked.

It was at that point they realized they had actually succeeded in whipping the place into shape, replacing messy disrepair with aisle after aisle of order and polish. The cash register at the counter stood gleaming at attention like a medal-bedecked Prussian general ready to march off toward war. Boxes of merchandise were sorted, stacked, and neatly bundled in the storeroom and adjoining hallway. They looked at one another with smiles on their faces, basking in the enormity of the task that had been accomplished and flush with anticipation for the future. They were ready to open their doors to the public.

Of course it wasn't as simple as that. They'd expected that several extra days would be required for inspections, obtain the correct permits, and jump through the proper hoops. The days they'd planned on needing dragged into weeks. The original date they'd set as their opening day had to be postponed. Setbacks notwithstanding, they refused to let themselves get discouraged. Tenaciously they persevered, persisting in making their way stubbornly forward through myriad frustrations, obstacle courses of Byzantine regulations, and other civic roadblocks.

Eventually all the heavy lifting and high blood pressure paid off. Indeed, a long, long time would pass before Eddie would begin to forget the vivid thrill he received on one seemingly ordinary winter morning in early March. Although Saturday, it was, like almost every day in his life during that busy time, a work day. He'd tiptoed around the house getting ready and making his own breakfast in order to let his wife and kids sleep in for an extra hour or two.

Outside, the bracing day was blessed with stunning blue skies and a hint of thaw in the air. An unusual amount of morning traffic clogged his route to work. He had rushed to his locker after reporting to the station for duty, worried he'd be late. In his haste, he almost overlooked the piece of paper he found taped to his locker door. This was curious. He wondered what the heck it was as he looked down at it, assuming it might be a note from Dennis, who had worked the previous shift.

The pleasant surprise took a moment for Eddie to fully process and digest. There was a delay in comprehension borne out of stunned disbelief. Then it hit him. The message registered. A wide grin creased Eddie's face. He beamed with pride; he thought he might have felt his heart skip a beat. The taped up piece of paper was from Dennis. But it was no note. It was a professionally printed flyer that announced the grand opening of their store.

.

Chapter 4

The grand opening of the store took place at 9 a.m. on St. Patrick's Day. Eddie and Dennis arrived early, just after daybreak, putting final finishing touches on the place and setting up 11th-hour gimmicks that had been wholeheartedly sworn by, or at least strongly recommended by, the various family members and friends who formed their respective inner circles.

Dennis, for example, had Uncle Mike, who hastened to cite his twenty-plus years in the retail industry when emphatically advising the inclusion of the gaily painted promotional sandwich-board sign they had ended up placing to the left of the front door, just past the corner of the display window.

Steve's cousin Robert, who made a living trekking all over Jersey peddling his goods at weekend flea markets throughout the state, had a brainstorm about moving the banner from its original position over the entrance and front window case of the shop. At Robert's suggestion, the tri-colored "grand opening" banner they'd rented for the day was stretched across the street out front, where it would be noticed by a higher percentage of street traffic.

Finally, the leasing of the life-sized balloon figure, whose limbs went epileptic when hooked up to an accompanying air compressor, was a worthwhile fragment that Eddie and Dennis had adapted from a much-larger list of opening-day pointers offered by Jerry in the firehouse's dressing room as Dennis, Eddie, and he were changing into civvies following a particularly grueling shift.

And now, after all of the plotting and figuring and wheeling and dealing and preparations and hassles and red tape and running around, after countless hours of hauling and lifting and hammering and sawing and scrubbing and sanding and waiting in line with their three-ring business check binders and forms signed in triplicate, the cash was on the barrel head. The time had come for Eddie and Dennis to launch their painstakingly crafted partnership into the rough seas of small business ownership and find out whether it would sink or float. Would they succeed or fail? How would they know? When would they know? These questions dominated Eddie and Dennis's thoughts that opening day morning, as the duo buzzed around their shop looking after details and making sure everything was perfect.

They were both in position at opposite ends of a display table that was to be moved from the rear of the store. Dennis paused before hoisting up his end to wipe a few beads of sweat that had accumulated on his brow. Meanwhile, Eddie stole a glance at his watch. It was 8:20 a.m.

"Well, we've got forty minutes to zero hour," he informed Dennis, his voice slightly tinged by the strain of nervousness and excitement.

"We'll make it. And I'm not just talking about being ready to roll by 9:00. I mean, relax, we'll make it."

"I hope so. I wish I knew for sure."

"I know so. We can't lose."

"I'll tell you though, even though it puts us under a lot of pressure right away, one good thing about throwing so much of our resources into investing in this first day is that we'll find out pretty soon. I mean, we should know within the first week or so if we've got something here or if we're headed for a belly flop."

"You worry too much. Quit worrying and lift."

"We got everything in the game here, Dennis. You tellin' me you're not a little anxious?"

"Sure, sure I am. Any business is a risk but … you know."

"But?"

"But I don't think you get how much the deck is stacked in our favor."

"What's that mean?"

"It means help me lift this table."

"No, really. A couple of advantages and ins do not make for a sure thing. Especially in such a competitive market. I don't see how we have any inside track."

"Just watch."

"Watch what?"

"Watch the number of people who walk through that front door today and tomorrow and the day after that. Watch how many friends we have. Watch how much money piles up in the till. Then talk to me. You'll see. Mark my words."

"I'm optimistic, don't get me wrong … but I don't have that kind of absolute confidence. I wish I did."

"You will. Give it time. And remember this conversation so you can tell all our buddies how, when you were stressing out, old Dennis was like Namath before Super Bowl III. Ready?"

"Yeah, I'm ready. Let's go. On three."

The table was being moved to a spot they'd marked off beside the sidewalk. The guys had had the foresight and imagination to get additional permits so they could set some of their merchandise on tables outside.

The idea of setting up outdoor vending was an inspired one. The open-air market turned out to be a significant factor in the ultimate success of the store's grand opening. Many people came by out of curiosity, and that brought a decent amount of impulse buying. It began straightaway, seconds after the old grandfather clock they'd restored, restrained, and coaxed creaking into the back corner sounded out nine loud bonging sounds , and Eddie ceremoniously unlocked the front door and flipped the closed sign over to read "open."

The day passed quickly in a blur of activity. It was a kinda family affair, with Dennis's father, his wife Linda didn't show because Dennis always said she was a nut, Eddie, and his wife, Renee, all pitching in to help manage a flow of customer traffic that exceeded their wildest expectations. By mid-morning, a genuine crowd had gathered to check out the wares being offered by the new establishment. At one point, the line to the cash register snaked all the way through the middle aisle to the front door. The steady stream of buyers continued uninterrupted until twenty-five minutes after the scheduled closing time.

Almost all of their friends and colleagues stopped in to show their moral and fiscal support. Indeed, because such a diversity of inexpensive merchandise was available, and because so many of the products were needed staples, few of the people who entered ended up leaving empty-handed.

The positive momentum that started that day carried through the first several weeks. On the consumer side, the store was a bona fide curiosity to the locals and commuters driving by. During the week, the place was crowded at least once a day (either at lunch time, quitting time, or both); on the weekends, aisles were clogged more often than not with housewives and township workers , teenagers, cops, firefighters, teachers and most importantly senior citizens which was the major reason Eddie said yes to take over the business with Dennis.

Working the register, Eddie was often shocked to notice the sheer density of the chatty, contented mass of customers who had compliantly, indeed enthusiastically, formed themselves into intertwining lines of nebulous humanity, teeming like algae, stretching toward the door like a strand of spilled coffee vaunting from the nibbled lip of an overturned Styrofoam cup. .

Eddie and Dennis fell into a well-oiled routine. When possible, fire department schedules permitting, they'd get together, fill out necessary orders, and go on purchasing runs for products they'd need for the coming week. In the evening, Dennis's dad would stop by. Sometimes he'd have merchandise they could use. Other times he'd have leads on where they could go shopping. His advice always seemed to pan out. It was uncanny. It got so whenever Mr. Thefmor cleared his throat, Eddie dropped what he was doing and listened to the old man's words. More often than not, he was glad he did. The old man's words were awfully lucrative.

After Dennis's dad would leave, the business partners usually ordered take-out so they could have dinner together and work on near-term business strategy plans (in between Dennis's myriad boasts and bullshit stories). Even when Sunday meals were impossible, once a week, without fail, the two would convene at the iron grate bench on the sidewalk with a quart of Chinese from the storefront restaurant around the corner or a pizza from the joint behind the hardware store.

One advantage of trying to target Sunday to work together was that it was also the day that the fire department schedule got posted. The chief never put it up later than 8:00. So after they'd finished dinner, Eddie and Dennis would usually cruise down to the house to check their schedules. Once they knew their hours, they'd put their heads together and carve up the week, sharing the store so it was always covered. If the store was open, one of them was almost always there. Sandra, Dennis's sister was an invaluable aid on the rare occasions that scheduling gaps needed to be filled.

Despite their best efforts to avoid difficulties and complications, however, scheduling did turn out to pose bit of an issue. For both partners, the demands of the fire department could be unpredictable. Eddie and Dennis, however, dealt deftly with out-of-nowhere situations that would have had lesser men at each other's throats. They did it by keeping an open line of communication, and each shouldered more or less equal burdens of unexpected shifts, double shifts, and lonely weekends.

The store could be hard work, and there certainly was a down side. But the way they divided up the hours and the responsibilities was equitable and fair. Although both men were working themselves to the point of exhaustion, there were no budding resentments to deal with. Both men had the satisfaction of knowing that the other was just as stretched out and harried as the other. Sweetening the pot was the fact that sales continued to grow briskly and an ever-increasing quantity and variety of high-quality, bargain basement merchandise always seemed to be both plentiful and easy to find.

The crowds continued to flock to their spot. More and more faces of repeat customers were recognized. Those who patronized the shop were good natured, cooperative, and liberal in their generosity. Like religious supplicants, they mindlessly but blissfully filled the bottoms of their empty baskets with a steady stream of easy-to-turnover merchandise.

Even with, the struggles, and hardships they managed to juggle all the additional responsibility. The huge personal risks they had taken were not in vain. Unlike the many small businesses that started up every single year, their store was succeeding. Times were good. The future looked bright. The horizons appeared limitless.

In the beginning, it was that way.

❧ ❧ ❧

Steely and straight-backed, George Thefmor took a handkerchief from his breast pocket, dabbed his forehead, and carefully desmudged his mirrored sunglasses. A thin groan escaped from between pursed lips as he grabbed the door and upper chassis with both hands and hoisted his frame out of his bucket-seated Lincoln.

Once in the open air, he patted down his combed over hair, adjusted his glasses, and checked his pockets to make sure he had not forgotten his wallet and keys. Everything was in order, and with his characteristic (and often secretly imitated) wide-legged stance, Mr. Thefmor swaggered across the sun-drenched parking lot and through the whirring automatic doors of A&P warehouse and regional distribution center located on the outskirts of Corrunoside's uptown industrial district.

Inside, George sauntered to the Security desk which was manned by his buddy from Bergen county P.D. and they both walked over to the floor manager's desk and the disinterested part-time receptionist. He demanded to see the man in charge of offloading the incoming grocery trucks. The college-aged kid, still pimple-speckled, looked at him quizzically for a moment before grabbing the phone. He paged a Mr. Dulles, his cracked voice reverberating, bouncing off beams throughout the high-ceilinged warehouse, squawking bird-like through a forest of static.

As he waited, George began shifting impatiently from one foot to another, grumbling something under his breath about how many more minutes he intended to allow to elapse before he would no longer be able to hold his simmering temper. But before old George's face had a chance to turn plum, before he'd even begun to raise his voice in ornery complaint, a figure appeared from a side door and strode purposefully toward the gated bullpen that separated the warehouse's skeleton office crew from the forklifts and pallets (but not from the sawdust and noise) of the storage area proper.

The pale, pot-bellied man who had answered the check-out clerk's page was shorter than most and seemed timid in his mannerisms. He had a slight over weight build and a well-manicured black mustache. His uniform was worn, and his hair was beginning to go. He was thirty-seven, but he looked several years older. Everything about this man reeked of disappointment and defeat.

George took one look at the guy and sensed blood in the water. He flashed his no-longer valid badge and ran through his routine. By the time he had finished talking, carefully alternating subtle threats with overt praise and promises, they were standing on a loading dock, beside an imposing pile of pallets and stacks of boxes that had been approved for distribution by the top man on the site.

George couldn't help but laugh to himself as he tooled his car around to the back and proceeded to load it to the brim with "used" and "damaged" merchandise. It was too damn easy; candy from a baby. And the best part was that there was no risk unloading the swag. He had the perfect spot—the store that he used to own, the store that was legitimized by the fact that it was now a brick-and-mortar reality and a level removed from him; it now belonged to his kid and his kid's clueless friend.

It was perfect: a flawless scam that could last forever. The sky was the limit as to how much money they would be able to bank. He thanked the man he'd just conned, but the stupid mark with the pot belly and bullied and browbeaten shell of his eager-to-please, please-take-from-me personality wouldn't hear of it. Anything he could do to support the department. The guy wanted, no craved, acceptance and camaraderie so badly, he'd give half his stock to get it. George stopped trying to thank the man; it was wasted breath. Instead he thanked the Almighty, arrogant in the armor of his sin,

His skin seemed to shine in the strong Jersey sun like polished steel. He imagined himself an avenging knight living way back when, in a more honorable time. He shifted the car into gear as if reaching to unholster a saber, then slammed down on the gas, squealing his tires as they searched for traction in a soft patch of asphalt before gaining hold and speeding off into the darkening horizon through thick clotted clouds of haze and dirt.

🔥 🔥 🔥

Between his family obligations, firefighting, running a business, and maintaining a regular schedule of exercise, Eddie was leading a packed life. Almost every minute of every day was spoken for. Time flew. At home, he watched with growing wonder and awe as his kids grew into little adults. Although his wife shouldered most of the domestic chores, Eddie was looking into the future and tried to do his best to maintain a presence and make time for his family. More often than not, he was successful.

After over fifteen years of marriage, he and his wife could both honestly say that they were still in love with each other, an achievement many couples of their age and duration could not duplicate. At the fire department, Eddie continued his expected ascent up the ladder. In 1989, for example, he was promoted to lieutenant. The talk around the house was that the brass was looking to kick him up to captain as soon as there was an available opening.

The store was almost organized and demanding a little less of the partners' time. As of late 1990, everything was humming along like a high-performance engine. Eddie should have felt content and joyous. And he knew that's how he should feel. But for some reason he didn't. He had a premonition that things were going too good to be true.

Shortly after he began to have this sense of dread, it started to become more and more clear that it wasn't simply in his head. Eddie was not a neurotic man who couldn't allow himself to be happy. Throughout his life he had traveled a straight and honest path. In return, he had been rewarded with his fair share of peace and contentment.

Normally, previously, he readily if humbly accepted his success as blessings and a sort of tangible affirmation or endorsement from God for being a good man and doing his best to always do the right thing. So Eddie was not the type of lost, confused soul prone to vague, free-form anxiety. But gradually, more concrete signs and manifestations began to appear that confirmed his worries as well founded and well grounded.

At first, there was nothing he could put his finger on. There was just a sense of instability and tenuousness, like if he poked at this thing was his life and his situation long enough, it would start to come apart. That made him back away at first, and leave that line of thought alone. Little by little, however, he started to face what was bothering him. Eddie thought more deeply than ever before about his agreeable nature and wondered if it was being taken advantage of by those in the department with a stake in his fortunes and fate.

He was, as has been noted, a rising star in the department. Most men don't rise so quickly without "guardian angels" upstairs. He knew there were big shots that had their eyes on him, who were grooming him for bigger and better things. But he had always perceived them to be benevolent, paternalistic types who ultimately had the best interests of him, his family, and the department at heart. He never thought twice about doing these higher-ups a good turn (whether it be his involvement in the Young Democrats, distribution of campaign signs for fire department–friendly candidates, or finding time to do roadside fund-raising for the department and other volunteer work). It wasn't shady. It wasn't exchange of favors, quid pro quo; you scratch my back, I'll scratch yours. It was in Eddie's nature to help out folks whenever and wherever he could. He saw nothing that could possibly be wrong or sinister about that.

But now he prayed to God for guidance and assurance that he remains firmly planted on the correct path, something he'd been so sure of just a short time ago. He felt increasingly unsure of and uncomfortable with the compromises he was increasingly called on to make as he continued to slingshot his way up through the department hierarchy. It seemed that the fat filthy blood suckers had the chief's ear and he needed to not make waves.

In Eddie's eyes, looking the other way when a buddy did something stupid wasn't a matter of shepherding his career and maintaining his high level of station house popularity. It was a loyalty issue to Eddie. It was a matter of not being a rat. Now, as his once simple life and the associated issues that surrounded it became increasingly complex, Eddie was beginning to wonder if his widely praised and heretofore blind loyalty would come back to haunt him.

The storm clouds that Eddie had foreseen on the horizon first began to gather over the store. Subtle issues arose at first, issues that when isolated could easily be explained away. These isolated incidents began to increase, however, until it was no longer possible for Eddie to ignore their existence.

Initial signs of trouble centered around merchandise that was accepted on days when Eddie was not at the store. Half the time, Dennis would be unable to produce a receipt for the products he had bought. The first few times it happened, Eddie had taken it in stride, figuring Dennis had simply been careless or lost the receipt. He duly logged the missing status of the receipt in the inventory paperwork and moved on to his next task without giving it too much thought. But it began to nag at him.

Then something else occurred that, in retrospect, should have set off even more of an alarm than it did. But once again it is perhaps relevant to mention that Eddie was slightly naive. And Eddie was fiercely loyal. And Eddie trusted, until he had ironclad reason not to. These qualities, of course, would later serve as the core ammunition that his enemies-disguised-as-friends used against him. But at the time, they were not second-guessed; it was the way he had been raised. It was what he thought was right. You see, Eddie was a good man. And like most good men throughout literature, throughout history, he would be compelled to pay a terrible price for his virtue.

That first pivotal event—the one he would years later realize had represented a crossroads, a turning point, and a signpost— had happened like this. Eddie was whiling away a Sunday afternoon by himself behind the counter, enjoying a close Giants game on a small black-and-white TV. It had been an ordinary day, if a bit on the slow side. Eddie had just put the phone in the cradle after talking to Renee (they called each other several times a day if it was a slow weekend and Eddie was alone in the store). He turned his attention to the front door when he heard bells jangling, indicating someone had come in. Eddie smiled warmly and waved at the tall, athletic-looking middle-aged man as he made his way slowly and mysteriously down the narrow center aisle. It seemed as he was casing our store.

"What can I do for you?" Eddie inquired once the man had made his way to the counter.

The man regarded Eddie with a pensive air and did not answer his question right away. He inhaled, splayed his meaty-fingered hands palms down upon the countertop, and turned his head taking in the dizzying variety of the various products stacked soldier straight upon rows and rows of shelving. After the silence had lasted just long enough to become uncomfortable, the man cleared his throat and responded.

"It's not what you can do for me mister. It's what I can do for you."

"I'm not sure I follow."

"I'm not here to buy. I'm here to sell."

With a small amount of difficulty, the man swung a fairly large satchel to the countertop, where it came to rest with a substantial thud. The man unzipped the brightly colored nylon pack to reveal a large quantity of disposable Eveready brand batteries. The selection and sheer number of batteries stuffed into the bag took Eddie aback for a moment. They were wrapped in plastic, and there were ample amounts of every conceivable type, shape, and size.

Although Eddie had no idea of the how's or whys behind the situation that was unfolding before him, he knew instinctively that the man and his batteries were trouble. He'd get to the bottom of it later. (Much, much later, when he'd learn from an accusatory prosecutor that such batteries had later been accepted by Dennis for resale in the store. They could be traced back to the nearby Eveready Battery factory, from where they had originated, and from where they had been pilfered by a Corrunoside police officer.) At that moment, the thing to do was politely and deftly extricate himself from the deal without causing any hard feelings. As it turned out, this was easier said than done.

"Listen," began Eddie's first attempt at evasion, "my partner does all the purchasing and makes those decisions, and he's not here today. I'm sorry to waste your time, but you'll have to come back when he's around."

"Dennis is your partner?"

"Yes."

"Well then we got no problem. He's the guy who sent me. He told me I should come down today. Said you'd take care of me. Said to drop his name if there was any confusion."

"I don't know man. Do you have receipts for this stuff? Friend of Dennis or not, I can't take in merchandise that doesn't have an accompanying receipt."

"Hey look pal. I guess I better straighten things out before they go off the tracks. It's my fault. I should have let you know from the jump. I'm a Corrunoside cop, Mr. Thefmor's buddy. Ok?" AND?

"Meaning what?"

"Don't you get it?"

"Get what?"

The exchange continued back and forth a few more times, but the communication breakdown between the two parties could not be overcome. It wasn't long before the police officer ended up throwing up his hands in livid frustration before turning on his heel to stomp out the door, his bulging bag of suspiciously acquired batteries still clutched firmly in hand.

It would have almost been funny if Eddie wasn't vested up to his golden years in the store. Still, it was hard to suppress a chuckle that night when he told the story to Sandra and recalled how red-faced and agitated the sour-tempered cop had gotten. He was furious. But not half as furious as Eddie was going to be with Dennis if what the cop said was even close to true.

They'd had their big, dramatic hash-out session two days later when they crossed paths while changing shifts. Dennis was going and Eddie was coming in. After a brief search, he spotted Dennis exiting the showers with a towel around his waist, on his way to dress. Dennis looked like he was in a hurry and appeared distracted, so much so that he almost bumped into Eddie, who had stepped in front of his partner, blocking the path to the lockers. Dennis looked up with a start. His hair was still wet. The sound of water drops hitting the tiles of the floor was amplified by a silence that hung in the air between them. Other guys, perhaps sensing that something was up, tiptoed around them instead of asking them to move.

The annoyance in Dennis's eyes instantly disappeared with the recognition of the figure standing in his way. If Dennis sensed that something was askew in the dynamics of their working friendship, if he was aware that both the scent and weight of confrontation were hanging in the air, he had the presence of mind not to show it. He stared mildly at his friend with the expectant gaze of a faithful hound.

This threw Eddie, as perhaps it was meant to, trying to deflate the head of steam that had guys stepping out of his way as he'd stalked all corners of the firehouse, on a singular mission to give Dennis a piece of his mind. But then Eddie flashed back to the sordid scene in the store, and the propane tanks of his ire opened up to flame anew. Purple jets of fire surged out from the cerebral regions responsible for the transmission of impulses related to the losing of one's temper. It was all he could do not to punctuate the cadence of his utterances with rhythmic finger jabs to Dennis's sternum. But that wasn't Eddie's style. He restrained himself, allowing his voice alone to deliver the message he had come to convey.

"Hey," began Eddie by way of greeting, marshaling his thoughts in order to choose his words carefully.

"Hey," responded Dennis in kind, the trace of a question in his tone of response.

He wouldn't need to wait much longer. He was about to find out what the hell, Eddie had on his mind. . He meant to get down to business and he did.

"Listen, Dennis, you got a minute?"

"Not really, to tell you the truth. I've got to change into regular clothes, then make it across town in time to relieve Sandra by 8:30. Remember? My sister made it very clear to us that she was more than willing to fill in but didn't feel comfortable being there any later than that."

Under the circumstances, the assumed familiarity and overstated concern for his sister which he could care less about served to further gall Eddie rather than pacify him. He felt himself slipping down the precipice of his self-control. When he spoke again, his voice was short and clipped.

"Your sister will manage for a couple of minutes."

"Yeah? Is something up?"

"Yeah. I only need a few minutes of your time, but we need to talk."

"Sure, sure," Dennis responded in a purr, adding as if it were an afterthought, "anything wrong?"

"Sort of ... yeah."

"Well you know I'm your friend Eddie, as well as your partner. You should feel free to talk to me about anything that's bothering you."

"Ok, it's like this. A couple of days ago I'm in the store and this guy walks in, a cop … he was looking for you or your father and—"

And you should have seen the series of pitch-perfect, perfectly timed faces of surprise and concern that Dennis had on tap as Eddie related the rest of the troubling incident. He never gave Eddie the chance to work up to any sort of direct accusation, stepping in with effusive apologies as soon as he was able to understand the gist of what had occurred. Dennis assured Eddie the situation had arisen out of a simple misunderstanding, explaining that he knew about the battery sale and had forgotten, due to sheer overwork, to mention it. As far as the lack of receipt and the attitude of the cop, Dennis appeared to be just as surprised as Eddie.

"If something isn't on the up and up, I want to know about it right away. You were right to come straight out with me about this stuff, and you were right to turn him away. I would've done the same thing. I swear to you, I thought the transaction was legit, and to the best of my knowledge, it was. The guy is a friend of my dad's. I had every reason to trust him. I don't know, I may be wrong though. You made the right call. Better safe than sorry. As far as him being rude to you, again, I'm sorry. I thought he was ok 'cause he's dealt with my dad in the past. As far as him implying any funny business, I want to get to the bottom of it just as badly as you do. Don't forget, my ass is on the lease and on the line here too."

But it wasn't going to be so easy for Dennis to slickly skate out of the situation with his patented mixture of spit and polish. Eddie had been there. It had just happened. The whiff of impropriety was too strong for Dennis to fan out of the room by just blowing some smoke.

Every time Dennis moved to dodge and obfuscate, Eddie parried with straightforward honesty, trying to communicate the crux of the situation and just how rotten it felt. It wouldn't have, couldn't have felt that way unless the rot was more than superficial. It had to run deeper than the cop who'd come in the door. He'd acted too "in the know."

Eddie had the sneaking, eerie suspicion that the cop was more in the loop than he was.

Dennis's denials, however, were consistent and airtight. He kept his head, his wits, and his calm. The end result was inconclusive. Dennis had muddied the waters enough to remain above definite suspicion, but from that day forward, Eddie's level of concern about the way the business was being run increased with each passing week. Now that his attentions had been aroused, it wasn't long before Eddie had collected a preponderance of questionable incidents. These incidents slowly but steadily chafed at his conscience, like sandpaper against sensitive skin, pressing constantly, increasing in intensity, until they rose to press against the levee of his trust like floodwaters gathering in a hurricane tide.

🔥 🔥 🔥

Occasionally there were days like this. Days that try your patience, grate against the frayed fibers of your very last nerve and threaten to snap it loose. Occasionally life can turn on you, make you wish you never got out of bed that morning. Make you want to press down on some cosmic rewind button, turn the calendar back a page to a slimmer number, and start all over again. But life's no movie and no one gave any classes. No second takes are allowed. So, occasionally, there were days like this.

Mean days, nasty and aggressive as a skel on PCP. Dark days, oily and toxic. Days choked in barbed wire and broken glass. Days that barrel down on you out of nowhere like some runaway locomotive. Occasionally there are days like this. They were a fact of life. Nothing to be done but endure and make it through. Wait for the wind to change back and blow in a more favorable direction. Luckily for George Thefmor, when he looked back, he had to admit that hard times had been a rarity. For several decades, connections, power, and money had provided effective insulation. They'd kept the wolves at bay since he'd been a young man. Since the day he joined the force to be exact, he'd methodically pursued and attained a formidable collection of friends, favors, and inside information. From this foundation, he'd steadily carved out a plot of territory he could claim as his own. Over the years, he'd managed to construct a humble but well-fortified little domain for himself and his family. It was an empire built on loyalty, secrets, and quid pro quo.

As his position in the department and in the PBA became increasingly prominent, he had watched with an almost skeptical satisfaction as his impressively diverse portfolio of assets accrued and his mini-kingdom grew at a measured but consistent pace, deftly straddling the border of legitimacy and lawlessness, balancing precariously on the edge of respectability. If only his seventh-grade math teacher could see him now, the one who had called him a loser and a hood before kicking him out of her class and into the waiting arms of the Brooklyn streets? He'd come a long way from P.S. #62.

But deep in his heart, he knew it was a house of cards he'd put together. It would only take one hellacious gust to scatter the fruits of his life's work to the four corners of the globe. This was the reason he was under such a cloud as he tooled his Lincoln toward the Meadowlands, trying to clear his head and sort out things.

He flipped a Sinatra tape into the cassette drive, lit a Blunt with his dashboard lighter, and pressed his foot down on the gas pedal for an extra push as he changed lanes. Once in the fast lane, there was almost a football field of clear asphalt ahead of him. He squeezed the pedal down further toward the floor and let his mind go slack as the engine roared.

Most of the days passed without hitch or hassle, steaming smoothly by on greased rails. But here we go again, the train wrecks, leaving a tangle of twisted metal and smoking ruin... From the moment he'd locked his front door behind him and struck out into the world, everything had seemed to implode.

It had started that morning with a call from his boy. Seemed the kid's partner, who they'd tried to keep out of the action, was asking questions that didn't have pleasant answers. Since he held a half stake in the business, his cold feet were jeopardizing the entire operation. He would have to be dealt with. Doing so would likely prove to be a delicate and treacherous proposition. They had limited options. They could deal him in, buy him out, eliminate him, or discredit him.

Dealing him in didn't seem plausible. The guy was a straight arrow. Nothing seemed to indicate that throwing money at the problem would clear it up. They'd just be giving him more to blow the whistle about. The business was a part of his identity. He was proud of what they'd built and always talked about his role in turning the thing around. So a buyout didn't look too promising. Because he was an up-and-coming big shot in the community, there would be hell to pay if he all of a sudden just up and disappeared.

That left the final option, which was the most complex and involved solution of them all. The scheme had the potential to backfire, to blow up in their faces. It had to execute flawlessly at every turn, and they had to depend on the hope that Eddie's seemingly endless reservoirs of goodwill, gullibility, and naïveté would not dry up until they had the time and opportunity to fashion the noose around his neck and pull it tight.

Chapter 5

*T*he long, drawn-out battle assumed epic dimensions, stretching across several weeks and several shifts. Who had the upper hand repeatedly changing as momentum see-sawed up and down? A murder of upended pawns littered the landscape, victims of a brutal war of attrition. What began as a relaxed social interaction, an almost capricious afterthought of a game (played with affably offhanded opening moves made with an almost exaggerated lack of interest by two colleagues conspiring to kill time), had evolved into a serious contest, a high-stakes showdown of competing intellects, a charged confrontation of wills.

Over the course of their chess sessions, as the amount of time they'd logged across the table from one another continued to mount, the mood of casual jocularity gradually eroded. The easy jokes and breezy banter was replaced by the steely silence of deep concentration. The atmosphere had grown tense, intense, relentlessly so. A small audience began to coalesce around the Spartan break room table, exchanging rushed and hushed raspy whispers in the extended intervals between each move, countermove, dodge, and parry.

Then, just when the suspense had built to a nearly unbearable crescendo, a sudden opening appeared like a busted seam in a pair of tight jeans, upsetting the applecart of equilibrium that had been carefully constructed over hours and hours of more or less even play.

A gaping breach in the white army's line of defense, dead center, between the coffee mug shadows cast upon the checkerboard battlefield, clearly visible to all but the least savvy observers. Sensing his edge, the black general maneuvers to exploit it with a blitzkrieg attack, sweeping his remaining bishop across the board with a bold diagonal swoosh. Pressing his apparent advantage, the black player exposes his queen, moving her forward to reinforce the penetration of the bishop. In doing so, he has fallen into a carefully planned and expertly executed trap.

White's ruse, a relatively simple ploy designed to unravel the solid web of black's defense, proves to be a resounding success. In the haste of his excitement, the black contestant has dangerously overextended his resources, rushing headlong into an ambush while simultaneously weakening his backboard, exponentially increasing the vulnerability of his king.

Reviewing their moves later on, the two foes will agree that the drawing out of the black queen represented the turning point of the entire match. Even the capture of the black queen, when it occurred a short time later, seemed a bit anticlimactic. Black attempted a valiant last stand, but white deftly anticipated the gambit, responding correctly to counter each phase of the stratagem, move by move, as it unfolded, adding insult to injury with the taking of a knight and two pawns.

The tide had turned decisively, and this latest sea change was final. The end game had commenced. Eddie had the long-reigning house champion on the ropes. He knew it. His opponent knew it. Barring a miracle or some unforeseen or overlooked contingency, Phil Zawatski (also known, at least in his own mind and according to his own braggadocio, as the Grand Master of the fire dept.), was approximately three moves away from being checkmated.

Some from among the modest crowd of co-workers who looked on began to murmur excitedly but reverently, taking care to keep all commentary below a sub whisper decibel level, as if in respectful acknowledgment of the event's auspiciousness.

Unpopped kernels of sweat beaded between the creases and crinkles of Phil's furrowed brow as Eddie leaned back in his chair with a studied, dignified, imperial air, stroking his chin with two fingers as he regarded the pieces before him. The chessboard he surveyed was also surveyed by the eyes of many others. Indeed, the humble game board was serving as the focal point of the entire room's attention. There was no mistaking the electric charge in the atmosphere. The zinging shock of upset crackled through the air like stun gun lightning. It was Eddie's move.

Following a tense interval of contemplation, after carefully checking and double-checking his defenses lest, in his enthusiastic zeal for victory, he left himself vulnerable for some desperate, last-minute Hail Mary back-door maneuver, he slid his rook across the board to go in for the kill. It was then the alarm sounded.

One of Phil's friends stepped forward and slapped him on the back. "Saved by the bell," he said. A gentle ripple of laughter passed through the crowd as they broke ranks, hurrying to gather gear and take their stations. Eddie couldn't help but notice that Phil didn't laugh.

Eddie was disappointed that he would not be able to finish Zawatski off until the next time they had down time together. But all in all, the sudden burst of action was a welcome distraction to the frustrations that afflicted his moonlighting efforts and gradually seeped into other sectors of his life as well.

The hassles between Eddie and Dennis were increasing and approaching crisis level in their intensity. For Eddie, the stress of the present situation was slowly but steadily draining the fun from the business. Perhaps most distressingly, it was impacting the way he interacted with others, wreaking havoc among other important realms of his life: misunderstandings with superiors at work, biting his wife's head off for no good reason at home. That sort of thing.

The store had been hard work, but it had also been invigoratingly exciting, a novel chapter embarked upon with great expectations. Now when he thought about it, the picture that formed in his mind's eye was an angry montage consisting of clashing colors and overlapping obstructions leaning upon one another in a domino-like pile. His thought balloons were overstuffed to bursting with the toxic helium of acrimony, ready to pop at the pinprick of what had become one extended hassle, smaller incidents, minor episodes, and occasional bench-clearing blowouts bleeding into intervals of uneasy peace. They eventually merged in Eddie's weary head to form an unbroken blob of white noise and intense aggravation...

Jesus Christ, it gave him a headache just to think about it. Every other shift (and since when, he thought, did he start using the word "shift" to describe his time there?!) at the store had been steadily transformed into a ball-busting struggle. Tedious. Draining. One miserable confrontation after another.

All of the arguments hewed to a common theme: Dennis's increasingly shady and suspicious business dealings. Not to mention the red flags raised by the increasingly suspect machinations of George Thefmor, their less-than-silent silent partner. Indeed, years later, thinking back on these times, Eddie realized that the only other place he remembered seeing so many red flags on parade was when he'd turn on the evening news and a correspondent was reporting on location from Moscow! (This was back in the cold war–era, at least a decade before the Soviet Union was finally defeated).

Jarred by the jolt of the old candy-apple-colored rig rounding a rough corner onto a sudden steep hill, Eddie shook free from the weight of the heavy thoughts threatening to pin him beneath them. Rolling the cerebral rocks away, he retrained his focus on the fire that he and his compadres would soon be in the thick of.

The engine gathered traction and speed as the hill leveled out, causing it to heave forward brusquely when the driver slammed on the brakes a little too late to facilitate a smooth approach toward the intersection it was, a four-way stop carved across the summit of what happened to be the highest point in Centerville County. The view was postcard scenic, the very definition of breathtaking, burnished with a rustic grace, the secret sacred heart of rich central Jersey, the reason they call it the Garden State.

They were headed toward an upscale residential neighborhood that rarely summoned them for anything more serious than extracting cats from trees. They negotiated a wide left turn, freezing the four-way traffic in place across the pavement-covered peak. They bolted sharply around the southwest corner and proceeded with all deliberate speed toward their fast-incinerating destination.

And, as they rounded the corner, there it was. Eddie nudged Jerry and Jerry nodded. From the up-angle down-slanted vantage point perspective of the hill, they were able to see for about a half a mile. Right where the buildings began to blur into horizon, an angry exclamation of raging orange flame shot up toward the mountain range clouds. Heat distortion arose around the edges of the fire, bathing the adjacent pavement and buildings in an eerie glow and bordering the scene with a dream-tinged aura of drama and danger.

Their destination, at first faint and vague (appearing as more of a distant concept than an immediate reality) quickly acquired concrete characteristics, looming larger and larger, betraying more and more detail as the engine catapulted purposefully and ungently toward the crackle and singe of the flaming structure. Not long after Eddie pointed out the site to Jerry, they arrived, pulling up short in a flourish of squealing rubber and brake pads.

Just before the engine had come to a complete stop, it began: a whirlwind of controlled action, a buzzing hive-like flurry of deliberate activity sounding out a symphony of sensory overload. — It was then the pounding hearts, rushing blood, surging adrenaline, straining muscles, stomping boots, torrents of jangling tools and whirring machinery, sizzling hisses emitted from unfurling hoses, urgently shouted orders mingling with grunts of acknowledgment and burdensome effort.

The next phase was automatic as the men succumbed to the trance state that characterizes unconscious labor, falling back on trained, ingrained routines, following the well-worn paths of their established patterns as they raced to their places, carefully retracing the steps of the fixed process they'd been taught.

It should be noted that the preceding description is intended to highlight the skills of these daring professionals. The methodical efficiency and precision with which the firefighter carries out the duties demanded of him.

Of course every fire emergency situation is different; every fire possesses a character that is unique. Therefore, each individual situation requires a slightly different set of responses and reactions. That's why, in addition to rote follow-through and military-style discipline, one of the firefighter's most important assets is the brain. The firefighter needs to be a thinker who can deviate from the established playbook when applicable, augmenting fluidity and flexibility where necessary and appropriate.

As fires go, the one that Eddie and his colleagues were facing was a formidable one. Before it would be defeated, this blaze demanded a good measure of their bravery and a great deal of their considerable instincts and talents. They had to summon internal reserves in order to remain cool and calm amid an excruciatingly stressful set of circumstances. In short, this particular conflagration would require more of what their hearts, minds, and bodies had to offer than they had at first expected or bargained for.

Initially there was little outward evidence to suggest that the call would turn out to be such a challenging experience. The first moments of the engagement passed unremarkably, everything going by the book and according to plan. Within minutes, the ladders were up, the hoses were fixed on their targets, the axing of a window had vented the building, and the search and rescue crew was suited up and ready to enter the building.

The building was a two-story apartment complex. They had an uncommon amount of quality intelligence about the internal layout of the place thanks to the fact that the woman who had initially phoned the fire in. After narrowly escaping the grasp of its searing tentacles, she was on hand to provide an accurate and detailed description of all the rooms, hallways, and staircases.

Within five to ten minutes, the Corrunoside company, aided by the volunteer Engine Company #1 (a crew from the adjoining town), had successfully isolated the blaze to a single first-floor apartment and the second-floor apartment directly above. Just when the call began to look like it would end up being a relatively easy job, complications began to arise.

Eddie's first inkling that the minor operation was taking a turn for the serious occurred when he saw Keith and Steve exiting the building without the residents they'd been sent to retrieve. Steve was coughing and wheezing and needed to support himself on Keith in order to stand and walk. Keith had an arm around Steve's shoulder and struggled to half carry and half drag him clear.

Eddie, who had been supervising and directing the main battery of hoses, quickly delegated the task to the most senior man he could find. He then ran to the two to see what was wrong and lend a hand. Steve was ghost white, grappling for each breath and seemed on the verge of total collapse.

Apparently the level of smoke infestation was unexpectedly heavy in the upstairs apartment. The two could penetrate no further than the hallway before Steve had been stricken by smoke inhalation, and the two had to beat a hasty retreat before they both succumbed to thick gray pea soup of poisoned air.

After confirming that at least one and as many as two people were still trapped inside, Eddie ran toward the ladder detachment as fast as his feet could carry him.

"Listen, we got a man down with smoke inhalation and up to two civilians caught inside the upstairs apartment. Help me raise a ladder to the balcony. I'm going in."

The firefighters were in the process of obeying the order when a lieutenant from the volunteer squad stepped forward to intervene.

"Nothing' doing'. Put them steps right back down where they were."

"Are you crazy? We got live bodies inside."

"Are *you* crazy? Let's grab one hot second here to take a step back and assess the situation clearly and coolly."

"No time."

"No time indeed. As in: at no time am I going to allow a brother of mine to shuffle straight on up into the hereafter."

"What are you talking about?"

"I'm talking about the angle of the flames and the heat emanating from the downstairs apartment. I mean, we got it somewhat under control, but she's still roaring. She'll still kill. And if the heat doesn't get you, the smoke will. Tell you what, show me where we can position the ladder without it and you melting into an aluminum crisp and I'll be the first to—"

"If we—"

"And even if you can show me that, how the hell are you going to get through that smoke carrying a body on your back? No. I won't allow it. We got to figure out something else and quick. This little back and forth we're having here, fascinatin' as it is, ain't saving' no one."

Feeling desperate and helpless, his heart sinking further toward despair with each passing moment, Eddie scanned the site to find a plausible solution. It was possible that he could find someone to override the lieutenant, but as he took in the scene, he realized that the goddamn lieutenant was 100 percent correct.

The fire had been confined, but even in its compacted state, it had a high degree of power and potential, remaining unruly and, as a result, was still quite unpredictable and dangerous. Huge curving sheets of wild flame, a full story tall, intermittently flared out from the bottom floor in an upward arc, like a blossoming flower. The angry orange petals licked at the bottom balcony and would more than likely engulf any ladder at any angle.

Because of the prodigious amount of uncommonly thick smoke billowing up from the flames, two of their better men, wearing almost a full component of safety gear, had narrowly averted tragedy. There was no room for the seventy-five foot snorkel to get close enough.

Then, –in mid-thought, was when he saw her frenzied face in the window. He yelled to get her attention and to get the attention of the ladder men who were in earshot. Eddie frantically gestured for her to open the window. No dice. The situation was turning dire. He thought his voice would grow hoarse from screaming before she heard him above the surrounding din.

There was a tap on his shoulder. A Corrunoside volunteer lieutenant had a megaphone he'd gotten from his truck. Eddie nodded his head in thanks, and wasted no time using it. It did the trick. Through the ever-thickening swirl of smoke, he saw the glow of recognition spread across her face, like the light of a brilliant sunrise across the dawn.

In her hand was a bundle of what Eddie presumed was valuables. Eddie directed her to drop it so she could work the window open. She did not comply. However, she did finally move to lift the sash. Shifting the bundle into her left hand, she leaned against the sill, and in one motion, using the strength mysteriously granted to those in mortal crisis, she threw the heavy frame of the window up and open with her right hand alone.

An eruption of acrid smoke poured up into the chill sky in a dark gray column that grew wider as it diffused. Holy shit. Now that the window was open and a plume of obfuscating smoke had been allowed to escape, Eddie saw, to his horror, that it was no bundle she was holding: it was a baby!

The baby's face was swaddled to protect it against the smoke, but even so, it was living on borrowed time. Despite the heat and danger of stray flame, Eddie moved as close as he could. He was adjacent to the building and directly below the window.

"Throw down your baby, I'll make the catch, I promise," Eddie called to the mother. The order threw her into a panic. Her head shook back and forth in an emphatic no. "I don't have time to argue with you. I know what I'm doing. Throw down the baby or the baby will die. There is no time for further debate. You don't have time to think it over."

Somehow he got through to her. Later she'd tell the press that it wasn't what he said but how he said it. The soothing competency underlining the urgency of the emergency gave her confidence and courage. She realized it was the right thing, no, the only thing to do.

Tears welling in her eyes, she leaned trembling out the window. "On the count of three," Eddie instructed, and, to his relief, she nodded in affirmation. On one, she christened the child's forehead with a kiss of tortured hope. On two, she tentatively extended wide her arms, holding the baby in her hands. On three, she carefully aimed at Eddie's outstretched, upturned palms and gently let her baby go.

The crowd of usually jaded "seen it all" firefighters watched in awed and petrified silence. They'd never seen this. The smattering of chorused "Our Fathers" and "Hail Mary's" abruptly broke off. Those who had been feverishly petitioning the Lord had ceased, mid-sentence, to stare open mouthed at the precious human cargo as it tumbled through an eerie, slow-motion descent that lasted at most three seconds but seemed to take hours. The tension was palpable. A squeamish few averted their eyes, but most watched intently, as if willing the breathing bundle home to Eddie's grasp with the power and intensity of their gazes alone.

With a tender smack and plop like a baseball homing into a catcher's mitt, Eddie caught the baby with sure hands. After pulling the swaddling from the child's face, he held her aloft, yelling "It's a girl!" as if he were a doctor or a midwife following a successful birth. Those gathered erupted into spontaneous cheers. He handed the baby girl to another firefighter and motioned up toward the mother.

"Now you," he implored.

She hesitated, wearing the same frightened look of denial and fear as when Eddie had first called for her baby. The Volunteer lieutenant joined into the cajoling, assuring the woman that both he and Eddie would catch her together. Every second was a black hand closing the book on her living days.

She was already woozy and disoriented from the smoke fumes. They had to reach her soon. Between the two of them, alternatively ordering her sternly and begging and pleading, they managed to convince her in what the paramedics treating her later estimated to be the nick of time. (Of course the fire no doubt did some convincing of its own.)

At any rate, she jumped. The two men caught her cleanly and without incident. The spontaneous cheers exploded once more, this time even lustier and more unbridled. The firefighters handed off the formerly trapped nineteen-year-old mother to paramedics. Jerry came up behind Eddie and clasped him affectionately on the shoulder.

The lingering fondness and familiarity of Jerry's grasp quickly embarrassed them both. Eddie pulled away. The motion was abrupt, but not overly so, just as the smirk on his face was reproaching but also warm and not unkind. "What?" asked Eddie, "what are you doing'?"

"You, man. Don't you get it?"

"What?" he asked again, this time with a tinge of impatience? After the day he'd had, there was no patience left in him for riddles.

"You did it again, brother. You did it again. Without even trying' to."

A reporter approached the two close friends. She broke into a typical question. Before she could finish, they answered her in unison:

"No comment."

They walked away, off into the proverbial sunset (but really just back to the fire station to shower off and fill out paperwork.)

It had started off being a more-or-less ordinary, albeit more active than usual Monday night at the Town Derby a neighborhood pub. There was certainly no hint in the air that it would be a night some folks would remember, in one way or another, for the rest of their lives.

Healthier than normal the place was packed especially for a weeknight crowd, owing mostly to the fact that it was football season. Indeed, the head count was so much healthier than average that Pete (the "Derby man" in the flesh, who was the pub's namesake and owner), the usually chronically cranky fifty-five-year old second-generation lifelong sole proprietor of the place, could not suppress a smile. Even for the heart of *Monday Night Football* season, tonight's take would be extra good.

If Pete knew anything, he knew his business, and he knew that the brisk business was not an anomaly of some mysterious phenomenon. It could be attributed to three simple reasons. First and foremost, the

Giants were on tonight, and they were playing their arch-rival, the Dallas Cowboys. With the teams tied for second place and in playoff contention, the game meant something. The victor would move within two games of the first place Redskins, while the loser would fall within striking distance of the fourth-place Eagles.

Second, the weather was bitter cold, classic drinking weather. Even most of your committed athletic types would be tempted to forgo a wind chilled jog, opting instead for a burger and a beer in the comfort of the oil heat.

The third reason for the enhanced crowd was no happy accident or fortunate circumstance. It was the big-screen television Pete had finally broken down and purchased the previous August, after much hand-wringing and loss of sleep.

For the first time he knew his decision had been a sound one. The place was packed. The kitchen was jammed with orders. The taps were flowing steadily, so much so that the bar was constantly wheeling out new kegs to replace the tapped-out Budweiser and Coors draft. Pete couldn't recall the last time he had had to reinforce the drafts this early when it wasn't a weekend or holiday.

It wasn't as if the place was claustrophobic or uncomfortably sardine-full like some dance club in the city. The room had a long way to go before it could be described as being filled wall-to-wall with people. But by shortly after 8 p.m. the bar, bar-tops, and surrounding booths were already full. "If this keeps up," mused Pete, "I'll have to take reservations."

A lively crowd of regulars had gathered at the far corner of the bar by the dartboard. Two of the guys were playing, and they'd attracted an audience. The dart contest was serving as an impromptu opening act for the Giants. No one was really interested in the pre-game chatter anyway. Pete still had the TV tuned low and the jukebox cranked high. Springsteen's "Glory Days" blared through the bluster of the unseasonably frigid Jersey night.

Because of the relatively packed house and all the activity, no one noticed or commented when the solitary black man entered quietly through the front door. He walked up to the bar, found and occupied the last available seat, and ordered a drink without incident or undue attention.

Not that the mere arrival of a person of color should or would necessarily cause a stir, but within the insular confines of the Town Derby, where the patrons all pretty much knew each from the old neighborhood and came from a decidedly narrow spectrum of working-class Italian, Irish, or Polish stock (or some mixture of the three), any occurrence of ethnic diversity was rather remarkable and notable. The bar had such fraternal club-like feeling about it that just about any stranger might feel a bit unwelcome, let alone a member of a minority.

The lone African American drinker got his beer, nodded a polite "thanks," and slid a single dollar bill across the bar as a tip. A few seats down from where he began to nurse his drink, three off-duty cops and one recent retired cop were engaged in boisterous chatter and horseplay.

When the oldest member of the rowdy foursome rose from his stool to take his leave, he was instantly assailed by streams of raucous protest that soon coalesced into a cohesive verbal landslide of good-natured peer pressure. Determined to reach the door, he patiently but firmly brushed aside the jibes of his mates as he tipsily rummaged through his pockets for his car keys.

"Thefmor, where the hell you think you're going?"

"It's past my bedtime, boys. I ain't no young buck like youse no more."

"What the hell? You're not even going to stay and watch the first half of the game?"

"I'm sure you'll tell me how it turned out."

"Aw, you're lettin' us all down old man."

"What can I say? When you got to go, you got to go."

"What for? You got a hot date?"

"I just got a lot to get done if I want to get down to Florida this weekend."

"Oh, big vacation. Well excuse us."

"No vacation. Work on the vacation house. The house that the dented cans built ain't gonna renovate itself."

"All right, all right, get out of here and go do your thing. Cryin' out loud, when a man is too busy making' money all the time to take a little nip with his buddies, on football night no less, something is wrong."

"Sorry you feel that way."

"Well I do. Now get while the getting's good. And give our regards to that boy of yours. How's he doing' anyway?"

"Not bad. He's crankin' along with the business. A few headaches with a goody-two-shoes partner who wants to do every little thing by the book, but we'll straighten it out."

"Sounds good. Tell Dennis we were asking after him."

"Will do. And thanks for the drink and the hard time."

"Don't mention it. That's what we're here for."

The trouble started about an hour after the older retired cop had made his exit. The game, along with the moods of most of the patrons, had turned sour. The second quarter had just kicked off and the Giants were already taking a pounding. Dallas, up 17-0, had the ball, yet again, and was driving.

It happened after Danny White, the Cowboy quarterback, had hit wide receiver Drew Pearson for twenty yards, a handoff to their star runner Tony Dorsett yielded a second consecutive first down when he scooted through a gaping hole up the middle for a gain of sixteen. Just like that, Dallas had a first and ten on the Giant thirty-four yard line.

There are times, even in the latter twentieth century, even in the supposedly enlightened Northeast, when it's downright dangerous to be a minority. There are times (i.e., Howard Beach, Queens, or Benson Hurst, Bronx, Brooklyn) when it can be fatal. For the black man at the bar, the relevant minority wasn't the color of his skin, although, God knows it couldn't have helped matters. He held minority membership that was much more offensive and provocative than his race: he was Cowboys' fan in a bar full of guys who bled Giant blue. Not only was he a Cowboys' fan, he had the unfortunate lack of sense and sensibility to be enthusiastically vocal about it.

On the next play, White dropped back and launched a perfect pass to Butch Johnson, who had run a short flare route about eight yards downfield. Johnson tucked the ball to his chest, broke the tackles of several Giant defenders, and turned up field for a significant gain. When the smoke cleared, the 'Boys were deep in the red zone for the fourth time in as many offensive drives.

The Dallas fan at the bar pumped his fist and shouted "Yessss!!!" in a way that would have made Marv Albert proud. Apparently this latest outburst was the last straw for the cops occupying the end curve of the bar. They looked at one another, exchanging silent venom, wordlessly goading and inciting one another to some sort of decisive action. The closest cop, who also happened to be the alpha male of the group (and used every possible opportunity he could to prove it), leaned over and tapped the shoulder of the Dallas fan.

"Hey pal, you mind shuttin' the fuck up?"

"Actually yeah. It's a free country, and I'm just enjoying a game and a beer. I'm a football fan, you know?"

"Oh it's like that?"

"Yeah it's like that. What's the matter, you don't like football fans?"

"No I don't mind football fans. I just don't like niggers."

He didn't know they were off-duty cops, schooled in the vilest of corruptions and used to acting with absolute impunity, doing whatever they wanted and getting away with it scot-free (as they ultimately would on this night). If he had known, maybe what happened next wouldn't have happened. But it did.

The words escalated until one of the off-duty boys lunged at the black man. The bartender, cursing like a sailor and brandishing a Louisville Slugger like he meant to use it, succeeded in breaking things up and cooling things off. The Dallas booster, although his feathers were ruffled, assumed that was the end of it. But he didn't feel comfortable watching the game at Pete's establishment anymore. He paid his tab and left, paying no further heed to the fuming trio he was leaving behind.

The aroused pack of cops, however, was not willing to let matters lie. A bit buzzed from the brew perhaps, the exiting Cowboys' backer failed to notice that they rose when he rose and followed him out to the parking lot. By the time he heard the savagely purposeful clomp of footsteps behind his back, it was too late.

He broke into a run, desperately striding toward his car, but the man he'd exchanged words with was able to get a hand around him and wrestle him down to the ground. Another officer clasped a hand over his mouth, while the other two dragged him around to the pitch-dark backside of the establishment, out of sight of the street and arriving or departing customers.

Over the next twenty minutes, they viciously and brutally beat the man within an inch of his life. When paramedics finally arrived (several hours later, after a drunken barfly had stumbled out back to vomit and heard weak gurgling and moaning), they were astonished at what they found.

"I thought I'd seen bad, but this is fucking bad. I can barely where the hell there's supposed to be a human being under all this blood and mess," one of the EMTs was overheard commenting to another as they slid the unfortunate victim onto a stretcher, hustled him into the back of the ambulance, and sped off in a hurried rush of churning gravel, sirens flaring and blaring like bloody murder. One of the off duty officers went to police headquarters and took a unit and followed all the way to the Hospital. Once there he beat the Dallas fan even more.

Chapter 6

The first rays of visible light were busting vigorously through the newborn day as the sun slid sizzling forward, making a spectacularly understated entrance, rising slow and deliberate between Jurassic buildings, peeking over jagged ridges of horizon, a poached egg simmering between the glint gray highlights of a frying pan sky. As dawn broke over the downtown business district, Eddie arrived at the store, pulling into his usual parking space. He reviewed a mental checklist of tasks he intended to accomplish by the end of the day.

Although it would still be several hours until the doors of the place would officially open for business, Eddie was eager to get inside, get busy, and hit the ground running in order to get a jump on his endlessly expanding workload.

Plus there was another reason, one more covert and less routine. As time continued its inexorable march, as the details of day-to-day life were dispensed with to the tune of honking car horns, roaring jet engines, droning dial tones, and other assorted white noise blare, as tasks were accomplished and errands run and to and fro movements from point A to point B were undertaken in an atmosphere of such rushed hustle and bustle that no one had much time to think about how quickly the days were running away like wild horses over the hills, about how many days, weeks, and months had fallen to the floor unnoted, unnoticed, like the paper leaves of a disposable daily desk calendar. As the Reagan decade ripened toward its waning years in a hazy cloud of cigar and smokestack smoke mixed with miscellaneous emissions of diesel, dust, and avarice amid the sounds of silence, the screams of Tiananmen, the wanton whoops of Wall Street, and the clattering clang of iron curtains falling from Berlin to Johannesburg, relations between Eddie and his partner had plummeted to an all-time low.

Eddie increasingly felt as though he were being ever-so-gently nudged out of the loop of his own business. He was determined to investigate until he got some answers and got to the bottom of whatever was going on. The more poking around he did, the less sure he was that he wanted to know the truth.

Apparently Dennis was duping Renee and therefore forming some level of collusion between Dennis and Eddie's wife Renee. Furthermore, their clandestine understanding had been flourishing for quite some time. Eddie had yet to confront Renee about his concerns; he almost couldn't bear to, but from what he had been able to glean thus far, Dennis was using his wife as a means to circumvent his concerns about proper receipt-taking, inventorying, and accounting.

The way the business worked was that one of the principles always had to sign for and approve merchandise. By virtue of the paperwork and Renee's position as Eddie's spouse, she functioned as a de-facto principle owner, endowed for all the practical purposes with the same level of decision-making powers as Eddie and Dennis, at least when it came to day-to-day matters. Initially Eddie thought this decision was a no-brainer.

He was even the one who suggested the arrangement since there were times when neither Eddie nor Dennis would be available, and Renee was the only person, other than his parents and children, who he truly trusted. Plus the store was bound to profit from her involvement. She was effortlessly competent. The woman truly had a head for business.

The move was also intended to serve as a reassuring counterweight against Eddie's lingering sense of mistrust toward Dennis. Eddie had figured it couldn't hurt to have an extra pair of watchful eyes in his corner. Only now he was forced to wonder whether the person those eyes belonged to was still completely on his side.

Over the months, a series of low-key, almost barely perceptible changes had taken place. The metamorphosis in the personality dynamic of the decision-making triangle was so minute that Eddie barely noticed. Except that he did. One or two things definitely stuck out in Eddie's mind. So, he did notice something that was an indescrible awry.

It is relevant to note that the process of detecting the evolving phenomenon wasn't easy. Dennis was a deft and subtle operator and Renee had always been a closed book, even back in the carefree beginnings of their love, so it was difficult to reconstruct the sequence of events with any real certainty. From what he'd been able to gather, however, was that Dennis had gradually convinced Renee that Eddie was being over cautious with the books and merchandise and that it was costing them business and potential profits. Dennis was able to color the conflict in a way that convinced Renee that she was really helping Eddie and looking after his financial interests when she was, in reality, betraying him.

All this and more was on Eddie's burdened mind as he gathered his papers, locked his car, and walked toward the front door of his store. The other major focus of his deliberations had to do with rapidly moving developments occurring across town at the firehouse. At least the latter situation was positive in nature. Despite this, it remained a source of stress because new demands on his time were being requested. Soon some serious decisions would have to be made.

According to most of the scuttlebutt around the station—and most of the rumors that tended to flow freely whenever the guys gathered together for barbeques, bachelor parties, and what have you—Eddie was first in line for a major promotion.

Eddie was modest by nature, so he tried to nip the proliferating buds of loose chatter that were blossoming all around him mostly out of a deep-seeded sense of humility and gratitude. He also didn't want to jinx his chances, didn't want to assume he was a lieutenant until they sewed (pinned) the actual bars onto his jacket. As fortuitous as the development was (the more substantial paycheck certainly wouldn't hurt and could, as a matter of fact, be put to good use immediately)—assuming it did go through, navigating the interminable labyrinths of department bureaucracy until it became finalized enough for the captain to announce it one morning at roll call—there were definitely significant drawbacks to consider.

After the pomp and circumstance died down, the promotion would mean a net increase in the amount of weight that Eddie was toting on his shoulders. More headaches, more responsibility, more pressure, more effort, and more time spent on the job away from the wife and kids. It also meant more time away from his business, which, for the time being at least, required his most alert attention.

In addition, his position on the firefighting "team" would be subtly but tangibly transformed. He was placed in a role in that required him to issue orders. They would be orders of do-or-die importance that would demand lightning-fast, flawlessly competent response. They'd concern the lives and deaths of his men and traumatized members of the civilian population.

Due to the nature of the firefighters work, it was necessary that these orders be followed unquestionably and without hesitation. Assuming, of course, that the promotion-related rumors were true—and when it came to this type of stuff, they usually were—news of this type usually emanated from someone in the know or someone who overheard something. Job-oriented information such as hiring, firings, promotions, or demotions was the one grapevine topic that tended to be based on hard facts rather than random speculation or lurid conjecture. Based on the past performance of the rumor mill, it was a good bet that Eddie's elevation to lieutenant would occur. Most likely, the decision had already been made and was now enmeshed in the process of slowly but steadily making its way to Eddie's home station house, guided by a relay of desk jockeys who passed it like a baton through a maze of paperwork, triplicate signatures, ink stamps, and approvals. For this reason alone, in order for the integrity and effectiveness of Eddie's leadership to be firmly established and remain intact, it was crucially important that he be unanimously, no, universally perceived by all station-house personnel, from the chief down to the stray Dalmatian, as a viable authority figure.

A certain distance had to be established between Eddie and the guys. For one thing, he had to cease thinking of them as "the guys." He could no longer afford to act informally, pal around, and be seen as one of them, a friend. He had to withdraw from situations that tended to undermine his hierarchical position and placed him on a casual or equal level with the colleagues who would, with a stroke of the chief's pen, suddenly become his subordinates.

In the context of day-to-day living, the practical implications of Eddie's potential promotion would be myriad and far-reaching. For example, there would be no more off-duty poker or billiard games, no more invitations offered or accepted for weekend cookouts with everyone's wives and kids mingling and frolicking by the pool or playing volleyball on a lush, leafy green sea of well-tended, meticulously manicured backyard. The conspiratorial camaraderie of stealing away with two or three buddies for a "quick one" at the corner bar right after quitting time, those days would soon be over as well. It would probably even be wise, Eddie reflected, to refrain from the heated competition of the break-room chess matches they played to pass the time between emergency calls.

The realization that distinct changes were in store, at least on a social level, filled Eddie with a softly flickering sadness. Despite his misgivings, there was no doubt he'd follow through on the unpleasant measures, because they were as necessary as they were unpleasant. Still, it was ironic. Up to this point, he'd spent his entire career being known as a well-liked, gregarious person who was genuinely concerned about being approachable, friendly, and blending in. Now he'd have to be genuinely concerned about being respected, honored, and obeyed. From here on he'd have a foster a vague sense of impenetrability, the superior mystique of the supervisor. From here on the name of the game was separation from the pack in which his membership had heretofore been an unquestioned thing; it was such a given, so elemental and identity-defining, that he had taken it for granted. It's because of family and political influence that have caused cover ups is why the department often transferred someone in or hired from the outside whenever a higher-level position opened up. Though Eddie appreciated the common-sense wisdom that had inspired such a policy, he was also stirred by a secret pride that his stature as an all-around firefighter had been too imposing and the overall quality of his work had been too exemplary to pass over.

His close friends—Keith, Steve, Jerry, and at least for now, Dennis—would remain his close friends. In truth, there had been some abstract tension. Things were slightly strained at the moment as they scrambled to find sure footing amid the changing terrain. Nothing remarkable, mind you, or even clearly discernable, just a faint edge to some of their jibes. They'd taken to calling him "Lieutenant," "MacArthur," or "The Colonel" when they fraternized.

Eddie was certain, however, that they would come around. And they would. They were. The very fact and focus of their work-related teasing, sardonic as it may have been, was a tacit acknowledgment of the soon-to-be-implemented station house food chain. In other words, they had accepted the changes in their workplace circumstances as a given, even before they officially existed. No, he didn't have to worry about his key allies. These guys were his best friends. One thing he did not have a right to suspect was their loyalty.

The real threats would come from his rivals. Along with each new workplace success, along with every instance of official recognition (and over the years there had been many), Eddie seemed to acquire a growing number of enemies. Not overtly hostile foes, mind you, these were subversive cloak-and-dagger types who whispered their snipes in the dusty corners and forgotten corridors where they'd quietly withdrawn to nurse the venom of their jealousy in the shadows. He only knew of their existence because most of the shit they said behind his back got back to him. Their invisibility, however, made them no less real, no less treacherous. They were waiting for their opportunity to strike, biding their time, serpentine. They were the true stones in his valley. To avoid stumbling, he had to remain perpetually aware. Only his opponents could damage him now.

On reaching the front door of his shop, Eddie fumbled through his pockets, shivering against a vicious gust of frigid air as he searched for and then located his heavy jangling keychain. Exhalations of his breath jetted through the pitch of night in elaborate plumes, then billowed and dispersed like dry ice smoke. He was so deep in thought about the potentially pending promotion and the pressures that awaited his attention inside that he almost didn't spy the little butterfly of paper that fluttered to the ground at his feet as he turned the first of a series of keys in the first of a series of padlocks. The door swung open with the heavy grating growl of a cracked safe, and Eddie moved forward to cross the threshold, pausing to pick up what he thought was a piece of trash.

Trash may have been an appropriate word to use to describe the folded sheet of loose-leaf paper trembling between Eddie's fingers. Trash was not, however, its literally intended purpose. It was not something meant for the wastebasket, although perhaps that is where it belonged and where it should have been immediately thrown like so much debris. Although such an impulse emanated from Eddie's gut to cross his mind, he did not trash the note, the note that had been written specifically for his eyes to read, then purposefully and carefully tucked in the shoulder-high space between the doorjamb where a break in the mortar caused a wallet-sized gap between the door and the wall.

Instead, he read it, wishing he hadn't even as his eyes scanned the crudely handwritten words of the message. The writing on the page contained a simple declaration, twice underlined: "Your wife is cheating," it read. And then, in slightly smaller print, there was a number to call, presumably to be used if he wanted filled in on all the lurid details of her entanglement. The number was written across the bottom, like in a tabloid advertisement for a novel consumer product: for more information, to learn more, call, further inquiries directed to—that sort of thing. Written in neat, red ballpoint, word for word and letter for letter, just like that. There was no further information, evidence, or incriminating details. So it was easy not to believe, especially for someone who didn't want to believe.

Eddie pushed the troubling message to the back of his mind and got down to business. He straightened the shelves, unpacked some boxes, tidied up the front area, and then retired to the desk in the back to do some paperwork and try to piece together the puzzling clues to the interlocking jigsaws of deception that were beginning to box him in at every turn.

As he discharged his daily duties, working through his personal checklist of things to do, Eddie found himself frequently slipping into deep and vivid reverie. The primary topic of all the memory-dredging daydreaming was, of course, Renee.

There might have been other players and other plot points, but she was always the main character, the protagonist, standing center stage with the defiant flashing gleam in her eyes that he had fallen so madly and passionately in love with all those years ago. All those years ago ... it doesn't seem like it all happened so, so long ago. He had met her in high school, on the first day of his senior-year AP English class. She walked in a sliver of a second before the bell rang, wearing a long black cotton dress. Her eyes were as aquamarine as a shivering, choppy flank of Atlantic Ocean basking off the sandy shore down at Wildwood in the radiant sensual heat of mid-July. She sat in the empty desk behind him. She tapped him on the shoulder. He felt a chill run up his spine. She asked him for a pencil in a voice both soft and gravelly.

Eddie turned around and looked at her, really looked at her, for the first time. She was a vision of angelic grace, imbued with the mystique of the eternal. Her shining head of hair cascaded down to her shoulders, crashing there and curving back up to her face in Niagara plumes of blond. Her gaze was downcast, innocent, and demure. It was right then and there that he fell in love with her. But it took three months before he worked up the courage to ask her for her phone number.

The courtship was short and intense. After their first date, which took place on a Saturday night (they went to go see a varsity basketball game in their school's cavernous gymnasium), they found time to see each other almost every other day, if not every day. They took numerous trips over to Coney Island (where they shared their first kiss atop the old, creaking Ferris wheel) and weekend escapes down the Garden State Parkway to the Jersey shore They spent several Friday nights at an intimate Mexican restaurant in the city's West Village, a romantic senior prom night that Eddie saved countless weeks of part-time paychecks to pull off (he rented a limo, took her to dinner at the South Street Seaport, and took her on a cruise around Manhattan after the dance was over), and took camping trips to Bear Mountain on the first spring break they shared as a couple.

After an interval of time that was surprisingly brief to everyone but the principles involved, Eddie proposed. Even Renee had realized by the way he looked at her on those early dates as they strolled down the boardwalk just past sunset that it was not a question of if; it was a question of when. By the time he'd actually popped the question, they'd both long since realized that they were meant for one another. Eddie, of course, knew from the first night he took her out that he wanted to be with her for the rest of his life, knew that he wanted her to be his wife.

Still, when the time came to do the damn thing, he pulled it off with uncommon style and aplomb. This happened in the winter of 1968. The proposal took place four months before Eddie's graduation from Corrunoside High, during the midnight hour of a frigid February snowstorm. They were staying the night in a tiny motel on the outskirts of Vernon Valley, the night before a ski trip with some friends. Lying next to each other in bed, Eddie asked Renee to light the candle he'd placed on her nightstand.

When she opened the cardboard matchbox, there were no matches inside, only a beautiful diamond engagement ring. Eddie dropped to one knee and asked the question. Renee answered yes through a veil of joyful tears. There wasn't the slightest hesitation in her response or her voice. That night, they listened to the Johnny Maestro and the Brooklyn Bridge and made love for the first time. Renee was a virgin. Eddie was not, but he might as well have been. Until then, his sporadic handful of romantic experiences (if they could even accurately be labeled as such) had consisted of furtive fumbling in the backseats of cars, on the couches of somebody's cellar-slash-den while Zeppelin blasted from the stereo upstairs and the air pump sound of a keg being primed swooshed down from out of the backyard, or under blankets back in the patch of woods that surrounded the desolate dirt road dead-end where all the high school and community college kids used to go park and make out.

He'd never shared real intimacy like this. Never had the time to take his time, to not have to look over his shoulder or at a clock (that inevitably ticked off the time left before a parent's return), to be able to stay beside his woman all night, or to be able to wake up next to her in the morning. Hell, he'd never even shared an actual bed with another woman before.

So it was all more or less new to him as well as her. And it was wonderful. They shared it together, both feeling at least a piece of the passion and the innocence felt in the conjoined hearts of the first lovers on that first day, before the apple, before the fall. If, at that point, you told either one of them they'd have a long relationship but that it would end in an acrimonious divorce, both would have looked at you as if you were crazy. And to look at them and say that, the way they were then, you'd have to be crazy, you'd have to be out of your mind.

For the rest of the summer that followed his high school graduation, Eddie worked like a man possessed. He had three regular part-time jobs and was often able to pick up odd jobs around the neighborhood. Renee worked as well, as a waitress and cashier at the soda fountain of the corner drugstore. The McCrory's management staff never gave her more than thirty to thirty-five hours a week. As she settled into the routine she'd follow through the sultry weather months, she often found herself with an excess of time on her hands, killing hours here or there, waiting for Eddie to get off of work at one job or another.

While she sort of resented all the time Eddie spent that he could have spent with her, Renee knew he was doing it for the two of them, for their future. The harder and longer he worked, the sooner they could afford to marry and set up a home together. Despite being well aware of the financial facts of their life, Renee could still drive Eddie to distraction sometimes with pouted, silent moods and complaints about neglect. It's awfully hard to be forward looking, think in terms of differed gratification, and hold fast to a long-term viewpoint when you're barely eighteen years old.

By the end of summer '68, Eddie had met the monetary objectives he'd set for himself. However, he realized that his exhausting triathlon of part-time jobs was simply not going to cut it when it came to establishing the stable domestic foundation upon which he and Renee could build a family. It was during this period that he first considered joining the fire department.

Actually Eddie's initial area of interest was the police force. Several of his relatives had been on the job, and Eddie had always viewed the life of an officer with a reverent mixture of interest and respect. This idea was eventually drowned by Renee's endless reservoir of strenuous objections to such a dangerous line of work.

"Marrying a firefighter is bad enough," she'd say, worked up almost to the point of tears, "but if you're careful and you follow the rules, at least you have a fighting chance. I won't have to sit up nights wondering if the man I love has been shot or stabbed or worse." Because he loved her, because he couldn't stand to see her upset, he promised her he'd never don a blue uniform and carry a badge and a gun.

His final vocational decisions were temporarily set aside while Eddie enrolled in classes at Centerville's County College to pursue a degree that he hoped would dramatically expand the amount of available career options open to him.

One thing Renee's fears could not erase was his sense of patriotic duty. At this particular point in history, the carnage in Southeast Asia had reached a crescendo. War was raging, and there was no escaping the reality of the conflict. The blood of their brethren was inked dark and bold across the newspapers laid out on their lawns in the morning and splattered like snowy static across the TV at night, Cronkite peering out from behind the screen of the rabbit-eared black and white box of electrodes and pixels and light. Many of their friends were already in Vietnam, or preparing to go. A handful of people they knew, or people that knew people they knew, had perished within the last twelve months.

Despite protesting harder and more stridently against his involvement in the war than the members of the Chicago 8, Renee could not dissuade Eddie from what he felt was his obligation to volunteer to do battle against the enemies of our nation. She tried everything to make him stay, or at least wait until his lottery number came up. From begging, cajoling, and pleading on one end of the spectrum to empty threats to leave on the other, no technique was effective. Neither the sweetest honey nor the vilest vinegar even showed signs of getting through to him. All of her efforts seemed to be to no avail.

As it turned out, this hyper stoic attitude was a conscious decision on Eddie's part and far more difficult to follow through on than he ever let her know. His feelings for her hadn't changed in the slightest, nor did the lunar hold she exerted on the tides of his blue trench heart. But when push came to shove, his love for his country trumped his love for his woman. He hid the stigmata of emotional wounds she had inflicted upon him and went about his business as if he were immune to her entreaties. He wasn't of course. But that doesn't mean he had any intention of allowing her, or anyone, or anything else (including the big, fat, coveted college deferment that he could have easily fallen back on), to stand in the way of fighting and, if necessary, dying for his country.

So it happened, after a difficult, emotionally draining weekend of tears and long walks and talks early that first Monday morning of October 1968, Eddie reported to the U.S. Navy induction center prepared to leave the woman he loved and the future he was building to turn himself over, heart, mind, body, and soul, to Uncle Sam.

That night they met for dinner at the local burger joint. Renee was calm. Having cried herself dry, she had finally resigned herself to the fact that he was going and she would be a mistress to Vietnam, some far-off place she probably couldn't have found on a map to save her life and had never even heard of before it was all over the news.

Eddie had entered through a side door, surprising her with a kiss on the cheek before sliding into the seat opposite her. She greeted him with a pained, silent nod and returned her gaze to the menu she was intently regarding despite the fact she must have seen it 1,000 times and probably could have read off the items verbatim with a blindfold over her eyes.

"I don't think they changed anything on there since last time," offered Eddie, tentatively testing the waters between them with a weak attempt at humor. She didn't laugh. The carefree chatter of happy couples in the surrounding booths and tables only amplified the silence fiercely lurking between them. Eddie took a second stab at conversation, pointing toward her open menu with a plastic fork.

"So ... you know what you want yet?"

"I'm not hungry."

"C'mon honey, you got to eat something. You can't starve yourself until I come back."

"Maybe I'll starve myself so you don't go."

"Well I'm not."

"What?"

"Going, that is. I'm not going. Satisfied?"

"What happened?"

Her mouth fell open as he brought her up to date. As he related the story of the day's events, he felt himself journeying through an entire range of emotions. On the one hand, he was relived that he wouldn't have to leave her to ship off to some horrifying jungle perdition of bungee spikes and exploded limbs. On the other hand, he was bitterly disappointed, even a touch ashamed (although even the grizzled old Marine recruiters had taken time out to let him know he had nothing to be ashamed of) that, due to what amounted to a technicality, they had slapped him with a 1-Y classification. In the process, they denied him the opportunity to protect the embattled American ideals he held dear, prove the mettle of his patriotism, and show his gratitude and appreciation for the country that had nurtured, raised, and protected him.

It all came down to a simple, stupid wool allergy. It sounds like a little thing, but it's not. U.S. military uniforms are made out of wool. Standard issue bedding is also made out of wool. Bottom line: you can't be an American soldier if you are severely allergic to wool. And Eddie was. The absurdity of it would have made him laugh if he hadn't felt like screaming or crying. After climbing mountains of emotional obstacles, bravely facing down the fear of war that bristles in the heart of every man, and hardening his heart to Renee's pleas and most of all he wanted to be with his buddy Gino, they'd sent him home for a reason so obscure it had never even crossed his mind.

The next few weeks required quite a bit of adjustment and refocus. All of a sudden, instead of shipping off to Southeast Asia, Eddie found himself more or less at loose ends, still in Jersey, still trying to plan his long-term future and figure out, over the short-term, what his next move was going to be. Despite reeling from the unpredictable turn of events that had terminated his military career before it got off the ground, Eddie earnestly threw himself into making preparations for the rest of his life.

After gamely trying to follow the student path for almost two semesters, Eddie realized he was not cut out for the long, droning days in the lecture hall and the sleepless nights packed with endless readings from thick, incomprehensible books and monotonous studying that comprised academic life. In early '69, Eddie decided to quit college so he could concentrate on and have more energy for working the long hours demanded of ambitious young men who were just starting out and attempting to make their way in the world.

By this time, his incessant labors had yielded enough savings for a down payment on a small house. Shortly afterward, he married Renee in a small ceremony in the church they had both grown up attending. Never had he seen her so beautiful. Never had he felt so proud. He'd had no idea what happiness a little love could bring.

They spent a week-long honeymoon in the Pocono's at a quaint and quiet chalet decorated in dark woods and silvers. They built fires in the fireplace, ate decadently rich and warm stews, broths, and bisques in the hotel lodge restaurant, took long, leisurely walks in the bracing mountain air, and shared their deepest secrets, their most cherished dreams, and their visions for a future together that was just beginning. Their horizons seemed limitless, their possibilities endless; they were so in love with one another they felt as if their swollen hearts would burst.

Making ends meet was a problem for a while, especially since Renee was still in school and could only contribute a part-time check towards running of the house and paying the bills. Thus, Eddie was always moonlighting and taking on extra work where he could find it. A friend of Eddie's who also had a new family and shared his predicament recommended that Eddie apply to join the Corrunoside Volunteer Firefighting Company.

Although it was volunteer work and there was no salary as such, there was a small stipend that was distributed among the men based on the amount of fires they extinguished over a given period. Not only would the small amount of supplemental income be welcome and helpful, advised his friend, but it was also an excellent way to get one's foot in the door of the department. Everyone knew that the paid force drew most of their recruits from the ranks of the volunteers. The extra kicker, the bonus, the icing on top, was that Eddie had wanted to be a firefighter for a long time and was only biding time until the right opportunity came along.

So Eddie took the advice. It turned out to be one of the best decisions he ever made. His application was accepted, and he so excelled at the job that in September '70, after only six months, he was hired onto the standing Corrunoside force as a full-time firefighter. Pleased with his job and in love with his wife, Eddie couldn't believe his luck or that things could get any better. He was wrong.

A few weeks after he'd been inducted into the force, on a Friday night, they were off to see a film when Renee nonchalantly announced that she thought she might be pregnant. She was. Their firstborn arrived in 1971. They named him Dominic, after his maternal father's brother. Two more boys, Justin and Colt, followed in fairly rapid succession; Justin was born in '73, and Colt arrived in '78.

Eddie's unrestrained rush of memories were abruptly cut off by the loud clanging ring of the office telephone. He picked up the receiver. It was a routine inquiry from a potential customer. He answered the question then set the phone gently back into its cradle. With an aggravated sign, he surveyed the mounds of paperwork. To his left was a pile of correspondence that Dennis had neglected to take care of. To his right was the receipt log that he was forever trying to decipher, rectify, or at least make some sense of.

Eddie pushed the paperwork forward and rested his head on his desk. It just defied understanding. Such promising beginnings, such potential, such hope. Since those early years, those ignorantly blissful early years, he'd dutifully done everything he was supposed to do. He'd been at the right places at the right times, volunteered for the right causes, canvassed and lent support to influential politicians and decision makers. On paper his life should be cruising along, the picture of perfection.

Instead it was a mess, more of the mess than the reams of papers currently splayed across his desk. He stared at a framed, wallet-sized portrait of his wife that looked up at him from the far corner of his desk. Her eyes were brimming with innocence and goodwill. She looked like the last person on this earth who could or would hurt him, who could or would hurt anyone. How could it have come to this? Was the rumor true, or did it simply represent the mean-spirited machinations of a jealous, petty person? The subject exhausted and vexed him. The very possibility was unbearable to even think about.

Chapter 7

Eddie dusted himself off and forced himself back into reality. No use feeling sorry for himself or wasting away half the day daydreaming about the past. Time to get the day under way, he decided. Looking at his watch, he saw that a big chunk of the morning had already been squandered. He rose from his workspace to perform the routine functions that needed to be completed each morning before customers could roam the aisles and make purchases.

Stepping behind the counter, he flipped the switch to turn on the register. The computerized screen warmed and whirred into digital consciousness. Next, he double-checked the locks on the glass-encased valuables. He unlocked the door before going to the display window, where an orange and black "closed" sign hung in a prominent position, centered over meticulously stacked rows of showcased merchandise designed to entice passersby into the store. He removed the sign from its suction cup hook and flipped it to the "open" position.

Open for business, Eddie thought, stepping back toward the aisles with a sense of expectation, as if waiting for something to happen. Outside, the morning had begun to ripen into rush hour. Traffic had picked up, but pedestrians were still few and far between. Eddie surveyed the scene for a moment before returning to his desk.

Still distracted, he aimlessly shuffled his paperwork. Eddie wasted another few minutes drifting through mists of reverie, of choices made, of paths not taken. He resolved to put his musings behind him, and with a deep sigh, pushed back from his desk. The wheels of his swivel chair squeaked as they rolled backward. Eddie stretched to reach for a stapler situated on a nearby shelf. Startled by the jangling of the bells over the front door, he almost lost his balance.

Catching himself, Eddie lunged forward. He was ready to forget about the stapler and leave the paperwork behind until later. He made his way to his familiar position behind the counter to greet the first customer of the day.

The interaction is a strange one. Another cop was looking for merchandise the store did not stock. If that was the only queer aspect of their exchange, Eddie would not have thought twice about it. However, the confrontation infused Eddie with an unmistakable sense of deja vu, as though he was playing and re-playing a part in an endlessly looping film. It was as though he was stuck slogging through repetitive takes of the same scene, over and over again. He knows his lines and can anticipate the other guys' responses.

The reason was simple: the dialogue, with minor variations in syntax, blocking, and casting, had happened many other times over the past few weeks. The similarities and patterns were impossible to ignore. There was a series of common threads that connected these incidents in Eddie's mind.

The "customer" was always a law enforcement officer looking for a special deal. He spoke in a strange sort of clubhouse code that Eddie was clueless to decipher. The tension builds as miscommunications mount. As best as Eddie could determine from the context of the increasingly heated exchange, the man is looking—more accurately, expecting—to buy tools or dog food at an extreme discount. There is an air of thuggish entitlement in the officer's attitude. Eventually the cop adopts a rude demeanor, becoming agitated and annoyed when it becomes clear that he is not going to get what he came for.

"Look, pal, I've been here like a thousand times. Been coming here ever since the old man owned the place. This is the first time I've had any sort of problem. I'm not trying to jam you up here."

"I'm not trying to make problems. It's just that we don't have tools and we give most of the dog food to the Corrunoside pound." Just ask Ann Bentovr.

"Sure, sure … I'll play along. I need to know a password or something?" Ya why don't you try Macavellian.

"I'm afraid I still don't know what the fuck you're talking about."

"Give me break. Don't tell me I came all the way down here for nothing."

And on and on it went like that, until the cop exits, hostile and frustrated, slamming the door behind him. Eddie stood open mouthed behind the counter, stunned and suspicious. Eddie tried to remember where he had seen this jerk off before. Then it came to him he was a sheriff in the county and a good friend of the Thefmor family. Eddie would come in from time to time and see him and Dennis whispering in the back. (Later Eddie would see him again, standing security in Judge Dolfman's courtroom.)

Later in the day there was another occurrence that, at the time, lodged itself in Eddie's mind as curious. In retrospect, the incident would make more sense and assume more sinister overtones. Around 4:00 in the afternoon, Dennis arrived to relieve Eddie so he could get ready for a shift at the firehouse.

Unknown to Dennis, Eddie didn't have to be at the station until 6:00. In the interim, Eddie planned to grab a bite to eat and just hang out at the shop until was time to report for duty.

When Dennis arrived, the two partners exchanged greetings and made some strained small talk. Eddie excused himself without mentioning to Dennis that he will be back.

After walking around the corner to a local Subway fast-food joint, Eddie gathered his food and headed back to the shop. After rounding the corner, he noticed a couple of guys walking into the store so as he approached he took a look through the front window. He saw an animated conversation between Dennis and two young men with faces that Eddie recognized right off the bat. They were volunteer firefighters, younger guys, rookies or close to it. They'd worked together once or twice at some point over the past few weeks. It was not uncommon for volunteers and regulars to work the same fire.

Eddie had never seen the two men in the store before, but that wasn't what initially caught Eddie's notice. Rather, it was the intensity of the unfolding tableau that attracted Eddie's attention. There were always young volunteers hanging around the store when Dennis was working. From time to time, Dennis would use some of these guys to help stock shelves, take inventory and work the register. Eddie had his wife and sons pitch in when the workload got heavy. Dennis never asked his wife to help is because he wanted to keep her in the dark. But to each their own.

Dennis had the floor. His body language was uncharacteristically stiff. Whatever the subject was that they were discussing, it was clearly a stone serious matter. The two men huddled around him were keenly focused, seeming to hang on his every word as they gave him their undivided attention, faces fixed in expressions of acute concentration. As they spoke with one another, Dennis made hand motions that seemed to pantomime the use of a firearm. Eddie observed from outside until he began to feel uneasy, as if he were eavesdropping, despite the fact that he could neither hear the words nor read lips.

As soon as Eddie walked through the front door, he was greeted by an immediate hush. All conversation ceased in the blink of an eye. Eddie felt like he was back in high school and had caught a clique of disloyal friends who were talking behind his back.

Eddie introduced himself to the volunteers, and then directed a simple question at Dennis, which he tried to pose in an offhand manner. Dennis tried to make his answer sound casual. Both tried too hard, and the exchange was painfully predictable. All that was left unspoken spoke volumes. Certain uncertainties and uncertain certainties hung in the air, thick as smoke.

"What are you guys talking about?"

"Nothing much."

It was a personal problem and they asked me not to say anything.

OK

It was right about this time that the arson epidemic began. Area firefighters found themselves struggling to shoulder the extra burdens that were now thrust on them. Eddie, Dennis, and the rest of the firefighters were forced to work longer hours and respond to more calls.

For Eddie, the arson outbreak marked the beginning of a particularly exhausting and frustrating period. Due to his position of leadership within the fire department hierarchy, the draining demands on Eddie's time and energy were particularly acute. It fell on him to coordinate the extra hours, fill scheduling holes on short notice, figure out strategies to stretch taxed resources, maintain morale, and make sure his weary charges were not cutting corners on safety issues and standard procedures. At the same time, the demands of home, family, and business, not to mention Dennis's myriad financial shenanigans (which he was still trying in earnest to get to the bottom of), did not abate in anyway, shape, or form.

The fires began in empty buildings, mainly construction sites, and warehouse dumpsters throughout Piscatstown, Corrunoside, and spread to similar targets throughout Centerville County. It didn't take a top-notch detective to figure out that the fires were being deliberately set and that a serial link existed between most, if not all of them. That is, one person or group was responsible for the entire wave of destruction.

Even before it was officially determined that these were arsons, the more experienced firefighters who responded to these conflagrations had little trouble identifying and pinpointing the source of the crimes and reconstructing the probable sequence of events leading up to and including the blaze from evidence they found left behind (in more or less plain view) at the scene. Because the methods varied very little from site to site, it was also a fairly simple process for even a mildly observant investigator to connect the dots between the targeted structures.

Again the correlations made were not the result of keen investigatory prowess; the arson incidences were linked by a standard set of ingredients and a very obvious signature. Targets were always empty, merchandise was usually damaged, and in cases where merchandise was not damaged, the buildings that were incinerated had all belonged to the same developer, who happened to be a major contributor to the local Democratic Party and to Corrunoside's fire department–friendly mayor.

The arsonist or arsonists demonstrated very little variation in the techniques employed to start the fires. There were always several ziggurats of wadded-up newspaper and kerosene-soaked rags. This kindling, in turn, would be doused in gasoline. The entire pyre could then be ignited with the shot of a well-aimed flare gun. While chewing it over among themselves, the veterans on the force had drawn several conclusions that seemed to have strong circumstantial support.

Clearly, whoever was perpetrating these acts had a good idea of what he or she or they was/were doing. The sites were always vacant, so no one was ever hurt. The gasoline-soaked pyramids were strategically situated to optimize the spread of the blaze. Finally, the point of ignition was always set at the weakest, most flammable point of the structure.

That said, the tell-tale traces they left behind were easy to find: the spent flare, the smell and other traces of gasoline, some burnt paper and the trail of soft, clean ash, leading to some residue of the material utilized to spread the fire from room to room. The arsonist or arsonists knew what they were doing, to be sure, but they weren't so adept at covering their tracks. Eventually the firebug or firebugs would be caught. It was a matter of time.

The following week Dennis asked Eddie if he would run down to the storage center for some price-marking guns and some other merchandise they had left unclaimed when they had initially opened the store. Eddie agreed and, on a rare night off a few days later, took a ride down the storage facility to obtain the needed supplies.

When he arrived, he immediately sensed something was askew. After unlocking the first trailer, his worst fears were confirmed. The trailer's interior, which had been meticulously organized the last time Eddie had seen it, looked as though it had been hit by a tornado.

Labeled boxes had been ripped open, merchandise littered the floor, and packing materials were strewn everywhere.

As his eyes adjusted to the darkness, he followed a musty breeze, searching for its source until he spied the gaping hole that had been carved into the far wall. From the markings on the metal, it was clear that the intruder had used some sort of torch to gain entry. There was a smoothly congealed solder along the lip of the hole in the wall. The culprit had found a thin layer of unreinforced sheeting and then used the tools of his trade to strip off the siding like the side of a soda can.

Eddie exited the storage space in a state of disbelief. The surrounding areas were empty, except for a group of guys standing around a trailerless rig parked in an adjoining parking lot. With no other leads or ideas, he decided to approach the group of guys to find out if they'd seen anyone suspicious lurking around the lot or the surrounding warehouses, if they'd heard anything out of the ordinary, or even seen anything at all.

Crossing the pavement, Eddie hesitated. Some of the guys had come into clearer focus and looked like rough customers. He didn't want to unwittingly start any trouble. He continued haltingly for a moment, and then made up his mind to go over there. He was overreacting, he decided. These were working men just like him; they'd be glad to help him out if they could.

Waving a greeting as he walked toward the driver's side of the cab, however, he was thinking that maybe his initial instinct had been correct. Far from being welcomed into their midst, Eddie felt the unfriendly shiver of a chilly reception. He was met by silence and piercing stares. He felt like an uninvited guest intruding on an intimate ritual. Oh well, there was no turning back now. Clearing his throat, Eddie hailed the man behind the wheel of the rig. "Hey there."

The man behind the wheel nodded his head but gave no response. His face was fixed in a frozen scowl, most likely meant to ward off any further attempts at conversation. Despite his misgivings, Eddie persisted, establishing eye contact and accenting his next question a genial nod:

"Could I have a word?"

"What's the trouble boss?"

That last word spit through cobra lips, pursed and spiteful, dripping with venomous sarcasm. Unsure of his footing, Eddie kept talking, trying to adopt the friendliest tone he could.

"No trouble, just need your help if you can. I don't know if you know old man Thefmor but—"

As if a magic password had been uttered, the entire atmosphere was transformed by the mere mention of Dennis's father's name. The driver's scowl curled into a benign smile as he dropped his guard and began to speak. As he did so, the tense, threatening poses of the six or seven guys around him instantly relaxed. Eddie, who was feeling like a Christian in the Coliseum, was well aware of the radical climate change. A sense of relieved ease spread through his bloodstream, calming the armies of aroused adrenaline that had stood by, armed and on high alert.

"Oh, you should've said. How's that ole Weasel doing these days?"

"Fine, fine."

"That's good to hear. Shit, me and him had ourselves some times back in the day. I bet he hasn't changed much."

"You got that right. He's still the same guy."

"So listen, you said you needed a hand with something."

"Actually I'm looking for some information. We just got broke into."

"No shit."

"Yeah, they hit us pretty hard. So I was wondering if you've seen anything, anything out of the ordinary ... anything at all that might—"

The impact of what Eddie saw effectively reached down his mouth into his voice box and removed the rest of the words he was about to speak. In the course of the conversation, the trucker had been leaning closer and closer in Eddie's direction. He finally decided to hop down from his cab so Eddie wouldn't have to shout up to him.

In the process, in the sliver of an instant before he slammed his door shut, the entire inside of his truck cab was exposed for Eddie to see. Jammed between the driver and passenger seats were a portable pony tank and an acetylene torch—exactly like the one that had been used to rip open the trailer.

"There's always creepy characters lurking around, but I haven't noticed anyone poking around over there by the old man's trailers. Hell, I would've gotten involved myself if I had."

"Uh … yeah … I, uh—"

He stammered and stumbled as the men watched him with a curiosity that, with the slightest touch, with the most subtle push from any direction, could easily be molded into something else. Although what happened here barely lasted long enough to register on any clock, it was a critical juncture.

A brisk gust of air stirred the snack wrappers and industrial debris in the far corner of the lot. Absentmindedly, Eddie noticed that the wind has shifted; so would the mood of the group he had so amiably confronted if he failed to grab hold of himself and raise his voice as if nothing at all had changed.

He knew he must pretend he hadn't caught them red-handed with an acetylene torch. What he said wouldn't matter as much as how he said it. He had to restore his confidence before they realized it had been shaken. He had to set them at ease before they realized they've been given reason to tense up. He had to recover without further hesitation. He groped for words, a word, and any word.

"Damn."

Gaining a bit of traction now, he shook his head and emitted a slow whistle of stunned regret.

"Mr. T. is going to be pissed. This is not going to be a pleasant message to deliver."

"How much do you estimate they got?"

"Couple hundred bucks' worth of stuff. But it's the principle, the utter disrespect that someone would just waltz in, load up, and drive off. You're sure you can't think of anything I can tell him? Point him in the right direction?"

"Man, I wish I had something to give you. None of you guys … I mean, you boys didn't see anything did you? Speak up. This here's a friend."

Assorted choruses of "no man" and a synchronized shaking of heads followed.

"All right, then. Thanks anyway. Listen, I'll catch you all later. I better get a move on and break the news. Geez, he's going to be pissed."

"Not if he's insured."

Eddie was already backpedaling toward the trailer to clean up and straighten out what he could when he heard the driver's curious response to his farewell. At the time it didn't make sense. Now it's all too clear.

By the time Eddie finished securing the trailer as best he could, the parking lot was empty. The men, despite their obvious guilt, made a point of not hightailing it right away. .They did not even look guilty. In fact, they even acted in a manner that could only be described as casual. There was an aspect of their overall attitude, as least it had seemed to Eddie that almost implied everything had been prearranged, so they had nothing to hide. As Eddie's shock faded, he gathered his wits and decided he should report the theft.

Eddie met the police at the scene of the crime. He told them about the torch, gave them the name of the trucking company, and generally walked them through the entire evening, explaining what happened from the time he arrived at the trailer. To say that the officers treat him brusquely and dismissively would be an understatement.

"So let me get this straight. This is not your trailer, and this is not your stuff. You're not sure what has been taken, but you are sure that this mysterious truck driver and his buddies are the culprits." All his buddies I think were Volunteers from Engine # 2's co.

"Look Officer Sharken". "It is Officer Sharken isn't it?"

"Tell you what, if you don't get out of here, I'll arrest you!"

When Eddie got home, he called Dennis. He seemed philosophical about the loss, calm about everything, until Eddie got to the part about the gang of truckers. At that point, his demeanor changed, and he tried to make a big issue about it, not so much about the theft itself, but about Eddie's set of decisions and reactions to the situation.

Dennis became even more agitated when he found out the police had been called. "Listen," he scowled, "this is our business, not police business. You should have at least given us the option of trying to take care of it ourselves before you called it in. That wasn't right. I should've been consulted. I should've been the first call."

The next day Eddie saw Dennis when he arrived to put in his time at the store. To Eddie's surprise, Dennis's father was there. After a short time beating around the bush, the elder Thefmor got to what they both knew was the point of his visit.

"It's a bitch about what the hell happened isn't it?"

Eddie figured the question was a rhetorical one because Mr. T. did not pause for his answer.

"Hell of a thing. You know son, back in my day, back when I owned the store, this sort of thing never would have happened. Where do these guys get the balls?"

When he paused for a breath, Eddie almost had the chance to respond "I don't know." But before he could open his mouth, Mr. T. was off and running again.

"You say you got a look at the guys who did it?"

"Yeah."

"Then why the hell didn't you do something about it?"

"With all due respect Mr. Thefmor—"

The old man thrust his hands in the air in a gesture of resignation and surrender. There was no need for Eddie to finish the statement. He wanted to pursue the matter further, but what good would it do. The guy's son is his partner, like it or not. The subject was dropped.

Hector was a good, honest guy, but a little weak. His father was a Lt. in Corrunoside's Police Dept. He and Eddie had been colleagues for years, and although they rarely socialized or otherwise knew each other outside of work, they both liked and respected each other. Hector had a theory on the fires. He had heard some uncomfortable things. He had seen some fishy, unexplainable phenomena with his own two eyes.

Not sure of his footing or how to proceed, he decided to Eddie, a decision that would loom large in both of their futures. He trusted Eddie, took him at his word. Hector could see his own values in the straight-up way Eddie conducted himself. One morning during a personnel meeting, Eddie invited anyone with any knowledge of the arsons to come forward, promising they would be shielded by anonymity. Hector took his offer to heart and, after a sleepless night or two, decided to confide in him, to unload the increasingly heavy burden of his growing concerns, and ask for advice.

The next time they were both on duty, Hector found Eddie in the break room. Eddie was relaxing over an early evening meal of lasagna that his wife has fixed when Hector approached his table. Eddie greeted him with a friendly, warm smile that gave Hector the courage he needed to not change his mind.

"Hey Lieutenant, this seat taken?"

"Of course not."

"Can I sit here?"

"Absolutely."

"I wanted to—"

"What's up?"

"Got a minute?"

"Sure, what's on your mind?"

"Can we … uh … speak in private? It's a personal matter. It's somewhat serious."

The pair adjourned to Eddie's office. Hectors words have the strength and impact of sledgehammers. They have the power to shatter illusions and crack the foundations of long-held ideals. Eddie at first couldn't believe his ears. Eddie didn't even want to consider the possibility.

His first reaction was to lash out at the messenger sitting in his office daring to bear what he knows will be extremely objectionable news. Eddie wanted to respond rashly, to rise and defend, to challenge, to admonish, to berate, to threaten, to dismiss, but didn't want to upset him. Wisely, however, he held his tongue and reserves judgment until the full story was on the table. This gave him time to collect and calm his thoughts. By the time Hector reached the gist of his conversation, Eddie's mind had been blown like demolished drywall.

"I believe I know who's setting these fires."

"What fires?"

"The arsons."

"Really?"

"Really."

"Well speak up."

"You're not going to like it."

"Why not?"

"I, um, think it's some of our guys. Well, not *our* guys …, you know, some of the volunteers."

"That's a pretty serious accusation Hector."

"I know. But I can back it up. I wouldn't be in here if I couldn't."

"You've got proof?"

"Not quite. Not yet. But I have managed to gather some evidence that I believe you might find compelling. Just bear with me for a few minutes. Hear me out, ok?"

Eddie heard him out. What he heard was plausible and persuasive. He had no reason to doubt the man across the desk, a levelheaded man with impeccable integrity who had nothing to gain and everything to lose from the disclosures he made. The disclosures had a troubling consistency and sang out with a ring of truth. Although much of the evidence he presented tended toward the circumstantial (overheard snippets of conversation, secondhand allegations, etc.), when taken in its entirety, it all added up to a fairly convincing case.

Accusations rooted in hearsay might not convict a criminal in a court of law. However, in the privacy of Eddie's office, when shared between two like-minded colleagues with no impure, ulterior motivations or particular axes to grind (except for their desire to safeguard the honor and dignity of their profession), Hectors words were as profound and damning as a pistol shot in a parlor of pretension packed with pretenders telling nothing but lies.

His bombshells now dropped and exploded, Hector had no more to say. Eddie was speechless. They sat across from one another. A lone finch streaked past the window. The room had become a stifling nest of dust and air. Eddie felt claustrophobic, as though a great weight was pressing down on him. Sounds of clinking silverware and other break-time activity penetrated the walls from outside. In his gut, Eddie was already convinced. But his heart, his stubbornly faithful heart, did not want to believe his ears.

Even so, the more he thought about it, the more it made some sort of twisted sense. There was motive. There was opportunity. Other puzzle pieces began to fall into place. Volunteers are paid a prorated stipend based upon the number of fires they fight. The arsons, therefore, would net a direct and significant financial benefit to the volunteers who may be setting them. Many of the fires targeted the buildings of a single developer. Again, this developer happened to be a major contributor to the current Democratic regime.

For many years, the local government had been in the hands of a mayor who was good to Eddie and good to the department. He was an old-school traditionalist who tended to "dance with the folks that brought him" into political office, meaning that, as a loyal personal friend of Eddie's, he never forgot the up-and-coming firefighter's tireless volunteer work and campaign-organizing activities.

Over the years, he'd done his best to demonstrate his gratitude, serving as a sounding board, a resource, and an advocate who subtly attempted—completely within the bounds of propriety—to lend a hand when he could to help boost Eddie's prospects for promotions. He also never forgot that the fire department had always endorsed him and had voted as a sizable and influential block for his successive candidacies. Thus, he'd always been extremely responsive to any fire department–related issues or problems. The department had always been properly funded, even during the years when massive Reagan/ Bush budget cuts left other departments with old trucks and fraying hoses.

With the rise of a new younger Democratic Party on the local and state political landscape, however, the mayor and his allies knew they were facing unprecedented reelection challenges. One could speculate that the firebombing of the mayor's primary funding source was designed to be an act of political intimidation. The fire department, especially the new generation of volunteers, was no longer monolithically loyal to the old Democratic Party. The mayor and his allies were accumulating increasingly stiff opposition, both within and outside of the department. A new political faction had formed and wanted a turn at the helm. Both common sense and human nature suggested that if they felt locked out of the action, they were likely to attempt to break through the lock by any means necessary.

There were other reasons that might motivate volunteers to risk such a criminal misadventure: insurance fraud, resale of merchandise missing from many of the torched warehouses, But it was only additional speculation. To pull off such an intricate operation they'd need to find a fence. All of a sudden, the far horizon of Eddie's mind was seared by the recent flashback of Dennis and his closely guarded interchange with the two young volunteers.

No. Eddie was probably letting his anxieties run wild. He assured himself he was jumping to conclusions. Dennis might be shady, Eddie figured, but evil? It was too much to process all at once. Still, during unsuppressed moments, Eddie's worries bubbled to the surface of his consciousness, and he began to ask himself ever more prickly questions. If there was corruption, it wasn't likely to have been dreamed up by a few knucklehead twenty-year-olds. He had to wonder how deep did this thing go? Where did the rabbit hole end?

The sad reality, however, was that Hector and Eddie needed more, much more, before they could even begin to move forward in any way, shape or form, never mind the kind of ironclad proof they'd eventually need before they could act to put a stop to the destruction. There was, as of yet, no smoking gun. Eddie rubbed his eyes wearily, realizing that he and Hector had sat in silence for an unnaturally long period of time.

"Geez, Hector. Do you realize what you're saying?"

"I do."

"Look, first of all, I'm with you on this. I'll back you up all the way. But without hard-and-fast proof, there's not a whole hell of a lot we can do."

"I understand."

"You may want to keep this under your hat for now. I hope you understand I'm not trying to get you to hush up. I'm talking about for your own protection. I'm talking about your career."

"Too late."

"Who knows?"

"I went to Chief Rumpkey yesterday."

"Who else knows?"

"Just you." So if it goes any further other than the Detectives it's the Chief not me.

"I'd strongly advise you to keep it that way. The truth is always an endangered species, but this is a whole new ball game, uncharted territory. This is explosive stuff. This is going to be a scandal of major proportions when it finally hits the fan."

"I'm aware of that. That's why I felt it was so urgent that I come to talk to you. You're the only one I can think of that I can trust a hundred percent."

"I appreciate that. You did the right thing."

"Yeah? Squealing on the brotherhood? Then how come I feel like a rat?"

"Ask yourself how you'd feel if you'd stood by your code of silence and someone got burned alive. No, I'm with you. This has to end, and it will end here. We just have to be careful about how we go about ending it. Listen, the so-called 'brotherhood,' we don't start fires; we put them out. Those guys ... I don't know, Hector, I just don't know.

I do know that you're not alone. We need to start poking around and documenting what we find. Keep your eyes and ears open, and I'll do the same."

Just a few days later, Hector disappeared from work. Eddie went to see the chief and ask him what happened.

"Where's Hector?"

"Transferred. Up to the north end."

(The "north end" station referred to was a tiny outpost in a dull suburban pocket in the extreme north corner of the town, far away from any potential action, or even activity. It was where the chief traditionally sent the inept, the out-of-shape and the ready-to-retire.)

"Wow. All the way out in the boonies. He must've done something really bad to get himself shipped off to Siberia. What happened?"

"Nothing happened."

"He's a decent firefighter. Why'd you … what got him sent him up there?"

"His big mouth."

This was the point at which Eddie realized the seriousness of the situation and has his first inklings of the depths of the possible cover-up. He was forced to wrestle with the distinct possibility of widespread corruption within the department. If anything was going to get done about the arson crimes, if anyone was going to be able to get to the bottom of them, it was going to have to be him.

Protected by the clout of his tenure and his influential friends in the upper levels of the political hierarchy, Eddie felt as though he was the only person who could safely speak out without fear of reprisal or retribution. At least, this was what he believed at the time. The ensuing years would teach him a bitter lesson. He will learn the lesson well. Now he knows. No matter what. No one is untouchable.

Chapter 8

The sizzling gust of a flare gun split the night air. Impact, a cascade of sparks and smoldering. An entire complex of uniform warehouses lit up eerily against the growing back light of a maturing fire. The cavernous structures squat side by side like airplane hangers, row upon row steadily became more illuminated as the blaze gained light and strength. Tendrils of flame felt their way out of a ravenous, insatiable center that crackled like boots on twigs as it fed on fuel provided by its original source.

The exact source point, where ignition initially occurred, will later be identified by investigators as a solitary, single-roomed wood-framed office building neatly tucked between two identical steel storage facilities. The sheer massiveness of its surroundings had shielded and concealed it, dwarfing its potential vulnerabilities and its visibility in an industrial forest of towering metal. Until now. Its frame, its roof, its walls, and all its contents going up in flames like a box of tinder.

A light-colored van and a four-door sedan fled the scene in a hail of gravel. At the entrance gate, they peeled off in separate directions. The van headed left, out of town; the car turned right, in the direction of downtown Corrunoside. After several screeching corners and hairpin turns, the car sped down Plaintown Avenue... Seemingly out of nowhere, the flashing lights of a police cruiser appeared as the Crown Victoria fish tailed into a haze of exhaust to give chase.

The driver of the pursued vehicle gunned the accelerator, as if contemplating a run for it. Thinking better of it, he slowed down, and switched lanes, decelerating toward the curb, working his signal blinker to acknowledge the flashing lights in his rearview.

The cars pulled to a stop as if connected. An eternity of waiting ensued. The officer observed the jittery movements of those in the car. Finally, the officer got out of his car, turned down the squawk of his walkie talkie, and approached. The driver's side window was down, and the man behind the wheel was already offering up his papers. The officer took wordlessly as he shined a light on the interior. Inside sat four young men, all taut as the string on a bow. His instincts told the officer that there was more to see than met the eye. *No reason to overreact*, he told himself. It may indeed just turn out to be a simple traffic stop.

However, he'd heard about the arson on the police radio, and this car fits the description of the one that was seen speeding away from the scene. The atmosphere is rife with tension. A pervasive silence exacerbates this tension. Not a single word was exchanged until the officer cleared his throat to speak:

"You know why I stopped you guys?"

"Yes sir. I suppose I was well over the speed limit."

"Could you do me a favor sir, and step out of the car?"

"Is that necessary? My father's a captain in the fire department." What's your father's name Swetpee...? Still.

"I'm afraid I'm going to have to ask you to go ahead and comply anyway."

In a flash, as speech is processed and becomes recognition, the surprise in the eyes of the driver turned to fear. Gingerly, he stepped out of the car. His three passengers are directed to follow suit. Any thought of verbal protest, physical resistance, or even the notion of stalling for a while is nixed by the timely arrival of two more police cruisers.

The passengers exited, exchanging frightened, furtive glances at one another as they do so. The cars of the backup officers both pull to a halt at the same time, as if synchronized, in a clean crunching of hard tires on loose asphalt.

Two of the arriving officers introduced themselves to the arresting officer and offer to pat down the four detainees. They are then ordered out of the vehicle. This enabled the arresting offer to return to his car and run the driver's licenses he collected. As he strolled back to his car, nothing in the officer's demeanor portrays anything out of the ordinary. Concealed behind his badge and his blues, however, his heart beats one million miles an hour as he opened his front door and reached for his radio to call the license in to dispatch.

There's a strange response from the dispatcher when he spells the letters of the man's last name into his handset. He can't be sure because of the distortion and noise on the line, but the dispatcher seems to emit a faint but audible gasp of recognition. "Are you sure?" asks the dispatcher. The officer reads it again, carefully enunciating the consonants and vowels of the long Italian surname.

As dispatch checks the document for validity and/or attached warrants, the enormity of the moment sunk in. What a monster collar it would be if his hunch checked out. He'd be in the papers. He'd be a local hero. His family would be proud. To bag this kind of collar, being a rookie and all, being fresh out of the police academy, it was unheard of. Speaking of "unheard of," Officer Mulberry had been working solo when he'd managed to pull off the I.D., the chase, and the initial stop. The puck had hit the back-net mesh unassisted.

He had to keep his emotions bottled up, at least for now, he reminded himself. The guys may have solid alibis, perfect explanations for their whereabouts. If it was a case of mistaken identity, and it still very well could be, the entire exercise would be meaningless. Until a thorough search had been executed, there was no use in speculating; it was impossible to know for certain.

Meanwhile, a thorough search of the vehicle was performed by the fourth and fifth officers to arrive. The second and third were still patting down the driver and his passengers. What the stop revealed was a flare gun under the passenger seat, accelerant in the back, kerosene-soaked rags, and other various implements of arson. Caught red handed with the damning evidence, one of the detainees blurts out:

"Listen, I can explain everything. This is nothing more than a big misunderstanding. See, we're volunteer firefighters. This is stuff we just now recovered from the site of a fire. We're investigating to see … we think it might have been set deliberately. We're volunteer firefighters, all of us. We're currently transporting–"

"Shut up!" snapped one of his partners, his voiced pitched in a loud hiss, "Say nothing until we get downtown and the attorney arrives. Say nothing at all. Understand?"

Back Officer Mulberry's car, the dispatcher finally came back onto the radio band, heralded by a crackle of static. The license was clean, and the identity of the driver was confirmed. The officer thanked the dispatcher and hooked his mouthpiece back onto the radio set. He scooted out of his seat, slammed his door, and went to confer with his colleagues.

Two of the four guys who'd responded when he'd called for backup had already gathered to confer. . One of the officers moved to make room for Officer Mulberry. Mulberry nods in greeting, and the other officers acknowledge his nod with nods of their own.

At this point, the officers who searched the car shared their findings. Mulberry's original suspicions that his late evening speeder is no ordinary traffic stop are resoundingly confirmed. They lined up what they had, mixing hard case facts with experienced conjecture to form an overall picture of events. They re-created the sequence of the crime with what will later be confirmed to be amazingly uncanny accuracy. They compared notes on the exact proximity of the crime and possible escape routes utilized by the other vehicle, still at large.

They also decided, without much deliberation, to haul all four suspects downtown. It's a no-brainer. They are practically around the corner from the arson site. The suspects fit the description. The evidence is there and then some. "It simply doesn't get much more open and shut," observed one of the cops. Mulberry turned on his heel to give the arrest go-ahead to the officers who had patted down the suspects. They were one step ahead of him, however, and were already busy reciting Miranda monologues to their captive audience.

Although it wasn't necessary procedure, Mulberry returned to his radio to call the dispatcher to tell her what he and the men discovered. He told her of their plans to bring the entire carload of suspects in for questioning and put them behind bars, at least until bail could be set at some point over the course of the following day. His thinking in doing so was that since four suspects would tax the holding-cell facilities, they would appreciate the courtesy of the heads-up.

He also wanted a paddy wagon sent out. With three cars on the scene, they could actually handle it without one, but this was a big moment in his career and therefore no time to be doing things half-assed. Might as well take the extra time to do things right and take all necessary precautions.

It would take a little longer to get the whole thing wrapped up, but Officer Mulberry didn't care. The longer this lasted, the better. This was his moment, and he basked in it. Indeed, he was so distracted by the siren songs of impending glory that it took him a while to realize when, in the middle of his transmission to dispatch, he suddenly found himself speaking to dead air.

Haltingly, he asks, "Is anyone there?" There was no answer on the line. Just a long low wolf whistle of distortion. He was about to switch channels when the dispatcher came back on the line.

"Officer Mulberry, please stand by."

This was a bit odd, but Mulberry let it go because he was making sure that proper protocol was being followed. He could say it now. Its official: This was his first major collar. With any luck it will beget many more. After all, from the way some of the guys had been talking about this case, these arrests could represent the mere the tip of the iceberg of a scandal. Mulberry smiled to himself in a self-satisfied way. He thought of newspaper clippings yellowing in an old scrapbook.

"Dispatch, I've got four suspects on that arson. Requesting a wagon. I'm bringing them all into Headquarters."

"Copy that. Please stand by." Are Volunteer Tippler's and Biscoe's sons with that crew?

Affirmative.

Another eternity of waiting, not just for the prey now but for the predator as well. What was the snag? Why the hold up on a routine call to dispatch? Finally the line crackled into action again.

"Officer?"

"Reading you loud and clear. Over."

"Let them go."

"Excuse me?"

"Let them go."

Fuck. This can't be happening. Not a chance. No way.

"Negative."

"It's not a suggestion. It's an order."

"An order? On whose authority? Who the hell do you think you are to give me orders? I want to speak your supervisor right away please."

"I'd be glad to, officer. Sergeant Tippler, she's the one who issued the order anyway, not me."   I'll bet she's screwing the chief again. Dammit.

The supervisor got on the horn and confirms the order. She patiently but firmly explains that she absolutely and without question does have more than enough authority to do what she's doing. "Officer, your job will be on the line should you refuse to comply. Understand?"

And then he understands. The apparent recognition of the name when he originally called it in. The mysterious phantom pauses and dead air on his end while frantic discussions and calls up the line were likely going on the other end. The fact that these guys are volunteer firefighters and you have to have a hook to get on the job there in the first place. The informal network that fed recruits to the fire department included many of the same people who had pull with police department bigwigs. There was more cross-pollination going on between the two departments than there was going on in a greenhouse.

Officer Mulberry wrapped things up with the supervisor, assuring her the suspects would indeed be freed. He is not inclined to ask (being far too disgusted, sick to his stomach, and bone weary with disillusionment to boot), but he's sure that if he had bothered to inquire, odds were he would find that the surname of his primary suspect was identical to the surname of the shifty but haughty woman who had just pulled rank on him from the safety and shelter of the opposite end of the line, where no one has to look you in the eyes.

Bottom line: He had no choice. There is nothing he could do about this. At least right this instant. Oh later, sure, he could lodge and file a complaint, air his grievance and allow it a full hearing, whereupon its merits would be judged by the very people he's accused. Of course he could go over their heads or outside the department, to internal affairs, or even the press ... if, that is, he wants to be ostracized by peers who will despise him with the passionate intensity of young lovers and earn a career-long reputation as a snitch and troublemaker that will hang around his neck like an albatross for the next forty or fifty years. And who knows—possible indictment if it reached too far, to someone powerful.

The arsonists, caught dead to right, were going to walk. Lucky for them, they had powerful friends. The officer is beyond disappointed; it goes way deeper than that ... his faith has been shaken. He'd heard that this was the way things sometimes worked, but he hadn't wanted to believe it. Now he had to.

Officer Mulberry walked up to the road shoulder where the four cuffed suspects sat in a neat semi-circle. Mulberry called the other officers out of earshot and shared the foul news. The two newer guys let loose with torrents of cursing and righteous indignation.

The older two members of the blue quartet reacted less dramatically, tending to exhibit a more resigned, knowing air, at least when compared to the histrionic tantrums of their inexperienced counterparts. The older hands acted as if this had happened to them before. Most likely, it had. One just shrugged and grits his teeth while the other scowled as he shook his head slowly and ruefully.

The suspects were all trembling fiercely, all pale as zombies and, while not exactly sweating bullets, are sweating bullet-shaped beads, the size of swollen jungle raindrops in thick and substantial increments across their furrowed, troubled brows. , The entire crew had managed to drench themselves in a deluge of their own perspiration. They couldn't have looked any more guilty had the word itself had been tattooed in neon ink upon their foreheads.

All four men braced themselves, fearing the worst, as they heard the resoundingly sullen footsteps of the gruff, irritated cops approaching them from behind. They all heard the jingling of keys behind their backs as, one after another; they were unceremoniously uncuffed and released, let off with nothing stronger than a stern warning.

The pardoned men milled about for a moment, lingering around the curb, rubbing their wrists, looks of confused disbelief on their faces. Two or three mouths gaped open in jaw-dropping shock at their stunning good fortune. No one, the cops included, could quite believe the sudden turn of events.

"Go on, get out of here … before we change our minds," Mulberry growled, hardly able to hide the desperate frustration he was trying to keep from boiling over.

The officer's words provided the necessary stimulus to jolt the men from their trance and sent them scuttling toward their car.

"They … they're really letting us go," one said to another.

"Shut up!" was the savagely whispered reply.

The driver had recovered his bearings, however. It was he who had the presence of mind to request that the confiscated pieces of evidence is returned, thereby eliminating the possibility of investigators picking up their trail again at some point down the road, if and when the political winds changed direction.

Since time was of the essence because the driver and his men were actively investigating a recent fire and undoubtedly hot on the heels of the "real" arsonists, and since technically, the objects were not part of any existing criminal investigation (as the driver so helpfully pointed out), the cops had no legal grounds to maintain possession of the seized items.

In an absurd scene that flirted shamelessly with a brazen surrealism, two of the cops helped load what amounted to a fire-starting first aid kit back into the trunk of the probable perpetrators. The driver, taken aback—not just by the sudden turn of the tables but also by the unexpected level of cooperation he is receiving from his local police—arched an incredulous eyebrow at Mulberry, as if to ask the obvious question that hangs in the air.

"Somebody upstairs likes you … and it ain't God," is how Mulberry answered the silent query, dismissing them with a curt wave, staring off bitterly into the distance and darkness as he sent them on their way.

🔥 🔥 🔥

Eddie attained the rank of full captain in the spring of 1990. After all the struggling, all the favors and volunteer work, all the effort he had expended above and beyond the call of duty, all the treacherous rescues carried out with little regard for his own life and limb, he had finally made it. Although the promotion represented the attainment of an ambition he'd held close to his heart, sacrificed for, and worked extremely hard while chasing after it over the course of multiple decades, the achievement, due to the configuration of current circumstances, was somewhat bittersweet.

The day of the promotion and the attendant ceremony might have indeed been a crazy, blinding, splash of sunshine, scattered like buckshot, dappling Eddie's life in a bright sizzling glow, but, alas, this illumination could easily prove only temporary, and Eddie knew it. There were dark clouds looming on the horizon. Foremost among them, the closest, most fearsome thunderhead, and the one that was so engorged with rain that it threatened to burst over his parade the soonest, was shaped like the store.

According to several relatively reliable sources that Eddie had been able to jigsaw into a coherent picture, the rumor around the firehouse and in related circles was that the store was being watched, that it was under investigation by a special interagency task force put together by the newly elected mayor.

The stated job of the task force was to root out old Democratic Party patronage and graft and other general forms of corruption (so that it could be replaced by new younger Democratic Party patronage and graft and other general forms of corruption). The actual role of the task force was to target the real and imagined enemies of Mayor Yulency and his friends. .

The narrow election of the new mayor posing as a reformer and cost-cutter (the sleeves up and broom out pose, of course, was pure hypocrisy. All the questionable practices of the previous administration had been retained. In addition, many more had been added.) Would prove to be another serious thorn in Eddie's side. It occurred shortly after he had been installed as captain and immediately made Eddie's day-to-day life more of a hassle. He had to claw to get funding and assistance from city hall for core fire department needs. Under the previous administration, anything the department required was there for the asking.

To make matters worse, the new administration made no secret of the fact that they viewed Eddie with mistrust and hostility, due to the fact that he had been a close friend of and an influential, effective, high-profile campaigner for the previous mayor. At that time in Corrunoside, the Young Democrats and local Democratic Party machines were nothing more than two competing factions of business interests and loosely allied coalitions of powerful men. Since Eddie was widely associated with the old Democratic faction, it had been made known to him, in no uncertain terms, that his career would be stuck in neutral for as long as this mayor reigned.

The thing was that Eddie knew this, and he was fine with it. He'd made it to captain in record time anyway; Deputy Chief could wait. There was enough on his head. What Eddie didn't know, and what he wouldn't have been fine with, was that the new administration was not content to let Eddie languish in benign neglect upon some dusty fire department side shelf. They had made the decision to destroy him and had set a concerted plan in motion to do so.

There was plenty of timely prodding from old man Thefmor—through intermediaries naturally, never directly—and other well-connected enemies from various sources, including, as the latter part of this chapter will chronicle, influential decision-makers from within the upper echelons of his own department. They included folks Eddie considered to be as close to him as family, or, if not literally as intimate as his biological family, he believed so deeply that he took it for granted, that they shared membership in the type of family structure that is forged of comrades-in-arms who risk their lives together as a matter of course.

Little did Eddie know, and this is part of the tragedy, that by the plans he was making and the plans he had laid, he was playing right into the hands of those who wished him all sorts of ill and had banded together to make every one of their nefarious wishes come true.

Down at the store, relations between Eddie and Dennis had reached such toxic levels that the situation between them could no longer be characterized as a cold war. The frozen expanse of cold war never thawed, erupting into open and intense, impassioned hostilities. They now despised each other.

Dennis hated Eddie for being such an unforeseen and intractable problem. He was too much of a square to be cut in on the action but not enough of one to continue to dupe for much longer. Eddie hated Dennis because he was imperiling his life and dreams with his sleazy dishonesty. The friends turned foes were diametrically opposed. They would, at steadily decreasing intervals, explode into draining arguments that imperiled merchandise and came dangerously close to fisticuffs. These outpourings of animosity were punctuated by extended periods of hostile silence.

It was no way to live; a solution had to be found. One night, up late, half watching a television screen he was not paying attention to, he'd found himself brainstorming about the problem. In a flash, Eddie figured he'd figured it out: they would dissolve the partnership. Either he would buy Dennis out or Dennis could buy him out. It was elegantly simple. It was basic common sense. Why hadn't he thought of it sooner? One or the other that's it.

The answer, he realized sadly, was that he'd first wanted to give Dennis the benefit of the doubt. And when that was no longer possible, he wanted to have faith that Dennis would come around and do the right thing before too long. By now, however, it had been too long. It was no longer possible to maintain faith in Dennis's eventual goodness. Right then and there, Eddie decided to throw in the towel on the partnership he'd grown so many gray hairs and worked so hard to salvage.

He broached the subject with Dennis the very next day when they were changing over shifts at the store. Eddie had decided that he'd flat out ask Dennis to sell his share of the store. If that didn't work, he had plan B, which was to offer to sell out to Dennis. Eddie cleared his throat and began his rehearsed pitch. Dennis was on his way out the door when Eddie hailed him and asked for a minute of his time. Dennis rolled his eyes but he paused in his tracks, waiting to hear what Eddie had to say.

The ensuing conversation went smoothly, far more smoothly than Eddie had expected. Of course he hadn't expected to get set up like a bowling pin either, but that was precisely what was happening. Behind all the smooth talk and niceties , Eddie was not only being fleeced, he was being set up to be left holding the bag of several bad and criminal business decisions made by Dennis and his dad.

Dennis made it sound like the decision to sell was the hardest, most torturous decision he'd ever been faced with in his life. He brought up his father, the generations of Thefmor's who had toiled under the shop's rafters, the hope that his future son, currently nonexistent (a status that was highly unlikely to change), would get a piece of the thing. He pulled out all the stops. It was a real tear-jerker of a performance.

Finally, after much huffing and puffing and miscellaneous fanfare, he said he'd think about it. "Let me sleep over it tonight," he'd asked, and Eddie had, of course, readily agreed, relieved that it was at least officially on the table as a viable option that would go a long way toward helping him navigate his way clear of the mess he found himself mired in.

In reality, both Dennis and his father had been wishing desperately for the exact scenario that Eddie was now proposing. They were salivating over the prospect of getting out from under the potential criminal liabilities connected to the store now that they'd exploited every angle to bleed the place dry. They had spent years using it as a front and a base to pull off a stunning range and variety of ethically challenged misdeeds.

It was more than they could have hoped for actually, because they'd expected to have to bring up the proposition themselves. Had that been the case, they would have had to offer to sell at a bargain price to sweeten the deal and ensure Eddie's buy-in. Now the need for all that had been eliminated. As soon as he left the store, Dennis found a payphone and rang up his dad with the fortuitous news. Together they schemed out all the ways to get the most exorbitant price possible for the place out of Eddie.

The next conversation took place a few days later. After some cursory hemming and hawing that even Eddie realized was more for form than for substance, Dennis consented to do Eddie "the favor" of letting him buy out the balance of the business. He would do this, he said (really hamming it up) for the sake of future peace between them, even though it would cost him dearly to walk away from a shop he helped make a success, as well as break his heart to walk away from what had been a multigenerational family business.

With this foundation for negotiations set, Eddie and Dennis began hammering out a price. Eddie got conned into paying about 20 percent above and beyond the fair market value of the place, but not because he'd allowed Dennis to pull the wool over his eyes. He knew he was getting ripped off a bit, but Dennis's asking price with within the bounds of reason, albeit on its outer edges. At any rate, Eddie was willing to pay the extra money to obtain a degree of piece of mind and avoid the melodrama, histrionics, and hassles that would accompany a drawn-out period of haggling with Dennis and his dad.

Sure they got a little extra out of him. In return for the premium he paid, however, he'd gotten rid of them. With one fell stroke of the pen, the ordeal was over, cleanly and completely. He had extricated himself from a dangerous downward spiral of a situation. There was no more quicksand to pull himself out of. No more feeling like he was in over his head, drowning in a blinding morass, danger lurking in lagoon shadow perimeters as he flailed about helplessly. It was over. He was free and clear. Or so he thought at the time.

Meanwhile, the arsons continued in earnest. The fires were starting to make headlines, bold banners of cold, hard newspaper ink that began to weigh on Eddie's conscience like fetters. Hadn't he done all he could? Even though he thought his younger friend was acting overeager and moving too fast, Eddie though it went against his better judgment and instincts to lodge such a serious accusation against his brothers without the smoking gun of iron proof.

Despite all that and several other gnawing uncertainties, he had supported Hectors whistle-blowing attempts and clean-up efforts 100 percent. He'd served as a loyal ally, an unofficial investigator, a sounding board and a leaning post, sturdy, sure, sincere. Any way you sliced it, he'd gone to the mat for him, and there was no denying that.

He had even, a few days after he'd inquired and found out about Hectors disappearance from the schedule, changed his mind and called an immediate meeting with the chief to talk about the allegations he'd heard from Hector (and, subsequently, from many other sources). All this activity, whether undertaken alone or in coordination with Hector, had yielded nothing productive. Nothing happened at all, except Hector had been transferred and Eddie had been ignored.

After weeks of deliberations (during which time three more arson strikes helped ratchet up urgency), Eddie decided on a second appointment with the chief. This time he would not be ignored, shooed away, and sent packing so easily.

This time, armed with a sheaf of new evidence he'd compiled in his off time, he was prepared to take this thing as far as it needed to go. He was ready for a confrontation, prepared to take things as high upstairs as was necessary. Indeed, he planned to keep ascending the fire-department hierarchy until he'd achieved some measure of satisfaction. If that didn't work, he had his aces in the hole to resort to: he could always go to the police or the papers, or both, with everything that he'd heard and compiled, or at least threaten to do so.

Even he wasn't sure that he would ever be able to come close to being prepared to take that step, but the brass at the department didn't have to know about his misgivings and the illogically lingering endurance of his misplaced, tarnished loyalty. Maybe the simple suggestion, this time with some real teeth behind it, would be enough to force their hands into doing the right thing.

So Eddie made an appointment with the chief and voiced his objections in sterner terms. Whereas before he merely stated concerns, this time his tone was bold and declaratory. He spoke of the arsons and the rumors surrounding them, if they were true, as blight and a shame upon the fire department.

He presented the evidence he had (much of it new), communicated both the devastatingly damning direct quotations and incriminating innuendoes he'd heard, and pressed upon the need for a full and proper investigation. He made it clear that he would not rest until he'd been satisfied.

The chief listened intently, then apologized to Eddie, frankly admitting that he hadn't followed up on his first inquiry, but only because he "just hated the think that any one connected with the fire-fighting profession could possibly be tangled up in this awfulness." The chief continued, "I just wanted to give those boys the benefit of the doubt. But," he added, "these papers here, they raise questions that demand answers. So all right," he concluded, "you have my word. I'll personally check into it."

The chief, however, wasn't content to stop there. He proceeded to continue glad-handing Eddie, making vague half commitments and stalling for time with such a polished, practiced political smoothness that Eddie left the meeting believing he'd really accomplished something and made an impact that would result in decisive action. In reality he'd just hammered the final nail into his own coffin. Forces were aligning against him.

Roughly five minutes after Eddie left, the chief pressed a button on his intercom and summoned his longest-serving and most-trusted assistant Captain Biscoe. The chief asked him to close the door behind him and indicated the empty chair situated directly opposite the business end of the desk. Dispensing with further preliminaries, the two men got right down to business. .

"I just had an appointment with Eddie, the captain over in precinct #1."

Indicating, as he speaks these words, the now-occupied visitor's chair, with the same gesture he'd just used when it had been empty.

"Yeah? What about it? Why you telling' me this? Trouble?"

"You could say. He's squawking like he knows something about who's been setting the fires. Has some crazy idea that there's volunteers mixed up in it."

"That's nuts. That would implicate our own kids. We can't have that."

"Even if it's true. Hey, I'm joking!"

"What? Oh, yeah, yeah."

"Listen, you know and I know that this guy's allegations are baseless. He obviously has some ax to grind with the new power structure and has decided to buck the current rather than adapt."

"So what's the problem?"

"Well the thing is, I know this guy, have known him for a long time. People like him, trust him, believe him … he gets rolling on this story, it might stick, and regardless of what the facts are … lot of people we know could stand to get hurt by a scandal like this."

"So what now?"

"I don't know. That's what called you in here to kick around. Any ideas?"

"Eddie huh?"

"Yeah."

"Isn't he in business with Thefmor's kid?"

"Right."

"Thefmor Senior used to run the place."

"Right again."

"And wasn't Thefmor's old man pretty underhanded and rotten, I mean, business wise?"

"To the core. He was a real son of a bitch."

"Isn't the handed-down business currently under investigation?"

"Yeah, but it's more of a formality, kind of on the back burner. The department checks out all the guys who are serious moonlighters at one point in time or another."

"Well maybe it's time we found out the exact status of the investigation and put some resources and manpower into it. Put it on the front burner and turn up the heat. See what boils over."

"I like the way you think. Get on it. I will too. In fact, if you'll excuse me, I've got a couple of calls to make right away."

"I'll let you get to it."

"One more thing."

"Ok."

"And listen careful."

"I'm all ears."

"Be careful. Just between you and me, the old man is pretty well hooked up."

"Well so are we."

"Very funny."

"Who's kidding'?"

The chief emitted an annoyed exhalation before plowing ahead. When, he asked himself, did the simple, boldface truth start pissing him off so much?

"No, I mean, he's connected to some pretty shady puppet masters. Real heavies. And ruthless. I'm talking about guys who have too much pull to get dragged into this. Hell for all I know, I might even be talking about the guys that sign our paychecks."

"So how do you want this thing handled?"

"Tread lightly and accurately. Or else you're liable to step on the toes of some powerful friends and some powerful enemies. Remember, these are guys who could flush our careers down the toilet with one phone call. If they feel any heat, fall under even a hint of suspicion, if they are made to feel threatened in any way, shape, or form, they'll crush us. Simple as that. End of story. Unless we find an effective way, right off the bat, to let the big shots know that this is a pinpoint investigation. We're out to solve a very specific problem."

"I'll convey the message."

"Very good."

"When do I move on this?"

"Yesterday. If you only take one thing away from this meeting, let it be an understanding of the urgency of our situation. This guy … the position of leadership and respect he holds on the force and in the community, who he knows, who he is, what he knows, the things he's bound to find out if he continues poking around, the way he's slowly but surely putting things together … he's a ticking time bomb. He's got to be diffused, one way or another, ' cause if he goes off, the explosion will rock the foundations of this entire town—fire department, police department, city hall, chamber of commerce. Put it this way: he's liable to blow all of our asses to kingdom come!"

"Don't worry Chief; the bomb squad is on its way."

Chapter 9

Eddie received a couple of company merit awards in the summer of 1990. After all the struggling, all the favors and volunteer work, all the effort he had expended above and beyond the call of duty, all the treacherous rescues carried out with little regard for his own life and limb, he had finally made it.

Although the his promotion and awards represented the attainment of an ambition he'd held close to his heart, sacrificed for, and worked extremely hard while chasing after it over the course of multiple decades, the achievement, due to the configuration of current circumstances, was somewhat bittersweet.

The illumination could easily prove only temporary, and Eddie knew it. There were dark clouds looming on the horizon. Foremost among them, the closest, most fearsome thunderhead, and the one that was so engorged with rain that it threatened to burst over his parade.

According to several relatively reliable sources that Eddie had been able to jigsaw into a coherent picture, the rumor around the firehouse and in related circles elsewhere was that the store was being watched, and that it was under investigation and under continuous surveillance by a special interagency task force put together by the newly elected mayor and his right hand hatchet man, an ex-FBI agent by the name of Paul Munsterhed, who held the title of Director of Public Safety. Eddie felt pretty good that an ex-agent was holding the position of director because he believed that at least Munsterhed would be a man of integrity. He couldn't have been more wrong. More politicians had their hands in his pockets then carter has liver pills.

The stated task of the Munsterhed-led task force was to root out the patronage, graft, and other general forms of corruption associated with the old regime (so that it could be replaced by the patronage, graft, and corruption of their new regime). The actual job of the task force was to target the real and imagined enemies of Mayor Disbarr and his friends.

The narrow election of a new mayor posing as a reformer and cost-cutter (the sleeves up and broom out pose, of course, was pure hypocrisy. All the questionable practices of the previous administration had been retained. In addition, many more had been added.) Would prove to be another serious thorn in Eddie's side.

The new mayor's swearing in ceremony occurred shortly after Eddie had been installed as captain. The Disbarr administration immediately made Eddie's day-to-day life more of a hassle. He had to scratch and claw to get funding and assistance from city hall for core fire department needs. Under the previous administration, anything the department required for the safety of the public and men was there for the asking.

To make matters worse, the new administration made no secret of the fact that they viewed Eddie with mistrust and hostility because he had been a close friend of and an influential, effective, high-profile campaigner for the previous mayor.

To fully understand the nature of the precarious position Eddie now found himself in, it is necessary to comprehend the convoluted workings and the Byzantine ins and outs of the political scene in which he was a player.

At that time in Corrunoside Township the old Democratic Party was in a position of unchallenged dominance. The young Democratic candidates were lucky if they could eke out a victory in a race for dogcatcher. This is not to suggest that the old Democrats represented a united monolith. Far from it.

Although it is true that everyone joined together when faced with a serious external threat to party supremacy, and/or during major election campaign years (i.e., during races for governor, U.S. Congress, or president), for all intents and purposes, the local Democratic machine was actually comprised of two rival organizations within themselves that were constantly maneuvering behind the scenes in a fight for control.

The existing schism was not the result of conflicting principles or ideological differences. The only issues at stake concerned the manner in which the spoils of patronage, city contracts, and job appointments were carved up. The two competing factions simply represented opposing groups of power brokers, political movers and shakers, officials, bureaucrats, volunteers, business interests, loosely allied coalitions of powerful men, and their sympathizers.

On one side stood the old guard, populated by the civic leaders, administrators, backstage decision makers, and puppet masters, who had traditionally monopolized all levels of elected office in Corrunoside, wielding absolute power over the local government apparatus for over a generation. The opposition was comprised of relatively recent converts. The new-school faction had only been in existence for five or six years and, during that time, had to be content with a somewhat subordinate role in party affairs and direction.

That was, until the elections of 2000 rolled around, and the old guard underestimated the charms of a smooth-talking upstart mayoral candidate and suddenly found themselves displaced by their intraparty foes. Stam Disbarr, the man responsible for wrestling the upper hand from the traditional leadership, promised sweeping changes and reforms. In reality, he merely changed the cast of characters who had free access to dine at the tax-subsidized feed trough.

Since Eddie was widely associated with the traditional faction, it had been made known to him, in no uncertain terms, that his career would be stuck in neutral for as long as this mayor reigned.

Eddie knew this, and he was more or less fine with it. He'd made it to captain in record time anyway. Deputy Chief now had to wait. There was enough on his head. Still, make no mistake about it, he wanted the job if there was any way he could salvage it. For this reason. He decided to visit the new mayor to see if there was any way they could see clear to hash out their differences.

According to Eddie's admittedly naive thought process, he was, after all, a firefighter—first and last. At the end of the day, fire-department appointments should be based on merit. Ideally they ought to be placed above politics. He had worked for the other guy; so what? That was all in the past now. What real conflict did they have? Maybe the new mayor would agree with Eddie's perspective. Maybe he wouldn't. At any rate, it was worth a shot. Stranger things had happened.

Eddie went into the meeting with a nothing-to-lose attitude. He was expecting anything, so it would have taken a disaster to disappoint him. As it turned out, he left the mayor's office far from disappointed. In fact, he was startled to find himself more and more pleasantly surprised as their talk continued to unfold.

Eddie introduced himself to the mayor, whose demeanor was disarmingly warm and respectful. Mayor Disbarr said he praised Eddie's work, putting him immediately at ease by letting him know that he knew who he was and, moreover, was aware of his outstanding record and work history.

Wasting no time, Eddie spoke frankly about their political differences and the things he'd heard through the grapevine about his career being put on ice. The new mayor reacted with what appeared to be genuine shock to the news that his office was somehow planning to blackball Eddie. He hastened to assure Eddie that there was nothing whatsoever to worry about. Skeptical, Eddie politely pressed him on specifics.

"Before the election, everyone from your predecessor's people on down to my house supervisor had flat out promised me the position of deputy chief. I was told point blank, more than once, that I would be the next deputy chief of the Corrunoside F.D."

"And?"

"And according to the scuttlebutt I've been hearing down at the station, the husband of the secretary of that union is your choice. What union? You know lets not play around. Who, Captain Soupe?

He's weak and has no leadership skills. I know and he's never worked on the floor with the men. Don't worry that's not gonna happen. Now everyone's telling' me I can forget about it. That I got no chance. I know things change, but I feel that I've earned that position. It would be a shame if—"

"If we let politics get in the way of picking the best man for the job? No way. Not this mayor. Listen, I don't know what you've heard, but I can assure you … I mean the boys are going to be boasting and rubbing in the upset, but I hope you don't seriously think that I'm going to hold it against you and forget about your dramatic rescues and service to the department because you were a volunteer for a political opponent of mine."

"So I'm still going to be the—"

You'll have the position you were promised. You have my word on that. It's no problem. No problem at all. Just one thing, Eddie."

"Yeah, sure."

"Just stay out of trouble. Make sure you stay out of trouble, you know, keep your nose clean and the job is yours, no problem."

So except for the mayor's quizzical last statement (Talk about your left-field remarks! *Where in the heck did that come from?* Eddie remembered thinking at the time.), Eddie left feeling reassured. Had he known then what he knows now, he would have been anything but reassured. Of course the mayor was lying. The job that was at issue was the least of it. The question of who was going to be the next deputy chief had already been settled. It had not been settled in Eddie's favor.

Not that Eddie wasn't prepared for such an eventuality. It's just that he had assumed that getting pushed aside as deputy chief would be the maximum repercussion he'd face for his vigorous backing of the losing mayoral horse. He had no idea how vindictive these people were. No idea how far they were prone to take things.

What Eddie didn't know was that Disbarr's boys were certainly not taking a wait and see approach. Their plans for Eddie began where Eddie's worst-case scenario ended. "Worse comes to worse," he had told his worried wife, "my upward mobility will be impaired for a few years. Until we can get the old mayor back or someone new is elected that's not so close to all the rivalries and infighting and all the other b.s." Rather than being content to let Eddie languish in benign neglect on some dusty fire-department shelf, they had made the decision to destroy him and had set about a concerted strategy in motion to do so.

Make no mistake about it; Eddie had been singled out long before he'd ever made his appointment to go see the mayor. Indeed, the only reason the mayor had so many fawning facts at his fingertips concerning Eddie's stellar and inspiring record was because he and Munsterhed, his trusty diabolical scum bag sidekick, had recently been through Eddie's file looking for dirt.

Although Disbarr's crew would develop a reputation for going after political foes with a vengeance and would certainly have moved on Eddie in due time, it should be stated for accuracy's sake that Eddie's systematic dismantling, its speed and its severity, didn't occur in a complete vacuum.

There was plenty of timely prodding from old man Thefmor, who was only too happy to furnish forged documentation and sworn affidavits filled with lies that facilitated unquantifiable savings of law enforcement time and taxpayer money, yielded tantalizing shortcuts, put investigators of various stripes on a scent and then, whenever necessary, pointed them in the right direction.

He did this through intermediaries, naturally, never directly, first to accommodate an informal probe that originated out of the mayor's office, and later to provide key support to the internal fire department investigation that would, in conjunction with task force findings that just happened to be released at a conveniently crucial juncture, spawn the involvement of several police departments and, eventually, attract the undivided attention of not only the county prosecutor's office (the appropriate venue for the things Eddie was to be accused of) but also pique the apparent interest of law enforcement elements placed significantly higher up on the proverbial government food chain.

In fact, the old man, by his lonesome, was so helpful that a source in the county prosecutor's office was heard to comment, in the aftermath of everything, that there might not have even been an initial investigation of any kind had it not been for the well-placed distributions of Mr. Thefmor's "evidence." Scandalous is not the word for it. And the blanks haven't even been filled in yet.

In addition to the mayor's office and Dennis's dad, Eddie was grappling with other well-connected enemies (although at the time, he was completely unaware of this reality, unaware that this struggle existed, unaware that any of these wolves were after his throat … perhaps because so many of these would-be grapplers wore their sheep's clothing so well, constantly smiling at him, offering toasts to honesty and honor, and proffering hands to shake in friendship) including influential decision makers from within the upper echelons of his own department.

Of all the wrongs that were and would be done to him, the worst among them revolved around certain choices that were made and behaviors that occurred within his own department, indeed, under the roof of his own firehouse. When he found out about it, it had to be one of the details that cut the deepest and hurt the most. It had to be the bitterest pill, hard to swallow to this day.

The sheer complexity of the network of crisscrossing, cross-pollinated, interoffice alliances, contacts, friendships, and aligned business interests that would soon, indeed had already, begin to waylay Eddie's fortunes was astounding. It is far too twisted and convoluted to even begin to discuss. To lay out the full family tree of Eddie's enemies, along with an accompanying explanation of how they came to be in league with one another, would either confuse an average reader or else put him or her to sleep.

Suffice to say, Eddie's betrayers and back stabbers were legion. They worked in unison to place numerous obstacles in Eddie's path and build an overarching matrix of pitfalls that was extensive and ultimately impossible for one to defend against. What was happening to Eddie, what would happen to Eddie, fit the Webster's Dictionary definition of conspiracy.

In the spheres and arenas closest to Eddie, however, a bit of clarifying detail can't be avoided. Here the sordid trail has to be traced. The fallout from this particular web of family, friendship, and professional relationships will prove to be the most devastating.

But there is another reason it is crucial to untangle the labyrinth maze of contacts, connections, and collusions that were woven both within and between the fire and police departments by those closest to Eddie, those who regularly came into contact with him, those who looked him in the eye, slapped his back, then walked away, secretly using their sway to forge unholy alliances against a man they had to know was innocent.

That reason is justice. Fairness. Decency. Liberty. The reason is that it is important to expose the fact this can happen, that this did happen. In America. In this day and age. Certain agreements were made on quiet golf outings, over drinks at the corner pub, and in rushed and harried code over the clank of coffee cups in busy offices. As a result, a man was marked for utter ruin, a man who in no way deserved it. It is important to write that down, to read that out loud. Ideally, to hold accountable those responsible.

Nothing else, however, these words should still be written if only to chronicle that it happened, that crimes occurred, that trusts were broken, that a genuine American hero was cut off at the knees. Redress may be late in coming. It may not be attained in this world. But at least people know. Once they know, they will care, and be enraged by the awareness that a grave wrong has been committed.

Ignorance is suffocation. Knowledge is breath. The truth is a wind pushing air into Eddie's weary, fire-scarred lungs. The further his story spreads, the louder his voice will become. Until one day he is able to shout his story from the rooftops, shake the steel beams of skyscraping privilege, and cause trembling in the towers of men in high places with the thunder of his simple righteous eloquence.

He won't need to speak in meter or rhyme. He won't need presence or poise or a keen sense of time. All he'll have to do is rattle off the basic unassailable facts of his story. But all this is getting into big-picture stuff, and the big picture gets painted one brushstroke at a time. In order to continue, the narrative must first return to more pedestrian matters. Namely, the mundane nuts and bolts of inter- and intradepartmental betrayal.

Now it gets a bit complicated: The chief of the fire department was close friends with several fire-department captains. These captains, in turn, had sons who were on the volunteer squad, many of whom were also part of the gang that was committing the arsons. (Many of these volunteers also worked with Dennis in the store.) Therefore, the chief had a number of personal and professional motivations to facilitate a cover-up that would silence Eddie and squelch the arson investigation.

Apart from the embarrassment it would cause him if and when his entanglements with these criminals came to light, it would have shown how very close to these guys' and their fathers he really was. His best friend, who was promoted with him on the same day (the former to chief and the latter to captain), was Captain Biscoe. The son of Captain Biscoe, a Corrunoside volunteer firefighter, would later be identified as one of the ringleaders of the arsonists. The relationship between the chief, the arsonists, and their families was, in fact, so cozy that Biscoe's son, along with three of the other arsonists, were hired for a side job painting the chief's house.

Another important relationship is the one between Dennis, Dennis's father, and the chief of police. Dennis's father had known Chief Cowardly and the chief's father since his days as a uniformed cop. Police Chief Cowardly's father, as a matter of fact, was Dennis's godfather. This is an important link to note because Dennis, via his police department contacts, was more than likely able to serve as a conduit, feeding information and fueling suspicions about Eddie both within and between the two departments.

Of course the fire and police departments weren't exactly as separate as church and state; there were many men in both departments who wanted to see Eddie taken down—even his envious, jealous insecure brother. There is little doubt that these men had extensive contact with one another, socializing and comparing notes. The world these men operated in was an insular and self-validating one; once an idea took root and a problem was identified, an aggressive group-think tended to prevail until said problem was rooted out. There is little doubt that Eddie was victimized by this very type of thoughtless feeding frenzy. If at any point one of these guys had pulled back and said, "Wait a minute, we're mistreating one of our own," events may not have proceeded as they did.

Now the reason that Disbarr and his entourage were so sore at Eddie had nothing to do with arson. Their jihad against Eddie was fueled by a perceived political snub. As city manager, Eddie's mother-in-law had been the de facto number-two person in charge of the old regime. Most agreed that other than the mayor, who was the acknowledged boss, she was the most important decision maker.

She held so much power because she had a key hold on the party's purse strings because she was a super-experienced, accomplished, skilled, and effective grant proposal writer. She had an uncanny knack for sniffing out new sources of funding. She also had an encyclopedic knowledge of paperwork and filing deadlines. Over the proceeding decades, the government bureaucracy had run smoothly as a Rolls Royce engine thanks to her oversight.

After the election that changed everything, Eddie's mother-in-law was aggressively sought after by the new regime. She rebuffed all efforts to co-opt her services. Through the mayor's intermediaries, Eddie was asked to approach his mother-in-law and help change her mind. He refused on principle; he felt it was unethical and condescending. The lady was an adult. And his elder. She could make her own decisions.

Plus, why risk rocking the boat with his wife on the off chance she might find his political maneuverings offensive? Mayor Disbarr and his boys never forgot the perceived slight. They vowed revenge. Now, they were in a prime position to take that revenge.

Little did Eddie know—and this is part of the tragedy— that by the plans he was making and the plans he had laid, he was playing right into the hands of all who wished him ill and who had banded together to make all of their nefarious wishes come true.

Ironically, things were, for the time being, good even as the sinister plot against Eddie's good name had already been put into motion, was winding through its early stages, but still needed a decent amount of time to ripen. In the interim, there was calm before whatever storm might be looming. For a short sweet period of time directly following Dennis's divestiture in the store, business ran more smoothly. What had become an almost normal daily routine of emergencies and conflict began to recede into the rearview mirror of the past.

For Eddie, life in general became far more peaceful and calm. Until it had ended between them, Eddie had failed to fully appreciate the grinding damage that the partnership had extracted. The squabbling and stress had taken its toll on his health, happiness, and well-being. Now he had time to heal.

The tranquil operations of the store overlapped with a period of optimism at the department. Eddie believed that he had the ear, confidence, and renewed commitment of the department brass. It was his belief that they would get to the bottom of the arson any day now.

It was an ascendant period in his family life, his relations with his wife, and the quality of his on-the-job performance as measured by the ferocity and fearlessness he displayed when fighting fires and fighting to requisition needed supplies for his guys.

During the agonies, humiliations, and overwhelming tornadoes of upending turbulence that would follow, Eddie would look back at the above stretch of time as a brief, blessed oasis of hope and stability. Alas this charmed era was not fated to last long.

The first indication that Eddie's troubles were not quite behind him was slow in dawning. Its onset slowly came over him like the subtlety unfolding symptoms of some exotic flu. There was a creeping realization that there were elements of strident discord lurking in the shadows of his apparently harmonious surroundings.

As time passed, Eddie realized that despite the chief's assurances, it was increasingly apparent that not only was the department not aggressively pursuing the leads he'd furnished, he began to suspect that nothing was being done at all.

Meanwhile, the property damage and number of individual incidents continued to mount unabated. The pace of the arsons actually seemed to increase for a time. Several people narrowly escaped being burned alive following the torching of an apartment complex.

On another alarm a complex was supposed to be empty but trapped inside was the real-estate executive who had bought the building and supervised its renovation. He was on the second floor, using a flashlight to show off the almost complete results of his efforts to his wife and a party of several of their friends after a night on the town. Although apparently an accident, it was still a sobering and harrowing rescue for the guys who were there. It underlined the inescapable fact that if the arsonists weren't stopped, they would just keep going on and on, getting progressively bolder, taking bigger risks.

If they were permitted to keep on going, it would merely be a matter of time before they seriously hurt or killed someone. Eddie had the horrific realization that he would be at least partially to blame if any innocents ended up in the burn wards or worse as a result of the extended arson spree. All of the ingredients of a recipe for a catastrophe were there, just add an unlucky janitor on a night shift or a homeless guy trying to escape the cold, only to find himself caught at the wrong place at the wrong time.

The other thing was that Eddie also began to realize the mayor had lied to him. After several delays (no doubt designed to delay and defray the issue while lulling Eddie into a false sense of security), the new deputy chief was announced … and it wasn't Eddie. Instead, he had to grit his teeth and be a good sport as the man who was his polar opposite and perhaps his chief rival, George Soupe, a training captain from headquarters and a person who had no clue about working fire scenes but with a well-earned reputation as a shifty double-dealer, who Eddie couldn't stand. He was crowned with the laurels of the prestigious position that only a few weeks ago was Eddie's by foregone conclusion.

Through the friends he still had in city hall that had managed, despite the transition, to retain their jobs, Eddie decided to do a little digging. Had the mayor ever intended to honor his commitment to Eddie or was he lying from the jump? What Eddie found out was that the job decision may have had less to do with him and more to do with Soupe, or more precisely, Soupe's wife.

To be fair, even if all bets were off and all job appointments went under review to be reconsidered in the wake of a new administration's arrival, no objective manager could honestly look at the way Eddie and Soupe stacked up against each another and pick the latter candidate. Eddie obviously held the edge, both in terms of seniority, job competence, popularity among the men and most important not a rat. Eddie was a man's man (at this time their were no woman on the dept).

When one really breaks it down, Eddie would win the nod by any measure. For example, Eddie outranked his adversary by virtue of being named a shift captain the previous winter; Soupe was still a training captain. In the words of one of Eddie's colleagues, who rode the same engine as Eddie for many years, "Soupe had done nothing to deserve the job. Eddie had done everything."

The move only made sense once Eddie became acquainted with the qualifications of his counterpart's wife. As it turned out, she was, as he thought, one of the officers in the most powerful union in the state and held extremely influential sway over their public relations arm. When messages were molded for media consumption, she had input. With her on board, Mayor Disbarr's faction had the potential to sew up a major power base, a harvest that could, over the years, yield an uncountable amount of votes and money. It was hardball politics. It was unfair. But it was reality. Eddie had to grin and bear it.

Right on the heels of the Soupe's promotion, disappointment Eddie's fragile sense of peace absorbed another blow. Through well-placed friends, the investigation rumors that had been swirling around the station house and the store were substantiated. Although his friends were able to break the news that the store's dealings were being looked into, they couldn't definitively tell Eddie whether the scrutiny had teeth. In other words, did the investigation have the potential to result in departmental disciplinary action or even charges being filed?

They suggested Eddie visit the prosecutor's office and inquire about the status of the inquiry. It couldn't hurt, they advised, to show he had nothing to hide. Maybe, they speculated, he'd get lucky and the prosecutor would lay his cards on the table. (Although Eddie couldn't for the life of him imagine what those cards were.) His friends urged him not to worry. After all, he'd done nothing wrong.

The drawn-out nature of the ordeal, along with all the attendant uncertainty, began to weigh on him, however. He could not follow the advice he received to visit the prosecutor's office because he had already taken that step several months before, while he and Dennis were still partners. He'd even dragged Dennis along, against his will, to face the music. All they'd heard at that point were sketchy whispers about the store being under some kind of surveillance, which the prosecutor they spoke with would neither confirm nor deny.

He remembered that day well and thought about it often, wondering if he'd helped his cause or dug himself into a deeper hole. Against Dennis's strenuous objections, Eddie had brought all their books downtown for the prosecutor to examine. *Why not?* He'd thought at the time. Since there was no willful mismanagement or wrongdoing, let alone purposeful fraud, how could it hurt? But the move had hurt. In hindsight, it had completely backfired.

While the prosecutor was reviewing the account books, he came across three items of merchandise that were not accompanied by receipts. Therefore, there was no way to trace their origins and how and if they'd been properly sold and paid for. When questioned by the prosecutor about the mysterious items, Eddie was flabbergasted.

Dennis had promised to be more careful concerning documentation; he promised that receipt-less transactions were a thing of the past. That was a major part of the reason Eddie had the confidence to meet with the prosecutor; he'd been assured the books were kept in good order. As a result, he'd inadvertently added fuel to a fire that he'd gone to extinguish.

His closing exchange with the prosecutor had been troubling to say the least.

"Sir, we've cooperated fully, so I would hope—" If you want to know more about the receipt less items talk to Dennis, I have no clue.

"And we value and appreciate your cooperation. This kind of open attitude is always taken into account."

"But I was hoping you might be able to tell me something, anything about what's going on? Are my partner and I in some kind of trouble? Should I get a lawyer?"

"I'm sorry. As much as I'd like to help, I can't comment on the status or even the existence of any potentially ongoing investigations."

Ready to give up, Eddie turned to leave the man's office and walk into the bathroom where Dennis was waiting for him. Before he reached the door, the prosecutor halted him.

"Eddie?"

"Yes sir?"

"Do you know anybody political?"

"Political?"

"Yes political … someone who could help you out if things get messy."

"I don't know, I guess."

"I'd start thinking about talking to anyone you might know with any influence or pull."

"What does that mean?"

"It means what it means. I've said far too much already. Good luck. I wish you the best."

With that, the prosecutor motioned to the door of his office and Eddie let himself out. As soon as Eddie and Dennis were out on the street, out of earshot of the courthouse, Eddie wheeled around with a snarl and grabbed Dennis's collar.

"You son of a bitch. You set me up in there."

"What are you talking about? As I recall, it was I who told you that no good could come of this."

"You vowed to me that the monkey business with the receipts was over. You lied. You looked me in the eyes and lied right to my face."

Dennis shrugged.

"Shit happens," he replied. You should have kept two sets of books like my dad did.

Eddie pressed his face close to Dennis's. The veins in his neck were bulging. Dennis had never seen him this angry. Both were awash in the rush of adrenaline that directly precedes a fistfight.

"If you ever buy or sell merchandise without proper documentation and receipts again, I swear to God I will break your neck."

Dennis pushed away, turned on his heel and walked away briskly to put some distance between himself and his irate partner. Over his shoulder, he taunted, "I'll just start doing it when I'm working nights when you're not there. You won't know what I'm doing."

Eddie recalled all of this word for word, because it was the exact moment that he realized for the first time that he was sure he wanted to sever their partnership as soon as possible.

Then and now, Eddie vaguely suspected Dennis, his father, and their connections for his rising tide of misfortune, but he had nothing remotely solid to even begin to go on. It was just that the timing of the store sale was, in retrospect, too perfectly providential for Dennis and his father to be coincidental. As soon as Dennis bailed out, the heat began to come down. So Eddie had an idea that Dennis and his old man might be behind some of his woes. But these were just passing thoughts. They were never pursued or pieced together. Eddie had no idea how deep the rabbit hole went.

Chapter 10

As the arson headlines continued to multiply, mounting pressure from state officials was being applied on both the fire and police departments of Corrunoside. It was made abundantly clear that heads would roll if the culprits continued to evade justice much longer. Whispers of corruption and cover-up, attributed to anonymous sources, had started to appear in the local press.

The quotations bred speculation that, in turn, assumed a life of its own. The mushrooming mess spread like a toxic cloud, ultimately attracting the attention of the governor's office and state attorney general. Assuming that the word on the street was accurate, Trenton was preparing to clean house, assume control, and take over the investigation if results were not forthcoming soon.

How soon was soon? That was anybody's guess. The nebulousness of the situation made for unsure, footing, causing an unprecedented amount of tension and surliness around the firehouse. The prevailing winds of paranoia swirled with merciless unpredictability, ruffling almost everyone's feathers.

It was against this backdrop that the plague of firebugs struck again. It was late, well after 11 p.m. The night had been unusually slow and uneventful: no calls at all, not even to rescue a treed house cat. Instead of battling deadly flames, the men on duty were fighting boredom, trying to stay alert in case they had to snap into action.

Eddie was the captain on duty and was in his office catching up on paperwork. A half-hearted chess game was in progress, but most of the guys were hanging out, relaxing around the television. They were watching a Devils-Canucks game that had just been sent into overtime on a Vancouver power-play goal with less than twenty seconds left in the third period. There were a few scattered curses at the timing of the alarm. Even the most colorful of the epithets were without conviction, however. These guys were quite used to having their sports contests interrupted at a moment's notice.

By the time an anonymous tipster had finally called in the fire, it had been blazing for quite some time with unbridled intensity, rearing and kicking with furious equestrian flourishes, running in place on crackling hooves, like bunched-up racehorses with coats of blinding orange flame and wispy, gray-black soot-stained manes.

The engines arrive in a breakneck jangle of noise, screeching around a sharp corner, thundering down the access road with the *sturm und drang* of Old West Calvary. The din of blaring sirens punctured the post-midnight silence, multicolored lights strobed against the deep indigo night, high beams piercing through billowing smoke.

Pneumatic hiss of breaks as the two red trucks park perpendicular to one another. Hoses are hustled into action and trained on the remains of a sizzling house. Despite their casual professionalism, efficiency, and jaw-droppingly amazing response time, the red-helmeted rescuers are too late. Within minutes of their arrival, the structure had burned almost completely to the ground. The wan glow of soggy embers scattered about the concrete foundation were the only remnants of the building that had stood there just a few hours before.

A horror of realization settled over the men as they began to pick, sift, and sort through the rubble and debris. If this home had any inhabitants, no one had even a remote chance of making it out alive. To the relief of all assembled, however, it soon became apparent that the house had long been abandoned. Before long, one of the men found the tell-tale signs of a flare gun–fueled fire, at which point the cause of the blaze was clarified beyond the shadow of a doubt.

On the way back to the station, an interesting conversation took place between Jake, an observant new probie, and Eddie's old friend

Jerry. While they were riding back to the station beside one another on the inner-side seats of one of the fire engines, Jake gave Jerry a gentle; nudge in the ribs with his elbow, then began to speak in a near whisper, almost under his breath. At least it seemed that way to Jerry, who had to strain to hear him above the raucous chatter of the other guys and the clang and clatter of the rig they were riding in.

"Was it just me, or did you notice the vehicle tearing ass up the access road entry on our way in?"

"Yeah," Jerry shouted.

"Sshhhhh!"

The probie, who was catching on quick to the taboo topics of the station house, put a quick finger to his lips and indicated the other ears surrounding them with a furtive side-to-side glance that suggested there might be an unexpected unfriendly or two among the brothers they were riding with. Jerry, who was by now privy to the aggravations that Eddie's concerns about the arsons and the possible connection of the perpetrators to the department had caused him, understood straightaway and lowered his voice. He couldn't help but marvel at Jake's instincts and his perceptive discretion.

"Now that you mention it, yeah."

After pausing to make sure no one had taken an interest in listening in, Jake continued. "A light-colored van right?"

"So it wasn't just me who spotted it."

"I don't see how anyone could miss it."

"How come you didn't say something?"

"We were on our way to a fire. Excuse me if I was a little distracted."

"No, you misunderstand. I'm not trying to be accusatory, I was just curious. Remember, I'm the new guy. I probably get more juiced up with fear and adrenaline that anyone else. I mean, it wasn't a priority to me either at the time."

"Right."

"Right. But now—"

"But now, you can bet I'm going offer up my two cents about it. That's for damn sure. These guys—and I don't care who they are—these guys go against every last thing we stand for … matter of fact, risk our lives for."

"I agree. But you know—"

"No, I don't know. Fill me in."

"I hear that whoever is doing this has got a lot of well-placed friends. I'm sure you heard what happened to Eddie's buddy Hector. He was lucky to avoid getting shitcanned. Word has it that only due to Eddie's intervention and Hectors father being a Lt. in the Corrunoside police department and being promised with a promotion that Hector only got shipped out instead of fired. (It was at that time the Corrunoside Police dept was informed and should have known who the arsonists were). Some people are saying that since the elections, Eddie lost a lot of pull. I even heard from some of the new recruits that Eddie himself could end up on the chopping block if he keeps squawking about the arsons. What do you think they'll do to us? And even if we wanted to do the right thing and take this somewhere, who knows who you can trust around this place?"

"I do. I know just the guy we need to take this to."

"You sure about this guy?"

"Positive. I'd bet my life on him. In fact, over the years I have … any number of times."

"Who is he? Do I know him?"

"You were just talking about him."

Thus, once again, and on that very night no less, matters relating to the arson rampage were to be dumped back onto Eddie's lap.

When the crew that had responded to the arson returned to the station, Eddie heard them pull into the garage. He hadn't accompanied them on the call; he was among those left in reserve in case another emergency occurred in the meantime. Around the time that the men who had fought and subdued the abandoned house fire were cleaning themselves up, Eddie decided to take a break from the mountain of managerial paperwork he was wading through to grab a bite to eat, hear news of what had happened, and spend some time hanging out with his guys.

Eddie emerged from his office and made his way to the kitchen and dining area. He grabbed some ground beef from the refrigerator and began preparing a late-night meal for himself, taking care to fix an abundance of extra hamburger meat for anyone who had worked up a hunger. He was flipping the patties over in the pan when Jake and Jerry came out from the showers and took seats at the communal table.

Captain John De Nuzio, who was usually posted at another house but was pitching in at Eddie's house for a few shifts while they were shorthanded, due to injuries and vacations,, had also wandered into the room, drawn no doubt by the smell of frying sirloin (He was another useless lazy fat bastard). After greeting the trio and being assured that his presence wasn't an intrusion, he pulled up a chair and sat down. Firefighters Jake and Jerry worked with Captain De Nuzio for years and knew him well so they felt comfortable at the same table.

Eddie turned the burner down to low then sat down to relax as well. After a brief exchange of pleasantries and some cursory commenting on pro sports and current news events, the subject turned, as it often did in those times and parts, to the arsons.

"Guess you heard about it by now," began Jake, breaking a brief silence, "you know … that this was yet another one that was no accident."

Both captains gave nearly simultaneous nods, somber and sober expressions breaking across their faces like clouds spreading over the sun. Eddie let out a deep, burdened sigh, and then pushed away from the table in order to tend to his cooking. Jake went to the overhead cabinet and fetched some paper plates and condiments.

The topic remained on the table, but an awkward pause had ensued. Every member of the usually loquacious bunch seemed to be at a loss for words. Something more than idle shop talk and the predictable ritual of providing a play-by-play re-cap of the torched house was in the air. The two captains, feeling distinctly out of the loop (even though they had no idea what the loop concerned or contained), exchanged curious glances.

At the same time, Jake and Jerry locked eyes. The silent communication taking place between the latter pair, however, was of a different type than the befuddlement being expressed by Eddie and Captain De Nuzio. Clearly they knew something. With an impatient and not very subtle arch of his eyebrows and a "come-on already" look on his face, the veteran seemed to be urging the probie to come out with it.

But Jake seemed as though he would be more comfortable with Jerry stepping up to take the reins of the conversation at that particular juncture. For one thing, he knew that Jerry and Eddie had been friends for years. Also, due to the obvious gravity of the situation, he preferred to defer to Jerry's seniority and experience. Jake didn't mind going out on a limb for what he thought was right; he just didn't want to find himself out there all by himself. The clock on the wall ticked off several piercingly uncomfortable seconds. The two captains waited while their men hashed out the rest of their wordless negotiation.

Jake was still struggling to find his voice and get his words out when finally, Jerry made up his mind to speak. He drew a deep breath and, without further hesitation, dove in.

"Me and the rookie … we think we saw something," began Jerry.

"Think you saw something?" prodded Eddie.

"We saw something," Jake confirmed.

"We were on our way to the fire, all juiced up and ready to face who knows what, so it didn't quite register at the time. I mean, my heart was beating a mile a minute at that point. I was thinking about making it out of that death trap oven alive, not about playing detective. Still, it stuck in my mind and when Jake here mentioned it afterwards—"

"We turn the corner in the rig onto the access road on the way to the cul-de-sac where we can already see the fire blazing away down at the far end. Most of the guys were staring down the street at where we were going. I mean, that fire was roaring. Anyway, the thing that distracted my attention was the approach of a car engine. Now there is only one way in and one way out of that cul-de-sac, so I figure whoever is tearing ass down the road, more likely than not, was involved in setting the fire we were on our way to fight."

"So did you guys … I mean were you able to identify the vehicle?"

"We saw it clear as day. It was a tan van."

"A tan van? Are you absolutely sure?"

"Positive."

"We're both sure. Jake saw it too, with my own two eyes. No question. There's no question at all."

The quartet is frozen into stunned silence by this revelation and all that it implies. Eddie shook his head in disbelief. Captain De Nuzio let loose a low whistle. It was Captain De Nuzio, who eventually spelled out what all the men were thinking, why all their jaws were gaping, why they were all staring at one another as if to say "holy shit, what now?". They exchanged meaningful looks loaded with significance and portent.

"So … uh … tell me something," said Captain De Nuzio, "doesn't Swetpee's kid own a tan van?" I asked the chief about that van weeks ago.

"Funny, I was just sitting here thinking the same thing," commented Eddie.

"Oh yes, he certainly does. Captain Swetpee's son definitely has a tan Chevy van. The family lives in my neighborhood. I see Junior and his buddies tooling around in that thing almost every single day," stated Jerry.

"He's on the volunteer squad isn't he?" asked Jake.

"He sure is. Stated Jerry and so are all the boys he pals around with."

"Jesus Eddie, something just struck me like a lightning bolt."

"Well out with it."

"Remember when Dennis still half-owned the store and I'd come in to shoot the breeze with you all?"

"Yeah, what of it?"

"You always had me or Keith or Steve … or one of your sons … or your wife helping out whenever you needed an extra pair of hands. Now when Dennis needed someone to pitch in down there, he always used—"

"Holy smoke, Corrunoside's own volunteer firemen!"

"Not just any volunteer firemen. Dammit I knew I recognized those boys more than just in passing. Those were Swetpee's kid's posse … his closest pals. You think it's just a coincidence,' cause I don't."

"Damn, that son of bitch. No wonder, no wonder." All their father's are Rumpkey's best friends.

"What?"

"Don't worry about it; just a lot of queer doings and goings on that I couldn't understand for the life of me are beginning to make a whole lot of sense."

"You don't think Dennis—"

"No, I don't think, I'm positive. I just need some time to back it up. I'm telling you guys this is huge. Huge. You know, moving forward here, we—all of us—need to be careful how we step, how we handle this and where we take it."

"Any ideas?"

"Well we still have no out and out proof."

"Yeah but we *know* now, *we know*."

"Oh man, I can't believe I have to explain this again. This is like deja vu. Listen, I know and you know and they know but without proof, it's just hearsay, witness testimony. Solid witnesses you guys are, but it's your word we have and his word and that's all we have. Remember what happened to Hector? I'm not saying he's been blackballed, but damn, he was in the heart of things and he had a bright future. Then he tries to blow the whistle and they exiled him way out to station 45. buried the guy in the freakin' boondocks, where nothing ever happens, where there's almost never any action at all. That means there's no chance to shine, no chance to advance up the ladder. And that was with me having his back. I was firmly in his corner and threatened to make a big stink about it. I'm not blowing my own horn, but facts are facts; if I hadn't intervened—and believe me when I say I did all I could, everything I could think of to protect his ass—used my influence, called his father, put my reputation on the line, if I hadn't done that, honestly, the guy might not even be a fireman any more. My involvement may have kept him from a suspension or a termination, but other than that, I couldn't do anything for him. Man, they put him so far back on ice he might as well be fighting fires in Antarctica. We need to be careful or it's going to be more of the same shenanigans. The bad guys will find a way to slither away yet again and we … we'll just get burned. We'll just get burned."

🔥 🔥 🔥

Either the men were overheard during their post-midnight meal or someone confided in someone they shouldn't have. Maybe the visiting captain was not to be trusted or perhaps he simply didn't take heed of Eddie's words counseling caution. Whatever happened and however it happened, there was a leak. Consequently the confidential kitchen conversation made its way right back to the chief.

Roughly ninety minutes after the words had left their mouths, Chief Rumpkey's sedan came roaring into the fire-station garage. Pushing several curious onlookers aside to clear his path, the chief stormed up the stairs toward Eddie's office. Eddie heard the thudding echo of boots approaching. The slapping of the soles pounded in his temples, exacerbating a fledgling headache that had been threatening to blossom into a migraine all day.

From the angry sound of his boss's steps, he was able to guess who it was and why he had come. Bracing himself for the impending confrontation, Eddie leaned forward in his chair and prepared to face the music.

Moments later the chief stormed into Eddie's office, pushing the slightly ajar door wide open and stepping inside without waiting for an invitation. The man was fuming. Lurid green and purple veins stood out in sharp relief against his pale, blood-drained face, pulsating in his neck and his forehead.

Eddie was reminded of the cartoons he'd watched with his son, the ones with steam engine sound effects that were accompanied by the visual imagery of animated kettle smoke emanating from the character's ears to express exaggerated anger and rage. Eddie was prepared for some fireworks. In decades of interaction with this man, he had never seen him in such a state.

"Chief? To what do we owe the honor of this unexpected visit?"

"Cut the b.s. You know why I'm here."

"Get Captain De Nuzio in your office, now. I want to talk to you guys."

Captain De Nuzio was called in, the door was closed tight, and the chief proceeded to spend the next fifteen minutes on a rabid tirade, berating his two captains about the dangers of loose talk and unsubstantiated rumors. (Neighbors had described the van weeks earlier and Captain De Nuzio did report it.)

"Listen, I have nothing to hide or cover up. Eddie, I gave you my word I'd look into this and not rest until I got to the bottom of it, and my word is my bond. But when you guys go rogue and start wantonly spreading slander around the house, people's lives get ruined. It's reckless and it's irresponsible. You have no idea what kind of damage can be caused. The worst thing is that you guys have no basis for this shit. Believe me, if I had the goods on these guys, I'd move, I don't care who they are or who they know. But as it stands now, there's a good chance that you are impugning reputations that don't deserve to be smeared."

"With all due respect chief, this is not about sniping or backbiting or engaging in petty gossip like you're making it sound. This is about the integrity of the department. It's bigger than you or me or Captain De Nuzio. It's not about any individual."

"Ah, but that's where you're wrong Eddie. Do I take it personal? Yeah I take it personal. Of course I take it personally. How could I not? It's no secret what we're talking about here. You know I'm friends with some of these guys. Me and their fathers go way, way back, for years and years, and years. So when you spread this mess about them, you're directly attacking me. When you refuse to give them the benefit of the doubt, you refuse to give me the benefit of the doubt. Don't you trust me Eddie?"

"Of course I trust you. But put yourself in my shoes. You want me to tell my guys to ignore what they've seen? Just refuse to believe their eyes because it makes things complicated and uncomfortable."

"Oh come off it Eddie. We're not talking about a smoking gun. If we were, I'd be first in line to bust these guys. Again, it wouldn't matter who they were. It wouldn't matter if they were my own mother and father. But the reality is, you got nothing. We're talking about some van you may or may not have seen in the dark careening down an unpaved access road on the way from a fire."

"Still, these guys know what they saw, and I have complete faith in their abilities. Remember, it wasn't just one guy; it was two … both saw the exact same vehicle. Both of them are highly, highly credible. They have no ulterior motives, no axes to grind; their credentials are unimpeachable and their motives are above reproach. I have absolute confidence in their powers of observation. Yes it was dark. Yes they were distracted. However, they are competent professionals. I would have no problem putting my life into their hands, I have before and I will again, so I think we can be pretty sure of their ability to identify a simple van."

"Let's suspend our common sense and put reality aside for a moment and assume you're correct, that here was indeed a passing glimpse, a phantom sighting of this mysterious tan van. What then? Has the case been solved? Should I go and round up suspects on the basis of that information? Is this tan van definitively linked to the arson because it was seen in the general vicinity? Are there no other tan vans in the state of New Jersey, or do you think Swetpee's kid drives the only one? I mean, what shade of tan are we talking here? Tan? Off-tan? Brown? I can't believe I have to tell you guys this shit. It should be self-evident. To want me to move on the basis of a possible sighting, well it's just patently absurd. And then to call my morality and commitment to the arson investigation into question due to this ... its borderline insubordinate. I take it as an insult. I've said it before and I'll say it again: I want these guys every bit as bad as you all do. It's a blemish on this department and my administration. It's an embarrassment and a shame and an outrage. Especially, especially if it turns out to be an inside job, which, excuse me, I'm not as ready to accept as you guys are ... until I've got some damn strong evidence that's been corroborated and stands up to scrutiny. I don't know, maybe I'm wrong, maybe I'll end up standing behind all you boys for too long. If that's the case, don't worry, I'll be held accountable for it. I mean, don't you see? Don't you get it? To find some firemen scapegoats, trump up some charges, and hang them out to dry, that would be the easy thing to do at this point, the easiest thing, the path of least resistance. You know how hungry they are in the prosecutor's office to pin this on one of our guys, to string up a fireman from the old regime? What a trophy! It's all they talk about. It's a virtual obsession with that bunch. Get a fireman no matter what it takes. Do you know how bad they want to generate the slightest excuse to embark on a department wide witch hunt in order to make big names for themselves and decimate the old guard? They are salivating at the prospect, practically foaming at the mouth. Imagine the headlines and the photo-ops and the righteous breast beating. The voting public will undoubtedly be dazzled by the sheer spectacle of their little circus. They'll fall for it. Eat it up like pro wrestling. Shit, what's the damn difference between politics and pro wrestling these days anyway? I don't know. I do know that, odds are, everyone in their office automatically gets reelected next year. And me, I'm being offered a guaranteed way to cover my ass and keep my job. All I have to do is go along to get along. But I can't do that. At least not yet. First I need proof. Until then, excuse the hell out of me if I'm not willing to throw our guys to the wolves until I'm positive that's what they deserve. I'd do the same for you guys, and I hope you'd do the same for me. That's what brotherhood is about. It's called loyalty, trust, giving the benefit of doubt to those who have earned it. It's called standing behind your men until I'm certain, absolutely certain, that they are in the wrong. You wouldn't respect me if I wasn't willing to stand behind you guys until the bitter end. I couldn't call myself your chief otherwise. But don't think I'm not staying up at night worrying about how to bust these bastards, whoever they are, before they burn someone alive. No one has to remind me what the stakes are here. But don't make me out to be the bad guy here 'cause I don't choose to do something rash and maybe blow the whole hunt for these guys. How we go about it—the strategies and tactics—that's my call. I call the shots. Remember that. You report to me, not vice versa. I'm getting really, really tired of having to justify my actions to employees. Eddie, you know me, you've known me for years. I'm not some power-hungry egomaniac who gets off on blustering and swaggering around the station house pulling rank. Believe me; it doesn't make me feel good to have to break it down to you guys like this. I can't believe I've got to spell that out, but you guys make me feel like I do."

"Whoa Chief, whoa. This is insane. We're talking about five minutes of idle chatter in a private setting between confidants. (Eddie's words "private" and "confidants" are drawn out and accompanied by a laser-sharp glances of suspicion directed at the other captain, who furtively averts his gaze. It is at this point that Eddie realized who the weak link was and why he was taking heat from the chief in the dead of night. Whether intentional or not, he was never to find out for sure.) That is getting blown all out of proportion. Let's back up and call time out for just a second. No one here is questioning your authority or your ethics. There is certainly no hint of accusation intended here in any way, shape, or form. You're my chief, Chief. I'm 100 percent loyal to you. Just tell us what you want us to do and we'll do it."

"Simple. Keep your mouths shut. You guys want to be Encyclopedia Brown and Sherlock Holmes and continue on with your amateur sleuthing, fine, be my guest, but keep it to yourself, at least until I say so. Did it ever occur to you that, far from supplementing our efforts and helping us along, your meddling may be counterproductive to the ongoing investigation? You may unwittingly obstruct what we're doing or spook folks back into hiding who we want feeling safe and secure so we can flush them out, follow their movements, and catch them red-handed. We've been hot on their trail for quite some time, but they've always been able to stay a half step ahead of us. Clearly someone on the inside has got their back. They've been underestimated more than once and have, we think, been tipped off and warned whenever we've gotten close to closing in on them. More than once, they've miraculously slipped away when we thought we had them cornered. On top of that, they've already proven themselves to be incredibly resourceful, astute, and slippery on their own. For obvious reasons, this probe has to be conducted covertly, behind a veil of strict secrecy, or we'll never take these guys down. As a result, you have no idea where we are in this investigation and no clue about what we know and what actions we are planning to execute. Take my word for this Eddie, and mark them well, no good can come out of your actions, no good can come out of it. Steer clear. Give it a rest and let me do my job. That's a direct order. Disregard it at your own peril."

"Chief, I got to be honest. After all these years working together, I can't believe what I'm hearing. Is that a threat you just made?

"Geez Eddie, get it through your head. The sooner you get it through that thick Guinea skull that I'm your friend, the better. I'm not threatening you, I'm trying to protect and look out for you. I'm trying to look out for everyone in this department who's got the balls to dress out in a uniform and strap on a helmet. If you ever take my advice on anything, hear me out on this one: You do not want to get mixed up in this mess or you will be sorry. I'm not saying another word on the subject 'cause I can see you're taking me all wrong. But do yourself a huge favor and squelch this fucking crusade immediately. For your own good. I'm on it. I won't rest until the case is solved and these sleazebags are brought to justice. I'm on it I tell you. For God's sake Eddie, let me do my job."

"If I want to keep mine."

"I didn't say that."

"You didn't have to."

Eddie's retort concluded the tense conversation. In an apparent effort to claim the conversation's last words, the chief opened his mouth to speak but then abruptly thought better of it. He gave a theatrically dismissive shrug of his shoulders meant to dispel, to literally shrug off Eddie's final contention as far too ludicrous to even warrant a response.

The expression on the chief's face was one of indignant denial. Quite notably, however, the chief did not say anything verbally to refute the explosive charge, backpedaling out of Eddie's office, leaving Eddie's parting shot to hang ominously in the air like a suspended cannonball. With nothing left to say, Chief Rumpkey nodded gravely at his men and quietly took his leave. Coming in like a lion, exiting like a lamb.

🔥 🔥 🔥

Early the next morning, the chief was back on the job. He looked worn, tired, and stressed out; he looked as if he hadn't slept for several nights. His usually impeccably pressed clothes were shabbily wrinkled, adding to his state of general dishevelment.

His secretary, Nadine, was shocked and concerned about the dark rings under his bloodshot eyes as he stomped heavily past her desk into his office without his usual warm, friendly greeting. In fact, he'd said nothing at all. She couldn't help but notice. She also took notice of his closed door and the uncharacteristic silence behind it. Both of which were oddities.

Usually Nadine found herself surrounded by so much noise and bustling activity that she had trouble concentrating on her work. Usually the chief's door was wide open to a host of gregarious, backslapping, good old boy visitors who came and went informally, without scheduled appointments.

Everything about that morning was highly irregular. It was a feeling Nadine couldn't quite put her finger on. She'd been employed as Chief

Rumpkey's secretary for three years. Until that day, work had been such a pleasant place she actually looked forward going to every morning.

There was a collegial, light, almost fun vibe about the job. They worked hard and with a great deal of efficiency, but there was very little drudgery involved. She felt challenged by her responsibilities and appreciated by her boss. Moreover, the compensation was good. On several occasions, she told her friends how lucky she was to have found such a cool position.

Today, however, was as different from the rest of her tenure there as night and day. A gravely serious, somber atmosphere had settled over the office. A crushing heaviness had descended that was so tangible it seemed it could be cut with a knife. The chief's caring, sweet demeanor had curdled and turned sour. For no apparent reason, he was in a terribly nasty mood. For no apparent reason, he'd snapped at her several times.

All of a sudden and out of nowhere, the chief's management style of solicitous kindness and respectful flirtation had been replaced by rude sarcasm and malignant disapproval. It seemed she could do nothing right that morning. She began to brace herself whenever she heard his office door creak open, expecting to be assailed by a scathing comment and a scowling attitude every time he exited his office. More often than not, he managed to exceed her expectations.

The phone rang ceaselessly, but Chief Rumpkey wasn't taking any calls. Nadine spent the bulk of the morning trying to ignore the air of combustible tension and scrawling down message after message until her fingers grew sore from writing.

Just before noon, as Nadine was packing to go to lunch, the chief emerged once more, brusquely instructing her to clear his schedule for the rest of the day and handing her a list of names and numbers to contact.

The chief wanted all of the men on the list summoned to his office immediately. No excuse for absence would be acceptable. They were to drop whatever they were doing and show up right away. "Or else," she was told to tell them. Those were the exact words she'd been instructed to use: or else.

Right off the bat, Nadine recognized most of the names on the paper. They were as familiar as the office wallpaper. In fact, Nadine had even gone out on a few dates with one of the guys on the list, but it hadn't worked out. Anyway, they had remained friends so, although it would be a little weird to call him, it wouldn't be that bad. (It was certainly better than the alternative: asking the chief, in his present black mood, if she could avoid the call. She shuddered at the thought.) The men on her call sheet all had one thing in common: they were members of the south ends Corrunoside's volunteer firefighter force. Many enjoyed a good degree of popularity and prominence in the community. But that's not where she knew them from. She knew them through the chief. She'd seen many of them at the office Christmas party. Others she'd often seen around the office when they came by to visit with the chief, either by themselves or with their fathers.

The chief went way back with the fathers of most of the men on the list. Over time, he had gotten very close with a couple of the listed youngsters as well. They confided in him and asked him for advice, letters of recommendation, help with job troubles, and other such things. As Nadine dialed the first number, she idly wondered if the meeting she was in the process of coordinating was in any way connected to the chief being so ill-tempered and out of sorts. It was none of her business anyway. At any rate, the sooner she did her job and dispensed with the assignment, the sooner she could escape to the reprieve of her lunch hour.

Although some arm twisting and schedule juggling was required, Nadine was able, within a half-hour, to convince everyone of the chief's dead seriousness and persuade all the boys to hurry in at the same time. The earliest possible time that everyone could make it downtown at once on such short notice was 2:30. She set the meeting for that time and went to inform the chief. For the first time that day, she saw a glimmer of his old self. He forced himself to smile at her and tell her what a good job she had done. Nadine went off to lunch feeling much better.

Lunch and the early part of the afternoon flew by. Before she knew it, the clock was ticking toward 2:30. There were a few follow-up phone calls to make, coordinating stragglers, admonishing latecomers to double time it to the office, and reminding them that harsh consequences would be in store if they failed to do so. Still, it was quarter to three before everyone was assembled in the outer office, another fifteen minutes until the chief could see them, and another fifteen minutes that he intentionally made them wait.

The half hour the assembled volunteers spent in the outer office was nerve-racking to say the least. Although they tried not to acknowledge it, everyone present (with the exception of Nadine) knew that the group possessed another commonality besides volunteer firefighting.

More than one of the volunteers was trembling. More than one had broken out in a cold sweat. More than one was wondering if he'd been set up, if they were going to walk out of Chief Rumpkey's office in handcuffs. They looked at each other and Swetpee's kid said remember what Dennis said: if anything happens ask for our lawyers. They looked at Nadine, trying to get a clue as to why the hell they were there. During the time the arsonists spent waiting on tenterhooks, not a single word was spoken until, after what seemed to the men like centuries of waiting, the intercom finally buzzed, and Nadine ushered them in to see the chief.

The chief was at his desk when they entered the office. He instructed the last man entering the room to close the door, and he gingerly did so. For a two-minute eternity, Chief Rumpkey just shook his head sadly while staring at the men, all of whom he knew, some of whom he knew extremely well. Finally, the chief rose and spoke.

"I'm going to get right to the point. We all know why I called you guys in."

The chief was almost overwhelmed by a cascading chorus of earnest no mans, nada, and I have no ideas.

"You're the ones. You're the crew who has been setting these fires. I can't believe—"

At this point the Chief was interrupted by a louder crescendo of no ways, absolutely not, and `I swear to Gods. Chief Rumpkey shouted them down.

"Shut up! Listen up you fucking assholes. It's bad enough what you're doing. It goes against everything we stand for, everything we are. But to add insult to injury, you're not even being careful. You're getting sloppy, cocky, leaving traces. People are coming to me ready to blow whistles. It's everything I can do to hold them off, and now I've put my job and reputation in jeopardy. This is outrageous and it's got to stop."

The men started to protest their innocence again, this time more vigorously. With an arrogant grunt accompanied by a raised hand gesture that promised he'd smack the next kid who kept it up, the chief quickly and violently cut them off.

"This conversation is over. I don't want to hear any of your bullshit. I just called you in to say that if you are doing this shit—and the reasonable doubt is getting to be slim to none here—but if you are doing this, I can't protect you. Word is spreading. Everybody knows."

"But we're innocent," yelled Swetpee's son, "we can't help it if we have enemies that are jealous of who we know and—"

"For the last time, shut up! I've heard enough crap out of you guys to last me a lifetime. Look, you guys say your innocent, and I want to believe you. I know you all. You've been good kids for as long as I've known you. So maybe you're being framed, maybe you've been wrongfully accused whatever. At this point, it doesn't matter. To be honest, I don't care to know what the particulars of the situation are. I was willing to turn a blind eye to all your rowdiness, but now it's beginning to affect me, my life, and my career. So, let's for the sake of argument, we'll say you guys have done nothing wrong. But if you have, if you guys are the ones responsible for these arsons—or forget that, if even one of you guys was even peripherally involved in setting even one of these fires—I want you, right now, to cut it out, knock it off. You understand me? Knock it off. That is all. Now get out of my sight."

Chapter 11

A postcard-perfect Sunday. Late September. Bright sunshine. No clouds in the sky. A light, steady breeze. Indian summer temperatures. Eddie and Dominic, his eldest offspring, had managed to carve a few precious hours out of their busy schedules to enjoy some rare father-son time together.

They'd spent the morning taking advantage of the mild weather to complete some light yard work that Eddie had meant to get around to for weeks. The constant, exponentially multiplying demands of home ownership had, due to pressing necessity, been subordinated to the more immediate needs of the fire department and the store.

Happy to reconnect with his son and relieved that he had caught up on his growing backlog of small but nagging household chores, Eddie had cleared the afternoon of all obligations and was planning to spend a lazy afternoon hanging out with Dominic watching NFL football on TV.

Drawn by the blue skies, balmy breezes, and bronzing rays of the uncommonly beautiful day, the men elected to eat lunch outside on the back porch. After polishing off a small pizza, Eddie and Dom retired to the living room with towering glasses of ice-cold lemonade, just in time for the opening kick-off.

Father and son shared an energetic first half on the edge of their seats, exchanging spirited high-fives with one another, raucously debating the merits and drawbacks of various players, and directing loud cheers and jeers at the television set.

At some point shortly before halftime, the intensity of the duo starts to wane. For one thing, the home team had begun to pull away from its opponent, taking a two touchdown lead, making the game less of a nail-biter and more of a foregone conclusion.

For another, the exertions of the morning, coupled with the stress and strain of their various labors from the previous week, were finally catching up to them, steadily sapping their enthusiasm for the action taking place on the gridiron and slowly sinking them deeper and deeper into the luxuriously plush embrace of their overstuffed seat cushions.

Lulled by the whirring air conditioner and satiated by their midday feast, Eddie and Dom grew increasingly sluggish and heavy-lidded. The beginning of the second half found Eddie and his eldest boy laid out in comfortable repose, Dominic sprawled across the recliner and Eddie stretched out on the living-room couch.

For at least one blessed afternoon, both father and son had successfully pushed aside the myriad cares and worries and burdens of their daily existences, managing to attain states of complete relaxation and utter contentment. Safe and secure in the embryonic privacy of the family home, they rest; breathing sighs of satisfaction, exhaling long and slow as satiated smokers, lounging in the cool flickering darkness, sipping on arctic soft drinks, watching their beloved New York Giants overrun the New Orleans Saints.

Just when it seemed the day could not possibly improve any further, it did. Midway through the fourth quarter, the phone rang. Both men were jolted out of a state of semi-sleep by the sudden clamor. Eddie fished for the mobile handset, found it under the end table, and mouthed a drowsy greeting. As soon as he realized who was on the other end, his face lit up and he nudged Dominic excitedly, a huge smile on his face.

"It's for you."

Dominic took the phone. The conversation was brief.

"Hello? Yes, this is Dominic. Who is this? Oh, Ok. Well yes, yes, of course officer. Yes of course. I'll be right there. Ok, I'll be right down. Goodbye. And thanks."

After he hung up, he turned to his father, a broad smile ringing both of their faces.

"Dad that was the department, the police department." It was a Lt. Daniels

"Ya I know him that's Lt. Jack Daniels."

"They want to see me."

"I know."

"Right now."

"Well, you better get down there."

"Do you know what this means?"

"I do. Your turn on the list must have come up."

New recruits in the Corrunoside Police department were ranked according to a list. When openings occurred, the next name on the list was the next job candidate. Through friends in the police department, Eddie knew that Dom's name was due to come up soon.

"Well, I better get going."

"Son."

"Yes."

"I want you to know that I'm very, very proud of you."

Eddie extended his hand for a shake, but Dominic ignored it, grabbing his dad in a massive bear hug.

Down at the station, Dom's excitement level was high. He bounded up the station house steps. Inside, however, things took an unexpectedly negative turn.

Instead of being ushered into the office of a Lt. Daniels or some other expected bigwig, he is led to seat at a table in a bare, intimidating interrogation room. After being left to wonder why he is there for about twenty minutes (and shivering in the uncomfortably cold air conditioning), two plainclothes officers, detectives Malaka and Toilette, entered the room, pull up chairs, and sit across from him. They introduce themselves.

"I'm Detective Malaka and this is Detective R. Toilette. I want to say hello, and I want to thank you for your prompt response to our summons."

"Hi, and you're welcome. Only I wasn't aware this was a summons."

"Well, not in any legal sense. I want to make it clear that we consider you here on a completely voluntary basis. If it any time you wish to leave, be our guest."

"Have I done something wrong detectives?"

"You? No of course not. The reason we asked you down here is that we wanted to ask you a couple of questions about your father … just any observations you may have made while volunteering at his store."

"You're asking me about my father? That's why I was brought down here? I thought my number came up. I thought I was being officially told that I had a job on the force. I got to tell you, this is a really, really sneaky move."

"Be that as it may, and you're free to formulate your own opinion of me, in my eyes I'm simply doing my job. I apologize if you find that offensive."

"What I find offensive is to be ambushed here under false pretenses."

"Hey, nobody promised this was going to be a job interview you were coming down here for."

"Nobody told me I was coming down here for an interrogation either."

"This is not a legal interrogation."

"What's the difference?"

"The difference is, let me reiterate once more, you are free to go at any time. We only thought you might be interested in helping your father out. You know, maybe our interest in him is misplaced. Maybe you could provide the piece of information that clears him of suspicion. Cooperation is always the easiest path."

"Am I under arrest?"

"Of course not."

"Then I'm free to go?"

"Of course, we only wanted to give you and your dad a chance to get your side of the story onto the record."

"Right. I don't know a whole lot about all this, but I do know that this kind of stuff should all go through my dad's attorney from now on. I think we're done here. I'm leaving."

"That's your prerogative."

Detective Malaka shrugged his shoulders theatrically and cleared a path for Dominic to leave. Not another word was said. Still, Dominic was in a cold sweat as he shut the interrogation room door. It is on wobbly legs that he heads to the parking lot and his car. He can think of nowhere else to go but straight back to his dad's place to apprise his old man of the bad news.

When Eddie heard the story, he did his best to suppress his rage. For Dom's sake, he acted like the incident was no big deal, does everything he can to minimize events. But it is a big deal. Some jerk in the department has targeted a completely innocent member of his family.

From the looks of Dominic, the whole incident had shaken him up pretty good. Dom wasn't not the only one shaken up. Eddie, in addition to being mad as hell about the situation, was more than a little bit scared. This was his first inclination that when dealing with the random, petty, and immensely massive nature of the powers involved therein, being innocent may not be enough.

۷ ۷ ۷

After repeated reassurances, Dominic calmed down enough to leave. After he left, Eddie made some phone calls, poked around, and asked some questions. It didn't take long for Eddie to figure out who the prime mover was behind the Corrunoside Police Department's little Gestapo ambush of his boy. It seemed that Detective Malaka had a son Dominic's age who aspired to become a police officer.

Malaka's kid was directly behind Dominic on the list. In addition to the bonus of rattling Eddie's cage by hauling Dominic in for questioning, if Malaka could paint Dominic with the same brush that

Eddie is currently being smeared with or even succeed in throwing a little suspicion his way, his kid can easily leapfrog into position to be hired by the department.

Malaka's name was disturbingly familiar to Eddie. They were already budding enemies due to an incident that took place not to long before. Eddie had been on duty when a call came through concerning a residential fire in progress. When the men and the engines reached the address, they found no smoke and no fire; it had been a false alarm. Procedure for false alarms dictates that, after the fire department processes the scene and compiles an incident report, the police conduct a separate walk-through of the premises and question any persons of interest.

During the police walk-through of this particular house, a tremendous amount of petty vandalism and serious property damage occurred. Furniture was broken; epithets and threats were carved into wooden tables; filed paperwork had been pulled out of filing cabinets and strewn about the place; drawers were pulled from bureaus, then upturned and emptied; rugs were stained with eggs, milk, and urine; foodstuffs from the refrigerator got splattered against the wall; and a large potted palm had been defecated in.

The whole thing was a huge potential embarrassment to the city and many other power brokers and, therefore, kept far under the radar. But Eddie heard through the grapevine that the entire false alarm and subsequent house trashing were acts of reprisal against a whistle-blower in the police department who many of the cops viewed as a rat for reveling the unspoken rules and regulations of police culture, thereby bridging the blue wall of silence.

After doing some digging on his own, Eddie heard that a patrolman called in the false alarm, so that the police could strike back against an Officer Davis, who was the only man to tell the truth concerning the police beating of an innocent local man in the parking lot of a local pub. On every street corner in Corrunoside some one put signs that said Ron U Rat.

Eddie was only involved in the matter peripherally. The police who perpetrated the false alarm and accompanying sabotage blamed both crimes on the firefighters. Eddie was, as usual, an outspoken advocate for his men. He knew that the stories of the police who were involved did not align and failed to hold up to scrutiny.

Enraged that dirty cops would cast such poisonously corrosive aspersions at his men just to shield their own wrongdoing, Eddie vigorously made his case, quietly but firmly making it clear to all relevant authorities that he would not stand for a whitewash of the guilty cops that would use his guys as scapegoats.

Despite the fact that nothing ever came of the matter and no formal action was ever taken, Eddie's aggressive style managed to ruffle the feathers of numerous law enforcement professionals. Sergeant Figuttles among those offended was the man who led the raid of the whistle-blower's residence. And none other than Detective Malaka, ended up catching a lot of heat over the matter, not as much as he should have, but more than he had bargained for.

Although he had faced no lasting consequences for his actions (such as the potential prison time for such a heinous criminal act), Malaka felt as though a dark cloud had settled over his career and, by extension, his life. His life and career were almost interchangeable entities. EVIL

First, he was written up by a superior for an unrelated offense. His superior, who had never taken any form of disciplinary action against him before, made it plain that he'd gone a slap on the wrist for an infraction, any infraction, he'd been barred from officially punishing Malaka for the anything related to the actual vandalism of the other officer's house, due to the fact that it would leave a record and an accompanying paper trail that an intrepid news reporter might be able to sniff out.

Next, suspicion about his involvement in the planning and execution of the sabotage—along with speculation about the potential leadership and crucial organizational role he was alleged to have assumed—was strongly hinted at in a key written performance evaluation that could have brought him a long sought-after promotion and raise and had it not contained such damaging, ultimately damning innuendo.

The reality was that Malaka dodged a bullet. (The rumor was that he caught a councilman coming out of an adult store and he was going to let it out of the bag). Neither the police nor the politicians had any interest in allowing the unsettlingly despicable details of Malaka's thuggish strong-arm maneuvering to enter the public's realm of awareness.

In Malaka's own warped mind, however, he'd been unfairly singled out as a lone fall guy because he had the balls to do what everybody else in the department had felt like doing. From Malaka's point of view, he was the victim. The primary person he blamed for this victimization was Eddie.

They'd only exchanged words on one occasion, and then only briefly. Both men, however, had come away from the short exchange with a piercingly fierce, gut-level dislike for one another that was almost primal in its intensity. It was in a random hallway of the police headquarters that their paths had first crossed.

Malaka was on his way in to answer some questions. Eddie was on his way out after a meeting with the police chief that he had requested to make sure that it was understood, at the highest echelons to which he had direct access that his men had engaged in no wrongdoing. It was Malaka who confronted Eddie, reaching out for his shoulder as he strode past.

"Hey Mac ... hey, excuse me. You got a minute? I wondered if I could have a word with you."

"Sure. What's on your mind?"

"You don't know who the hell I am, do you?"

"Can't say that I do. What's this all about?"

The conversation deteriorated from that point, becoming less and less civil with each volley and response. The gist of it, however, was that Malaka promised Eddie he'd remember him. Someday Eddie would be sorry he'd ever heard the name Malaka and for dragging his name through the mud with wild allegations.

"I'm not accusing anybody Mister. I'm simply making sure everybody knows that my guys had nothing to do with any false alarms or house trashing of one of our brother patrolman," Eddie had recalled saying.

It was to no avail, of course. Malaka was past the point of dialogue. He wasn't listening and did not bother to respond. He had simply repeated his promise, spun on his heel, stalked down the hallway, and plowed through the staircase doors, out of sight.

Despite his many corruptions and flaws, Malaka would prove to be a man of his word. He had certainly wasted little time making good on the promise he'd snarled in that neutrally colored, blandly carpeted bureaucratic hallway such a short time ago. And Eddie already felt sorry he'd ever heard the name Malaka. Before long, he'd be much sorrier. His nightmare was merely getting under way.

🔥 🔥 🔥

About a half-mile before they'd arrived, the first thing the firefighters became aware of was the smell. The stench, a mingling of aromas including scorched tar, melted petroleum products, and a not-quite-definable cocktail of various chemicals, was awful, almost unbearable. A dense black smoke of burning rubber snaked unsteadily upward on the wind, meandering into the sky.

Seconds after the scent had first assailed them, the men piled purposefully out of two trucks that had pulled into the parking lot adjacent to the fire. Unless you were a local, you would be unable to identify the burning structure through the oozy thick darkness of the smoke, fire, haze, and assorted debris. Everybody on the call, however, had grown up around Corrunoside twsp, or lived there long enough to know what was happening. The local Midas muffler shop was in the process of burning to the ground in a blaze of foul and acrid flames.

The fire turned out to be a memorable one, fairly remarkable for several reasons. It took quite a bit of time to get the stubborn fire under control. Also, several firefighters were overcome by noxious fumes and had to be treated at the local hospital. Finally, and perhaps most notably, this fire marked the grand finale of a harrowing serial string of deliberately set blazes. The Midas conflagration was the fire that brought the arson rampage to an abrupt end and resulted in the apprehension of the elusive culprits.

As soon as the call came through, some of the more seasoned veterans immediately expected another occurrence of arson. Midas shops, predominantly constructed of metal and glass, are not exactly tinderboxes. Also, the timing was right. Following the established pattern of the arsonists, investigators had expected that another strike was imminent.

When it all came down, however, it was not ripe timing, veteran hunches, or detailed, cutting-edge forensic investigative technologies that tripped up the perpetrators. Instead, it was old-fashioned police work and lightning-fast follow-through that finally did the trick and yielded the high-profile collars.

The first break in the case occurred when an anonymous fireman phoned a police sergeant with information about who was involved in the arsons and where they might strike next. This sergeant happened to be an upstanding member of the department, so instead of suppressing the lead, he clued in his officers on what they should be looking for to catch the criminals and prevent the next arson.

To a surprisingly substantial degree, the efforts of the police were aided by their prey. The so-called perfect criminals finally made several costly mistakes. Whether it was the result of overconfidence, hubris, or just plain sloppiness on the part of the fire starters remains unclear to this day. Unlike many of the other arsons, this one took place in broad daylight. An alert officer on routine patrol (who had been briefed by the sergeant that very morning) spotted a van that matched the description of the one that had been linked to the arsons. It was parked directly across the street from the Midas.

Inspecting the scene, the officer detected signs of forced entry and immediately called for back-up. Had this initial call for back-up (not to mention the four subsequent calls) not been mysteriously delayed, the muffler business might well have been salvaged and the bad guys would have likely been caught red-handed inside.

By the time the responding officer was finally able to summon help, the blaze was well under way and he was miles away, in a hot pursuit car chase straight out of a Hollywood movie, complete with hairpin turns, triple-digit speeds, and narrowly averted collisions.

In the end, the officer got the guys. Five of them to be exact. Before the fire site had even cooled to the point that it could be searched and the tell-tale flare could be recovered, the band of arsonists was already in the process of being booked and fingerprinted. They turned out to be the same exact group of guys that Chief Rumpkey had warned a couple of months earlier. And they all had worked with Dennis at the store at one time or another. Every last one was a volunteer firefighter and friends of Dennis's.

Word of the bust spread through the Corrunoside firefighting community with wildfire speed. In the firehouse that day, there were enough feigned expressions of shock and surprise to put a stage filled with actors to shame. Guys who had pretty much known all along what was going on had to pretend that the news was some kind of bombshell revelation.

It turns out that a huge number of the men knew to some extend tidbits of information that they should have shared or revealed more of the arsons than they had let on. To the enduring shame of the department, the identity of those behind the arsons was a dirty little open secret. If they were searingly honest with themselves, most of the professional firefighters that had knowledge would have to admit to varying degrees of guilt.

Within an organization vested with so much public trust and so much social responsibility, even mere silence in the name of minding one's own business constitutes a form of obstruction of justice.

"I don't want to get involved."

"I'm no rat."

These are not excuses when lives are on the line. Deep down, they all knew it. Only Eddie and a handful of other guys had done what they could and behaved with the honor and decency that their commitment to the department and to public safety had demanded and expected of them. The only reward Eddie could expect for his exemplary behavior would be silent resentment, unconscious and unspoken reproach, and the knowledge that he would now be more of a marked man than ever. (Director Munsterhed needed only one more thing a leader of the pack). Guess who?

When he was apprised of the news by a probie who had knocked on the door of his office where he was finishing up some outstanding paperwork, those disturbing realities were the furthest thoughts from his mind. At the time, Eddie felt vindicated. Many of his troubles, he believed, would simply wither beneath the sunshine glare of truth that seemed to be bursting out everywhere, shredding countless cloud layers of obfuscation and deception.

Unable to help himself and nearly overwhelmed with relief and elation, Eddie decided to take a spin by the fire site on his way home from the station. By the time he saw the muffler shop, only a pitiful, smoldering husk remained of the sleek, shiny, modern-looking storefront he'd driven past just the day before. Through his air-conditioning vents, Eddie crinkled his nose at the offensive odor of singed oil, burned rubber, and molten rust. The mixture was stubbornly persistent, lingering in his car long after he had passed.

Although Eddie didn't stop, he decelerated until he was moving slowly enough to take in the entire scene. The tableau was a sobering one. A mass of police cars and several fire trucks were parked at skewed angles within a roped-off area in front of the former car maintenance shop. Eddie strained to catch a glimpse of the guilty parties, not knowing that they had been tracked down off site and already taken into custody. All Eddie had heard was that the arsonists had been apprehended after burning down the muffler shop. He wasn't told of many key details until later that evening.

The most arresting image that struck Eddie wasn't of one of the guilty men being led away in handcuffs. The man that attracted Eddie's attention may indeed have been guilty, but he was not a member of the group who had directly participated in the arsons. In Eddie's mind, however, he had aided and abetted them so much he might as well have been shooting the flare gun himself. So intently was Eddie staring at his boss that he almost rear-ended the car in front of him.

The troubled brow of the fire chief, Eddie had blindly trusted for so many years was gleaming with a dripping sheen of profuse sweat. The chief was leaning against the tailgate of his Bronco, bathed in perspiration, pale as a dead man. Eddie flinched when he thought he saw the chief lock eyes with him and catches him staring. Then he realized the chief might have been staring off in his general direction but what he was actually seeing was nothing at all. He had the 1,000-yard stare of the freshly traumatized. His gaze was frighteningly empty.

As Eddie pulled away, his last glimpse was of the chief leaning against the edge of the truck, which seemed to be the only thing propping him up on his feet. He appeared shrunken, hunched over, guilt-ridden, and utterly defeated. The full awareness of just how much trouble he was in appeared to be hitting him square in the face, over and over again. Heavily, wearily, the chief shook his head and buried it in his hands.

Turning a corner and disappearing from sight, Eddie shook his own head and whistled a long, low note to himself. He wasn't angry or vengeful or jubilant. He was just relieved that the truth would no longer be squelched or spun or diluted to a palatable strength. It would all come out in the wash, was what Eddie kept thinking as he continued to make his way home. All the dirty laundry would soon be hung out to dry. That was Eddie's expectation. As the rest of the story will demonstrate all too clearly, the only thing hung out to dry would be Eddie.

That night, when Eddie arrived home, he was disconcerted to find that all the lights were out and nobody was there. He had sped the rest of the distance from the muffler shop because he couldn't wait to share the good news of the bust with his wife. Now she was nowhere to be found. Eddie took a shower, fixed himself some dinner, and settled down in front of the television to wait for her.

By the time he heard her car pull in the driveway, it had gotten very late, well past one in the morning. Eddie woke with a start that almost sent him rolling off the couch. He realized that he must have fallen asleep while he was waiting. He stole a quick glance at his watch. According to the time, he'd been asleep for at least four hours.

It was not at all like Renee to stay out so late and not even leave him a note to let him know what was going on. In fact, except for special occasions and the odd night out with friends or family, Renee hardly ever left the house at all for social reasons.

Why now? A sudden surge of raw jealousy coursed through Eddie's veins. He suppressed it. In all their years of marriage, she'd never given him any grounds to be suspicious of her and, therefore, she deserved the benefit of the doubt. He was not going to jump all over her for no good reason. Still, Eddie couldn't help but wonder where the hell had she been all this time.

As he heard the key turn in the deadbolt, Eddie rose to greet her but then thought better of it. Instead, he rested his head back on the couch cushion, not quite feigning sleep but also not making it obvious that he was awake.

Renee entered the foyer then paused, waiting for her eyes to adjust to the dim light before proceeding any further. The TV set was providing the only illumination, so it was dark enough for Eddie to observe his wife without her being able to watch him watching her. Why hadn't she flipped on the light? Eddie wondered. Was she being considerate for his sake or was she being sneaky?

Thinking about it for a moment, Eddie reached the unfortunate conclusion that the latter explanation was far more plausible. Blinded by the dark, she had not yet noticed him across the room on the couch.

Thus, there was no reason—besides, of course, stealth—not switch on a light. Also, she had removed her high heels and was tiptoeing toward the staircase as quietly as possible.

As she walked across the room, Eddie found himself assailed by a cornucopia of clashing scents. She was, for some reason, wearing her best perfume, and lots of it. For Eddie, this was a red flag. Very rarely did the bottle of extravagant French stuff leave her vanity drawer. He couldn't, for the life of him, remember the last time she'd worn it for him. Perfume was not the only odor clinging to her clothes. The other scents—bar scents, the faint mingling of secondhand tobacco and some fruit-based liqueur—were far less pleasant.

When she entered his field of vision, he saw that she looked absolutely stunning. No doubt about it: in her silk blouse and knee-length skirt, she was dressed to kill. She had to pass by the couch on the way to the stairs. This was the point that Eddie chose to speak to her. He nearly startled her out of her skin.

"I've been waiting up. What happened to you? I was worried. You can't leave a note?"

Recovering herself almost instantly, she spun a tale about an old college roommate and a last-minute outing. There were holes in her story, but he couldn't bear to think about that. He believed her because he wanted to believe her, because he didn't want to think about what the alternatives were to believing her. The next day she apologized and said it wouldn't happen again. It appeared that everything was forgotten.

Chapter 12

The stunt Detective Malaka had pulled on Dominic (calling him into the police station under the pretense of a job interview, and then giving him the third degree) failed to yield any incriminating information that could be turned into ammunition against Eddie.

That wasn't the point of the exercise anyway. It was well known that Eddie was a devoted family man and that he was especially close to his sons. Any attempt to get at Eddie by way of his children (a tactic of the SS in WW 11), although extremely unethical and unfair, was bound to have a devastating impact.

Once Malaka had figured this out (or, more accurately, once someone had pointed it out to him), he wasted little time zeroing in on and exploiting the weakness. Thus, although the interrogation had ended before it began; it managed to serve its intended purpose on a number of levels.

Malaka sensed that his gutless power play had been a roaring success. He was all smiles after Dominic stormed out of the interview room. Malaka commented to his partner, "We really rattled his cage."

"The kid?" Detective Toilette had asked with a nonchalant shrug of his shoulders as if to ask "so what?" Toilette obviously didn't think it was very difficult to ambush an unsuspecting young man, (Toilette was really a fair guy it's just that everybody would shit on him) flashing guns and badges and authority and shake him up. He wasn't sharing Malaka's sense of pride. It certainly hadn't been one of his finer hours. In fact, he wasn't at all feeling very good about himself, his partner, or what they'd just been a part of. He hadn't become a cop to play underhanded storm-trooper games that used sons against fathers and tried to pit them against one another.

"No, his old man."

"How can you tell? He wasn't even here."

"Oh, he'll be here. Mark my words. It's a matter of time. We're in the homestretch now. This is what's known as the end game. We're about to crack this case wide open."

"What case?"

"You'll see."

"I hope I do and damn soon, 'cause all I see now is an overeager partner with a Paul Bunyan–sized axe to grind."

"Hey now, hold on just a minute. What are you implying?"

"I don't imply anything. I call 'em like I see 'em. This Eddie character, I don't know yet if there's fire to go with the smoke signals people have been sending us about him or if it's just a bunch of hot air being stoked by rivals. I do know that you have had a hard-on for him from day one."

"Look, I won't deny I don't like the guy, but this isn't personal. He's dirty and I'm going to prove it."

Malaka rose to exit, his face contorted in an ugly, power-maddened mask of hypocrisy and false righteousness, the same dangerous combination of zeal and blindness that burned witches at the stake, launched inquisitions, and inspired crusades. In the old days, they spoke about these types of men in fear-hushed whispers, cursing them as despots and tyrants. Nowadays, they simply call them terrorists.

Toilette walked out of the station to get some air, worry and guilt creasing his thoughtful forehead. Detective Malaka's brow betrayed no such self-doubt; it shined smooth under the glow of the overhead lights as he swaggered back to his desk, patting the gun on his hip like a cowboy, a smug smirk curling up toward a nose that smelled blood in the water. He could not help himself from salivating as he sat at his desk, imagining Eddie's reactions, savoring his simmering revenge.

In his wildest fantasies and daydreams, however, even Malaka was unaware of how completely he had achieved his objective. The Dominic thing was utterly maddening to Eddie. It had gotten under his skin in a way that few things had before. Several days had passed since the event. Still, Eddie could barely sleep nor eat. Whenever he thought about the incident, it made him so angry he had to summon all of his self-control to keep his temper in check.

In addition to the anger Malaka's violation of decency inspired, Eddie was tormented by an ever-growing sense of helplessness and fear. *What would Malaka and his cronies pull next?* He wondered. *If they didn't respect family boundaries, was anything off limits? Where would it all end?* Questions like these were constantly on Eddie's mind. He was in a state of unceasing and relentless tension, bedeviled by a sense of impending doom, like a condemned man waiting to be escorted to his demise.

After a few days of wrestling with the problem on his own, Eddie decided he could use some advice, or at least some sort of a sounding board. He turned to his old friend Keith for guidance, one of the few people left that he was sure he could trust. They met over coffee at the corner deli. Keith tried to keep it light, making a joke about the dark rings under Eddie's eyes.

The truth of the matter, however, was that Keith was concerned. He'd never seen Eddie so frazzled and burdened. His longtime friend had been under serious pressure before. Indeed, it was a key part of both of their job descriptions. Until now, the Eddie he knew had thrived under stress and strain. This time, though, was clearly a different situation.

Eddie filled Keith in on the basics of the situation, which came as no surprise. Keith had heard rumors about the investigation, so he more or less knew what was going on.

"The thing is, I honestly haven't done anything wrong, so I'm tired of sitting back waiting for the other shoe to drop. I want to get out in front of this thing."

"Ok, so let's figure it out. What's that best way to do that?"

"Well, I was thinking I'd grab the bull by the horns, just go down to the police station tomorrow, confront Malaka, and find out what their intentions are."

"If you do that, and I'm not sure that's the right way to go about it, but if you do that, you'd be crazy to walk in there without an attorney."

"I suppose you're right. I just don't like the message that sends."

"Eddie, this isn't some cop procedural show on TV, where everybody plays fair and by the book and does the right thing. This is real life. You've got everything on the line here, your business, your family, your reputation, your freedom, your life. If you decide to go downtown, don't do it without your lawyer."

After a bit of deliberation, Eddie chose to follow Keith's words of cautious counsel. Bright an dearly the next day, he called and made an appointment to come down and talk to Detective Malaka and Detective Toilette. At 2:30 the same afternoon, he arrived at Corrunoside police headquarters with his lawyer, Lou Delomre, by his side.

At the front desk they gave their names and stated their business. After a fairly significant wait, a side door opened and a uniformed officer appeared and motioned for them to follow. Eddie and his attorney were led up a flight of stairs and down a hallway into an interview room. Inside the somber, sterile room, Detective Malaka, Detective Toilette, and a serious-looking, slight, bespectacled man in a suit and tie were already seated around the far corner of a large rectangular table.

Cursory greetings were exchanged as Eddie and Mr. Delomre took their seats opposite the trio across the table. Mr. Delomre began the discussion, inquiring about the identity of the well-dressed but over weight, pocked marked and ugly as sin, stranger in their midst. The woman was introduced as Det. Kathy Hober. She was present; it was explained, to serve as a representative from the Prosecutor's office. With the hind of scotch in the room she could have been from Benigan's who knew.

"Although I serve as a special investigative detective attached to the Prosecutor's office, I'm here in a completely unofficial capacity,"

Det. Hober stated. "My purpose today is to serve as a liaison between the police department and the Prosecutor's office and report back to the prosecutor's on what transpires during the course of this meeting. **_MEANING_** (Lets see how stupid this lawyer is so we can screw his client) that is unless, of course, there are any objections to my presence."

"This is a highly unusual occurrence," commented Mr. Delomre.

"It's a highly unusual case. Listen, you two set up a meeting with the two detectives in charge of this investigation, not with me; I understand that. But let me just say that my attendance at this meeting may very well end up being most advantageous to your client."

"How?"

"Well, my interest here is to find out if there is any substance here, if this case is worth pursuing to the next level. If I am able to obtain satisfactory answers to my questions, we might be able to close the book on this entire matter today."

"I don't think I'm comfortable with the appropriateness of—"

At this point, Eddie put a hand on Mr. Delorme's shoulder to cut him off. He stared across the table, looking straight into the PROSECUTORS investigator's cold and gray eyes.

"I've got nothing to hide," Eddie asserted. "She can stay."

Mr. Delorme's knee-jerk reaction was to protest his client's decision, but one brief look at the determination etched across Eddie's face stopped him in his tracks. His decision was final. The experience Mr. Delorme has accrued as an attorney had given him enough insight into human nature to know there was nothing he could say that would persuade him otherwise.

Before they got under way, Malaka couldn't resist making a comment about the incriminating image projected by Eddie being "lawyered up" before any formal charges were filed.

"Why would an innocent man—a man who insists, who swears hand over fist that he's got nothing at all to hide—why on earth would an absolute angel such as this decide that the only safe course of action is to only show up here if can hide behind the protection of a fancy mouthpiece, rather than hashing things out and clearing things up man to man? He claims his only aim is to shoot straight and speak plain, but then he goes and shows up here with an expert double-talker in tow. Honestly, it really just doesn't make any sense to me."

You piece of garbage. After what you did to my son are you kidding?

Eddie just couldn't keep quiet following Malaka's inflammatory soliloquy; Eddie had to clutch the sides of his chair with all his strength to avoid doing something rash. The days and nights of suppressed anger toward his persecutor rushed to the surface, but Eddie bit back as much of his rage as possible, trying to keep his cool and summoning the wisdom and strength from the Gods and maturity he needed to not grab Malaka by the throat and rip his heart out through his neck.

Calling on every possible molecule of self-control and discipline, Eddie dug his fingers deep into the cheap, cracked pleather-cushioned arms of his chair until his knuckles were white. Breathing deeply, in and out, concentrating on maintaining his impassive facial expression so he wouldn't give Malaka the satisfaction of seeing him too upset, Eddie allowed the most of the sting of the insult to pass over him. Thankfully the detectives selected this interval to open up the manila folders in front of them and get down to business without further taunts or provocations.

For Eddie, the next two hours were a revelation. As Malaka and his partner barraged Eddie with a series of rapid-fire questions, he was stunned by both the scope and sheer outrageousness of the allegations they confronted him with. All of their queries either directly pertained or were somehow related to the business practices and finances of the store.

One saving grace was that the early phase of the interrogation focused on accusations that were so absurdly outlandish and easy to debunk that much of Eddie's apprehensions and tensions eased. He had a relatively simple time explaining himself and was able to offer a fair amount of corroborating evidence to buttress his assertions.

Initially, at least, Eddie's explanations appeared to convince the trio of skeptical investigators before him. What he could read of their attitudes led him to believe that things were being cleared up and that he had a legitimate chance to resolve the entire matter before it went any further.

It is important to point out that from this first sit-down onward, Eddie's version of events will remain consistent and unchanged. Moreover, Eddie could provide concrete substantiation for every statement of fact he made that is in any way doubted or disputed. He and his attorney were able to offer up a serious amount of meticulous and credible documentation to support the veracity of their version of events.

Even Malaka later admitted to his partner that, throughout the session, Eddie appeared to be the epitome of cooperation and sincerity, answering questions truthfully and completely, even when his lawyer objected strenuously or advised him to remain silent.

Despite the vocal exhortations of his attorney to restrict his answers to the subject at hand and to truncate his replies as much as possible, Eddie elected on several occasions to volunteer extra information where he felt it was relevant. His general demeanor was open and unguarded.

Eddie was pleased to finally know exactly what he was facing and be able to respond to it. Ever since he first caught wind of the murmured rumors about the store's questionable business practices, he had been waiting for this day: the day he could finally go on record with his side of the story.

Although most people would be threatened by the prospect of being questioned on police turf by adversarial detectives, Eddie, after all that he had been through and all the backdoor whisperings he had to endure, was actually eager to push the entire affair into the open light of day. He believed that once he was able to talk frankly with the authorities and disclose everything he knew, all misunderstandings would be eliminated, the matter will be put to rest, and his name and reputation restored.

There was no question in Eddie's mind that he had done the right thing by dealing with this mess head on. Throughout the duration of the entire session, there were only a few times he questioned or second-guessed his decision to assume such a forthright stance. It was toward the end of the meeting when doubt reared its head for the first time.

Eddie's guard had been lowered slightly as a result of his exemplary success he had establishing his innocence. On all counts, he'd demonstrated himself to be an aboveboard businessman unjustly accused of wrongdoing.

Every question that had been raised about the store's finances and record keeping had been answered to the best of his knowledge. They may be able to charge him with sloppy record keeping and a few minor accounting errors, Eddie figured, but that was about it.

Furthermore, all the ledger entries that have been called into question were throwbacks to when he and Dennis were partners. Malaka himself conceded that the books had been immaculate since the date Eddie had taken over.

As the meeting wound down, Eddie had reason to feel pretty positive about the interchange. Then Malaka pounces. In an instant, the accusations bandied about the table geyser skyward from misdemeanors that can reasonably be attributed to carelessness or negligence to willfully intentional felonies.

Eddie could hardly believe his ears: Malaka had accused him of being a thief. Not in so many words, of course, but the clear implication is that the store is dealing in stolen goods and goods obtained improperly by various public officials.

These are serious charges. Eddie was thoroughly unnerved to find himself under the ugly taint of this type of suspicion. He is, in fact, completely blameless. The basic fact is Eddie did not know. He and his lawyer had come prepared, toting in all kinds of files and paperwork. However, records of the specific merchandise and particular transaction receipts that Malaka asked about were nowhere to be found.

Perhaps Dennis swiped them to protect himself. Perhaps Dennis was engaged in activities that he didn't want connected to a paper trail. The problem was that Dennis might indeed have been involved in shady dealings. Eddie can't begin to hazard a guess. Only Dennis can help them get to the bottom of this topic. Eddie told his questioners they would have to ask his ex-partner because he honestly has no idea what they are talking about. He has to plead ignorance. He has no choice.

They appeared to accept his word, at least at this preliminary stage, but there was no denying that the gap in his testimony looked bad, made him seem evasive. It erased a lot of credibility he had accrued in the previous ninety minutes.

Malaka had touched on stolen goods earlier in the interrogatory. However, he had done so in a manner that had been patently absurd, twisting Eddie's confrontation with the truckers at Dennis's father's trailers to make it seem as if he had been complicit in the robbery. In fact, he'd been the one to report it to police. Perhaps Dennis's father had been trying to set up Eddie and that's why he had been so miffed over Eddie's decision to contact the authorities after the incident.

Malaka's questions about the store were much more disconcerting than the obvious fishing expedition about the truckers. They were specific and numerous. He made it seem like Eddie and Dennis had been running a fencing operation.

Eventually the questioning moved to another subject, and Eddie recovered his poise. The rest of the sit-down was relatively painless. Malaka gave a brief recap of the ground they'd covered, looked at his watch and then across the table at Eddie and his lawyer.

"That should about do it."

"We can go now? We're all finished here?"

"I think we're adjourned. Unless you or your attorney have any questions of us?"

"Just one," interjects Mr. Delorme, who had been conspicuously quiet for some time.

"Fire away."

"What is Eddie's current legal status?"

"Legal status?"

"Yes, is he for example, going to be classified from here on out as a suspect, a person of interest, or what?"

Is my client a target or under arrest, is an indictment being considered."

I'll just say he not under arrest.

"That doesn't exactly answer my question."

"Come down tomorrow and drop by my office. I'll be able to give you a definite answer pending our review of the case file following today's meeting.

"I'll be in your office first thing in the morning."

"Fine with me. I'll have the coffee ready."

As Eddie and Mr. Delorme rose from their chairs, Malaka put a palm to his forehead, and then makes a gentle, almost apologetic motion with his other hand and requests they wait for just a second.

"Just one more thing."

Who does this guy think he is, Columbo? Eddie remembers asking himself.

Mr. Delorme asks "What's the problem now?"

"No problem. It's just, while I've got you guys here; there was just one issue I wanted to clear up. Hopefully we can wipe the slate clean right here and now and I can get it off my plate. If you can bear with me for a brief moment, I'll be right back."

With that, Malaka rose nonchalantly from his chair and left the interview room. When he returned a few minutes later, he had a thick file folder under his left arm. He plunked it down on the table and opened it wide, allowing Eddie to get a good look at its contents.

Eddie only needed to read a few random lines off the proffered paperwork before he realized what the thrust of Malaka's next few questions would be. A wave of horrified disbelief washed over him; it is a sensation not unlike the one feels while embroiled in a nightmare, only there is no waking from this surrealism. Coolly, Malaka continued to execute his game plan.

"As you know, we've had a rash of arson-related crimes of late. I just want to establish what the extent of your involvement was in these crimes."

What? Are you nuts? What the hell you trying to do?

"Anything I heard I told the chief and also watched and heard one of my men, Hector, tell Chief Rumpkey who one of the arsonist was…"

Malaka bulldozed Eddie's subsequent protests with mounds of superficial evidence linking him to the suspects through the store. Actually, the only links between the arson suspects and the store existed because of Dennis, who had hired some of the men to help him out. Malaka also accused Eddie of knowing about the crimes but failing to come forward and report them to the proper authorities. Despite the fact that this was patently untrue, Eddie had no proof to support his denials.

Malaka and Eddie both knew if the detectives had hard evidence, Eddie would be in handcuffs. Eventually Malaka ran out of gas and the proceedings came to a close, for real this time.

Eddie left the station cautiously optimistic, feeling that, despite the bumps in the road at the end of the meeting, his proactive approach toward the situation had done his cause more good than harm. His initial confidence, however, began to ebb as the day wore on. By evening, Eddie was chafed and agitated by the questions he was unable to answer and the implications that Malaka was able to make as a result.

The main thorn in his side was, of course, the idea that he was somehow complicit in the horrific campaign of serial arsons that did over $5 million in damage to his own community, shamed and stained the name of Corrunoside's volunteer firefighting tradition (and, by extension, all individual firefighters, volunteer or professional), and very nearly resulted in a slew of serious injuries and loss of life.

What was particularly maddening about Malaka's audacious charge, above and beyond its transparent motives (for example, that it was obviously driven on an organizational level by the political imperative that the police department "get a fireman, any fireman," and on an individual level by Malaka's personal animosity and twisted desire to avenge Eddie's spirited defense of his crew when Malaka attempted to use them to cover up his key role in the vandalism/intimidation of a fellow officer), was its utter baseless ness and absolute opposition to the truth.

In actuality, Eddie had risked his life on more than one occasion immersed in smoke and flames, a SCBA on his back and an axe handle, hose nozzle, or ladder rung in his hand, fighting the ravages wrought by the arsonists. He was the highest-ranking official in the department who dared to disagree with the prevailing view and the official party line promulgated by every member of the brass that the fires were being set by "a couple of neighborhood kids."

He was one of only two firefighters who questioned the progress of the internal investigation and dissented from its preliminary findings. When locker room rumors that implicated specific volunteers reached a crescendo and everybody else was busy contributing to the behind-the-scenes gossip while simultaneously conspiring to keep it secret, Eddie and firefighter Hector Idnal did not hesitate to follow established procedures and protocols, promptly reporting the information directly to the chief and appropriate personnel above him in the chain of command.

When the other firefighter was abruptly exiled to a rural outpost on the edge of the district (where nothing ever happened and there was no hope of advance) and Eddie asked why his friend was suddenly absent from the duty roster, he was told it was due to his "big mouth." With that statement, Eddie's superiors were delivering him the message, in no uncertain terms, that he could be next.

Despite the fact that he knew he was putting his career on the line and despite the frustration and alienation that comes with being a lone voice in the wilderness, Eddie persisted in his efforts to bring the culprits to justice. He confronted the chief on multiple occasions, even going so far as to threaten to take the matter outside the confines of the house. Each time Eddie was assured that the matter was being looked into and to the best of his knowledge, this was the case.

The only thing Eddie could possibly be guilty of, in relation to his actions concerning the arsons, was an abundance of good faith and trust. That he crusaded against the deliberate fires and did his best to do something about them, despite being thwarted at every turn. That he found himself accused of being involved was one of the bitterest ironies, among many, that he had to suffer. Many prominent men in the fire department knew much more about the identities of the culprits and did nothing to stop them. Why Eddie? It is a question that lingers to this day. If anyone *wasn't* responsible for the whole dirty business, it was him.

۷ ۷ ۷

Eddie spent another sleepless night thinking about his legal troubles. And he knew that there was only one reason why he was not 100 percent successful in answering all questions and laying the allegations lodged against him to rest. That reason: Dennis. His ex-partner represented the one missing link between Malaka's questions and the answers Eddie was unable to provide. They needed to talk to him.

While drinking his coffee the next morning, Eddie decided to call Dennis to air out things and try to get some sort of honest accounting of what had transpired. Eddie wanted a clearer picture of the liabilities he might face.

Eddie spent the next day and night calling Dennis's house, leaving urgent messages with his wife and on his answering machine. The next day, Eddie decided to pay his ex-friend a visit. He arrived on a chaotic scene. Through the front door of Dennis's house, mostly closed but cracked open about a half an inch, Eddie could hear the caterwauling of an intense, loud argument.

The first words Eddie was able to make out belonged to a screeching female. Her yelling was so agitated and unpleasantly high-pitched that it took Eddie a few moments to recognize that the voice belongs to Dennis's wife, who usually spoke in delicate, soft tones. In addition to the adamantly unusual tone, the content of her words are shocking as well.

"I can't believe you've been fucking her all this time. And of all people, that sluttish police dispatcher. Do you know how many cops went balls deep with her you bastard? How many people know? You goddamn lousy, no-good liar. The man I thought was a husband turns out to be nothing but a fast-talking con man. I hate you."

Eddie felt as though he had walked in on something he shouldn't have and almost turned to leave. Then he remembered the shame and shock of his session with Malaka and was seized by a determination that held him in place. He needed, no, he was desperate for answers. After a slight hesitation, Eddie knocked on the door. Loudly. He had to pound on the door to be heard above the din.

After a few more heated exchanges, the couple noticed the commotion at the door. Straightaway, they lapsed into an embarrassed silence. Another moment passed. Nothing happened. Eddie was about to knock once more when Dennis shouted "just a minute" from somewhere down the hall. A wait of several minutes followed before Dennis appeared, opens the door a bit further, and stepped forward to poke his face out.

"It's uh, not really a good time right now."

Dennis started to close the door, but Eddie blocked it with his hand.

"I don't care Dennis. We need to talk right now. If it wasn't super important, I wouldn't bother you, but it can't wait."

It was clear from the tone of Eddie's voice and his steely gaze that he would not be dismissed. Dennis stepped onto the porch and shut the door behind him. From inside, came more loud epithets, followed by the tinkling of breaking dinnerware.

"What's going on?"

"I talked with detectives yesterday, and they say I'm in a lot of trouble for all kinds of unkosher things going on at the store. It occurred to me that the only questions I was unable to answer were the questions that you have the answers to."

"So what do you want from me?"

"I want to know everything. What the hell's been going on? How deep in it are we? Come clean with me Dennis so I can be prepared for what I'm facing."

"I don't know what you're talking about."

"Have you been using the store to trade in stolen goods? Did you have anything to do with the arsons?"

"Of course not. I screwed up a couple of receipts. Don't start making wild accusations."

"These are not my accusations; it's what they are investigating us for. Listen, I need to talk with your dad as well, as soon as possible."

"That's impossible."

"Why?"

"He moved to Florida."

"When did this happen?"

"About a week ago."

"Fine, then I need some answers from you. Let's start with—"

"I'm sorry but I can't help you. You're on your own."

Dennis turned his back on his ex-partner and quickly darted inside.

Chapter 13

Immediately following his extremely disappointing and fruitless encounter with Dennis, Eddie found himself standing statue still on his ex-partner's porch, staring straight ahead, open-mouthed, alone. For a second or two he remained immobile, straining his brain in a vain attempt to process what had just happened.

Before he had the opportunity to sink any further into the numbing depths of the trance that was slowly enveloping him, Eddie's concentration was shoved back onto solid ground by a volcanic eruption of molten noise and tumult spraying through the window screens and spewing out of the spaces between the front door and its molding.

A minute or so after Dennis turned his back on Eddie and shut the door in his face, the angry rumblings inside the house resumed. Before long, the heated exchanges between Dennis and his wife were again gathering steam and intensity. An ominous, ugly pressure thickened the air between husband and wife, continuing to build until it finally boiled over in a cacophonous cascade of slamming doors and crashing appliances.

As the chaotic combustion careened out of control, approaching new crescendos and showing no signs of abating, Eddie shook his head in frustrated disbelief. Turning on his heel, he clenched his fists, thrust them into his pockets, and made his way back to his car. In Eddie's mind, he'd already written off the visit as a total bust, resigned to the realization that whatever he had hoped to accomplish would have to wait, at least for the time being.

As long as Dennis and his wife were busy spinning round and round, caught amid the gale force hurricane chaos of their disintegrating union, Eddie figured the odds were against him being able to obtain any of the answers he was so desperately seeking. Once he was able to comprehend the full extent of the marital implosion he'd had the misfortunate timing to intrude on, it became clear to Eddie that his chances of finding the piece of mind he'd come looking for were minimal.

Things were going nowhere. Progress seemed impossible. Eddie could think of nothing that would do any good at all, much less break through the present impasse to yield even the resemblance of a productive outcome. Regardless of how patient and tenacious Eddie was prepared to be, the reality of the situation was not likely to change. The end result (or lack thereof) would be the same, no matter how much time Eddie was willing to waste arguing with Dennis on his doorstep.

Sensing futility, Eddie decided to cut his losses and try his luck again as soon as Dennis's domestic maelstrom had calmed. After beating a retreat across his ex-partner's front lawn walkway, Eddie stood curbside, digging through his pockets to retrieve his keys.

The plan, at that point, was to get behind the wheel and drive away, without any further confrontation, without another word, or, for that matter, even a look back into his rearview or a glance over his shoulder. And that's exactly what would have happened had Eddie been physically able to enter his vehicle, had he not instead been seized at that moment by an ineffable force that held him in place, literally stopping him in his tracks.

From a place deep inside of him, a place so remote Eddie was barely aware of its existence came an abrupt surge of anger so powerful it sent him reeling. Eddie struggled to maintain his balance while being battered by a relentless onslaught of a primal fury that seemed to rise up in successive waves, cresting and crashing, again and again. Sweat trickled down Eddie's temples, down his arms, and down the sides of his legs. His heart pounded in his throat. Steadying himself against the hood of his car, Eddie was surprised to feel himself trembling all over with a rage he could just barely control.

He stared across the green expanse of Dennis's well-manicured lawn, resting his gaze on the ornate front door of the man who, in the guise of friendship and partnership, had managed to insinuate himself into every last nook and cranny of his life.

Now, after the touch of this malevolent Midas Muffler shop had turned Eddie's entire world to shit, after he'd completely taken advantage of and manipulated Eddie's trusting nature, after he'd cynically traded on the goodwill that he'd been shown, after he'd severely compromised Eddie's sense of safety, serenity, and security, damaged his friendships and family, ravaged his career, reputation, and future, perhaps even placed his very freedom in jeopardy, Dennis had the unmitigated gall to believe he could simply wash his hands and walk away from the very catastrophe that he'd been instrumental in creating.

The worst part about it, Eddie realized, was his own willingness to cooperate with Dennis's audacity. Dennis had summarily dismissed him, and Eddie was just about to let him get away with it. No more. As of right then and there, Eddie was through being a doormat. If Dennis planned on weaseling out of the share of trouble he'd caused, Eddie could at least refuse to make it easy. And he certainly was not going to tolerate being casually disposed of like dog shit on the bottom of a sneaker.

Summoning his courage and prepared for anything, Eddie went forth, purposefully and defiantly, retracing his steps back to Dennis's house. As he approached the front door, he balled up his hand and drew it straight up and back, until it was level with his ear. His intent was to pound with abandon, knocking for as long and loud as it took to be heard above the din within. But before he could strike his first blow, the door swung open. Dennis stepped forward and stood in the entranceway, not quite inside, but not quite outside either.

Although the two men occupied almost the same positions that they had only minutes before, the entire tone that had been set over the course of their previous interaction had changed. Eddie had shed his air of amiable reasonableness. There was a new iron in his approach. He was wary, firm, and determined, his face locked in a mask of grim resolve. Dennis, conversely, received Eddie much more receptively, discarding all traces of the combativeness and arrogance that he'd just displayed so prominently.

Dennis's decision to adopt a sympathetic, apologetic, nice-guy pose succeeded in throwing Eddie more than a little off balance. This was no accident; it was a calculated ploy. Like everything else associated with Dennis, it was nothing but another con.

Exhausted by the afternoon of emotional discord, his wife unloaded a few parting verbal salvos, whipped a glass vase at his head (which, due to a well-timed duck, missed its target by an inch or two, shattering spectacularly against the living room wall), then stormed up the stairs, locking herself in the master bedroom.

As the muffled sound of her bitter tears descended like a dark cloud from the second floor, Dennis started to follow but then thought better of the idea. Instead, he grabbed a broom from the staircase closet and began sweeping up the glass shards and other battle-related detritus littering the hard wood of the living room floor. While bending over to fill the dustpan, Dennis looked up from the debris pile. Eye level with the windowsill, he peeked out at the street from behind the front curtains.

Now remember, Dennis fancies himself to be an astute observer of character and an advanced student of human nature. Although his own perceptions of his skills in this arena are a bit exaggerated and grandiose, they are far from delusionary. Dennis's insight into the human psyche and its baser motivations is no less than his very bread and butter, the fundamental edge that enables him to get over and then get away with it, time and again, for as long as anyone can recall. Throughout his entire lifetime, he has abused this uncannily unerring ability to figure out what drives people and makes them tick at their core, working with and wielding this knowledge as if it were a secret weapon. It's actually one of his few genuine talents.

This is why, when he spied Eddie's Hamlet moment out at the curb, he only needed a quick read of Eddie's body language and facial expressions to be able to decipher the tempest brewing inside. From the look in Eddie's eyes alone, Dennis was able to conclude that he had pushed Eddie too far. Faced with yet another potentially volatile situation, Dennis decided it was in his strategic interest to give a little ground. Otherwise he'd have a two-front war on his hands, forced to juggle the hot potatoes of an enraged crazy wife who suspects (correctly) that Dennis has been screwing a female police dispatcher and an indignant ex-partner who suspects (correctly) that Dennis has been screwing him (although not quite in the same manner).

At any rate, it didn't take a relationship expert to understand that the sole reason Eddie had come back for a second helping of Dennis's B.S. was because he was spoiling for a fight. One up-close look at Eddie's flaring nostrils and face Dennis was positive he had made the correct decision. Right away, Dennis moved to diffuse the tension.

"Look, before you say anything, I really have to apologize to you for being so rude. Just forget about everything I said a few minutes ago and let's start over. I know you've got things you need to talk to me about. I'm just sort of … how can I put it … Having a bad, bad day."

"I guess I can understand that."

"So what's up? What's on your mind?"

"Listen Dennis, I know you've got quite a full-blown domestic crisis here, and I'd like to leave you alone, believe me, I really would. But I'm afraid I just can't. The thing is, I'm going through a crisis of my own, and at least part of what I'm going through is your fault."

"Eddie, we can go around and around here all day. I've said it before and I'll say it again. Whatever you are trying to insinuate, the fact remains that I did nothing wrong."

"Ok, ok, maybe fault is too strong of a word for me to be using. Bottom line, I'm being asked questions by police detectives that I don't have any answers for. The only place I can get these answers is from you. The only questions I'm unable to respond to are those that directly pertain to parts of the business that you were responsible for.

I need your cooperation to help me sort out this mess. I have to be as thoroughly prepared for this thing as humanly possible 'cause it's for real. The full weight of it is set to bear down on me in a big, big way."

"Look, I don't know what you've convinced yourself of when it comes to me, but I can tell you that I'm not trying to play games with you here, Eddie. If they've got you in their sights, it's only a matter of time before they come knocking at my door. Don't you realize that when it comes to this investigation, I'm on Front Street just like you?"

"Then let's put our heads together and hash out all the facts, no matter how sordid or unpleasant. I need to know what I'm up against. I need to be sure that those scumbag detectives won't be able to hit me from my blind side again. You say you're still my friend, that you always have been and that it's me that's been unfair to you, that you deserve the benefit of the doubt. Well then, prove it. Help me out."

"What do you want from me? What do you want me to do?"

"Buy me out."

"You want to resume the partnership?"

"No. Buy me out completely. All the way. Lock, stock, and barrel. You and your pop created this monster; the least you can do is get it off my back. How about it? C'mon. I mean, from a pure dollars-and-cents perspective, you'd be hard-pressed to find a more attractive business proposition. I'd be willing to sign over the whole shooting match for a rock-bottom price. We're talking pennies on the dollar. I'm offering you a real steal."

Perhaps initially at least, Eddie intended for the last word of his proposition to serve as a subtle dig. While passing through Eddie's lips, however, the sarcasm contained in the single syllable spilled over, drowning any subtext in oceans of obviousness. Despite the abundant amount of tension currently separating the two ex-friends and ex-partners, they couldn't help allowing a wry half-smile to pass between them. The moment passed in the blink of an eye, however. The stakes were far too high for plays on words or gallows humor.

"I'm afraid the remedy you propose is impossible, not to mention completely inadequate in terms of being a practical solution. It's out of the question."

"Why?"

"Well for one thing, I'm going through a divorce here if you hadn't noticed, which means I'm not exactly in a great position to be shopping for new business opportunities and real estate. I'm going to be forced to liquidate everything I've got, so it's not the best time to be acquiring additional assets. I don't know how much of the gory details you happened to pick up on while you've been standing out here on the porch, but to fill in whatever you might have missed and sum it all up for you, she's got the goods on me. She's going to take me for damn near everything I've got. I'll be lucky to have a pot to piss in when this is all over. Even if I wanted to hassle with the store again, I wouldn't be able to afford it, not for pennies on the dollar, not for a penny on the dollar. It's all very simple: I'm going to be very broke very soon. And at any rate, selling out would give you no protection from any investigation that is currently taking place. The idea is absurd on more levels than I can mention. If you wanted to sell out to me, why didn't you say so in the first place, back when we dissolved the partnership?"

"I did."

"You did? Yeah, ok, that's right. All right, so you did, but that wasn't the course of action we ultimately decided to take. So it's neither here nor there; it's ancient history."

"You're right."

"I'm right? Yeah, I mean yeah, that's what I've been trying to tell you. Listen, I-I—"

"Look Dennis, enough, ok? Enough. Whatever song-and-dance routine you're getting ready to lay on me this time, I don't want to hear it. You can just relax; there's no need for you to shift into weasel mode. You can spare me the lame excuses and skip the slippery squirming. Do me a favor and save us both the embarrassment. I didn't expect to sell you the store today. I was only being half serious when I brought the idea up in the first place, way back when. It's certainly not why I've been calling and calling you, leaving stacks of urgent messages that have all been ignored. It's certainly not why, after coming all the way over to your house, squandering an entire afternoon trying to work things out with you in person, man-to-man, and receiving, as a reward for my efforts, a curt "go fuck yourself" and a slamming door, I decided to swallow my pride and come back here to make a final attempt at resolving the few loose ends that remain between us. For some crazy reason, I thought we might try behaving like human beings, no lawyers, no lawsuits, keep our sharks in their cages where they can't do any damage, see if we can't hash out an understanding on our own, just you and I, save a little cash and avoid some bloodshed."

"Let me make sure I'm clear on all this. All you want from me is help with filling some of the gaps that have been found in the shop records."

"That's it."

"So we talk things over, work things out, and reach, as you say, an understanding. And you're willing to give me your word that there's nothing up your sleeve? You're willing to swear to me that the small print of whatever quote-unquote agreement we reach won't contain some kind of cleverly concealed stipulation designed to saddle me with a backdoor deed transfer?"

"C'mon Dennis, you know darn well that's not my style. I've never operated like that, and I never will. There's not even any legal paperwork I'm asking you to sign. As a matter of fact, the only place I need you to put pen to paper at all is on a few ledger entries where you entered the transaction but forgot to write down your initials. I might remind you that the decision to provide me with some of the tools I need to nip this whole scandal in the bud is a decision that serves your interests as well as mine. You might be out of the immediate loop of questioning and you might've washed your hands of the heat I'm now feeling when you sold your share of the store, but you know as well as I do that you're not out of the woods for certain until this thing is resolved. The statute of limitations hasn't expired, and all they have to do is widen the scope of their little fox hunt."

"Unlikely."

"Unlikely but possible. For crying out loud Dennis, I'm not asking for your first born here. All I need for you to do is go over the books with a fine-tooth comb. If you can lend me a hand to provide some answers where I don't have any, so I can back Malaka off a little, it might make all the difference. You're of course aware I could've handled this through formal channels. Instead of hiding behind a mouthpiece and going after what I need that way, I'm coming to you honorably and honestly. I'm asking, ex-partner to ex-partner, fireman to fireman, making this appeal as someone who was once a very good friend. Malaka's turned my life into a nightmare jigsaw puzzle. If I can't solve it for him, I'm in trouble. In the meantime, key pieces are missing, many of which you happen to hold in your possession. That's why it's so important for you to help me look under the couches and carpets and find them. I need any stray pieces, so to speak, that you may have lying around. Desperately. I promise you, I'll never ask you another favor. You'll never see my face around here again. What do you say? Yes or no?"

"Yes. Of course yes. If you're saying there's something I'm in a position to do on your behalf, something that'll help remedy this fiasco they're putting you through, I'm all ears. If you were listening, you could've skipped the big speech. For crying out loud, I already apologized for how I treated you before. I was out of line. I'm willing to help you anyway I can, within reason of course. We've had our ups and downs but, Holy Mary; you think I want to see you in this kind of situation? What exactly do you need me to do, and when do you need me to do it?"

"All I need is for you to initial the ledger entries where they're missing next to the transaction notations that you made ... oh, and add more detail on some individual line items. I indicated the pages in question with Post-it notes, which lead you right where you need to go. Just add what info you can where you can; if you can't remember, you can't remember. The main thing I need your help with is figuring out how to get to the bottom of the several complete blind spots the investigators found in the records, places where there is no documentation to be found at all. Granted, the absolute gaps occur rarely, but as I'm sure you can understand, they are particularly incriminating to me. I'm sure that together we can dig up some data or figure out how to furnish a plausible explanation. Normally I wouldn't get so worked up about a few misplaced files from God knows how many months ago, but you've got to realize that this Detective Malaka, who already seems to have an axe to grind with my name on its blade, has latched onto our record-keeping lapse and fixated on the mistakes as excuses to make mountains out of molehills. Anyway, I'm starting to ramble. The point is that if you can see fit to give up like half an evening this week to review the records kept from the beginning to the end of our partnership, it will enable me to address the suspicions of the investigators in a satisfactory manner."

"You want me to finish going through everything in a week?"

"Well, as soon as possible, the sooner the better, but that said, there is a little bit of wiggle room in the week-long deadline if you get extra busy on other stuff or find that you need some extra time putting everything together so it's up to snuff. I'll tell you what. The deadline for my next session with Malaka is two weeks from today. And that was the absolute most my lawyer could get. If I string him along even twenty-four hours past that, I'm likely to be hauled out of my house in cuffs in front of my family and the neighbors. He threatened as much, although not in those exact words. The reason I said this week is because I'm planning to go out of town in a few days. But I've got three more days before I take off, and I plan on being gone for a week. So if you can get through everything by the time I get back, which gives you ten days, that'll give me a few days to review whatever alterations you've made and get up to speed before they grill me. If I bring the records to you within the hour, all the ledgers, everything, can you commit to getting everything carefully looked over and back to me in that amount of time?"

"Sounds like enough time to do what I need to do."

"I mean a thorough job though. As I said, I need you to go through it all with a fine-tooth comb. Fill in all the blank spots, completely answer every last Post-it query that I put in the margins, and add the missing details that need to be added so I can at least face these investigators with a full set of records. Can you do that for me?"

"Wha'd I just say?"

"Ok man. Just making sure. I don't want to be out of state losing sleep because I'm worrying about what's happening back home."

"Are you planning on heading for the hills or what?"

"Believe me; I'd be lying if I said the thought never crossed my mind. But no. I'll return on schedule to face this crisis like a man, even though it may be the death of me. I just need a breather before they set their big dogs loose on me, which, from what I hear, is going to happen any day now. So as you might imagine, all this unyielding strain has got me about ready to crack. To prevent my getting fitted with a straitjacket, I decided I'd better get away from it all—surprise the wife with a little vacation—while I still can. Soon I may not have the option of leaving the jurisdiction."

"Where you off to?"

"North Carolina. Find a quiet lake and forget for awhile. But I can't do that unless you're totally on board and willing to cooperate with what I'm asking. I want to know that when I come back, I'll be able to give them the answers they're demanding and get them off my back for good."

"You have my word."

"That's what I'm concerned about."

"What's that supposed to mean?"

"Just kidding. I'll be right back with the materials. Needless to say, guard them with the utmost care, as if they were essential to your life, 'cause they are essential to mine. Please, please don't lose track of them or let them get damaged in any way. Anything happens to this stuff and my goose is cooked for sure."

"You have nothing to worry about. Listen, I know I have zero credibility with you at this point, but believe it or not, I only wish the best for you and your family. Yes we've butted heads recently, and there's been some bad blood, some nasty accusations thrown back and forth, but in the long run, there's too much history between us for me to simply write it off as if it never happened. As far as I'm concerned, you could never be a stranger I'm indifferent to or an enemy I want any part in helping to take down. No matter what, I still care very much about your welfare. I welcome the chance to contribute to your cause, even in this small way, by doing this minor thing. Maybe someday, far down the road, you'll find it in your heart to trust me again. Maybe years from now, time will heal the wounds we've inflicted on one another, and we can summon the forgiveness necessary to bury the hatchet. Whether that happens or not, I'm in your corner and on your side. I want to see you get out from under this. When it's all said and done, I hope I'll have played a small role in helping that happen. At any rate, it isn't right what they're doing to you. A lot of the boys don't have the balls to say that out in the open for fear of becoming the next fire-hat trophy targeted to go up on the Prosecutor's mantle, but that's what everybody thinks."

"It relieves me to hear that. And you didn't have to say all that. But I appreciate it Dennis. I really do."

"Don't sweat it. Just go home and bring me back the demon ledgers so I can exorcize them and you can start packing your bags. By the way, I think it's a great idea for you to get away from all this and come back with a fresh perspective. Relax and enjoy yourself. And you can get on that plane with a clear head and an untroubled mind; rest assured that I will keep the documentation safe and secure. The records will not leave my sight unless they are under lock and key. I won't lose track of a single page."

Inside, the phone began to ring.

"I better grab that before she does and World War III turns into World War IV."

"Say no more. We're done here. I got everything I needed to say off my chest, and we're on the same page. I've already taken up enough of your time. Good luck with the missus."

"Thanks. I'll need it."

Eddie took his leave feeling a lot better about things as Dennis opened the door and disappeared behind it with a friendly wave designed, as was every word he'd just uttered, to be warmly reassuring. Once inside, he picked up the closest phone and spoke in the receiver.

"Hello?"

"Hey, it's Lonnie. What the hell's going on? I told you we needed to talk today. I thought I impressed on you how important it was."

Lonnie, the caller on the other end of the line, was a volunteer firefighter who had worked at the store when Dennis and Eddie were partners. He was also one of the alleged arsonists.

"So we're talking. What's the problem?"

"I tried you twice before and couldn't reach you, and that was after this morning when your wife pulled the phone out of the wall screaming about some policewoman down at dispatch. So this time, after I had to let it ring six or seven times, I was starting to get a little nervous that you were trying to blow me off."

"Not at all man. What kind of guy do you think I am? I know better than that. Granted, my dad may be a pretty big-time heavyweight, but nowhere near big-time enough to give the dodge to someone so famous he's got his name and picture plastered all over the *Star-Ledger* and the *Record*."

"Infamous is more like it. So what took you so long to pick up the receiver? Things still blowing up with the wife? Is this a bad time?"

"Yes and no, but don't worry about it. It's as good a time as any. She wasn't why I couldn't get to the phone anyway; she's holed up in our room. I was out front talking and got a little distracted by the conversation. That's all."

"That's all? Anything I ought to be filled in about? Anything that needs taking care of? What was the deal?"

"Nothing you need to worry about at this point."

"You sure?"

"Sure I'm sure."

"So who was it?"

"I'm not going to name names over the phone. Put it this way: it was just some asshole I had to bullshit."

"Do I know the asshole?"

"You know the asshole. It's the one we're helping to bend over for our cowboy cop friend to make sure he doesn't decide to fuck us instead."

"And?"

"And for both of our sakes I had to take my time and make sure I bullshit him real well."

"And?"

"And ... I did. Of course I did. Now let's stop wasting time with trivia and get down to business."

🔥 🔥 🔥

Early the next morning, a portly man in a rumpled suit was in the process of clearing his credentials at the front desk of police headquarters when a swaggering, gray-suited, gold-badge-wearing middle-aged man with cold, ruthless eyes and salt-and-pepper hair came forward to wave him through to the inner heart of the building.

Delorme, who was flustered after facing heavy traffic that caused him to be five minutes late for his promised assignation with Detective Malaka,. He followed closely behind the faintly grinning police investigator, huffing and puffing and half jogging to keep up with Malaka's brisk power-walk pace as they made their way through a maze of corridors and stairwells, finally arriving at the detective's office.

Malaka opened the door, walked in, and sat behind his desk. He gestured for Delorme to take a seat on one of the two chairs situated across from him. Taking stock of his surroundings, Delorme was surprised by the mounds of clutter strewn about the room. It seemed out of character for Malaka, who struck the attorney as fastidious and efficient. Ignoring the stacked towers of boxes and files, Delorme peered out the window behind Malaka's head, which offered a pleasant panorama of trees and sky.

"That's a nice view you've got there Detective."

"Not to appear rude, Mr. Delorme, but you'll have to excuse me from participating in the dispensing of standard pleasantries. You see, I'm rather pressed for time. A couple of unanticipated matters have come up concerning my caseload that I need to attend to as soon as we finish here. Now according to my schedule, we're here to discuss the exact state of affairs concerning your firefighter, Eddie."

"That's right."

"What exactly can I do for you? What do you want to know?"

"I'd like the courtesy of a frank assessment of where things stand and how far this investigation is going to go. As you know, I requested this follow-up to our first sit-down so that I could give my client a more detailed picture of his potential legal liabilities regarding your investigation. You had said you needed time to process the results of our first conversation. I'd like to know what your perspective is on that conversation since you've had time to analyze what you heard. I'd also like to know if there's been a report on the meeting and, if so, be apprised of its overall findings and general point of view. Now we're set to meet again in about two weeks, at which time Eddie assures me, he will be able to address any and all of the remaining allegations he was unable to answer due to the involvement of his ex-partner. So the million dollar question is, assuming he is able to rebut these allegations and allay the suspicions raised against him to your satisfaction, can I safely assume we will be able to wrap up this matter at that juncture and he'll be able to put it behind him and move forward?"

An eerie, disquieting chuckle escaped Malaka's pursed lips. Catching himself almost immediately, his normally rigid countenance transformed itself back to stone. It was a scary and intimidating thing for Delorme to witness.

"What's funny?"

"I apologize. It's just that things have moved far beyond the point you seem to think we're at. The first interrogation raised more questions than answers, no charge was conclusively or compellingly rebutted, and whatever alibi he is able to fabricate following a second questioning session after he's had ample time to better construct his story will not be the least bit convincing. We are here today to show each other our cards. I'm afraid the deck is woefully stacked against your client. The upcoming meeting is a mere formality, a favor to the uniform, not the man."

"With all due respect, you seem to be nursing a grudge. You're not even giving my client a fair chance to answer for himself."

"On the contrary. Due to his honorable position and profession, he's been treated with kid gloves. We have not, to date, embarrassed him in his community and dragged him in here like a common criminal. Despite an abundance of evidence, he has not been placed under arrest. Instead, he's on more than one occasion and in more than one setting, had the benefit of polite, informal meetings at which he's been given every opportunity to explain himself. Instead, the hole he is standing in keeps getting deeper."

"You mention an abundance of evidence. All I've seen—"

"Mr. Delorme, we're here as two professionals to clear the air and pull back the curtain on precisely where things stand following an exhaustive investigation during which, I might add, your client has been given every benefit of the doubt imaginable. Lack of evidence? My good man, that is the most absurd utterance to come out of anybody's mouth in connection with this case yet, and I've been privy to more than a few so that's saying something."

Mad at the direct insult, the normally difficult to rile Delorme was agitated and decided to meet bluster with bluster, challenge with challenge.

"Then show me something tangible. Anything."

Malaka waved his hands in a vague circular motion.

"Take a look around."

"I don't follow."

"Do you think I operate in this helter-skelter manner on a day-to-day basis? These paperwork skyscrapers were assembled in anticipation of our one-on-one today."

"Meaning?"

"You still don't get it? Ok, I'll spell it out. All of these boxes and files and depositions and photographs and surveillance reports and paper mountains that are crammed into every possible corner and crevice of this office, they all relate to one suspect: your client. This is the raw material compiled over the course of our investigation. This is only a sampling mind you. There is more."

The fire in Delorme's gut was extinguished with a gurgling hiss as the blood drained from his face. He was at a loss for words. Noticing, Malaka stepped forward to fill the void.

"We are well past the point of explanations and artful dodging. Well past the possibility of closing this thing down quietly and going away. We are to the point of the consequences and hard choices that come with serious criminal prosecution. We are to the point of wrapping this stuff up into tidy boxes, shipping them over to Detective Kathy Hober at the PROSECUTORS OFFICE and start convening a grand jury, and obtaining multiple indictments. Make no mistake: we will get multiple indictments. We've been meticulously preparing our case, as you can clearly see. We've got more than enough incriminating material to satisfy even the most rigorous grand jury standards. Some of the financial fraud and thievery is egregious, not to mention that involvement in massive and multiple arsons corresponds with double-digit prison terms. Juries are particularly hard pressed to forgive firemen who set fires."

"There was no involvement, absolutely, my client, there was no, none—"

"Save the rhetoric and denials for the judge. You're going to need all of your Perry Mason skills to get this man out of incarceration before he starts drawing Social Security."

"We can show, I mean we can dispute categorically—"

"Let me give you some free advice—if you're really interested in acting on behalf of your client's best interests. Don't come to the next meeting carrying a sheaf of excuses. Come ready to deal. Maybe we can be flexible in order to avoid the taxpayer burden of the trial and the community burden of the associated shame and tarnish. Maybe we can be really flexible if he comes clean on the arson thing, testifies and helps us develop a more airtight case against the actual doers than we've already got. Think about it. Talk to your client and get back to me. But don't dawdle. Generous offers have quicker expiration dates than gallons of milk."

"This is outr—"

"Come on, Delorme. Look at this preponderance of evidence. You really think I'd be talking like this if it was all circumstantial."

Delorme began to protest again, but couldn't find legs solid enough to stand on. He'd been pulverized into jelly. Cut off at the knees. He wondered what would happen if he tried to rise from his seat. Defeated, he hung his head.

"I'll … I'll talk to my client."

"You do that. Now if you'll excuse me, there are some serious developments that demand my attention, and so I'd like to cut this a bit short if there's nothing else."

"There's nothing else."

Malaka showed Delorme the door and walked out behind him. As they parted company in the hall, Malaka did the "one more thing" number he learned from the '70s Peter Falk detective show *Columbo*, which was his favorite.

"Listen Delorme, I know you're overwhelmed. But you'll get it together, sooner than you think. You'll talk to Eddie, and you'll both get fired up by his misplaced and deceptive sense of righteous indignation. By tomorrow you'll be wondering if I'm bluffing. Be assured, I'm not. For the sake of your reputation and your client's future, I sincerely hope and pray that you take that to the bank, 'cause you can bank on it. It's a sure thing. Hard as currency. That's all. Anyway, I've got to go.

I'm overdue for my next appointment. I'll be seeing you soon. Hearing from you sooner if you know what's good for Eddie."

Delorme exited on marshmallow heels and glass toes. With every step, he felt he'd sink into the floor or shatter across it. The problem with Delorme, besides the fact that he wasn't a very good attorney and tended to get over on clients by bragging about who he knew and how long he'd been practicing, was that he cut corners. The last thing you could accuse him of was being thorough.

Case in point: the morning meeting with Malaka. Delorme never even looked at the so-called evidence mountain ranges chaotically piled across the tableau of Malaka's normally pristine office. If he had, he would have quickly figured out that Malaka was indeed bluffing and full of shit, boldly and hugely, with all his might and all the chutzpah he could summon (and he could summon quite a bit). Had he bothered to look, Delorme wouldn't have found a single piece of paper relating to his client or his client's case. The truth was that out of a week's worth of options the chief had given him, Malaka had picked the day of his meeting with Delorme to move the contents of his office from his department's old section to its new one. The clutter on the floor, coffee-table, bookshelves, and filing cabinets represented the totality of his case files, both active and archived. Eddie's stuff wasn't even among the debris. It was all in one of Malaka's desk drawers, which it didn't even fill.

🌿 🌿 🌿

During the time that all this gamesmanship was taking place between his attorney and his official tormentor, Eddie was blissfully oblivious. He had taken a drive to the local mall, where his travel agent kept her office. As Malaka was issuing Delorme the bum's rush out of his office, the agent was issuing Eddie two tickets to Lake Norman, North Carolina.

Plowing through a mid-day crunch on the Garden State Parkway, Eddie rushed home with plans to take his wife out to an unexpected lunch and surprise her with the tickets. His wife had already gone to lunch, however, before Eddie had even cleared the first toll booth. And she hadn't gone alone. It was many years later before he would find out that accompanying her to her meal that day was a man who was probably Eddie's 2nd most damaging nemesis, one the man who was at the helm of the anti-Eddie crusade currently under way. That man, of course, was none other than Corrunoside's Mayor.

Today, however, Eddie was determined not to let anything kill his positive outlook. He had dropped off the ledgers and was confident that Dennis would provide the information that would put a stop to the misunderstanding that had been causing him so much stress. Plus, he was going on a real vacation for the first time in as long as he could remember. It would be a much needed respite. He needed the time away from the investigation, and he and his wife needed the time to reconnect and repair the damage that all the recent problems had caused.

The rest of the day was spent running errands that had to be taken care of so he could leave. Near the end of the day, still riding a wave of upbeat and hopeful feelings, he dropped by Delorme's office to see how things had gone with Malaka.

The meeting was a rocky one, with Delorme suddenly running scared and talking deal and Eddie "you have to be out of your rabbit asses mind" reiterating his absolute innocence until he was blue in the face. Not wanting to ruin the rare momentum of his mood, Eddie cut Delorme short, explaining: "When I get back this will all be resolved. I'll have the books, the proof of my innocence. We'll be able to meet with them and clear up what we couldn't. And I'm going to work on lining up the evidence to blow this arson thing out of the water."

"You don't understand, Eddie."

But Eddie was already on his way out of the office, his heart already on the beaches of North Carolina.

Once getting to Carolina, Eddie and his wife had a great time. The tensions between them seemed to melt away. They got along with a passion and friendship they hadn't known since the early days of their marriage.

Eddie also got a handle on his anxiety regarding the investigation. He was innocent, and that was the bottom line. That assurance carried him through his vacation, through the airplane ride back to Jersey, and all the way into the next day, when he called to confirm his meeting with Delorme to go over what Dennis had added to the ledgers. That assurance stayed with him until the moment he arrived at Dennis's house, on his way to Delorme's, to find out that all of the records were gone.

They had mysteriously disappeared, lost into some black hole. Dennis claimed with all his heart that they'd been stolen; he even had one of his fathers buddies help Dennis with a false police report. Eddie was finally past listening to obvious B.S. stories. Now not pages, not single ledgers, had turned up missing, but any and all records there had ever been a partnership and every single daily transaction were flat out gone, vanished into the ether.

Eddie felt himself slip into a physical tailspin. He felt claustrophobic, as if things were closing in on him. He didn't know what he was going to do now. Where he would go from here, he had no idea.

Chapter 14

According to Eddie's original post vacation plans—a schedule that had been purposely packed sardine-tight so he could take maximum advantage of the energy generated by his rare respite to systematically and efficiently knock down each of the problems he faced—he had set up an appointment with his lawyer that was timed to directly follow his visit with Dennis.

The original idea was that Eddie would pick up the revised ledger set and deliver them, without delay, to his attorney's office. That way there was no way for them to get misplaced, and every explanation Dennis had furnished would be fresh in Eddie's mind. His lawyer would then ask him a series of questions, double-check everything for accuracy and legality, and that would be that.

The next day the prosecutor would get a phone call from Eddie's lawyer. Had the call gone smoothly, there was a very good chance that all financial questions could have been settled on the spot. Had the scenario unfolded as it was designed to, it is conceivable, indeed quite likely, and Eddie could have taken the legs out from under his case in a single afternoon of well-coordinated errands and meetings?

Instead, Eddie found himself sinking deeper than he had ever imaged possible, down into the bowels of a quicksand pit that, just hours ago, he had seemed on the verge of being able to escape. Now there would be no talk of escape, only survival. Now there would be no fixing the damage, only damage control.

The inopportune timing of the disappearance of the ledgers and associated financial paperwork made Eddie look guilty as hell, even though he had nothing to do with it, even though he'd been on vacation when it had happened.

No judge was likely to recognize such fine distinctions and give a good man the benefit of reasonable doubt, especially when they smelled the blood of potential cover-up in the waters, and especially when they had the sole authority and discretion to turn a routine case into a high-profile media event, making a name for themselves, staring down stern and severe as stone gargoyles from their exalted perches, basking in the glory of absolute power, meting out justice from on high with cameras rolling and mobs of so-called reporters crowding the courthouse steps, jockeying for prime position like vultures swarming a fresh kill. And, especially when, after it was all over, they could mount the trophy of a high-ranking firefighter's head over their fireplace.

Eddie wasn't stupid. He knew all this. He just didn't know what to do next. He felt like God had judo-kicked him in the side and, in the process, caved in his entire world. In the absence of the ability to think of any better course of action and out of sheer robotic momentum, he decided he'd go ahead and keep his previously arranged appointment with his lawyer, even though the whole point and entire reason for the meeting had been blown out of the water by Dennis's treacherous act of self-protection.

Well, Eddie figured, he'd have to break the news to Delorme anyway. It was the kind of thing to do over the phone, and now was as good a time as ever. Besides, there were few people he could think of that he needed to see and talk to more desperately at this point than his lawyer.

As morning slid toward noon, it had turned into an unseasonably, unreasonably stifling day. Outside a vicious, vindictive, scythe-shaped sliver of sun was slicing through clouds and sky, indiscriminately assailing pedestrians and pavement with wave after wave of merciless heat. No wind. Dead calm. Nothing much moved. Whatever was moving, inched heavily and sluggishly forward in jaundiced increments, leaving snail-trails of sweat sizzling on the griddle-hot sidewalks.

Delorme's office was on Third and Main, only about a football field away from where Eddie had found an open parking space. Despite the brief distance between car and destination, he was dismayed and frustrated to find that his newly laundered and pressed dress shirt had gotten soaked before he reached the air-conditioned refuge of his attorney's office.

After a few minutes waiting in the reception area reading a *Sports Illustrated* while standing directly beneath a powerful stream of arctic breeze that he'd discovered laser-beaming out of a kick-ass ceiling vent, Eddie was ushered through a pair of double doors and beckoned down a narrow hallway by a pretty, young, petite paralegal with little round glasses and dark hair pulled back into a tightly wound bun.

In no time, they were standing outside the closed door of Delorme's private office. She tapped gently on the frosted glass panel the bore her boss's name and quietly but politely took her leave as Delorme opened the door and invited Eddie inside. Eddie stepped toward the well-worn, unfortunately all-too-familiar visitor's chair as Delorme shut the door behind them both.

The client and the attorney settled in to conference with one another. Each could not help noticing the stricken look on their counterpart's face but elected not to comment for fear that they were merely projecting their own issues and mind states on one another.

There was a brief silence, neither party really wanting to or knowing where to begin, before Delorme (figuring that he was being well paid to do so) took the initiative. As he absentmindedly shuffled some paperwork on his desk, he cleared his throat with a flourish, took a deep breath and looked Eddie directly in the eyes. Delorme looked down at the desktop, where he'd placed his folded hands, seeming to contemplate the intricate matrix formed by his folded fingers as he began, slowly and deliberately, to speak.

"I'm afraid I have some really bad news."

"That's funny. Well, actually, not at all funny. It's just the same thing, word for word, that I was about to tell you. I also have some really bad news."

"You want to go ahead and go first?"

"No. You go ahead."

"Ok, here's the deal. While you were away, I had that one-on-one that Detective Malaka had promised me the day we had our introductory get-together. It was sort of pre discovery to see where we stand."

"And where do we stand?"

"I got to tell you, it ain't good. It ain't good at all. Malaka is loaded for bear. He showed me a museum hall full of evidence and surveillance they've been collecting on you. Of course our one saving grace, our one ace in the hole, is that we've finally got the books in order. Let me see the ledgers and related paperwork you've got and we'll go from there."

Each word Delorme spoke hit Eddie like a sledgehammer, swinging down from on high. When the missing data was requested, Eddie physically flinched.

"I don't know what to tell you Lou."

"Please don't tell me we didn't get the holes filled in."

"That's not what I'm telling you."

"Good."

"No. No good. What I'm telling you is they're gone, they're all gone."

"But how?"

"I handed them over to Dennis and he flat out said they were stolen."

"But there's no way to prove that."

"Don't you think I know that?"

"I'm sorry. I'm sorry. What's done is done. We just have to figure where we go from here. Grand jury will convene in a few weeks. I think they'll indict. After that, a guilty plea is our only logical option. Maybe I can work out a deal. They drop this weak arson tie-in; we keep you out of jail."

"But I can't plead guilty. I didn't do this shit."

Don't you remember what was said to me the day I went to clean out my locker?

Capt. You really didn't know who was setting all those fires. NO!!
"GOD, EVERYBODY KNEW, EVERYBODY"

"At this point, that may be the most irrelevant fact of the case."

"If I did … you know, plead, could you work it out so I could stay on the force?"

"I highly doubt it. We'll see what we can work out, but bottom line, you've got to start thinking about making a deal, especially with the books gone. They were our last hope."

"But they were stolen."

"I know that and you know that and this Dennis character knows that. The court, the people who count … not so much."

🔥 🔥 🔥

So Eddie was left with a dire set of facts to mull over. He spent the next week or so basically waiting for the axe to drop. Bright and early one morning it did. Delorme called with the news that the grand jury would convene on such-and-such a date and that was that.

The grand jury proceedings would determine if enough evidence existed to indict. As Delorme and the prosecutor had their preliminary meetings and showed each other some cards and held others back, it became apparent that the arson beef was nothing more than a reputation-killing red herring.

Sure, they'd use testimony alleging that Eddie had some sort of connection in order to destroy his character and credibility, but as far as hard evidence or surveillance footage of any kind, they had nothing. No formal charges would be brought tying Eddie to the arson defendants; it would just be a tar-brush they would use in a vague and deliberate manner to smear his name. What Eddie did have to worry about, according to Delorme, was a slew of charges related to the allegation he had knowingly received stolen property. Eddie figured that since that charges were complete B.S., he had at least a 50-50 chance. He was wrong.

The grand jury proceedings were a farce. A circus. Public officials lied under oath. Police investigators lied under oath. Dennis, in order to save his skin, lied under oath. The only witness who told the truth was Eddie, but that didn't matter. When all was said and done, Eddie found himself formally indicted by the State of New Jersey for a series of thefts that, if committed at all, had been committed by his partner and without his knowledge.

"So?"

Eddie was back in Delorme's ugly but comfortable visitor's chair, the one he'd grown so familiar with, the one he'd grown to hate. He was more or less asking how he should proceed now that his nightmare had transformed into reality, now that he found himself officially under indictment.

"So? So! I know you don't like it, know you don't want to hear it, but you've got to rethink this stubborn position, change your mind, and enter a plea of guilty. I know it isn't right, but we're not talking about what's right; we're talking about what we can salvage. I'll get pre-trial intervention, save your pension, keep you out of jail. Hey believe me, I know it's far from the best of circumstances for an innocent man, but it's the best that we can do."

"Don't tell me you know. You're not the one getting railroaded."

"Eddie, you've got to be reasonable. The deck has been stacked against you."

Delorme may have said more, but Eddie had already jumped up from his seat and stormed out of the office. As far as he was concerned, the meeting was over.

A few days later, Eddie was on his way down to the courthouse to drop off some documents so they could be admitted as defense evidence. Calendar-wise, his actual trial was still hanging out there on a relatively distant horizon, slated to commence several months down the road, but certain deadlines had to be met well in advance.

For one thing, all defense-related materials intended to be introduced as evidence had to be submitted by the end of a particular business day three full months in advance of the commencement of the opening proceedings of his case. This gave the prosecution a reasonable time span to thoroughly examine the materials and formulate an adequate and appropriate rebuttal.

In the interest of fair play, it should be stated that all materials related to the prosecution's case were also under the same deadline pressures. Because of the superior resources of the prosecution (including the fact they had the whole State of New Jersey behind them, which included but was not limited to an entire squad solely devoted to the investigation of Eddie's store and a phalanx of lawyers to assist in his subsequent prosecution, while Eddie had only himself and one incompetent, easily intimidated, overpaid lawyer to look out after his interests), in reality, the establishment of such a rigorous, early deadline clearly served as a de facto advantage for the state.

It was already late afternoon by the time Eddie had freed himself of his daily obligations, weaved his way through cross-town traffic, and found himself a parking space within hiking distance of the courthouse. He was in major hustle mode as he jerked his car into park, ripped the keys from the ignition, bolted out the door, pulled a crucial sheaf of files from his backseat, locked up, then half-walking and half-running, made his way through the labyrinth of the corner parking garage toward the battery of courthouse elevators awaiting him across the street.

Amid the adrenaline and stress generated by the rushed and hasty nature of his time-sensitive mission, despite the tunnel vision and blindness to any and all distraction that such an endeavor demands, he was ominously aware of a foreboding sensation running up and down his spine. It dogged him, nagged at the back of his consciousness, it was with him the whole time he was pinballing through thruway lanes and gunning his engine to beat yellow lights.

The feeling, the instinct, the whatever you want to call it that lets you know you're going to be in danger the instant before you're really in danger, never left him. He would have sworn of a stack of King James Bibles that someone had been following him ever since he'd left his house. Paranoia, they call it in clinical terms. Well, except in cases such as these, when the subject is completely correct in his assumptions, when the worst possible fears that said subject can bear to fantasize have actually become a tangible part of his day.

Eddie was being followed, tailed on his way to the courthouse by a gray sedan that was careful to hang back in traffic by two or three car lengths. He was shadowed on his way inside by two imposingly large men in forgettable everyday clothes.

After conducting his business with the clerk of the court's office, Eddie stopped at water fountain that stood directly outside of the fourth floor's men's restroom. It was there the two oversized sinister figures accosted him, and Eddie realized, too late, the reason for the hunted feeling he thought he'd been imagining all day.

Before Eddie could yell for help, one of his assailants had a hand over his mouth. The other applied a choke hold on him. Half shoving and half dragging, the two men grappled Eddie, who was struggling like hell, into the nearby men's room and out of sight and earshot of potential witnesses.

Once they dragged him through the restroom doors, they pushed him roughly against the wall of a bathroom stall. One man stood guard at the door, while the other held him still with both hands, invading his space and putting his face right into Eddie's. It was only at that precise moment, after all the noise and confusion and abject terror of the abduction, that Eddie realized who his tormentors were: the detectives were assigned to his case!

Malaka, of course, was the alpha aggressor, the one who had his hands on Eddie and was roughing him up. His partner was participating, but seemed to be hanging back as much as possible; he wore an almost embarrassed expression on his face throughout the whole ordeal. But Eddie couldn't see him at the moment; all he could see was a super-sized, super-agitated Malaka, loud and clear, up close and personal, so much so that Eddie could identify every imperfection, pockmark, and pore on his ugly mug of a face.

Eddie's and Malaka's faces were so near one another that when Malaka spoke, Eddie could smell the stale tobacco and liquor on his breath. The odor mingled with the aroma of cheap cologne and sweat that rose from Malaka's body, adding to the already sharp sense of nausea afflicting Eddie. Malaka's teeth were faintly yellowed, and his lips were snarled in the menacing rictus of a smile.

"So punk, you figure you'll take us to trial, slug it out, air all the dirty laundry, and bring a couple guys down with you if you're gonna go. Gonna plead not guilty. Gonna be a big hero."

"That's not what I'm—"

"Shut the fuck up."

This instruction was accented by a breath-stealing knee to Eddie's chest that knocked the wind out of him. Having made his point, Malaka continued, "I'm doing' the talkin' here for once. Not you, not your union delegate, and certainly not your bullshit lawyer. That ok with you?"

Eddie nodded, still too bereft of air to form words if he wanted to, if he wasn't scared silent in the first place anyway.

"That gonna be ok with your esteemed counselor? Oh wait a second; I don't see any lawyers here. No cops. No cons either. Just a few guys settling things the basic way, like they have since the beginning of time. Well let me make it even more basic for you then."

Malaka pulled a Glock 9mm pistol from a shoulder holster and pressed it to Eddie's left temple.

"It's as basic as this pal. You wanna be the big whistle-blowing hero, we know you know the whole story, and we know you know how deep it goes. You wanna sing out all that shit like some rat canary in court, I'm going to find you. I'm gonna put two right in your fucking skull. And your kid will never be a cop. Understand?"

Eddie just looked at his persecutor, eyes wide, thinking about how he was a sworn officer of the law. He thought about how this was going down in the State of New Jersey, one of the original states in the good old U.S. of A. His musings went no further, however. A pistol whip from Malaka brought him back into the here and now.

"I said, do we understand each other? Here's the part where you talk. I want to hear you say you understand what I'm telling you here."

"I understand. Plead out. Plead guilty. No trial or I'm a dead man."

"Oh no. Well you get it, but you really don't get it. See you might walk out of here, watch some *Rocky*-shit on the TV, and find some personal courage that steels you to the point that you don't care about your well-being, you'll just want to do 'the right thing' [this phrase is spit out dripping with venomous sarcasm], the stand-up thing, the integrity thing, and you'll say 'fuck it.' You'll go through with it, you'll break our little agreement we've reached in here, and you'll go ahead and testify."

All the time that Malaka is speaking, Eddie is reassuringly shaking his head no. Malaka picked up on this and began to mock Eddie, shaking his head in a similar manner.

"No? No. I know Eddie, I know, but you might, you just might. That's why I want to help you out by giving you extra incentive. I'm going to make your agonizing moral dilemma an easy thing for you. So listen up: point blank, you testify and not only do I blow your head clear fucking off, I also come after your family. I lock up your kid—your son—for the same shit we're charging you with. Your wife gets run off the road and disappears, etcetera, etcetera. Get the picture?"

Eddie got the picture. But just to make sure, Malaka left him with a parting shot, a brutal elbow to the diaphragm that slumped him to the floor. Before leaving Eddie in a hump of hurting humanity, Malaka meticulously unbuttoned his holster and put his pistol back inside of it before leaning down to repeat and rehash the general gist of the threats he'd just made and make sure Eddie agreed to keep quiet about what Malaka called "the nature of their little conversation."

Eddie was amenable, and Malaka figured he'd made his point. Eager to make his getaway, Malaka wasted no time grabbing his partner and hightailing it out of the courthouse men's room, leaving Eddie gasping and groaning, sprawled helplessly beside a bank of gleaming urinals.

🔥 🔥 🔥

Driving home from the courthouse, pale, shaking, and shaken, not five minutes after he'd been victimized by the casual thuggish ness of Malaka's menacing assault, a queer thought popped into Eddie's mind from out of nowhere.

It came to him while he waited for a red light to turn green at a downtown intersection its arrival was, in fact, so quirky, inappropriate, and misplaced that it actually ended up gouging a deep slice of light and levity that, for at least an instant, succeeded in piercing the almost-material thickness of his heavy, brooding mood. It cut like the blade of a circular saw, carving through Eddie's compressed layers of rage and fear, displacing, for a moment, the sensations of helplessness and abject terror he was experiencing.

"At least things can't possibly get much worse," was the oddly comforting cliché that bubbled up from Eddie's subconscious. He derived a significant amount of reassurance from the simple truth espoused by the realization. He also found it more than somewhat funny; it succinctly encapsulated and efficiently captured the sheer absurdity of the situation he had so speedily found himself descended into and gotten mired in—not to mention the shoulder-shrugging palms raised to the sky in complete frustration, Murphy's law-abiding "fuck it all" aspect of complete resignation the phrase implied.

It did not exactly make him laugh. More accurately, it inspired the briefest hiccup of a rueful chuckle. *It can't possibly get much worse. At least things can't possibly get much worse.* He repeated the phrase to himself over and over, with slight variations, repetitious and drone-like as a mediator's mantra, until he caught himself saying it aloud to himself in the empty car.

Turning the corner onto his home street, Eddie was snapped back into the pressing reality of present trauma by having to quickly and sharply turn his steering wheel to narrowly avoid an accident. By the skin of his teeth, he was able to avoid being run off the road and into a head-on collision with he hard-packed, raised bank of grass that traveled in terraced ridges across the hilly front yard of his neighbor.

The cause of the dangerous and instant twist in Eddie's (heretofore serene) traffic-related fortunes was a careening caravan of three jet-black Chevrolet Suburban SUVs that burned Firestone rubber and kicked up loose grains of asphalt as they plowed forward in unison, speeding, veering violently from one edge of the undersized stickball-, touch football-, and street hockey-playing child-frequented road to the next. They sped out of the low-impact community street with their snarling, steaming, high-impact machines spewing diesel and dust and threats of destruction.

The dark trucks that blew by Eddie were piloted by a trio of drivers who appeared to have coordinated and developed a certain aesthetic of collective aggression that characterized their driving style.

The necessary navigation correction their hazardous road hogging required that Eddie perform a lightening-fast 180^0 spin that called for the type of radical and instinctual feat of double-handed panache usually only demanded by certain discriminating NASCAR devotees. Even they restrict this uncommonly superior level of automotive performance expectation to an elite coterie of top-tier, bona-fide racing stars as the Gordon's, Earthward's, and Waltrip's of the world.

But Eddie pulled off the challenging maneuver, swerving precariously to the right and then to the left, all the while maintaining balance and control, seeking and finding a small safe patch of road shoulder on the opposite side of the road. He and his humble vehicle skidded into stillness, weathering the oncoming storm of steel frames and sheer tonnage.

With the offending procession steadily receding into his rearview, Eddie shifted back into drive and kept on moving. After the day's despicable, demeaning, and discouraging events, nothing was going to get between Eddie and the comforts and solace of his home and family, if he could possibly help it.

As it turned out, something quite substantial was going to get between Eddie and the comforts of his home and family, and there was very little, if anything, he could've done to help it. The something was simple animal fear. Ironically, the same thing Eddie was running home so desperately to escape was the identical thing he was on his way to find. Worse, he'd have the misery of watching as the horrid affliction was deliberately spread to and through his family.

Being intimately and recently well-acquainted with his dreaded emotional state, he had developed a particularly keen insight into the precise nature of its punishing tortures. Eddie was in a rare position to empathize with what his family was going through. He knew exactly how they felt. Same as him. And that was he realization he almost couldn't stand. It almost drove him right out of his mind. Of all the dirty tricks and de facto crimes heaped on the man, the way they terrorized his family had to be, by far, the hardest thing for him to take.

The renewed drama Eddie was on his way to walking in on would be generated by a parallel incident that had taken place at Eddie's house during the brief time that he'd been gone. Coincidentally or uncoincidentally (by this time, the reader is invited to speculate), what went on at Eddie's home occurred at almost exactly the same time that Malaka had blustered through his gun-wielding shakedown in the courthouse men's room.

When Eddie pulled into his driveway, he could already sense that things were terribly wrong. The peaceful, calm sense of order that usually emanated from the well-kept, ordered, and organized home was replaced by chaos. The first thing Eddie noticed was the open front door. Papers and files had been scattered across the front lawn.

Terrible as the day had already been, Eddie tried to write off the oddities and formulate some explanation. Once he stepped out of the car, this became impossible. His wife ran out the front door, her eyes puffy from crying, and her face manic with the rabid panic of fear. She ran to him as if she were running for her life itself.

Dropping everything he held in his arms, he ran to meet her. They caught up to one another in the middle of the front yard. She threw her arms around Eddie's shoulders and slumped into his chest. When words finally came through the borderline hyperventilation of rapid breathing, they were spattered and scattershot, short, sharp, and disorganized. Eddie had to strain to understand. At first he thought she'd gone crazy. He couldn't believe his ears.

"The government … the feds, I mean they said they were FBI … they were dressed in suits and ties, armed to the teeth … flashed badges and said they had warrants and everything. The FBI raided our house … tore through everything … left everything a mess … threatened me … threatened Dominic and the family … threatened everyone, talking about 'your husband better rethink his plea; he has no idea of the powerful forces arrayed against him.' Oh Jesus … oh shit. Eddie, honey, what's happening here? Oh God, oh my God. Eddie, what are we going to do?"

Chapter 15

"Don't worry. I'm here now. We'll figure something out. We'll get along. We always do."

"But I'm really scared Eddie, really scared."

Eddie was cradling his wife right out there in the middle of his yard, on the front lawn, where she'd swooned in his arms. For just that moment in time, the world seemed to shrink away, leaving just him and her.

He didn't care about neighbors, about appearances, about rumors, about the court of public opinion. All he cared about was comforting the woman he loved and providing her with the support she so desperately needed.

They remained out there, locked in a frozen solid embrace, for ten, maybe twenty minutes. Eddie held and fortified Renee in the steel cocoon of his chest, shoulders, and arms, whispering reassurances until she eventually came around.

Once Renee had a chance to catch her breath and regain her composure, once Eddie had a chance to process some of the unbridled havoc he'd just come home to, she took him by the hand and led him inside. He had thought that some of what she had said at the peak of her hysteria had been ravings and wild exaggeration.

He clung to the vain hope that things were much less serious than she was making them out to be. When they'd been out on the lawn, he kept thinking, *once I get her calm, the better we'll be able to put this all into perspective.* By that, he meant shrink the situation down to manageable size.

To his growing alarm, he found himself facing the exact opposite. The calmer Renee became, the more meticulously she was able to fill in any blanks she'd left during her first few disjointed, spitfire attempts at narrative. The additional details she was able to recount grew more numerous, disturbing, and, well, detailed.

As she spoke, each tone more measured than the last, her words acquired a terrible resonance, compounded by Eddie's slow but steady realization of the fact that her accuracy or sense of perspective was now beyond reproach. She had clearly gotten her bearings back, and everybody who knew her knew that, bearings intact, this was an eminently stable woman, not prone to exaggeration or hyperbole. She was at her best under pressure, and didn't rattle easily at all.

If anything, Renee had actually understated the seriousness of the incident. (Her initial spillover on the lawn had flooded past a number of key events, resulting in several omissions, each more troubling than the last.) It only took one look at the interior of their usually immaculate, intricately ordered household to drive this point home.

Eddie stood in the foyer trying to make himself believe he was trapped in a vivid and extended nightmare, a nightmare from which he would soon awake. No dice. This was real, real, real; shit didn't get more real than this. Eddie sweat cool beads of moisture that needled him with chilly discomfort from head to toe, from what seemed like 1,000 different microscopic, seam-like openings that split the salt-slickened patina of his suddenly shimmering skin. He was breathless and speechless.

The scene suddenly liquefied, swimming by in an underwater blur. He reached in vain for a wall, a piece of furniture, anything that might steady his upright position as he no longer trusted his feet. His knees buckled and sent him sprawling. But, at the crucial moment, his wife put a steadying arm on his shoulder.

Then he remembered that, even though he'd never felt more alone, there were others involved; his family was at stake. They'd done nothing.

It was his blind trust and naiveté that had brought this entire trouble home to them. So the way he figured it, he had an obligation. He had to be strong. He couldn't fall apart. He would pull himself together, if not for himself, for them. They needed him now more then ever. They all depended on him, looking to him for the next move to be made. He simply didn't have the luxury of falling to pieces.

Taking a deep breath, then another, then another, he quietly rearranged and repaired the shattered puzzle pieces of his mental jigsaw until they fit together firmly enough for him to survey the scene that had thrown him so off balance.

He had psyched himself up to deal with the realities of the present situation in a focused, detached, and methodically efficient fashion, navigating whatever twists and turns might still lurk around the bend. Eddie could now maintain a level-headed equilibrium. Still, the visions that greeted him on his entry simply would not, could not, and did not compute.

The house was an absolute disaster area. Everything had been turned upside down and pulled inside out. It looked as if a bomb had hit it and then a gang of looters had followed along in the wake of the explosion, just to do more damage and spread more chaos.

🌿 🌿 🌿

After letting Eddie set for a moment, while he was standing stock still in the foyer, still just coming to grips with the full extent of it. Renee approached Eddie, took him by the hand, and led him inside. Quietly they toured the rooms together. She led the way, as if the story was too terrible to tell with words and all she could do was offer mute pictures, mute portrayals.

Eddie took it all in: the shattered mirrors, the drawer-less dressers, contents of the empty drawers strewn randomly about the general vicinity, layer after layer of rudely ripped off bedding, knife-slit mattresses, slashed pictures, and slashed canvases of paintings pulled off the wall. The destruction was almost unfathomable the way it just went on and on.

There are apologists for this sort of thing. Folks who step up to the plate and swing a bat on behalf of the bureau, aiming for the cheap seats with that old saw about how lawmen aren't gods, how even lawmen make mistakes, and how these boys were just doing their job. Well, it's important to point out that that line of drizzle just doesn't hold water in this instance.

Just "doing their jobs" doesn't account for all the malice they put into it and all the pleasure they took out of it. These boys left their mark, wanted everyone to know how much fun they had, how much they'd enjoyed their work. They took their time sending unmistakable messages and making precise statements.

For example, it takes a black-belt-level sadist to enter the room of Eddie's youngest child, take the time to select what—from position and wear—is obviously one of the child's most favored toys, hack it to pieces, and then crucify the remains on the child's bedpost. That was exactly what one of the more exuberant and darkly humorous of the agents decided to do.

Just "doing their jobs" doesn't explain, nor does it justify, the fact that for several years, Eddie was constantly made to feel targeted, as if he were living as a hunted underground dissident in a fascist state, always being followed, harassed by macho, power-drunk officials, with all the machinery of state power behind them. These were officials who got off on and derived amusement out of the occasional dropping of breadcrumb hints that were carefully designed to intimidate him further.

Purposely and methodically, as if they were following some sick, sadistic textbook, Eddie's well-connected, well-coordinated gang of tormentors kept him in a constant state of anxiety, kept him wound up tighter than a bale of copper wire. Sporadic episodes filled with unremitting fear and terror served as the only punctuation from the monotonously routine atmosphere of ominously impending doom that Eddie was forced to live under throughout the period chronicled here.

In the name of "the law," he was made to run wild-goose chases (standing in this line or that at some agency or another chasing an ever-changing, ever-growing portfolio of meaningless but required documents, then battling against the clock or cross-town or downtown traffic to get to the notary and/or his lawyer's office or the courthouse before close of business just so he could avoid the necessity of repeating the entire process from the beginning and being forced to endure the entire soul-numbing, through-the-meat-grinder routine all over again the next morning), slog across countless obstacle courses, and jump so many times through so many of their petty, pointless bureaucratic hoops that, without even realizing it, Eddie had began to follow instructions as if they were orders, discharging all charge-related tasks by rote, unthinking, instinctively responding to stimulus like a Pavlovian dog.

Action. Reaction. Stimulus. Response. Stimulus. Response. Before long, they'd broken a confident, competent, tough, proud, sovereign human being down to his basic animal essence. They'd eroded his sense of security until he felt exposed and vulnerable as the only creature of his kind left on Earth, the last prey remaining in a world teeming with predators. Before long, they'd reduced a robust, vigorous, poised man into a frayed pile of aggravated, raw nerve endings connected to haphazardly firing synapses, encased in a hollowed-out, haunted shell of quivering flesh.

This is how the justice system treated and was doing to one of America's bravest. This is the way they chose to thank him. And it was wrong. And people need to hear this story because it's the God's honest truth, give or take some event sequencing and a few names and dates. If it happened to a man like Eddie, it could happen to a man or a woman like you. So people need to speak up about this. People need to speak with other people about this.

Tell a friend about this travesty. Someday perhaps accountability will be demanded of the men behind the concerted plan to make

Eddie's life a living hell through systematic and sustained hounding, through periodic power moves meant to torture and terrorize.

If enough of you who read these words do speak up, justice will be done. And the Corrunoside fire and police departments, the Corrunoside volunteers, the Centerville County prosecutor's office, the mayor and director of Corrunoside, and all the minions in his administration, will have to explain why they did what they did to one of their own citizens, an honest, good-hearted person they were supposed to protect, serve, and represent; a fine firefighter and family man; an asset to his community named Eddie.

◟ ◟ ◟

After taking a visual inventory of the damage and disorder done to his house by the FBI agents in the course of their search, Eddie sat with his wife at the kitchen table, holding her hands in his own.

Gently he urged her to endure one last retelling of the day's events. This time, however, he wanted her to do her best to relate her tale in a linear fashion. He asked her to start at the beginning and concentrate on capturing everything that happened, in the exact order in which it happened.

"Do you think you might be able to do that honey? I mean, do you think you're up to it? We can do it later, but it's best to go over everything while it's fresh in your mind. Plus, we can get it out of the way and over with. What do you think?"

Renee said she thought it was a good idea to review the trauma, before it had a chance to fade and be buried. She said she didn't quite know what she was up for at the moment, but that now was as good a time as any. She said she knew what he was looking for as far as detail and comprehensiveness and accurate time line and that she'd give it her very best shot.

Then she smiled at him, closed her eyes, and inhaled and exhaled several times. Renee took her time taking each breath like it was her last... It was almost sensual the way she caught and released the air in her lungs, like a smoker really enjoying a deep drag. When she opened her eyes, she told what had happened.

"It all started when I was in the kitchen deciding what I should fix for dinner. That was when I heard the loud rev of engines and squealing tires. By the time I got to the living room window and saw the Suburbans in the driveway, there was already a pounding at the door. One of the officers had a megaphone and, just like in the movies, was yelling, 'FBI, open the door immediately!'

"Before I could even get to the door, however, it came blasting open. Thank God they hadn't been a few seconds later, because they would have caught me head-on while I would've been frantically trying to unlatch the door for them.

"They'd used one of those portable rams they show on the cop shows, but I mean, you wouldn't believe the force and the violence with which they took out our door! I'm positive that I would've been in the hospital right now had I been even a few steps closer.

"So, anyway, in comes a gang of four plainclothes officers, banging around and screaming, guns drawn, ordering me on the floor. For all I know at this point, this is a ruse and I'm about to get gang raped and brutalized by four criminals.

"Eventually I'm searched, I mean, pawed all over. Every time I think about it, my skin crawls and I want to run to the shower. Don't get me wrong, they were professional about things; there was nothing tangible I could point at as improper, but still, even when they are on their best behavior, a full-on search, especially for a woman ... well it's quite the degrading process, to say the least.

"After all this I'm allowed to get up and take a seat. Two of them interrogate and try to frighten me with veiled and not-so-veiled threats, while the other two tear through the house looking for who-the-hell-knows-what.

"It's at this point they flash their badges and identification to let me know that they're really with the federal government. Once they let this sink in, they tell me to tell you that you had better listen to all the friendly advice you've been getting and plead out your case, or else."

"Or else what?"

"That's what I wanted to know, so I asked. One of the agents drew a finger across his throat and the other agent says 'or else, this is just the beginning of the hell we are going to put you through.'"

"And then what happened?"

"I called your new lawyer, Mr. Blackburn , and he told me, to put one of them on the phone and he told them leave their business card and get out of our house. He then told me that we will deal with them later. He said he definitely felt that somebody purposely sent them. As of matter of fact Eddie went to their Office and questioned why they were at his residence. Their answer was it must have been a coincidence because there are no reports, no incident paperwork, and nobody remembers it ever happening. (Never another word from the FBI) Another coincidence, the director of Corrunoside at the time was retired from that same office.

"And then they just left. Left everything they'd overturned and messed up and rooted through and then took off, trailing more vague threats behind them about the decision I need to encourage my husband to make if he knows what's good for him and his family. You must have only missed them by five minutes. They tore out of the driveway right before you pulled in."

❦ ❦ ❦

Days later, after the sheer adrenaline panic had died down, after he'd finally been able to find enough peace to clear his head and think things through, Eddie was able to add two and two and come up with four. What could have gotten the FBI involved? Was the State of New Jersey now saying that he, Eddie, possibly committed federal-level crimes? No, of course not.

The only other explanation for the quartet of agents, and their timely arrival at Eddie's residence, was that somebody knew someone and was able to call in a favor and call in the big dogs for a day.

Eddie now realized how deep the proverbial rabbit hole went. The only person with that kind of power, the only person with that kind of clout, with those kind of connections, and with an actual career history as a employee/agent within the FBI, was the mayor's right-hand man and most trusted adviser: Corrunoside's esteemed director of public safety.

It was also at this point that he began to get a realistic conception of the mammoth conglomeration of interests that had aligned against him and were working against him, in concert, with a carefully coordinated— and devastatingly expert—strategic and tactical prowess.

It wasn't just elements of the fire department executive hierarchy and the mayor's office anymore; it had expanded beyond that. Eddie, one lone American citizen, suddenly found himself pitted against great strength, awesome forces, organized, terraced wielders of incredible quantities and qualities of influence.

The great regional power brokers and traditional political barons were nothing if not opportunists, and they smelled an advantage where Eddie's case was concerned. They saw Eddie as a convenient fall guy slash public service announcement example of the week, and they lined up to rail against Eddie, using as ammunition lies created and churned out by their own public relations mills.

Eddie consulted with his lawyer on Monday morning. It was then that he connected the many heads of the hydra he was up against. Articles had begun to appear about his case in the local section of the newspaper. They always included incriminating quotes from unattributed and anonymous but high-level sources in the mayor's office, the county commission's office, and the district attorney's office. Still smarting from the very physical intercessions endured by himself and his wife just a few days prior, Eddie, under tremendous pressure, made the fateful decision to wave a flag of surrender and see if the prosecutor's office would play nicely and live up to the promises they'd floated to Blackburn . Eddie's play was not to plead guilty, but to plead no contest and try to bargain his way out from the worst of it, to swim with the flow of the mighty state instead of against it.

The stress Eddie had been subjected to serve as the breaking point and the primary decision driver that morning. It's not quite as if it could be accurately said that Eddie actually broke down in Blackburn's office. No, what happened was much more subtle than that.

They were having coffee and discussing the progress of Eddie's case and the possibility of showing signs of giving some ground when Eddie's cup-holding hand began to shake and he could not stop it. He almost spilled the coffee.

It was exactly at that point in time that he became fully aware of the gut-wrenching strain the entire legal mess had wrought upon him, the years that it had aged him, and he began to allow mentally for the possibility of surrender, even though he was 100 percent in the right. In an ideal world, that would matter. In the real world, sometimes important decisions are based on expedience and fatigue.

Eddie shrugged his shoulders and faced Blackburn with upturned palms. He sat hunched for a time, palms still turned upward, in the dreaded visitor's chair, leaning intently forward.

There was a look of complete resignation on Eddie's face, as if he was saying "I give up, let's throw in the towel. Even though we're right, they've got too much might." That look on Eddie's face, that utterly resigned and hopeless look was a terrible thing to see.

After an uncomfortable silence during which both lawyer and client stared at each other and blinked a lot, Eddie finally spoke. "You're right and my wife is right. Heck, even the law is right about this one issue, though they're so twisted and wrong about everything else. But one thing is for certain: I can't fight them anymore. They're too powerful, too strong."

"So? What exactly are you saying to me?"

"Let's put out some feelers and see what they're willing to put on the table in exchange for a nolo contendre plea. Nobody testifies about anybody's internal, department-wide corruption, but then again nobody goes to jail either, we just call it a draw and all save face and go home and forget about it."

"Eddie, I got to be honest with you, I don't think anything short of a guilty plea will satisfy these sharks. In fact, I don't think anything short of an unconditional guilty plea will even bring them to the table. They smell blood in the water, and they are after your hide. It's as simple as that. They want to disgrace a firefighter and you fit the bill. And you, if I may be so blunt in saying so, have played into their hands, guilty or not guilty."

"So you're not even sure? My advocate questions my honor."

"Don't give me that load of you-know-what. The defense attorney is never sure, ever. We're always furthest in the dark. Did you do it? I don't care. The point now is to find the path of least resistance and the path that keeps you out of jail. Agreed? I mean, we're on the same page here, agreed?"

"Agreed."

"So, now we've come to a decision I can't make for you. I can counsel you on it, but you have to tell me what the next move is going to be. The ball is in your court, and you know what I think. It's your call. What's it going to be?"

"I'm going to cave. What other damn choice to I have? Float the possibility now, mind you, the possibility not the definite prospect, but the possibility of a guilty plea and see what we can get for it. I authorize you to make the deal if the deal is right. Let them know you have that negotiating authority. That will send the message that we're serious. Now let's see how serious they are."

"What exactly do you mean by 'if the deal is right'? You're leaving a lot open to interpretation, and I don't know if I'm comfortable with that. I mean I know you just want this over with so you can wash your hands of it, but take a minute here and think. This is an important part of the process. What are your deal breakers? At what point do you want me to say 'thanks but no thanks, fellas, but if that's your final offer, my client and I, we're content roll the dice at trial.'?"

"Well it's pretty obvious, isn't it? Jail! There's no way I'm going to just roll over and sign on the dotted line if there's any sort of stretch involved. Bottom line—main thing—just do whatever you need to do to keep me out from behind bars. Do not let them put me in a fucking cage for something I didn't do, understand? Under no circumstances will I take that lying down. That I cannot abide by. As God is my witness, no actual time or I swear to God I'll fight this thing to the death. If you can fix it so I'm guaranteed to at least walk away from this catastrophe with my freedom, then you can let them have all the rest of their petty victories as far as I'm concerned. I just want this to be over. I just want to be able to go home to my family and pick up the pieces of my life. I just want some peace, safety, and security to spend one night without knowing the relentless pressure and merciless stress of unending fear and worry. Any deal you can get that will allow me those simple reprieves I will sign, without going back and forth on it, without engaging you in debate on its finer points, in fact, without questions of any kind and without hesitation. That's a promise."

🔥 🔥 🔥

For several days after the decisive Blackburn meeting, it appeared that the shoulder-stooping burdens of the heavy-duty heat that, for an extended time, had been choking off Eddie's breath like an molten albatross necklace, digging into and crushing against his back like 1,000 steel beams, and pressing down harder and harder upon his existence, like the weight of the world itself, were at last beginning to lighten up and cool off a bit. The case was temporarily simmering on the back burner while Blackburn and the PROSECUTORS OFFICE hammered out the details of a trial-averting deal that, by mutual agreement, was designed and crafted to publicly embarrass, humiliate, and chastise Eddie and, by association, the old Corrunoside fire department and city hall leadership regimes to the maximum possible extent. In exchange, however, the stipulations of the deal would ensure that a declawed and defanged form of punishment would be meted out as Eddie's voluntarily admitted "crimes" were concerned.

Consequences and sanctions faced by Eddie consisted of a series of nonbinding resolutions and window-dressing proclamations that were passed by various government bodies convening on various levels.

The city and county commissions both weighed in and the New Jersey State Police Department contributed an investigator funded by a state legislature appropriation. But not one iota of federal resources was devoted to Eddie's case.

(Strangely, no federal-level law enforcement interest was shown, either during the jointly coordinated Centerville County and borough of Corrunoside's long-term, multi-agency program of investigation and surveillance, or at any time during the drawn-out proceedings of the subsequent criminal case.

Despite the cocky personas and ham-fisted, heavy-handed tactics adapted by the four G-men, despite their aggressive posturing during their repeated efforts at interrogation and the wantonly destructive rampage they inflicted on Eddie's house, the federal agents who so rudely and brusquely inserted themselves into the Eddie's legal affairs were clearly unauthorized to do so by the relevant authorities.

What they did was blatantly and brazenly illegal. To make a long story short, so many laws were broken by the FBI personnel who participated in the raid, search, questioning, and threat-making at Eddie's house, it would take an entire chapter to name them all. They should have all lost their jobs and been sent to prison for long stretches. Of course they skated. Eddie lost his job over this B.S. As of this writing, every one of the FBI thugs who raided Eddie's home remains in the employ of the federal government.)

Eddie faced official proclamations roundly condemning and censuring his questionable actions and judgment, as well as judicial scolding delivered directly from the bench, decrying, in the most sanctimonious (and, some would say, hypocritical) terms imaginable, the severe, irreparable damage his character flaws had caused in terms of the public perception and overall reputation of the Corrunoside Fire Department.

Eddie was also hit with a formidable slate of heavy fines. The toughest pill for Eddie to swallow, however, was not the public derision, the damage to his reputation, or the seriously severe bites that were taken out of his bank account.

For Eddie, the most devastating component of the agreement was the PROSECUTORS OFFICE insistence on a career-ruining dishonorable discharge, which terminated every vestige of Eddie's long-standing, proud affiliation with the department he loved so much and had contributed so much to.

The fire department had been his life. To separate Eddie from the department meant more than just firing him from his work; it represented a fundamental violation of his manhood and his dignity. Being a firefighter had made up a huge aspect of his overall identity. Now, in the blink of an eye, through no real fault of his own, it was all gone.

With the simple stroke of a pen and the crunch of a notary's seal, the bastards had succeeded in taking the one thing they had absolutely no right to lay claim to: his livelihood and his passion … his basic purpose, function, and reason for being … the job that God put him on this Earth to do, the job that He'd granted Eddie the innate talent and courage to do so well for so long.

To the petty paper-pushers, red-tapers, and rule-makers of the world, however, all this meant nothing. Thus, without giving it a second thought or losing a wink of sleep over it, these empty-suited bureaucrats, with their adding machine heads, soulless souls, and Lilliputian hearts, went ahead and stole the one thing Eddie thought he'd never lose, the one thing he thought that no one in their right mind or with any sense of fair play could ever deny him, the one thing he had clearly and cleanly earned with years of blood, sweat, toil, and for which he had boldly and willingly laid his life on the line and exposed himself to the most extreme dangers, again and again and again.

In general, the terms of Eddie's plea bargain were rough; in many ways, they were uncompromising. However, when it came to one of the most key and important components of the agreement, the prosecutor's office elected, at the last possible moment, to demonstrate some give and show the minimal amount of compromise and cooperation necessary to salvage, then seal the deal between the plaintiff (State of New Jersey) and the defendant (Eddie).

An iron-clad commitment was extracted from prosecutors that Eddie's guilty plea guaranteed, regardless of whatever arrangement was ultimately endorsed by the judge, his debt to society would not include so much as a single minute of incarceration time. Although Blackburn and the prosecutor's office were still negotiating precisely what the exact parameters of Eddie's restitution would entail, the looming, lingering specter of prison was off of the table for good.

In addition to the providential holding pattern that had briefly delayed all legal proceedings against him, freezing his case in stasis, halting all prosecutorial progress, and stilling the grinding gears of justice until they'd seized and slipped into a static state of suspended animation, Eddie's fortunes were further boosted by a different sort of reprieve, the nature of which was far more unofficial and informal.

News of Eddie's decision to go ahead and fold the potentially damaging, damning hand full of crooked aces and kings he was holding had busted out and was on the loose. Unengaged, it spread around more quickly than an overgrown, underbrush-fueled prairie fire during an arid, twig-snapping season. The message was disseminated so widely and traveled at such lightning speed thanks to the efficiency of both the fire department grapevine and the age-old, mouth-to-mouth telegraph of the streets.

Before very long, the word was out all over town that Eddie had decided to decline his right to a trial by a jury and would not be taking the stand on his own behalf. It was precisely at this juncture that the array of physical threats, nasty phone calls, FBI visits, detective-led bathroom shakedowns, and myriad other unpleasantries Eddie and his family had endured came to an abrupt halt.

It wasn't until a day or two had elapsed without incident of any kind that Eddie began to feel secure enough to let down his guard and relax. After so much unrelenting strain, Eddie was relieved that his hellish period of personal crisis appeared to be moving toward some sort of conclusion.

There were certain things about the resolution of his situation that had left a terribly sour taste in his mouth, but at the moment, he wasn't focused on the high price he'd have to pay to put this sorry episode behind him. At the moment, he was willing to do anything, make any concession, if it contributed toward the removal of the sword of Damocles that had been hanging over his head.

Eddie realized that he'd been carrying himself like a soldier in a war zone, ever vigilant, in a constant state of maximum alert, always tense as a drawn bow. The necessity of living in perpetual survival mode had exacted a brutal toll on his physical health, piece of mind, and family life. Now that he was experiencing his closest brush with calm and stability in quite some time, Eddie planned on taking advantage of the unexpected reprieve to catch his breath, recharge his batteries, repair the damage done to his and his family's well-being, and prepare for whatever was going to come next.

Since their vacation, for example, Eddie had often been short and snappy toward his wife. He was often so busy worrying about his own problems that he hadn't been sufficiently considerate of and attuned to her needs and fears. After all, she had borne the brunt of the FBI's invasion of their home. In addition, it was up to her to keep the home running with an air of normality—smiling, joking, and pretending everything was all right for the sake of the children—while their lives were crumbling around them.

It was Renee who had to show understanding and restraint when Eddie got moody or taciturn. It was Renee who bucked Eddie up whenever she saw that the whole draining drama was started to get the best of him.

Therefore, the top item on Eddie's agenda was to surprise his wife by doing something special for her to let her know that she was very much appreciated. He wanted to do something major for her, something big enough to send out the message of how much he cared for her, something big enough to let her know that he still loved her just as much as he ever had and that he was proud of her strength and composure. He wanted Renee to know he was thankful that she had loyally stuck by him and seen this thing through with him, sharing his fears, comforting his anxieties, facing things head on, refusing to hide from it or run away no matter how unpleasant and scary things got, going through every new wrinkle and unexpected complication of their hellacious ordeal as a team, as partners, side by side.

A lesser woman would have abandoned him. A lesser woman would have deserted him to avoid the inconvenience of the ongoing upheaval and to ensure the safety of her own skin.

❦ ❦ ❦

The next afternoon found Eddie busily following through on the plans he'd made to wow his wife as best as he knew how. He'd left the house around noon, telling Renee he was going to visit with his mother but that he'd be back before five and wanted to spend some time together.

"I'd like that," she'd responded, "I feel like we need to, we should talk about things."

Eddie completely missed the warning in her words, taking them at face value and agreeing that it had been a while since they'd had time to sit down together and truly communicate.

Eddie spent the next five hours in a cyclonic whirl of activity. By 4:30, he'd lined up a babysitter, made reservations for an expensive restaurant in the city that Renee was always saying she wanted to try and Eddie was always saying they couldn't afford, bought theater tickets to a Broadway show, and selected and purchased a breathtaking pair of diamond earrings.

Eddie's practical side could sometimes get in the way of his romantic impulses. It almost won the upper hand again when he saw the price of the jewelry come up on the store register. He got over the initial sticker shock, however, and told himself, *what the hell. She's my woman and she deserves it. If I have to scrimp and cut some corners somewhere down the line, so be it.*

Even though he'd finished his errands and still had a half-hour to spare until he said he'd be home, he ended up getting caught in traffic on his way out of Manhattan. He was further delayed by an accident-related snarl-up on the bridge.

Running late, he began to speed. Minutes later, a cop car appeared—seemingly from out of nowhere—flashed its lights and pulled him over. Once the officer found out he was dealing with a firefighter, he let Eddie off with a warning. After, of course, he called in to verify his license and registration. While it was nice to avoid what would have been a costly ticket, the damage in terms of lost time had been done. By the time Eddie pulled into his driveway, it was almost quarter to seven.

Eddie was perplexed to see his wife's car missing from the driveway. He didn't think much of it, assuming she'd run to the corner store or something. After all the activity and frustration of running around all day, Eddie walked through the front door and immediately plopped down on the couch and caught the tail end of the news.

When the news ended and there was still no sign of Renee, Eddie's level of alarm increased. He turned on the lights in the living room and the kitchen and began checking the answering machine to see if she'd left a message. Maybe she was mad that he was late, got sick of waiting, and had gone out to eat by herself.

After all that had happened, foremost on his mind was making sure she was all right. He asked himself *could she have been kidnapped.* The distressing thought spurred him into action. He walked through the entire house looking for clues. There was no sign of struggle, and since she was a fighter there likely would have been, so he was fairly certain there had been no abduction.

The mystery of Renee's absence was solved when he entered the bedroom they'd shared for almost a quarter century. Much of her stuff was gone. The rest was packed up and stacked against a wall. She hadn't been abducted. She hadn't been in an accident or hurt. And, she hadn't stormed out on her own or with her friends for the evening in retaliation for his tardy arrival.

Her stuff was gone. She was gone. She'd left him. For real. For good. She'd run out on him just when he needed her the most, when he was depending on her to get from breath to breath, as if she were his oxygen. There was a note on their dresser that was addressed to him from her.

Eddie picked up the note and read it, palms sweating and hands shaking with trepidation. After completing the note, he crumpled it up and let it hit the floor. Then he crumpled up and hit the floor. All he felt was pain. His whole world was pain. He felt, actually felt, a profound, nearly indescribable sense of loss that was concretely physical. There was a searing rip that tore through his midsection, as though a gaping hole had been gouged from his chest.

He could have sworn that he could actually feel his heart get heavy, go brittle, and break, all at once. It seemed to break more and more, into smaller and smaller, sharper and sharper pieces with each new breath he drew in. He had to remind himself to breathe.

He couldn't seem to get enough air into his lungs. The sensation reminded him of a Saturday afternoon, over two decades ago, when he was playing junior varsity football in high school and got the wind knocked out of him by a much larger boy.

It made him think about the time when he was a child and his pet goldfish had leaped out of its bowl. He'd found it in the nick of time, gasping for breath on his bedroom floor, in much the same way that he was now gasping for breath on the floor. Eddie remained where he had fallen for a long time before he even tried to pick himself up. What was weird, however, what was really, really strange, was that Eddie didn't shed a single tear. He was too deeply submerged in a state of shock to cry.

Chapter 16

In the weeks between the next phase of his case's disposition and the initial rent in the fabric of Eddie's life that followed Renee's unexpected disappearing act, something very unorthodox happened: Eddie began, as he always had when the odds were against him and his back was against the wall, to regroup, recuperate, and ultimately rally.

Like the '86 Mets storming back against the Red Sox to win the World Series in dramatic upset fashion, Eddie mounted his own dogged, gutsy comeback, surmounting unbelievable personal deficits in the process.

Not that he was about to bring home any championship rings or trophies at any point throughout this period, but in the midst of such trying times, he took stock of what he was made of and realized he could and he would make it through this. And if he could make it through this, he figured, he could make it through anything.

Before long, he was second-guessing his decision to throw in the towel on his legal battle. After a few consultations with his lawyer, Eddie began to seriously consider a withdrawal of his guilty plea.

His lawyer advised him to maintain the status quo unless or until he was absolutely sure about reversing his position.

On the particular morning currently being chronicled herein, their presence was required at a preliminary hearing. After a lot of back and forth about the pros and cons of possible strategies moving forward, Eddie was persuaded not to change his plea for the time being. The bottom line was that he still had time to demand his day in court if that was what he ultimately wanted, but this way he could at least have the option think it through further.

Due to a scheduling mix-up, Eddie and his attorney arrived at the courthouse over an hour early. Since they suddenly found themselves with unexpected time on their hands, Blackburn excused himself, explaining that there was some business he might as well take care of. Eddie watched as his legal counsel slowly disappears into a tide of people making their way toward a bank of elevators.

As Blackburn was trekking to an office at the far end of the building, Eddie remained immobile, glued to the spot where he and his lawyer had parted, not quite sure what to do with himself or how to pass the extra time he had on his hands. After a few minutes of aimless wandering through identical looking halls, he found a men's room and used it.

Afterward, while distractedly scanning the mirrors, light fixtures, graffiti, and the tiling on the walls (which, for some reason, noted were the same variety—except for a slightly different shade—as those on the floor) as he washed his hands, a surge of helpless dread rose, violent as a sudden wave. The force and speed of the internal swell jolted Eddie so harshly and physically that he almost convulsed.

The source of his discomfort was simple: he was flashing back to his last encounter in a courthouse bathroom. Eddie's abrupt anxiety attack was further exacerbated by the realization that he happened to have stumbled into the same men's room the two detectives had manhandled him into on that infamous day he would never, could never forget.

Drawing heavily on the inner strength and courage that had helped carry him this far through his ongoing ordeal, Eddie pulled himself together, washed and dried the cold beads of perspiration that had formed on his face and neck, then walked back out into the hallway that led to a bench outside of his assigned hearing room where he was to meet Blackburn in twenty minutes.

Eddie had decided to grab a soda and a newspaper from a nearby machine and just sit down, relax, read the sports page, and wait for his attorney to return. There was nothing else he could think of to do with the down time.

On his way back from the vending area, he thought he heard someone calling his name. A few seconds later, he paused at the sound of approaching footsteps hustling to catch up with him. But when he looked around, there was no one he recognized behind him. Writing it off as paranoia induced by the post-traumatic stress of his restroom visit, Eddie continued on.

As it turned out, someone was indeed trying to get his attention. Turning a corner, Eddie heard footsteps again. When he turned this time, he saw that he was being hailed by a man he vaguely recalled but couldn't quite place.

"Hey ... hey, buddy."

The man snapped his fingers and tapped his temple as if trying to recall a name that's right on the tip of his tongue. He retrieved the wayward detail and continued on.

"Hey ... Fre ... Eddie, Eddie. You're Eddie the firefighter, aren't you?"

"That's me."

"Remember me?"

"I'm sorry. I do but I don't. I'm afraid I can't quite place your name."

"That's ok. We only met once."

An awkward moment passed. Eddie expected the guy to explain himself further. When he did not, Eddie wondered what the hell—

"Can I help you?"

"Maybe, and maybe I can help you."

"I don't follow."

"You sure you don't know who I am?"

"I know we've met before. Hold on ... you're on the job, aren't you?"

"Yeah. I mean not right now, at this minute, as we speak, but yeah, I'm a detective."

"I guess I'm not too popular with many of you guys."

"Well you know actually, it's a funny thing. Not all of us have been able to swallow the party line on this one. Some of us are in your corner."

"When you say 'some of us,' what does that mean? One or two including you?"

"I think I could go so far as to say, pretty reliably and conservatively, that if we're not in the majority, we're damn close."

"Oh really? Is that so?"

It was hard to ignore the hostile edge that lined the otherwise casual and friendly inflections in Eddie's bemused/amused tone of voice. The man who had approached Eddie couldn't help but acknowledge it in his response.

"Listen, I don't blame you for being skeptical. Heck, if I were you, I would be too. I know it's hard to believe after all you've been through, but I swear on the Bible that it's true. You'd be quite surprised, I imagine, at the level of disgust many of us feel about all this."

He waved an arm over his head with the last two words to indicate the courthouse, the long and sometimes crooked arm of the law, everything, the whole ordeal.

Eddie was beginning to be impressed by the detective's apparent simplicity and sincerity, but he wasn't quite ready to let the detective know. However, regardless of whether he showed it or not, the fact was that, despite all the betrayals and let downs he'd been experienced of late, his first instinct was still to trust, not to doubt.

"Not all of us are proud of what's being done to you in our name. In fact, it's quite the contrary. I'd go so far as to say that a whole bunch of us are downright ashamed."

"I wish at least one or two of you would go ahead and speak up. It might be just the thing to help my cause."

"Well I've got to shoot straight with you there. I mean, you know how it is. It doesn't take much in the way of free speech to cost you your job these days. At any rate, I just came over here to tell you that we're pulling for you. You've got more friends on the force than you know.

"…"

"And I'm one of them. My name's Rich. I'm from the prosecutor's office. I know your son Dominic; I see him every day at the parking garage. I've told him how you were being railroaded by some of the detectives in my office." Especially by 1st assistant prosecutor B. Assale. You must know what he's looking for? Sorry no I don't.

With a familiar name to match the familiar face, Eddie was able to place the identity of his mystery supporter. The previous October, they had hit it off while jogging together at a March of Dimes event, helping to pace one another and spur each other onward.

An easy camaraderie quickly developed between the pair, and there had been ample talk of plans to hang out and grab a beer the following weekend. But as soon as the Sunday afternoon they'd passed together ended, they found themselves engulfed in their respective busy schedules, and neither of them had followed through.

"Oh that's right, now I remember you. From the charity run last year."

"Yeah. I just wanted to let you know that a lot of the boys on the force … well … we think you got a raw deal. We think, if you'll excuse my French, that you're getting screwed. We know a skel when we see one, we know a scapegoat when we see one, and we know how to tell the difference between them. We may not be in the best, most secure position to stand up and speak up about it, but that's where it's at. That's how we feel. Just wanted to let you know that you got all kinds of support from a lot of areas you wouldn't expect."

"Well, I do appreciate that."

"Yeah, and I just wanted to offer. If you ever need some advice or just need to vent about anything, you can always call me."

His timing so perfect, it's as if he'd planned a sales pitch beforehand, Rich emphasized his comradely offer with a smoothly proffered business card.

"My number is on the back," he explained.

And then with a wink and a slight smile, almost as an afterthought, Rich added "And don't worry; your secrets are safe with me."

"It might be good to have a sympathetic ear, assuming that ear can be trusted."

"Oh, without a doubt, without question."

"Good. I may take you up on that one of these days."

"Do that."

A slight, strained break came in the conversation. Eddie wasn't sure why the man, having said what he came to say, had still not taken his leave. Then Rich dropped a version of "the question" that almost all of Eddie's so-called friends had been asking.

"So, just between you and me, what are you thinking? What's your next move? If, of course, you don't mind me asking."

A sudden change in the weather. Eddie responded with traces of frost in his voice. "I'm not really at liberty to discuss my legal strategy."

"Oh of course. How stupid of me. It's just … yeah, well forget it. I'm afraid I've gone and stepped way over the line, crossed your boundaries and stumbled into prying territory, which, please believe me, was the furthest thing from my intention when I made the decision to introduce myself. I hope you'll accept my most profound and sincere apologies for that. Anyway, I'm still glad I got up the nerve to come and introduce myself. It was good touching' base and remember, I meant what I said. Also remember that I represent an unfortunately silent but fairly large constituency."

Dick nodded and turned to go. Eddie started to wave good-bye, but thought better of it right before the officer was about to disappear into the swirl of the crowd. Leaning forward and extending his reach as far as it could go; Eddie grazed his shoulder and got his attention.

"Hold on just a minute, if you don't mind. Before you do go, for the sake of curiosity, where were you going with that 'next move' question, if you don't mind *me* asking? What were you looking toward getting at? What do you really want to know?"

"Oh, no big conspiracy. Actually, nothing much that's really even that earth shattering. I was wondering about the veracity of something I happen to be hearing more and more of on the old blue grapevine."

"Such as?"

"Hey forget it. We both know I was out of line."

The shrinking violet act has its intended effect.

"No. Go ahead. It's ok, seriously."

"Like you said before … it might be dicey subject matter from a legal perspective. I wouldn't want to further compromise your position."

"Try me. If I cannot or should not give an answer, I won't. How's that?"

"Fair enough. It's just that all the scuttlebutt we've been hearing' up in the office recently says you might change your mind and decide to fight this trumped-up bullshit. I was wondering if there was any truth to that, but like you said, that gets into the realm of legal strategy and that's really none of my business. I'm sorry I even indulged myself by going there with you based on some dumb rumor that may not even have any basis in fact."

"Look here, even if I was thinking of changing my plea and going to war with these scoundrels, it's not something I've expressed to a single soul, outside of perhaps a blue-sky discussion or two with my attorney, which, to the best of my knowledge, are privileged communications. No offense, I'm pretty sure my esteemed and reputable attorney would not be willing to risk potential disbarment in order to share a hot tip with the prosecution team and the boys in blue and make sure they're stocked with fresh gossip."

Eddie paused for a moment to let his words sink in, and then continued. "So, whatever happens, I can tell you definitively that whoever passed that rumor along to you is either a liar or unwittingly or knowingly spreading the lies of another. Any talk along these lines is extremely premature to say the least."

"Understood loud and clear and over and out. You'll hear no more on the topic from me."

"Let me ask you, why do you want to know so badly? Why do you care about a rumor that I've just told you is definitely unfounded, especially at this early stage?"

"Well, if eventually the rumor were to hold any water, if there ever turns out to be any truth at all in it … well, what can I say … honestly?

264

To be perfectly frank—speaking for myself and quite a few others in the department—the bottom line is that you'd be our hero."

Dick's answer wasn't what Eddie had expected to hear at all, and it caught him off guard. If he was fazed by the direction their impromptu hallway exchange had taken, however, he didn't show it. Despite being moved by Dick's unexpected endorsement, Eddie was able to maintain a fairly blank poker face, nodding humbly to acknowledge the compliment, his lips pursed in neither a smile nor a frown.

Dick seemed to be scouring Eddie's reaction for some kind of a sign, but he couldn't detect a thing. Eddie's stance on the subject would've remained a mystery except that he couldn't help himself from taking a parting shot as Dick was making his exit, calling out to him before he get too far. "Hey!"

"What's up?"

"I might end up being your hero after all."

Suddenly, with that slight disclosure, it seemed a role reversal occurred. Now it was Eddie who wanted to stand around and talk further and Dick who seemed uncomfortable with the prospect of drawing out the conversation any further.

"So listen," Eddie continued.

But Dick now appeared distracted, tapping his toe like a man being held up with someplace to go.

"Excuse me for just a second Eddie," Dick interrupted, "sorry to be so rushed all of a sudden, but I just remembered an appointment. I've got to go."

The abrupt good-bye seemed strange. Even odder was the manner in which Dick took the nearby staircase, double stepping it all the way until he was out of sight. Eddie didn't think much of it at the time. He had much bigger fish to fry.

A few minutes later, Blackburn returned from his errand, hailed Eddie as he approached him from across the hallway, and, after a quick glance at his watch, indicated they should enter the room reserved for their hearing as it would soon be gaveled into session.

As Eddie entered the formal-looking little sub-courtroom (all wood paneling and a mixture of New Jersey and Centerville County state symbols and seals) with his lawyer in tow, he couldn't help but feel the abrasively acid nature of the toxic atmosphere in there. He felt as though he was on his way to his final sentencing, not a preliminary phase of a pending trial in which he was assumed to be innocent until proven guilty.

Soon the bailiff announced the judge and everyone stood up as he entered. The voice of the magistrate was hard-edged and booming. His owl-face, bespectacled, was pinched with wrinkles. Eddie stared up at the bench and tried to suppress images of classic old films with classic old hanging judges in them.

The early-stage hearing was specifically requested by Blackburn to address several troubling issues that had arisen between the handing down of the official indictment and the present.

Technically the proceeding constituted a preliminary phase of the trial. Blackburn had moved to condense matters, seeking a series of rulings that would resolve several outstanding requests, briefs, and petitions raised and/or filed by the defense. He had made this move in a conscious attempt to get on the good side of the judge, who had a reputation for being an efficiency stickler who liked to keep things moving along.

It quickly became clear, however, that Blackburn's strategy was not exactly having its intended effect. Blackburn began by addressing a few minor procedural considerations that he expected the judge to approve without comment. It was at this point that Blackburn and Eddie were rudely awakened to the fact that they were in for a long day.

"Your honor, defense moves that this case be diverted into the pre-trial intervention program as per our pending agreement with the prosecution."

"The motion for pre-trial intervention is denied."

Jaws dropped in the courtroom, and not only at the defense table. This was highly irregular, to say the least. Usually pre-trial intervention (P.T.I.) is worked out between the prosecution and the defense, with the judge merely serving as a rubber stamp. Most political figures and their friends in NJ receive PTI for much worst then what Eddie was being charged with, so what do you think Dennis was granted.

"But Your Honor, this is a routine request that is routinely granted. We were assured by opposing counsel that—"

"The motion is denied. That's final."

Similar requests for change of venue (on the grounds that the high profile of the case, the ample press coverage, and the small size and intertwined nature of the local community would make a fair trial impossible), recusal of the prosecutor (due to the prosecutor's prior history with Blackburn in which the latter once terminated the former from a job in private practice at which the prosecutor was an employee and Blackburn his supervisor. Several comments made by the prosecutor that had been overheard and/or passed along suggested he was in conflict due to the fact that he was out for revenge in this case and would ultimately act in an unscrupulous, unjust manner if given the opportunity to do so), and an attempt to call attention to possible evidence tampering were also summarily dismissed with a denial.

The reflexive rejection of the final defense motion was perhaps the most distressing. Evidence tampering is a serious allegation, and Blackburn was the type of attorney who was cautious and conservative enough not to even think of putting such an accusation forward unless he had some serious and solid documentation to support his contentions.

Before he could even move into the details of his allegations or even touch on the supporting evidence he was prepared to furnish, the judge waved a hand and slammed down his gavel, silencing the defense attorney, cutting him off mid-sentence.

"Let me get this straight counselor, so I can get a clear understanding of what is being alleged here. You're asserting that key evidence has been tampered with. Specifically, the evidence potentially exonerating your client has gone missing, replaced by fabricated evidence potentially implicating your client?"

"Well, in a nutshell, yes Your Honor. But if I can walk you through—"

"And this has been done by whom? An overzealous prosecutor out to get you because you gave him a pink slip almost a decade ago? A rogue police officer with a chip on his shoulder against the fire department?"

"No one is prepared to point fingers at any specific person or persons. What can be proven beyond a threshold of reasonable doubt is that—"

"That's enough."

"Excuse me?"

"I said enough. I'm prepared to rule on this matter."

"But Your Honor, I haven't even demonstrated—"

"Keep right on undermining me, son. But I want you to realize that every time you do so, you're flirting with a contempt charge. Is that clear?"

"Yes Your Honor."

"Now, back to the matter at hand. A serious allegation has been put forth by the defense. In the absence of corroboration from a neutral source, I am inclined to give the benefit of the doubt to the law enforcement professionals in the police department and the district attorney's office, both of whom have a long and esteemed track record of honesty, integrity, and professionalism. Their reputations speak for themselves, and nothing I've seen here today has convinced that they need to be impugned by the ugly shadow of a drawn-out investigation. In short, this sort of thing doesn't happen in Centerville County. There will be no official inquiry undertaken by this court into possible evidence tampering at this time."

"Permission to approach the bench."

"Permission granted."

Blackburn and the judge exchanged a few whispered words. Blackburn told the judge that Eddie's statement was tampered with." He said that 46.1% was missing and there was 12 minutes of complete silence. He also told the judge there are questions with no answers and answers without any questions. We had his statement authenticated by someone who works closely with the justice system and it came back the way I just described. Judge, I'm telling you, something's awful fishy here". From Eddie's point of view, the conversation did seem to be a little heated, although part of him wished that it had not been. Seconds later, Blackburn returned to the defense table. Soon afterward, the hearing was again gaveled into adjournment and motion denied.

While gathering up his files and papers, Blackburn leaned over to Eddie and commented, "Jesus Christ could have testified for this hearing and we still couldn't have won you a single motion in this courtroom, with this judge,"

Eddie nodded in agreement as his head swam with fearful portent and the ground seemed too desolately beneath his feet. He sat for extra moment to catch his bearings and digest what had surely been an ominous beginning to his case. Curious about the sotto voce exchange that had taken place between his lawyer and the judge just before adjournment, Eddie asked Blackburn what it was all about.

"Oh, that was just to set up a meeting in chambers after this, so that if we decide to go to trial... I didn't want the prosecutor to hear because as far as they know, we've still got a deal. I also wanted to protest the way the PROSECUTORS OFFICE has handed this case off from one prosecutor to another—that's how we ended up with my former employee—in order to get around the statute of limitations and make sure that no matter how long this thing gets drawn out, they can still go after you.

"Conversely, all other potential suspects that are vulnerable to charges of wrongdoing being brought eventually, your business partner Dennis, for example, are not being subject to the prosecutor shuffle. The end result is that you'll be the only scapegoat hung out to dry while all those who are really guilty will get off on a technicality that is being willfully engineered by backroom friends and contacts in the prosecutor's office. I just think that's blatantly wrong and unjust and I want to bring it to the judge's attention, for all the freaking good it'll likely do. I might as well stand on one leg and whistle 'Dixie.'

"But seriously, I think it's important, out of principle, just to lodge the protest and have it out there. There was a reporter here today from the local paper. I'm hoping maybe he'll pick up on all these discrepancies and maybe even report on the blatant biases being displayed by our steamroller judge." (Oddly enough, the reporter's story, although written and filed, was mysteriously quashed by his editors. The reason why remains open to speculation.)

As the hearing room emptied, Eddie followed his lawyer through the big wooden double-doors beyond the visitor's gallery, then out into the hall and into one of a bank of elevators. After a vertigo-inducing lurch upward, they exited onto one of the highest floors, Blackburn leading the way toward the judge's chambers. When they got within thirty yards of an open oak door, Blackburn nudged Eddie and pointed to their destination.

Emanating from the open door was the sound of booming laughter belonging to two or three men. Blackburn tapped lightly on the side doorjamb to indicate their arrival. They were both shocked at the identity of the company that this supposed "detached and neutral magistrate" was keeping.

The cozy trio they happened upon included the judge, Eddie's prosecutor, and an old, long-term crony of Dennis and his father.

At precisely this moment, Eddie had a flashback of leaving this very courthouse after one his first voluntary visits to the prosecutor, with Dennis by his side. Among other highly agitating, bothersome things said by Dennis on that day, was a flip comment he made in response to urgent questions about the integrity of the books. "Just keep two sets," Dennis had said, "that what my father used to do." Now, staring in amazement as an old friend of Dennis's and Dennis's father played patty-cake with the judge who held his future in his hands, and realizing how far, deep, and wide the Thefmor family contacts went, it occurred to Eddie why he was standing in the gallows and not Dennis or his father.

The arrival of Eddie and his lawyer broke up the judge's coffee klatch. Dennis's pal exited without offering any good-byes, followed by the prosecutor, who casually asked Blackburn if he and Eddie could drop by his office on the way out.

The face-to-face meeting with the judge began on a better footing than the hearing that had just preceded it. Blackburn confided the possibility that, contrary to the case's current trajectory, it still might eventually go to trial. The judge pulled out a leather-bound planner from his desk and courteously furnished Blackburn with an approximate time line of important dates, granting Eddie's attorney a maximum amount of latitude in his planning should the case go to trial.

Blackburn had less success when he tried to lodge a protest against the prosecutorial "rollover" practice the PROSECUTOR'S OFFICE was using to make a mockery of the statute of limitations concept. "There's nothing I can do about that," explained Judge Dolfman, "You'll have to take that up with the PROSECUTOR'S OFFICE"

Realizing they were getting nowhere fast, Blackburn decided cut his losses and get out of there. The final meeting of the day, an impromptu sit-down with the prosecutorial team, was a far more unpleasant affair. The moment Eddie and his attorney arrived, they noticed that a confrontational tone was being sought; the group from the PROSECUTOR'S OFFICE was seated in an accusatory circle and the scowls on their faces were two key clues.

Right away, they lit into the pair about the consequences of reneging on the plea offer. Veiled threats flew and "remember, this is a one-time only offer," seemed to be the most popular refrain. Over and over, they repeated that any delays, setbacks, or attempts to renegotiate the offer would result in the offer's withdrawal and that it would not be offered again.

Eddie and his lawyer were completely flabbergasted. They hadn't even made a final decision to take the case to trial, and they were already feeling the repercussions. As Blackburn moved to reassure the sharks, Eddie wondered, *how did this news travel so fast?* Then, almost right away, he answered his own question. It was Dick, the detective. The detective he'd decided against all odds and better judgment to trust.

❧ ❧ ❧

After the catastrophic courthouse fiasco, Eddie's woes were still not complete. That night he had an appointment with his estranged wife at her mother's house, where she was staying temporarily; to drop off some of the things she had left behind.

Eddie expected the encounter to be brusque and businesslike, strained. Instead, she came running out onto the front lawn to greet him in a virtual reprise of the day the FBI had invaded and sacked their house and privacy.

As it turned out, several incidents had combined to completely unnerve Renee. Among them was an intimidating series of collect phone calls she'd received from an inmate at Rahway State Prison. (This always happened after a motion was lost and Eddie refused a deal). Another coincidence

The implications of the phone call were chillingly clear. If Eddie's enemies could track down his wife and family to threaten them so easily, they could also track them down to follow through on the threats.

In addition, two of their boys had been accosted on the way home from school by intimidating police officers who claimed to be their father's friends and supporters. Once they'd introduced themselves, these characters launched into conversation that was more like interrogation, asking the question, "So, what is your dad going to do about his case?" in about fifty different ways.

Eddie just comforted her and assured her that he would do whatever was necessary to protect her and their family. He kept his uncertainties and fears to himself. He also kept to himself the fact that he was pretty sure that, since he left the courthouse, he was being followed by two detectives he'd seen following him before, in the same unmarked car they'd been using throughout the previous months of tailing him, just as he had been relentlessly followed in the weeks prior to initially accepting his plea agreement.

The totality of the entire day caused Eddie to think long and hard about what his ultimate decision would be. Events had made it clearer than ever that if he decided to fight this thing, there would be consequences, not just for him but also for his family.

He'd be plunging them back into the bad old days of constant surveillance and being followed, of policemen showing up to his workplace acting like friends but really just there on a mission to get information to convey to the PROSECUTORS OFFICE, of thuggish threats delivered anonymously via phone call. It would be back to the same dark days they'd just left behind them when he consented to sacrifice some of his dignity and cop a plea.

Chapter 17

After twisting in the whiplash wind of countless sleepless nights and bleary days spent in deliberation, after all the weeks of vacillating and hedging, of changing and rechanging his mind, Eddie ended up taking a deal and copping a plea. As he explained in his matter-of-fact, straightforward manner, "I took the deal that they offered and that's that."

In the end, the threats to himself and his family were too sincere and severe. Moreover, the slings and arrows were raining down from every discernable direction. The incoming fire of dirty tricks and ominous warnings emanated from so many sources that, despite vigorous investigative efforts to trace them to their point of origin, many remain enshrouded in mystery to this day. Remembering what his attorney told him "we couldn't win a motion in this judge's court room even if Jesus Christ testified"

Had he gone to trial, Eddie would have found himself standing alone in a quixotic battle against the combined powers of local, county, and state government. As daunting as that prospect seemed, it was exacerbated by the probability that the legitimate forces arrayed against Eddie only represented the tip of the iceberg.

Lurking beneath, hiding in the shadows of proper institutions, subterranean adversaries circled, smelling blood. These sharks swam in gray areas, evading the black-and-white certainties and absolutes that supposedly form the vertebrae of American justice. Sharks are called sharks for a reason when they behave as sharks. They are vicious animal killers, cool, controlled, without conscience, ruled by primal predatory instincts. These instincts are not governed by the niceties of law. Neither are they subject to its civilizing constraints. When it comes down to it covering up for a politician, who appointed the judges or prosecutors, it doesn't matter who gets destroyed.

It would have been one thing to roll the dice if there were only himself to consider. However, once complete innocents were thrown into the mix, and once his enemies had made it abundantly clear that they had no qualms about hurting those people to get to him, Eddie realized that he would have been gambling with chips that were not his own.

So it came to pass that in January 1996 (an unseasonably sunny and temperate day), after all the arrangements had been fixed and every one of the loose ends had been neatly tied in bows of compromise, Eddie found himself reprising a familiar role, assuming an all-too familiar position: propping his elbows against the shiny cedar of the defense table, fingers tracing trembling patterns in its deep, wavy grain strands, then blotting sweat from his brow as he loosened his uncomfortable tie and squirmed in his uncomfortable suit.

Steadying himself against a banister still slick from a recent coat of veneer, Eddie grimaced, enduring sensations of burning discomfort caused by the excess acid that had been swishing around in his stomach since he'd woke up just a few hours before.

Eddie surveyed his easily recognizable surroundings with a curious mixture of apprehension and boredom. *Yes. Here I am again and here we go again*, he sighed to himself, *back again … back to this place I know almost as well as and have seen about as much of lately as the living room of my own freaking home.*

Eddie was back indeed. Back among the burnished wood, somber hues, and painstakingly polished but still slightly tarnished plaques and patinas of the main Centerville County courthouse. Back fidgeting nervously as he swiveled his head, scanning the room, taking unconscious inventory of the various and sundry components that comprised his surroundings.

In a way he found it reassuring. In another way he found it eerie and unnatural. Nothing was out of place. Nothing was changed. Eddie was struck by the tone of continuity and consistency that ran through the entire room, from the way the judge wore his robes and pounded his gavel to the details of the décor he could reconstruct in his sleep (and sometimes, in his nightmares, did).

After weeks of hearings, motions, and filings, the courtroom experience had, by now, become almost a matter of routine for Eddie. On this particular day, however, the reason his attendance was required was anything but routine. Although the steady-state nature of his environment may have infused the proceedings with an ordinary and inauspicious air, the reality of the situation was as far removed from business as usual as possible.

For Eddie, the day's events would prove to be of monumental personal importance. More than merely representing a negative milestone—of even *the* negative milestone in Eddie's existence—the burden that Eddie now assumed threatened, over time, slowly and surely to bear its heaviness down upon him until it ultimately almost pulverized him.

That is because in January, 1996, Eddie entered the Centerville County Courthouse to officially plead guilty and be formally convicted of a crime for the first time in his life. Even though the agreement allowed Eddie to avoid the more serious charges he'd been indicted of and the terms of the plea deal knocked the charges down far enough for Eddie to be assured of averting jail time, albeit narrowly, it still called for Eddie's admission of guilt to a fourth-degree felony.

According to New Jersey State law, there are two levels of fourth-degree felony when it comes to larceny. On the higher tier of severity is having knowingly received stolen goods. Directly beneath that charge in severity was the one Eddie said was the only one he would plea to: knowledge of stolen goods but without having actually received stolen goods.

They—that is, the mayor's minions in the PROSECUTORS OFFICE—were asserting, and Eddie was being compelled to submit to the admission, that he knew what was going on under the auspices of the store that he was half-owner of, when indeed, he did not. After two years of getting to know the man through hours of long-distance phone conversations, reams of files and newspaper clippings, and countless questions, answers, clarifications, and revisitations (all in service of him telling me this story with enough clarity that I may have the opportunity to convey it to you), I tend to believe him.

Why? Because he's a straight shooter. He's never lied to me. In the two years that I have known him, his story has never changed. He has never deviated despite my having been beset by numerous personal problems that have disrupted and delayed the publication of this book and would have given him justifiable grounds to do so.

Also, after the investigation that lead up to his indictment, a detective Toilette from the Pros office that was working on the case told Eddie and others "nothing in the store was ever stolen." Help me out here, but isn't it the job of the detective to prove the guilt of the defendant? Aren't they—detective and defendant—in an inherently adversarial position? If an investigating detective, whose job consists of building a case against you, says that you are innocent, isn't that a pretty good indicator that you are?

Although it could have been worse, Eddie's guilty plea to a felony he didn't commit was far from trivial, and the consequences Eddie would face, both legal and extralegal, were far-reaching, diverse, and profound. The fact that Eddie was forced to lose face in such a public and humiliating manner, despite the fact of his complete innocence provided not even minimal solace. In fact, the knowledge of his innocence only served to torment him and cause him to endlessly second-guess his choices, pouring extra salt into his already festering wounds.

Thus, the decision to accept the plea was life-transforming in its significance. It marked the creation of a fundamental, foundation-rending rent, a turning point that would cause Eddie to veer off of the upwardly mobile ascending road he'd been traveling all his life.

Suddenly derailed from this steady path of happiness and progress, Eddie would spend the next several years on a hellish highway, careening downward in an out-of-control spiral whose slope dropped with stomach-churning steepness, plotting a direct course toward rock bottom realms of bitterness and despair.

The plea agreement represented a crude vandalization of the meticulously painted mural that had been Eddie's life to that point. In the center of the rendering, an ugly blot now obfuscated brushstroke upon careful brushstroke of achievement, leaving an indelible stain.

The ego-searing agony of the formal indictment, the subsequent conviction, the actual physical violation of being placed under arrest (along with its accompanying dehumanizing rigmarole), all of these things—as damaging in the extreme as they may have been to Eddie's mind, body, and spirit—combined paled in comparison to the aftermath he was compelled by fate to face.

Immediately after his sentencing, Eddie began serving a one year of probation. . While he found probation to be invasive and aggravating, and rancorously complained to his few remaining friends about the nuisance of having to report to his probation officer, his court-ordered obligations were not the true thorns in his side. The real pain was too tender to touch with casual conversation.

For Eddie, the most immediate, profound consequence of his decision to accept the arrangement proffered by the Pros. Office. Was the forfeiture of his post at the fire department? According to the final judgment, Eddie was not permitted to rejoin the force in any capacity. It was a life sentence. In fact, he could never again hold a municipal job. Eddie wasn't allowed to as much as step foot in his or any other firehouse.

Of all the unfair sanctions Eddie was to suffer and endure (the ruin of his reputation and good name, being saddled with all the baggage and loss of civil rights that comes with being identified as a convicted felon, and so on), the loss of his privileges as a working firefighter was the outcome that smarted and stung the most.

Throughout his career, as if born to his job, Eddie had seamlessly moved, rung-by-rung, up the fire department ladder. After decades of proudly wearing the uniform and becoming a widely respected and renowned leader of men in the process, he suddenly found himself reeling with the vertigo that accompanies the experience of having one's whole life implode, collapse, and tumble down like a burning tenement house. In one fell swoop, his entire purpose and reason for being had been taken away from him.

The fallout and aftermath neither began nor ended with Eddie's vocational fall from grace. Shortly after what was supposed to be only a trial separation initiated by the fear she felt due to the FBI raid and other chaotic events surrounding the case, Renee announced that she was leaving him for good. For Eddie, the news was absolutely shattering. It came at a time when he depended on and needed her the most. Like other married couples, they'd had their share of problems in the past. Despite their recent estrangement, however, Eddie had assumed that their love was strong enough to survive the ordeal and that, as they had during prior rough patches, they would see their way through their difficulties and find a way to salvage the damaged relationship and work things out.

Initially she had packed her bags and left him with dramatic and shocking suddenness, telling him that things between them were over and seeming firm and unshakable in her decision. After a short time away from the havoc of the house, she was able to calm down, collect her thoughts, and regain some piece of mind. At that point, her position on the future of their marriage had softened. For several weeks she was willing to discuss a possible reunion and defined her absence as a trial separation, explaining that she needed space and time to think, implying that the break-up might not be permanent. Eddie had been hanging onto that implication for dear life.

A few days after his sentencing, Renee called with the news that she needed to see him in order to discuss an urgent matter. Eddie assumed that, now that the dust was settling, she wanted to discuss reconciliation and figure out a way to put the sordid episodes of the past few months behind them. The longer it had been since she'd fled from under his roof, the more she'd been dropping hints that the current state of affairs might not be permanent.

Although Eddie was troubled by the finality of many statements she had made, and especially worried by the words she spoke the awful day she announced her departure, he also knew that the majority of their troubles had been external in nature (that is, directly relating to his lengthy legal persecution), so it was hard for him to believe that she was serious about leaving him forever.

Despite the writing on the wall that seems obvious in retrospect, one of the things that had kept Eddie going throughout the entire period of his investigation and prosecution was the belief, deep in the core of his heart that he and Renee would be able to reconcile and eventually reunite. Once the smoke cleared, he'd figured, they'd be able to pick up the pieces of the wreckage that had become their life, and share in the reconstructing and rebuilding of things together. His (perhaps overly rose-colored) dream was that they would learn from the turbulence and that the close call would ultimately bring them closer, making them stronger and better than they had been before.

Eddie was anxious but optimistic about their meeting and the prospects it held for the renewal of their relationship. *If all goes well,* he told himself, *and I'm able to express myself properly … put my feelings into the right words, today could be my first step forward, back on the route toward normality since before all this mess began.*

"Dear God," he actually prayed while on the way to meet her for breakfast at the local diner, "please let her see the horror of the last few months through my eyes. Help me to help her understand why I fell short and let her feel the truth of my sincerity … that I get it, I really, really get it. I get what she's been upset about and why she was pissed off and hurt enough to pack her bags and leave. I haven't been there for her, not in the way she needed me to be. I know exactly the kind of stress and anxiety she's been under. Matter of fact, I've been leaning on her too heavily at a time when she needed to lean on me. I've been too wrapped up in my own troubles to give full consideration to the impact all this had on her. The bottom line is that I haven't been the husband she needs and deserves. But I love her. With all my heart, I just want things to be like they used to be before this whole fiasco exploded all over us. Help me to explain what I am not articulate enough to explain. Help me persuade her. Help me put my family back together. Please don't let it be too late."

Getting out of the car on reaching the diner, Eddie bounded through the parking lot like a teenager on a first date. Although he was five minutes early, he was surprised to see that his usually chronically tardy wife was already there, secluded in a corner booth, nursing a cup of black coffee.

Demurely, Renee rose to greet Eddie as he rushed forward to embrace her. It had been weeks since they'd seen one another, and he missed her terribly. As he threw his arms around her, Eddie blushed, flush with excitement and youthful exuberance. She hung in his arms limply, unenthusiastically, barely returning the embrace. Sensing something wrong, he looked into her eyes. In the chill of her frosty gaze, he felt all his hopes evaporate into dashed, trashed illusions.

Instead of the teary wife begging for forgiveness that he expected, he found he was looking at a virtual stranger, whose cold and businesslike manner sent ominous shivers down his spine. Breaking eye contact, Renee gestured a sheaf of legal paperwork on the table.

"What's all this?"

"Eddie, please don't make this more difficult than it already is."

"I thought we were going to hold off on anything final. These are divorce papers."

"Yes they are. And I'm going to ask you to sign them with a minimum of drama and emotional blackmail. Please. For both of our sakes."

"But how could you do this Renee?"

"How could I do anything else?"

"You talk like you think I actually did those things they're saying I did." But Renee knew the truth. She knew he was being railroaded, and she knew they wanted someone else to be the next chief.

Eddie was vexed by Renee's silent pause. This was the last straw. He was about to lose his temper, but before he can do so, she ends the terrible agony of the silence, giving Eddie at least the minimal reassurance and vote of confidence.

"Oh, Eddie. You know that's not true. You know I know what happened."

"But so I didn't do anything wrong. If I didn't do anything wrong, and you even acknowledge that fact, how can you blame me for crimes you know I did not commit?"

"We've been over this a million times. I don't blame you for what they charged you with. I blame you for how it's been handled, how you failed to make me feel protected and secure, how you're back-and-forth stances of self-righteousness endangered not only you but me and the kids. I blame you for not opening up and communicating about where things stood, for trying to shoulder everything on your own instead of as a family, for not protecting us enough, for giving a man like Dennis the keys to the vault that held our future."

"You can't mean that."

"Actually I don't mean that. It's unfair. The whole damn thing is unfair. I mean it's not your fault. You've said you're the victim in all this, and I know that. But the tragic thing is that I don't care that it's not your fault. I don't have anybody to point the finger at and lay blame on. But it doesn't matter. The only thing that matters is that I simply can't live like this. I can't take it anymore. When I left, for the first week all I could do was mope around the house and cry. It was during that period that I was second-guessing myself and unsure of what I had done. That was right around the time I called you and suggested that we might be able to work things out."

"That's wh—"

"Just wait a minute. Hear me out. You asked me to explain, and I'm explaining as best I can. What happened was, in the middle of all that doubt and sorrow; I woke up one morning with the strangest feeling. You know what it was?"

"What?"

"Relief. Pure and simple. I didn't feel danger. I didn't feel stalked. I realized that there had been no suspicious people following me, no unmarked cars around the corner, no disturbing threats relayed through our children, no collect calls from Rahway State Prison, and no no-knock visits from FBI agents sent to intimidate us, threaten us all with incarceration, and turn our house upside down. Listen Eddie, I'm the same woman who married you, and I still love you. But the basic truth of the situation is that things have careened too far out of control for me, or any other person interested in maintaining their sanity, to remain immersed in. I love you but I've got to get out. And I know it's not fair to you. But, more important, I'm being fair to me, to our family. It's a matter of self-preservation, and it's a matter of providing them the shelter and security that this crisis has stolen away from them. I'm not leaving you; I'm leaving the crazy mixed-up situation. I'm tired of living in a state of constant fear. I'm sorry. You don't know how sorry I am [her voice cracked ever so slightly at this point before she visibly recovered herself and plowed ahead], but it's do or die time, a simple question of survival. I mean, look at me, have you ever seen me so harried? My mental and physical health is going down the tubes. I've no piece of mind. I can't eat, can't sleep at night. I'm just now, since taking the radical step of leaving you—and if you think this is an easy decision, you're nuts; it's the hardest thing I've ever had to do in my life—but I'm just now regaining a small modicum of calm and tranquility. But honestly, when I think of sacrificing that hard-earned tranquility in order to reimmerse myself in the toxic, unstable situation that has become our home life, I literally get physically sick to my stomach. Can you understand? I'm doing this because I have to do it. I don't have a choice. I've been beating my head against a wall trying to find one, but I just can't. I've thought this through long and hard and I'm absolutely sure. I'm dead certain, and I'm not going to change my mind. So I'm asking you, if you respect and care about me, to respect and honor this decision. Please don't fight me over it. Please don't make it harder than it already is for me."

"Renee, baby, I understand. I understand we've been through an extended period of absolute living hell. So I understand your decision and if you stick to this decision, I'll respect it. I'll sign the papers before I put the syrup on my pancakes. But the only thing I want to say is that the timing of all this doesn't make sense. To stick by me through all the shit and then to throw in the towel now? I mean it's all over. I pleaded guilty. The heat is off. We can start to rebuild again. And I can rebuild. I know I can. But to do that, I need you; I need you by my side." Renee shook her head in an emphatic no as Eddie stated his need for her. This exasperated him, causing him to lose his bearings and reiterate points he'd already made. "Don't you understand, I pleaded out so that we could begin to put this behind us? It's all over."

"All over? You know Eddie, if that were true, there might be a chance. But you're either pulling my leg, kidding yourself, or both. Over? No honey. It's just started."

"What's that supposed to mean?"

"Are the vicious whispers and gossips all over with? The friends— actually I won't say friends because we don't have friends anymore—the ladies at the supermarket who talk in hushed tones about my criminal of a husband and then abruptly shut up when they see me coming? What about the aftermath of the destruction that this has caused our family? Is that over? And what about you? You've changed so much as a result of this case. I feel like I don't even know you anymore. Your temper is shorter than ever, and you're always preoccupied. Over? This is only the beginning. Imagine you unemployed and at loose ends. Imagine how stressed out and bitter you're going to be as door after door gets closed on you. Who do you think is going to bear the brunt of that? You were neglectful and took me for granted when you worked at the firehouse, which was a job you loved more than life itself, a job you were willing to risk life and limb for. Tell me truthfully: if you couldn't fulfill your husband role at your apex, how are things going to be now? No Eddie, I still love you, but it just isn't going to work between us. Paint it however you want to paint it. I'm sure that in your mind right now I'm the evil betrayer who split when the going got tough and didn't stick by you when you most needed it. But in reality, I'm just saving you, me, and the kids from several years of ugliness and slow deterioration. I'm also doing it to ensure my safety and the safety of my family. For whatever reason, unjust as it may be, you've run afoul of some pretty foul characters. I can't lie awake anymore wondering what the next atrocity is they've planned for us. I'm sorry Eddie, I truly am. Someday I hope you'll understand this and forgive me. I'm doing this because there's simply nothing else I can do. I can see no other option."

In the ensuing days, a number of Eddie's so-called "close friends" would also terminate long-standing relations, many of them utilizing some variation of the final four sentences in the preceding paragraph.

Others didn't even bother to contact him and say anything at all, they just seemed to fade away and spin out of Eddie's orbit, as if he had somehow been tainted by an intangible impurity that had rendered him repulsive. Eddie understood. Sort of. The admission of guilt, painful as it was, had indeed tainted him and the department of which many of his friends were a part.

Thus when it came to his ex-colleagues, a complex web of mixed feelings developed. On the one hand, he felt bitterness at their disloyalty and lack of faith in him, a faith he believed he'd earned. On the other hand, he could comprehend the impulse to steer clear of anyone, even a brother, who'd been tarred by the brush of a scandal that had stained the good name of the department as a whole.

Although he liked to think he would have behaved differently, Eddie might have done the same had the shoe been on someone else's foot. He would swear the latter possibility was not even an option, but deep down he knew that he could not know for sure unless the tables had been turned. And there was no chance of that actually happening. Any speculation on the subject would have to remain theoretical.

There was, however, one exception among Eddie's dwindling social circle. One friend, a **Vietnam Vet** and Bronze metal winner, was unfazed by all the reputation-eroding legal bullshit slung at Eddie. One who maintained his position as a loyal, stand-up guy and who would go to war for him. Eddie always knew that he could depend on his life long buddy. This was a man named Gino, Eddie's best friend for the better part of four decades, a man who Eddie still speaks of as being closer than his own blood a man who Eddie reports was there in his darkest hour and whose support saved him from going over the edge or doing something stupid. A man who, even in the context of a "fictional" book, deserves his non fictional gratitude and respect.

"Not many people are lucky enough to have such a good and complete friend," "Even if they are that lucky, only one friend like Gino comes along in a lifetime, maximum. In a time of total darkness, he represented a lone bright spot. I'll always appreciate the fact that he and his wife were there for me when everyone else hung me out to dry."

🌿 🌿 🌿

Speaking of being hung out to dry, the Township of Corrunoside was busy doing to Eddie financially what all of his friends—except for Gino—had done to him socially.

Negations broke down over Eddie's severance compensation. According to his contract, he was eligible to receive a cash valuation of his sick time and other benefits. The calculated value of outstanding monetary reimbursement that Eddie was owed by the department exceeded $80,000. This was the case even and especially if Eddie was terminated from his position, and despite the fact that some form of wrongdoing had been alleged. This simple contractual clause was not being honored. Although neither the terms nor validity of the contract nor the exact dollar amount to which Eddie was entitled was ever in dispute, the Township of Corrunoside hired a high-powered lawyer in order to validate their unethical renege with a stamp of judicial approval. And what happened to his union? Vanished. Eddie and his lawyer sought, as per their rights, a public hearing on the matter.

The problem with a public hearing, much like the trouble with a trial, is that all of the dirty laundry of corruption could potentially be exposed if it were permitted to move forward. Therefore, as with Eddie's trial, Corrunoside officials began making a series of desperate chess moves in order to squelch the hearing or at least suppress any public record of the proceedings.

Through a series of intermediaries, Betty Mobil , a close adviser of the newly elected mayor Eddie suspected had a hand in his targeting and destruction, contacted Eddie's soon to be ex-mother-in-law, who had been a key political player, mover, and shaker under the old (and recently deposed) Corrunoside political regime. "If Eddie agrees to have the hearing in private," went the gist of her message, "we can do more for him. We'll make sure he receives everything he is supposed to get." (By having a closed hearing the cover-ups can still be covered up).

Needless to say, at the end of the day, representatives from the Township of Corrunoside again found a way to manipulate Eddie's goodwill and trusting nature. After agreeing to a private hearing, Eddie was indeed awarded the compensation he rightfully deserved. What Mrs. Mobil neglected to mention, however, was that the city had a right to appeal the ruling? Despite her repeated verbal assurances to the contrary when queried about this possibility, Corrunoside exercised this option.

The money was tied up in a series of appeals and counter-appeals. At one point, it looked as though the city would be able to evade its fiscal responsibility when Eddie's attorney failed to file necessary paperwork on time. The situation was so egregiously unjust, however, that a sympathetic judge granted Eddie another day in court. Seizing the opportunity, Eddie prevailed.

Corrunoside responded with yet another appeal, this time to the New Jersey State Supreme Court. In this venue, the team of high-powered attorneys hired by the city (at a cost that probably exceeded the amount of money in dispute) was able to get Eddie's award overturned. To continue the battle, Eddie would have had to take the fight to federal court. Afraid of exhausting the rest of his dwindling resources, he declined to do so. When all was said and done, the Township of Corrunoside was able to retain the money the Eddie had earned.

At some point during the time this saga was unfolding, Mrs. Mobil's son was hired by the Corrunoside Fire Department. Of course he may have been a qualified and deserving firefighter, and any appearance of systemic manipulation may have merely been a coincidence and not a case of quid pro quo for a dirty job well done. Throughout this narrative, however, an alert reader cannot help but be struck by the fact that the story of Eddie's abrupt fall from grace is rife with the occurrence of these types of "coincidences."

Afterword

You've just finished an entire tome devoted to the trials and tragedies of a firefighter named Eddie. The full extent of the consequences he suffered was massive, far-reaching, and ultimately life-shattering. Eddie suffered the public disgrace of being stripped of his fire department rank and unceremoniously excommunicated from his beloved firehouse and force forever. In addition, Eddie's private life was mercilessly invaded (both figuratively and literally), and the ordeal was directly responsible for the dissolution of his family.

Eddie's ordeal of officially sanctioned persecution gains an added dimension of outrageousness and absurdity when juxtaposed against and placed in the context of other fire and police officials who, far from being able to claim innocence in the compelling, evidence-buttressed manner with which Eddie states his case, were caught red-handed perpetrating a host of criminal activities, ethical lapses, and questionable behaviors.

Detective Malaka was never sanctioned for any of his abusive and illegal behaviors. Neither was his partner, who mostly looked the other way but sometimes participated in Malaka's unique blend of law enforcement. Eddie's complaints about Malaka's Gestapo tactics never even inspired so much as the hint of an inquiry from within or outside of the department.

The chief of police, chief of the fire department, the mayor, the director of public safety, and an array of suspect police and fire department captains were never called to account for their alleged ties to underworld figures, organized crime, and other sordid characters. No investigation was ever conducted into their unorthodox business dealings, conflicts of interest, numerous allegations of corruption, or most important, their ties to and knowledge of an extensive, sophisticated network of thieves (many of whom wore police and fire department badges) that profited from and traded extensively in public sector jobs, official perks, political favors, and a stunning array of stolen goods.

Where does the plague of arson suffered by Centerville County fit into all this? Did some or all of the above public officials enlist or encourage the ring of firebugs? Or did they, for a variety of reasons that they found advantageous, merely look the other way while it was happening? Were the arsons a result of a coordinated conspiracy designed to punish foes, enforce a dissent-silencing reign of terror, and mask massive amounts of theft and/or insurance fraud? Or did these public officials merely engage in a cover-up to protect friends and friends of friends? What did they know about the fires, and when did they know? Even if they only held suspicions, didn't their positions demand that these suspicions be shared with and reported to the appropriate authorities?

Alas, these questions of culpability remain unanswered because no authoritative entity ever bothered to probe the links that led from the arsonists to the top echelons of the chains of command at the fire department, the police department, and city hall.

Well, you may think, *perhaps at least the arsonists themselves had the book thrown at them since they were arrested with such ceremony.* As one of Hemmingway's heroes once opined wistfully, "wouldn't it be nice if it were true!" Not so. No arson ringleader served more than one year in prison. And we're talking over five million dollars in damage.

As far as the theft ring went, it was a deeply entrenched tumor with a complex web of tendrils emanating into the muscle and bone of the body politic, a cancer kept alive through generations from infusions of blood money and graft.

That fact notwithstanding, the powers that be had their scapegoat, and it was a slam dunk, the "lone gunman" meant that, conveniently, they could close a huge case by charging one man of limited means, who would be lined up against all the resources of the prosperous county office. He would have to make an expedient deal, and they wouldn't have to dig to deep or uncover any ugly truths about the bureaucratic brethren over at city hall and in the corner offices of the police and fire department brass they existed in symbiosis with. It all came down to dog-eat-dog politics, and Eddie was an easy mark. It didn't matter if he was innocent or not. They'd never have to prove anything. They'd make sure it never got that far.

"Did they end up getting his partner? His partner's father? At least some of the key players who were actually involved?" No, no, and no. Having publicly humiliated Eddie, having scored a high-ranking, up-and-coming, politically inconvenient scalp to show to all the voters come election time, the prosecutor was content to use his courtroom knowledge to manipulate the judicial process to let the statute of limitations run out on the men who should of at least been co-defendants, men who, according to the evidence—if one wants to bring evidence and logic and obvious issues of justice into this—should have been the only defendants.

If there was any wrongdoing at Eddie's store, it was only the tip of the iceberg. But that inconvenient fact was ignored, either out of prosecutorial laziness (it would have been quite a tangled web to completely unravel) or some more sinister motive. The reader will have to fill in the blanks on that one. However, if there was any wrongdoing at Eddie's store, it took place under the watch of Dennis and because of the involvement of Dennis's father. Outrageously, Dennis's father is free to move to his "house that the dented cans built" down in Florida, and Dennis is free to remain a Corrunoside firefighter! It also should be known that if Dennis didn't like the on coming shift he would either put a little liquid soap or cigarette ashes in the coffee or milk and on a few occasions he would leave ice cream and chocolate syrup with a melted down special treat of Ex Lax for the boy's. Ummmm Good (In a rather cruel irony that testifies to the existence of a higher, universal karmic justice despite the absence of appropriate Jersey justice, Dennis's throat … the throat that was responsible for voicing so many damaging lies … was afflicted with throat cancer.)

Perhaps the dandiest thing is, decades later, during the time of the writing of this book, PROSECUTORS OFFICE and Corrunoside still will not let poor Eddie rest. They have carried their mindless, reactionary vendetta against this man who dared, who had the audacity to stand up their sleaze across the generations. Eddie's son Colt was leaving a bar, the same bar at which an earlier episode detailed herein occurred when he was jumped by four men, one wielding a lead pipe. The fight had been completely unprovoked. They just came out of nowhere and started swinging. Despite taking some blows that could have been lethal and some blows that felt like they were, Colt managed to fend off his attackers and make it to the safety of his car. Battered and bleeding, he drove home.

Expecting to be plaintiff in a criminal case against his attackers, Colt was in for a rude surprise. They next day he was arrested and charged with assaulting the four men! The men claimed he had wielded the pipe. They showed their battle scars (inflicted in pure self-defense) as evidence of his ferocity and just down deep inside guts. Because of the climate of the times, a politically ambitious prosecutor bought their side of the story.

Colt was a police officer and his attackers were scum bag trailer trash that had been arrested many times before. Remember, these were the days of police violence and the bathroom broomstick, of the street vendor hit by forty-one police shots in his apartment vestibule as he reached for his wallet. It was a charged atmosphere, and Colt was called on to pay for the collective sins of his occupation and last name. See, the prosecutor who brought the charges against Colt was a defense attorney Eddie had fired tears ago for being an incompetent buffoon. So Colt was a convenient symbol. And, what the hell, it was an election year and pay back time.

Colt's trial was rife with the same kind of legal high jinks as his father's case had been. Detectives lied on the stand; witnesses were coached. The second time on the stand a girl had a sudden new version (just after the PROSECUTORS OFFICE met with her) and she now attributed threatening comments to Colt while he was inside the bar with the men. In fact, he had no interaction with the men. The jury took forty minutes to find him innocent of all charges. This anecdote may seem only tangentially related, but it was included because it provides an illustration of who these people are, these people who set up Eddie. Ruining Eddie's wasn't enough for the petty, vengeful bastards; they had to hoist his kid on a petard as well.

In fairness, it should be mentioned that civic corruption is not a phenomenon that is limited to Corrunoside. Corruption happens. Throughout the country. Throughout the world. The unique aspect of the Corrunoside experience has less to do with the crimes committed than the punishment meted out (or, more accurately, the lack thereof) to the staggeringly wide circle of officials who were allegedly engaged in misconduct. Eddie played the sacrificial lamb, while everyone went back to their day-to-day routines of petty and not so petty crimes.

Eddie was left with no recourse to combat the injustices that had been visited on him. According to his lawyer, the only option open to him lay in filing a federal grievance concerning the violation of his civil rights. He did so. It was denied.

Meanwhile, this thing, for lack of a better descriptor, this thing continues to haunt, continues to taunt; this thing won't let him be. This same thing that could've just as easily happened to you or to me. Remember that point. It is an important one. Eddie was a stand-up member of his community, a rising star in his department, a family man and a certifiable hero. And they did this to him. Despite all his credentials and all of his friends. Most of us don't command a fraction of the respect Eddie was able to earn. Therefore it is important to understand that if this sort of thing happened to Eddie, it could happen to you.

As we approach the conclusion of this novel, I'd like to be able to relate a moral or a kernel of wisdom that, as the more astute reader may have surmised is not possible. I wish in lieu of a happy ending, I could provide at least the reassurance that things are improving or some other related glimmer of hope. I wish I could, but I can't. The only moral is that injustice exists, and it is often allowed to flourish and triumph unmolested in a secure environment.

In the real world, nice guys do sometimes finish dead last, the right guy does not get the right girl, and they do not ride off into the sunset together as the credits roll. Not only do the good guys not take out the bad guys against all odds, it's hard to tell if there is even such a thing as good guys; that is, a group of likeminded, upstanding folk organized to contest and, if necessary, combat the forces of evil. Often there is just one solitary man. And, often, he is crushed beneath the weight of the burden he has elected, valiantly and heroically, to shoulder.

Eddie through his education, hard work and vigorous training thought of himself as being strong. He never wanted to be in the position of not being able to help or rescue someone nor able to free himself or any of his men from being trapped. Thus he always went into a situation with a positive attitude and always expecting the unexpected.

> ***With one swoop the almighty powerful took it all away.***
> ***You left my house and left me for dead.***
> ***Consider us even.***

> ***Will evil always survive?***

> ***The Characters, dates and events in this story are fictitious. Any resemblance to anything or anyone here is purely and totally coincidental.***

Appendix
Polygraph Results

WALL STREET INVESTIGATION SERVICES 80 Wall Street, Suite 717

New York, New York 10005

Mr. Jacob Evseroff, Esq. 186 Joralemon Street Brooklyn, New York 11201

CONFIDENTIAL ATTENTION:

Mr. Jacob Evseroff, Esq.

Fred Vickery *(Name of Subject)*

January 27, 1995 *(Date)*

ARRANGEMENTS: The above named subject was given a Polygraph Examination for the purpose of determining the truthfulness of the answers to the following questions. Subject signed statements releasing all parties concerned and empowering this examiner to disclose to those in authority his opinions, as well as information elicited during said test.

A four pen Lafayette Polygraph was utilized to register changes in blood pressure rate and strength of pulse-beat, galvanic skin response, and the respiratory pattern.

The purpose of this examination is to attempt to determine if the subject examined made a true statement as to all the facts related to business transaction he made with Mr.

Capfield, Manager of A & P warehouse in town of Corrunoside New Jersey.

The following relevant questions were asked with the indicated answers given.

1. Did you ever sign for dog food at A & P warehouse in Corrunoside New Jersey that you did not receive? Yes

2. Did you ever sign for dog food at A & P warehouse in **Corrunoside** New Jersey that was not given to you for your

use by warehouse manager Capfield?   NO

3. Did you make a false statement of receiving stolen property only because of threats made against you by Sergeant Kathy Hober of the Middletown Prosecutors office and Lieutenant Malaka of the Corrunoside Police department?   Yes

4. Did you admit in a statement on a tape recorder to theft by deception to Sergeant Hober of Middletown County Prosecutors Office and Lieutenant Malaka only after they made a threat against you?   Yes

5. Did you ever allow anything from A & P warehouse came into your place of business knowing at the time it was stolen?   No

6. Did you answer all of my questions about' transactions you made at A &P warehouse in Corrunoside New Jersey truthfully?   Yes

EXAMINER'S OPINION:

At this time a Stimulation examination was prepared and utilized with the key number being #7 (seven).

No deception was indicated in this subject's recorded responses to the relevant questions and it is this examiner's opinion that the subject answered all of

The questions truthfully.-

Edwin F. Lambert Polygraphist

TO;   Frank Bari, Esq.

186 Joralemon Street, 9th Floor Brooklyn, NY

SUBJECT. State v. Fred Vickery

Rebuttal to Gima Liar's Report of June 12, 1996

Mr. Liar's has identified eleven points at which the recording of the Vickery interrogation was interrupted. These are the same points initially referred to in the 11/9/95 Brady Report. There are slight timing differences found between the two investigators. The specific points are given in the chart below, along with the companion plot figure numbers from the Brady Report,

Koenig Time	Brady Time	Figure
03:55	4:07	40
03:54	9: 10	41
09:31	9:49	42
17:25	17:54	43
24:48	25:21	44
26:52	27:27	45
03:08	3:18	49
04:04	4: 14	50
08:00	8d3	51
09:14	9:29	S2
09:54	10: 10	53

Mr. Liar concludes that all eleven of these events were caused by the same machine control function. He claims that all were all pause stop, then pause restart" events. He claims to have performed critical listening, magnetic development, narrow band spectrum, physical inspection, and high resolution waveform analyses of both sides of the subject tape and on test recordings prepared on two tape recorders provided by The Prosecution. However, **he provides no scientific evidence** derived from said analyses to support his conclusions. Normally any plots, photos, and other data derived from an analysis are provided as an integral part of an investigator's report to substantiate the basis for his conclusions.

The theory upon which the process of tape authentication is founded is based upon the fact that ~ tape recorder will generate the same signature on the tape each time a specific control function is exercised. Thus, for a given machine every start signature should be the same, every stop signature should be the same, every pause signature should be the same, etc.

One should be able to extrapolate this theory to a copy of an original tape. If all of the repetitions of a specific signature are the same on the original tape, they should all be identical to each other on a copy tape, although they may be distorted (all in the same way) as a result of the copy process. Proof of this is found on the copy of the Vickery confession tape made at the Middletown County Prosecutor's Office on November 1, 1995.

Both investigators agree that the signature found at 00:06 on Side A of the tape is a start signature, as shown in Figure 37 of the Brady Report. Both investigators agree that the signature found at 00:14 on Side A of the tape is a start signature as shown in Figure 39 of the Brady Report. Although Mr. Liar does not specify a start signature for Side B, the signature found at 00:13 must be a start signature, since it is preceded by blank tape and followed by audio. This signature is shown in Figure 48 of the Brady Report. A comparison *of* the three Start signatures of Figures 37, 39, and 48 shows them to be quite similar to each other.

Both investigators agree that the signature found at 00:13 on Side A of the tape is a stop signature, as shown in Figure 38 of the Brady Report. Both investigators agree that the signature found at 17:40 on Side B of the tape is a stop signature, as shown in Figure 54 of the Brady Report. A comparison of these two stop signatures of Figure 38 and 54 shows them to be quite similar to each other.

Since the start signatures on the copy tape appear to be repeatable, and the stop signatures appear to be repeatable, it seems logical to assume that pause signatures, stop/start signatures, and any other signatures which the original recorder was capable of generating should also be repeatable. Mr. Liar concludes that all eleven points at which interruptions in the confession took place were made by the same pause function. If this is the case, then one would expect all eleven **signatures found at these points to be of the same format, Thus** signatures of these events are shown in Figures 40, 41, 42, 43, 44, 45~ 49, 50, 51, 52, and 53.

Starting with Figure 40$_t$ let us refer to this as Format A. Figure 41 <u>is entirely different</u>, so this will be referred to as Format B. Figure 42 is <u>different again</u>, so this will be referred to as Format C. Figure 43 is somewhat similar to Figure 41, so it will be considered as of Format B. Figure 44 is different from the previous signatures, so it will be considered as Format D. Once again, Figure 49 <u>is different</u> from the preceding plots and is considered as Format E. Figure 50 could be construed as similar to Figure 49, so it is considered as Format E. Figure 51 is similar to Formats 44 and 45 and is considered as Format D. Figure 52 again is a unique format and is referred to as Figure F.

Figure 53 compares favorably with Figures 44, 45, and 51 and is considered a6 Format D. It is thus seen that the signatures found at the eleven points of interruption are of six distinctly different formats. One can hardly then conclude that all eleven of these signatures were generated by the same control function, or even the same machine.

Mr. Liar states that "the recordings on both sides of Specimen Q1 have not been altered, edited, over-recorded, erased, and/or Changed in any manner. The information is continuous, except for the above listed record events." He does not go on to say, however, that Specimen Q1 i.e. the original tape made during the interrogation of Mr. Vickery on January 11, 1992. Neither has he submitted any scientific evidence showing that all eleven waveform plots display the same signature to support his conclusion.

A major difficulty with the subject tape is that it contains only 53 minutes, 07 seconds of the stated total 88 minute duration of the interrogation. Therefore, 34 minutes, 53 seconds, or 41.6 per cent of the conversation is missing from the tape. Unless this can be explained, and the 25 questions posed in the Brady Report can be satisfactorily answered, it cannot be determined if the subject tape is the original tape or an edited copy of the original tape. Even then, the ultimate proof would probably depend upon the appearance of the original recorder and examination of its control function signatures.

Note: The detective that testified about controlling this recording never was within 3feet of said recorder.

Conclusion: PERJURY

About The Authors:

Rich served as a volunteer in the fire service as well as the S.P.C.A. He joined the Professional ranks in 1970 where over the course of 22 yrs he had a distinguished and brave career. Due to his education and distinguished leadership skills he rose to the rank of Captain. He was a proud leader but most of all a proud father. He also achieved awards in life saving from the dept, as well as awards in bodybuilding and power lifting.

Matt Mahady is a freelance writer whose work has been published in numerous medical journals and trade publications. He also is a creative writer who wrote, directed and staged Where the Wind Ends. In 2001 and 2002 he was a member of the West Palm Beach and Delray Beach Florida Slam teams that competed at the national spoken word slam poetry competitions in Seattle Wash. In 2002, his competition piece was selected for the best of compilation that was published following the event. A volume of his poems, Midnight in Bushville was published in 2004.

Printed in the United States
203942BV00002B/130-177/P

9 781434 367488